THE BORDERLANDS PRINCESS

THE STONE CIRCLE SERIES
BOOK ONE

OPHELIA WELLS LANGLEY

The Borderlands Princess, Book 1 of The Stone Circle Series by Ophelia Wells Langley

Published by O.W.L. Publications, LLC

www.opheliawlangley.com

Copyright © 2022 Ophelia Wells Langley

All rights reserved.

No portion of this book may be reproduced in any form without permission from the publisher, except as permitted by U.S. copyright law. No part of this book may be reproduced in any form or by any electronic or mechanical means, including information storage and retrieval systems, without written permission from the author, except for the use of brief quotations in a book review.

All characters are a work of fiction, any names, places, or references therein are merely coincidental.

For licensing permissions contact: opheliawlangley@gmail.com

Edited by Jo Thompson

Cover by Nora Adamszki & O.W.L. Publications, LLC.

ISBN: 979-8-9862973-3-0 (ebook)

For those who have ever felt pulled in all directions and yet have found the space in the chaos to become your own person, and blossom, and grow…
Keep going. You have come so far.
Your ancestors would be proud.

CONTENTS

Pronunciations & Content Warnings ix

Chapter 1	1
Chapter 2	7
Chapter 3	11
Chapter 4	13
Chapter 5	21
Chapter 6	35
Chapter 7	53
Chapter 8	63
Chapter 9	71
Chapter 10	89
Chapter 11	101
Chapter 12	117
Chapter 13	137
Chapter 14	147
Chapter 15	157
Chapter 16	165
Chapter 17	175
Chapter 18	191
Chapter 19	197
Chapter 20	213
Chapter 21	215
Chapter 22	221
Chapter 23	229
Chapter 24	233
Chapter 25	245
Chapter 26	253
Chapter 27	257
Chapter 28	263
Chapter 29	269
Chapter 30	277
Chapter 31	283
Chapter 32	293

Chapter 33	299
Chapter 34	309
Content & Trigger Warnings	319
Acknowledgments	321
About Ophelia Wells Langley	323
Also by Ophelia Wells Langley	325

"We are at last perhaps what we are: uncombed, unclothed, mortal. Pulse and breath and dream."
   - Marjorie Saiser

PRONUNCIATIONS & CONTENT WARNINGS

Pronunciations:
  Sorcha - Sor-ka
  Conall - Con-uhl
  Achill - Ash-eel
  Geannie - Jeen-ee
  Gealaich - Gee-lach

TRIGGER/CONTENT WARNINGS:
  In an effort to be transparent, this is an adult dark fantasy romance, intended for audiences eighteen years and older. Please read the trigger warnings carefully. In order to avoid spoilers, you can find the content warnings located at the end of this book on page 319.

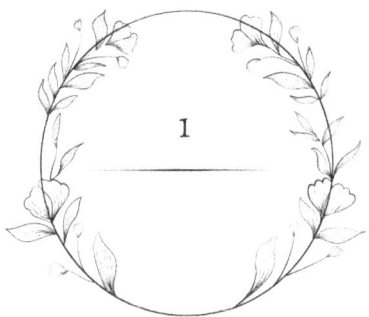

1

Seven more days, and I'll be married. A day I dread with my entire being since it will shackle me to the very creatures who almost killed me as a girl.

The Fae killed Geannie and now they expect me to be their Queen.

My fingers slide up to the chain hanging around my neck and pull the hagstone she gave me from between my breasts. The black stone shines in the bright light of day, the smooth stone cold to the touch though it had been resting against my skin the entire morning. I swallow thickly, the decades of grief settling like a stone in my stomach.

The coach lurches forward as we cross the Border. The invisible boundary between our worlds constricts my lungs and my ears pop. Our party clears the rolling fields, the landscape giving way to rockier terrain, deeper ruts in the hard packed road, and a lush forest with trees whose canopies seem to touch the dusk sky. We leave the cobblestone road behind and the light shifts slightly, brilliant hues of late afternoon brush the interior of the coach pink and orange. The gilded accents wink in the shifting light, glowing with extravagance, reminding me, yet again, that I am now a magic-less human in a powerful, magical world.

I press my forehead against the window. There are ten Fae in attendance, two driving the stagecoach, four at my flank, and then four at the front. I am severely outnumbered, so even if I *wanted* to jump out of this heavily gilded coach, they would catch me within moments. My fingers twine nervously in my mahogany-colored hair at the base of my neck, wanting to undo the intricate plaiting and pins, wear it down and free-flowing instead. Geannie would have snatched my hand away by now, ensuring my hair was still in its perfect style, tutting about and making sure that I look the part when I meet my betrothed.

The two Fae creatures driving the stagecoach are having a heated discussion and their voices raise in agitation, growing loud enough to filter through the window of the coach.

"Och! Are you daft? No way would the King believe it," one driver says hotly. "Besides, he'd have our hides if he caught us."

How I can hear them so clearly, I do not know, but I move to the opposite bench and slide the journal father gave me out of the way. I ride with my head tilted to the small window behind their seat and catch fragments of their frenzied conversation.

"We can easily make it look like an accident." The second driver says. His emphasis on the word accident has my heart skipping.

"What kind of accident? She's surrounded by Fae, the King's Guards, no less. This will never work," the first driver says, lowering his voice.

"I'd rather face the wrath of the King than ever deal with a human Queen." The second Fae spits the last few words. "She can rot at the bottom of a ravine, for all I care. Human trash." He grumbles and shifts in his seat. His tail flicks against the window and I jump, stifling a squeal as realization sets in: these Fae would rather see me dead than have a human as their Queen.

At that moment, the drivers yell and the coach lurches forward, throwing my head back against the driver's window. It careens backwards, coming to an abrupt stop, and I'm thrown to the floor, my forehead hitting the edge of the bench on my way down. My journal, cloak, furs and blankets scatter every which way.

Disoriented, head throbbing, stars dance in front of my eyes. I sit stunned on the floor of the coach, reaching up to touch my head. Cringing, my fingers graze a small gash and come away wet with blood. Shouts filter in from outside, angry voices shaking me from my stupor. If the drivers had planned this interruption, then my time is running out.

This is my chance.

Sweat lines my palms as my nerves wind tight, an invisible grip around my spine. I check my thighs and boots for my daggers, slowing my breath to stave off the anxiety. My hand dips down my chest, checking that the hagstone still sits there - a cool weight against my skin. I breathe a sigh of relief, knowing everything is in its rightful place.

Scrambling, I reach for my cloak and pull it on while listening to the commotion outside. A horse neighs loudly and the coach jerks forward, rocking to the side as the front end dips down and comes to a stunted rest.

THUNK, THUNK, THUNK.

Three arrowheads protrude through the ceiling.

Oh, no.

My heart beats in my ears and all I can hear is the whooshing of my blood.

Oh Goddess, oh Goddess, I think I might be sick. Shouts from outside the window close in, something roars and swords ring as blade meets blade.

Several shadows run past my window, and I scrunch down a little lower, hiding from view. I need to get out of the coach, but I am incapable of moving, struggling to find the courage. It is nonexistent. I know full well that I am an incapable human in the Fae lands. Though I have daggers, I lack any expertise in extensive hand-to-hand combat with creatures who can easily outmaneuver me.

I suck in a breath and reach for the handle, readying myself to jump, when the door behind me yanks open with such force that the whole coach rocks. Someone with large hands grabs my ankle and I yelp.

Oh, Goddess no.

"Got h—!" I kick out backwards with my free leg, the heel of my boot landing in the throat of an unknown assailant. He chokes and grabs his neck as he stumbles backward.

I launch myself out into the growing darkness, my boots squelch in mud several inches deep which is odd considering there wasn't any rain moments ago. I sink low to the ground and pull my cloak tight around my body, peering through the spokes of the wheel on the other side. I can't see my assailant anywhere. The shadowy figures all look similar as swords clang and giant Fae roar their battle cries in the middle of the road. A few bodies lay on the ground, but no telling if they're the guards who traveled with us or the unknown attackers so covered in mud and blood that their features were indistinguishable. One of the coach horses is dead, arrows protruding from his eyes and neck. His mate cut free, as the straps hang loosely from the harness and render the coach useless.

I'm a sitting duck. I need to move, but my legs are heavy, frozen in place.

Damnit, Sorcha, you idiot. MOVE.

The muck sucks at my boots, sounding so much louder than the rest of the fighting happening around me, as I slog around the abandoned carts.

I tuck my chin and pull the cloak low over my head, hoping to hide the fact that I'm the only human in this entire group and the obvious target. Roars sound behind me, almost human, as metal meets metal with a loud clang. I scurry to an overturned cart that sits off to the side and squeeze myself between the wheels and the front bench, putting solid wood at my back in case someone attacks me from behind. Some of my trunks have fallen from the cart and broken open. My dresses and undergarments are strewn about in the mud, tangled in the shrubs by the side of the road.

I move my hand over the dagger hilt in my boot, ready to

draw in an instant. But my hands are sweaty and shaking too much. Get it together, Sorcha.

Grunts and clanging echo to my left and through the axel I can see a very muscular, human-looking Fae with large curling horns fighting a guard. He thrusts a sword into his opponent, his blade coming away wet with blood. The guard groans, clutching his wounded left shoulder, and sinks to the ground on his knees, blood gushing from a near-fatal injury. Grasping his sword with both hands, the sheep-horned Fae raises it above his head and brings it down on the guard's neck, chopping his way through bone and muscle. The guard's head rolls away, landing a few feet away from his body. Gasping, I cover my mouth with my hand to keep from vomiting.

I don't stick around to see what the sheep-horned Fae does next, because I run in the opposite direction towards the woods, slip down an embankment on my side, and crouch at the bottom.

There!

A game trail between a few shrubs and the trunk of an enormous tree. Running as fast as my legs will take me, I head deeper into the forest and away from the melee behind me. I run until I'm out of breath, then slip around the base of a large evergreen tree and lean back into its trunk for support.

I take a few deep breaths and my heart rate slows, sweat cooling on my skin as the forest swallows all warmth from the last light of the day. The roiling in my stomach creeps up the back of my throat and I gag. Willing myself not to puke is like some twisted tug-of-war between my mind and my body as images replay the guard's head, rolling away from his body over and over.

My body loses the game and I lean over just in time to retch violently. When my stomach has finally emptied itself, I swipe the back of my hand across my mouth. Shaking from the cold and the exertion, I wipe at my forehead, wet with sweat, wincing as the rough wool scrapes across the wound on my forehead.

Rolling my eyes at my forgetfulness, I push off of the tree and head further into the forest. I bushwhack my way deeper into the woods and look for a place to lie low until sunrise. The path splits into two in the middle of a small meadow, and I hesitate, debating which direction to take. The night air sweeps in, and I snuggle deeper into my cloak as I head left, deeper into the forest. Old man's beard clings to the towering evergreens and redwoods, trees so large that it would take several humans to reach all the way around, their thick trunks slick with moss. The dampness settles into my bones the farther I get from the road.

A lone wolf howls in the distance.

Once I know I can make it through the night in the Land of Fae, I'll orient myself in the morning. I could just as easily slip away back to the human lands and make a legitimate run for my freedom. Right. That'll work really well, Sorcha, like you know enough about this place to get through this land on your own.

Large, lumbering footsteps sound from behind me, branches and twigs snapping underfoot.

TROMP. TROMP. TROMP.

Two people following me? Or just one? Oh goddess, I hope they aren't following the scent of my blood. Or vomit. Or human-ness.

My stomach clenches, and I can't hear much of anything now over the beating of my rapidly increasing heart rate. Still shaking, I slide my dagger out from its holster on my thigh and slink away further into the brambles and ferns as quietly as I can, hoping I'll find somewhere to hide and wait out the rest of the night.

I trot headfirst into bushes that scratch my arms and tear at my clothes as the thickets cluster ever tighter together, making a pathway through nigh impossible and forcing me to turn around. My cloak snags on the thick thorns, slowing me down.

"Ugh! Come ON." I yank and stumble backward, my back hitting something quite large, muscular, and sweaty.

"Well, well, what do we have here?" a booming voice breathes down on my head.

Shit.

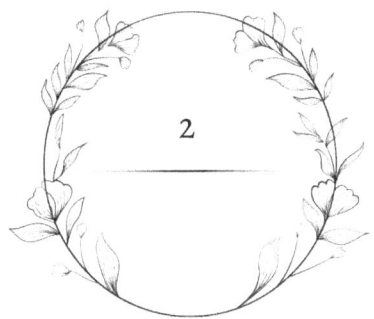

2.

Large hands grab my shoulders roughly and turn me around, throwing my hood off. Stunned, I look up into the yellow eyes of a Fae. But, unluckily for me, it's not just any Fae; it's the Sheep-Horned Fae That Likes to Behead People.

I'm not doing this tonight. I'm not going down.

But I stare, frozen in place, up at the horned Fae. He sniffs the air and a devious smile spreads across his lips.

"Princess." He almost hisses. He then leans down, peering into my eyes as I stand before him, unable to move. The musky scent of unwashed hair assaults my nose. He laughs, open-mouthed, and his foul-smelling breath washes over me. I scrunch my face to keep from retching again.

My hand grips the dagger tighter and then I lash out with my dagger hand, barely grazing his stomach. Shock registers on his face as he lets out an evil, bellowing laugh, throwing his head back. I take that moment to slide by him and head back the way I came, out of the brambles that have me trapped.

His hand snatches my trailing cloak and yanks. My head snaps back and I go down, his laugh reverberating through the understory. Rolling onto my stomach, I lunge forward on my hands and knees to get away when his hand snatches my ankle, pulling me back. My fingernails break on the hard ground, the unforgiving earth refusing to help me find a handhold.

"NO! No, no, no!" I scream and kick as he drags me back into the thicket. He flips me over and I keep thrashing, trying to make it impossible for him to find an easy way to hold me down and lop my head off. "Get off of me!"

I will not die tonight. I refuse. But Goddess above, if this Fae isn't extremely strong. He's a quick healer, too, because I see nothing more than the torn fabric from where my dagger nicked his stomach as he flips me over onto my back.

I scream again, kicking out at his ankles.

"Ah, ah, ah. Nice try, mortal." He lifts me off the ground with ease, throws me over his shoulder, and starts walking back to the road. I keep struggling, trying to get myself out of his grasp, but each step he takes drives his shoulder into my stomach and knocks the air out of my lungs.

This can't be happening, Goddess damnit.

I keep kicking and screaming, hoping someone from the road will hear me. I hit his back with my fists and mercilessly pull at his hair. He grunts and tightens his grip, shifting me enough to give me an idea.

Curling my knees up towards his shoulders, I twist on my hip, turning into his neck. I throw his balance off and he stumbles a little, which gives me just the right angle to open my mouth wide, bite down hard, and push off his horns while taking a hefty chunk of his skin away with my teeth.

"BY THE GODDESS!" he bellows. We go down hard as he falls to his knees from shock. Landing on my side on some rocks, I spit out a mouthful of his skin and blood. Dazed but not foolish, I take the split second I have, pop up, and run, weaving in between the trees.

"YOU'RE DEAD, MORTAL PRINCESS! DEAD!" I hear him yell behind me, grunting as he gets up. I glance over my shoulder and hope I've put enough distance between us. He presses his hand to his bleeding neck, blood pouring from the gaping wound, as he stumbles and groans. I push myself a little farther, putting my head down, and banking hard to my left, darting in between the trees. His blood fills my mouth, causing my stomach to roil as I spit out the remnants.

Oh goddess, oh goddess. Vomit creeps its way up my throat but I can't stop. I have to get away from here and go…

Where? To the Border?

I come to a skidding halt and try to figure out which way is which when I'm tackled from behind.

"UNGH!" Breath leaves my lungs and I'm thrown forward into the muddy path.

"You. Bitch." The sheep-horned Fae growls. "I swear to the Goddess when I'm done with you, no one will figure out who you were."

He raises his hand, and the hilt of his sword lands a swift blow to my temple. The world goes black.

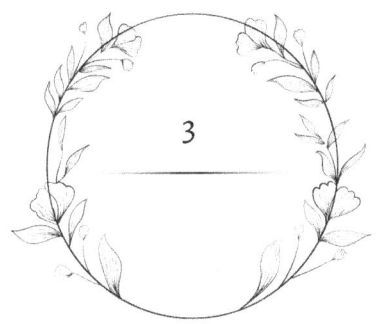

3

Strands of damp hair plaster my face, whipping at my neck in the winds as I turn my head, trying to track the wolves.

Howls punctuate the overgrowth, a warning call for my ears alone.

Picking up the pace, I try leaning into the gift of my earth magic, listening intently as a low humming leads me instinctively toward the stones. The moss grows thicker below my feet, and the ferns bow out of the way, revealing an ancient verdant trail leading that leads to the west. My heart lifts and I step quickly, weaving my way through. I thank the plants with my hands as I move past, vines and flowers growing where my fingers touched the trees.

More wolves cry, I count four separate, distinct howls coming from every direction, almost like they're herding me.

The farther into the woods I go, the clearer the path gets, finding the determination to run. I can still hear the river, the path meandering back towards its cliffs. I lean against a tree for a moment, looking down into the gushing water when a horse neighs in the distance and the rider's shouts carry on the gusts of wind.

Fog crawls around my ankles, slow like ghostly fingers, despite the increasing gusts of wind that tear through the woods. The forest floor disappears underneath the thick blanket of fog, forcing me to slow down and find my way over fallen logs and debris that I can't see.

The wind gushes through again. I can almost see a few large boulders, and a clearing appears through the bending trees.

My breath catches in my throat.

There!

It was only a moment, but a few standing stones shone in the moonlight. I am so close. Just get to the clearing...

The hair on the back of my neck stands on end as the creeping fog mutes all sounds, blanketing the forest in quiet.

No wolf howls, no wind in the trees. Just eerie silence, as if the forest has gone to sleep.

I slow to a crawl, holding my breath, sliding my feet carefully along the forest floor, mindful to not make much of a sound. Not like it would matter, anyway. The fog weighs on each inch of the forest and all I can hear is my heart beating loudly in my ears. I slide my blistered feet along the mossy undergrowth and I'm racing across the virgin ground, clambering over downed trees and branches, rocks, and dead fauna.

A wolf snuffles and grunts, sounding like it's a few scant yards away to my right. The fog creeps farther into the forest, dragging all sounds with it.

I can't trip... not now. Keep going. Keep going. Get past this fog, get into the clearing. Get past this fog, get into the clearing. Get past the—"Aargh!"

I slip on a slick rock and my grunt echoes throughout the eerily quiet forest. My left foot slides down a muddy hillside and the rest of my body follows, and then I'm falling, falling.

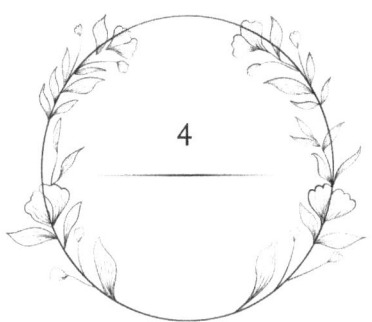

4

Jolting awake, I half expect to hear wolves howling around me. Instead, birds chirp outside a window and I swish my feet underneath cool, silky sheets and I snuggle a little further underneath blankets so soft they feel otherworldly in their divine comfort.

"Mmmm…" I hum, stretch, and crack the only eye that will open. Sunlight streams in through a lacy curtain and I inhale deeply the smell of cedar and fir trees, rain in the woods, and…

Bacon? Oh, goddess, I'm so hungry. My stomach grumbles and I launch myself forward in bed. Too quickly, because my head throbs tortuously and the world spins. I lie back with a groan and gingerly touch the side of my head. My temple feels tender as I graze over a bandage. Skimming my forehead, there's a smaller cut from the coach bench that has scabbed over.

The entire series of events comes rushing back, then. My eyes try to snap open, but my right eye must still be swollen, since all I can see out of that side is a blur. My fingers skim over the tender skin, gently prodding at the edges of my inflamed eye.

Leaning back into the pillows, I am resting in a four-poster bed. Heavy velvet curtains are tied back to reveal a sparsely furnished room. Directly across from the foot of the bed is a large wooden door with an engraved carving of an oak tree. A small chest of drawers with an oil lamp sits next to the door on the left.

Sunlight streams through the window and lacy curtains with early morning softness. Next to the window is an armchair, where my clothes lay folded up, looking devoid of all mud and blood. My boots are shining and polished. The remaining daggers are in their holsters, draped over the armrest. To my right is a small vanity and an adjacent stand with a washing basin, drying rags tinted with blood hanging from the rim. A few empty tincture bottles that are dark blue and green sit on the basin, but the handwriting on the labels is too tiny to read.

This doesn't feel like certain death. This feels like… an inn? But how in the hell—

A knock comes from the door, and before I respond, a Fae pops their head in.

"Oh, good. You're awake." An androgynous-looking Fae with short, shock-white hair says cheerily. "Can I come in? Excellent." The Fae pushes the door open with their foot since their hands are full of white linen rags and bottles of tinctures, then bustles in and sets everything down by the washing basin. They scoop up the bloodied rags and empty bottles and toss them into a bin outside the door, making themselves at home by tidying things up.

"Uh…?" I start, voice wavering. Panic creeps through my bones as I pull the blankets up to my chin and remember the last Fae who had his hands on me was none too kind, with a promise of death. "Are you… do… you…?" I choke up and my hands shake. I grip the sheets a little tighter.

"Oh, Princess. No need to fret. I'm with Lord Conall, of course." They scoff, waving off my concern with a flick of their wrist. The light catches their eyes as they walk to the other side of the room, a striking amethyst color against dark skin, and their white hair shimmers with streaks of silver. Pointed ears and ethereal ease wrapped up in billowing robes. A figment of my imagination has come to life before my very eyes. "I'm Thorne,

Royal Healer, cousin to Conall, Lord of the Borderlands and the King's Emissary. I hope you don't mind, but we found one of your nightdresses in your trunks and changed you whilst you were asleep. You were covered in mud and that awful Fae's blood."

"Oh. Lord Conall? What? Umm, no, I… how…?" I exhale and sink down into the pillows. The shaking subsides slightly the more Thorne talks, but I still can't seem to get rid of the feeling of strong, large hands grabbing at my body or the drivers of the coach talking about an accident happening to me on the way to the King.

"You're at the Land's End Inn, Princess," Thorne says with a chuckle. "Land's End Inn. Ha. Ha. Since we're so close to the Border?" Thorne looks at me expectantly, waiting for me to… laugh? "Never mind, then. The 'we' was me and the owner's mate. Let's get you seen to, as I have to report back to Mr. Tight—"

"Tight what, Thorne? Care to finish that thought?" A gorgeous, olive-skinned Fae fills the doorway. He leans casually against the doorjamb, muscular arms crossed over a broad chest. His jet-black hair is tied at the nape of his neck, revealing an angular jaw covered in scruff. Piercing green eyes meet mine and my heartbeat fills my ears. He cocks his head to the side and folds his arms over his chest. Frowning, he asks gruffly, "See something you like, *Princess*?"

I flush a deep red and blurt out, "I only have one working eye. I can't see *much*."

Thorne laughs, which turns into a cough, and asks, "How are you feeling, Sorcha?" Thorne turns to me, forcing a break in the staring contest between this immensely gorgeous Fae and me.

"I have an awful headache and I can't see out of my eye still, but all things considered… I feel okay?" I answer.

"She doesn't sound too sure." Lord Conall says. He looks at Thorne from the doorjamb with his head tilted and eyebrows raised. Haughtiness must be his default characteristic.

Thorne leans down, sitting on the edge of my bed. I pull my

legs closer to my body, instinctively putting more space between myself and the Fae. "I meant, how are you feeling, emotionally? You had a pretty... intense experience..."

"Oh! Well, that." I clear my throat, struggling to find the words for the anxiety that is threatening to shut me down. Uncomfortable with the quiet focus that hangs on my every word, I take a deep breath, but it comes in stuttered gasps.

Lord Conall rubs his jaw, the muscles in his forearm flexing with the movement, and says, "Give it time, Princess."

His soft lilt catches in my head, gooseflesh forming on my neck and down my arms as he lingers on my title.

He steps into the room and leans against the window frame, staring down at me through hooded eyes. The light wraps around him with an early morning glow. He looks utterly breathtaking, with the sunlight shining on his pointed ears. Lord Conall takes his time, considering me as he looks over my beaten face, the bandages, and the bruising on my arms.

I lean forward to adjust the blankets around my feet, eager to shift his attention away from my injuries. The blankets fall away from my chest, exposing my décolletage and the peaks of my breasts beneath the gauzy fabric. The lord's attention shifts from my face to my chest, lingering. Pulling the blankets back up, I shift slightly, covering myself.

"See something *you* like, Lord Conall?" I retort.

Lord Conall tears his gaze away, back up to my face, and he tilts his head, unamused. Correction - haughty and *patronizing* must be his default characteristics.

"Since you've just woken, Sorcha," Thorne says, "I think it's best if we try to get you walking about soon, since the *lord* over there wants us to leave quickly. I've got a few more of these tinctures for you to try."

Thorne lifts a bottle and eyes it closely, shaking the contents together.

"Right," I say, swinging my legs over the side of the bed. I stand too fast, my vision blurs, and I sway. My hands reach out for support as the world spins around me unsteadily. Spots float over my eyes and I feel like vomiting.

"Princess! Careful now…!" Thorne says as both Fae lunge toward me. Lord Conall reaches me first, grasping my arms, and helps me sit back down. We are so close that if I leaned in a little farther, I would feel the scratch of his scruff. Warm cedar and fresh fir mingle together under my nose and settle deep into my psyche, calming the fear that keeps threatening to take over. Instinctively, I lean in closer so I can smell him more deeply.

Oh goddess, Sorcha. You fool.

A flush creeps up my skin, and I try to pull away, but his body frames me in against the edge of the bed. I look up in his eyes and my breath hitches. An indiscernible emotion flashes across his emerald eyes before he tears his gaze away and looks at Thorne. He pulls away, an emptiness filling my bones and my arms burn from where his hands have been.

"Hmmm, well, that was a bit too soon, I think. Let's get you up more slowly next time, eh?" Thorne says. Coming over and helping me lie back down, Thorne fluffs some pillows behind my back. Their fingers, though featherlight and delicate, graze my bandage, causing me to flinch. Thorne withdraws their hand and looks at me with concern.

"I'll bring you up some breakfast, and Lord Conall can fill you in on the details. *Then* we will finish administering some of these tinctures and clean this wound on your head. Do you like your tea black and bacon burnt? Good, because there isn't really anything else this inn serves that's edible." Thorne says, giving Lord Conall a pointed look and leaves the room, not bothering to close the door behind them.

The silence is unnerving, so with as much authority as I can, I say, "Lord Conall, if you wouldn't mind…"

"Uh… filling you in? No, no, of course not. Would you like some water?" he asks, stepping forward.

His eyes travel over my face, taking stock of my injuries again, concern lining his features. I nod slightly; the movement making my head pound. He heads over to the washbasin and grabs a pitcher and a glass. Nausea swims in the back of my throat. I breathe deeply, hoping it'll keep the spins away.

"Thank you," I say. His hand cups my shaking one as I take the glass, ripples in the water giving away my nerves. I immediately bring the cup up to my lips and drink, if only to hide the fact that I'm still anxious. The cool water slides effortlessly down my throat, landing in my empty stomach with a resounding slosh.

Goddess, I'm hungry.

"May I?" He gestures to the armchair, and I nod. He moves my riding clothes off of the chair and places the pile on top of the dresser, gently smoothing down the shirt lapels as he does so. His fingers linger on the sleeves, and I notice that the tears from the brambles are gone.

"Did someone clean and mend my clothing? They must've worked in a frenzy to get them done overnight." I remark.

Lord Conall laughs. "Oh, well, it took them a while, but you've been asleep for almost two days. You received quite the concussion from that *animal*," he grumbles and rubs his jaw, pulling on his lower lip. He frowns and closes the distance between the dresser and the armchair in an easy stride. I catch another hint of fir as he walks past me, inhaling deeply as my heart rate calms. He lowers himself down into the chair, a faraway look on his face as he pulls on his lip.

"Animal?" I ask. "I thought he was Fae? Like you?"

"Not like me," he growls, looking at me directly.

The hair on the back of my neck stands at attention, and a shiver runs down my spine. I take another tentative sip of water and clear my throat.

"I have many questions, Lord Conall, about what happened during the ambush. And why it even happened. I heard…" I snap my mouth shut, deciding it best to not tell Lord Conall about the driver's plan just yet, in case this Fae is in on whatever they had planned as well. "I heard so much shouting when the fighting started that I just ran."

Lord Conall nods, taking a deep breath before he begins.

"Well, there's more history behind the why and the whom

that I should let the king tell you, but…" He hems and haws to himself for a minute, rubbing his jaw again and pulling at his lower lip while he thinks. "Since the peace treaty was signed a century ago, the Border between our lands increased. That meant more wards, more magic, for the Border to be strong enough to curb the killing between the humans and the Fae. It was intended as a way for both sides to cool off, and it wasn't supposed to last for a hundred years. But you were the first daughter born in the Salonen kingdom, and it just so happened that it took a while to get you Earthside. In the meantime, it was only a matter of time until certain factions of very radical-minded Fae grew in strength to keep the humans from fulfilling their side of the peace treaty. These factions of Fae want to keep humans out—for good. You're getting caught up in the middle because, well, you're the peace treaty."

"I see…" Images of Geannie laying in a pool of blood in the gardens have me shivering. "So, though the High King of the Fae has taken his vow seriously, the rest are not obligated to welcome me as Queen."

"Yes. You have quite a mountain to climb, Princess, and also a dangerous journey ahead now because of what happened once you crossed the Border. Touchy Thorne would say—"

"Heard that!" Thorne enters the room with a tray full of food: toast, several strips of slightly burnt bacon, and piping black tea with more in a little teapot.

My mouth salivates. I didn't realize just how hungry I was. A few flowers rest in a small teacup, and I smile at the kind gesture. Thorne places the tray next to me on the bed, and I can't wait to dive in. Before I consume like the starving patient I am, Throne holds out a tincture.

They shake it lightly in front of me. "Ah, ah! We need to get you some of this first to help with that headache and nausea."

The burning and bitterness sear my tongue, and I gag, grabbing some toast. I sink my teeth into the crust and a memory from the other night flashes in front of my eyes. A ghostly flavor of coppery liquid fills my mouth, as I relive the skin tearing away in between my teeth. The toast turns to ash in my mouth. I look at the rest of the food morosely as I place the bread back on my plate, struggling to chew.

Thorne reaches across the bed and touches my foot, squeezing it lightly. Their stormy purple eyes meet mine. "You did what you needed to—"

Lord Conall's green eyes flick to my bandage and he tilts his head as he regards me, thoughtfully adding, "To be fair, I have never known anyone to rip out someone's neck in order to get away from their assailant before. It was... effective."

"Effective? If someone could please tell me what happened that night? To the other guards, to the horned Fae?" I look from Thorne to Lord Conall, hoping at least one of them has an answer.

Lord Conall raises his eyebrows and looks at Thorne, who shrugs. Lord Conall hesitates before he answers, pacing in front of the window. Each time he passes, sunlight beams around his silhouette, haloing around his figure and highlighting his olive skin.

"Well, Princess, none of the assailants will live to see another day." His emphasis on those words should rankle me, but warmth pours over my body at the calm fury behind his tone. He looks at me, crossing his arms over his chest, waiting.

"Even the horned Fae?" I ask.

"Especially the horned Fae," he says.

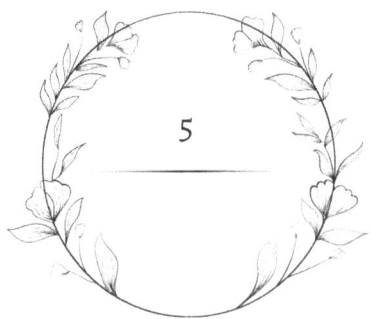

5

Thorne sits me down at the vanity to change the bandages on my head. The swelling around my eye has decreased enough for me to open it and Thorne grabs my face, turning my puffy eye towards them. Their fingers are gentle, featherlight against my skin, and press against the tender part of my injury.

I wince.

"This isn't taking as long as I thought it would for you to heal, which is lovely." Thorne hands me another tincture, and I swallow it down, holding my nose this time to stave off the earthy burn.

"Thorne?" I ask, hoping to get some answers from them. "Was Lord Conall there that night?"

They lightly dab some cream on my wound. It tingles, and I try to pull my head away. Thorne's hand reaches out and grabs my chin, keeping my head in place.

"Hmm? During the attack? Yes, he was." Thorne says. "Conall was to meet you once you crossed the Border, but apparently your party was late. So he set off down the road to see what had happened. When he showed up, they had already killed the horses, as well as most of the guards. The coach drivers, too. You disappeared into the woods shortly before he showed up, apparently. So he tracked you down via the horned Fae. Once you were safe, he then paid the innkeepers handsomely, so you'd have a place to heal before continuing on your journey." They turn back to me with a poultice that smells like lavender and apply it to the skin around my stitches.

"Oh…" I say, my eyebrows shoot up considering the additional details, but the pull of the stitches has me wincing.

"You'll soon find that Conall is nothing if not pragmatic. Less of a hassle to guard an empty inn," Their deft hands make quick work cleaning up the bandages and tinctures. "I'm going to leave your wound unwrapped since it's scabbed over, and I'd like it to get some air to finish healing properly. Keep this cream on it and keep drinking your tinctures and I feel confident that, given your progress today, we could leave the inn soon. In a few more days, we'll discuss taking the stitches out."

"Thank you, Thorne. I owe you a great debt of gratitude." I swallow a knot of apprehension. Is this what a Queen of the Fae would say or do?

Thorne's face registers shock at the mention of a debt.

"Princess," they say, "keep your debt. A debt to the Fae is not to be taken lightly. You should refrain from offering something you are not ready to fulfill just yet."

"I-I didn't know," I stumble, shame flushing my cheeks bright red.

"How could you?" Thorne smiles softly and reaches a hand to cup my cheek, "You should rest, Princess. Goddess only knows of your travails ahead."

I nod, closing my eyes as the door clicks quietly behind their exit, and a wave of exhaustion pushes down on my shoulders.

I turn to face the mirror, and as I lean forward to look at the cut from the coach, the hagstone from Geannie slips from beneath my chemise. The stone swings freely on its chain, glinting in the light as I close my eyes against memories that threaten to surface.

My rugged little feet slapping against the stone pathway as Geannie chases after me. I fall, hard, tumbling with gangly twelve-year-old limbs that slap against stone until I land at the base of the large fountain in the middle of the gardens. Her soothing voice murmuring as she scooped me up in her arms, a spoiled child princess all scraped up and weepy. Cinnamon and fresh baked bread still wafting from her hair, that scent alone could easily make all the aches vanish. She brushed the hair from my eyes and planted a kiss on my forehead as she tried to drag me back to the castle to finish my lessons when the air shifted. A smell of musk and lemon where no lemon trees existed in that part of the garden. The hair on the back of my neck stood on end. Stillness as the entire garden held its breath. Geannie pushing me behind her, shoving me in the direction of the castle guards, screaming at the top of her lungs. The last of her living breaths evaporate into a shrill scream to make sure I could make it home alive. A large, looming figure with a forked tail whipping in the sun behind them, the scent of musk overpowering everything else around me. Geannie taking the knife that was meant for me. Her blood splattering across the grounds at my feet, my eyes meeting the yellowed eyes of a strange Fae creature before I turned and ran back to the castle, never looking back.

Just a nursemaid, my father tried to tell me, as solace to her loss. But she was never just a nursemaid.

She was my everything.

Shaking my head, I swallow the lump of grief forming in my throat, and blink away tears that cloud my vision.

As kind as Thorne has been and as forthright as Conall has spoken, I am still uncomfortable being surrounded and outnumbered by the Fae. Magical creatures who want me dead. How am I supposed to defend myself in this land? I discard my shift in front of the mirror and cringe when my bruised and naked form looks back at me in the dying light of day.

Streaks of golden light highlight the curves of my neck and shoulders. My thighs, thick but muscular from riding horses, have bruises where I landed on the rocks. The cuts on my arms from the brambles are healing into tiny red welts. I look down at my ankles and see that there's an imprint in the shape of a hand from where the Fae grabbed me, finger marks reaching up to my shins.

My gaze travels over my softer stomach, the faint stretch marks at my hips and the tops of my thighs, noting the typical trademarks of a woman past her youth. What Fae king would want to marry a thirty-year-old, magic-less human woman?

Naked, I crawl back into bed and wrap myself in the blankets as a wave of homesickness hits me in the gut. Before I know it, I'm bawling underneath the sheets, ignoring the throbbing in my head and the nausea that follows. It doesn't take long for me to wear myself out. Exhausted, hurt, and feeling so much more alone than I have ever experienced in my life, my sleep becomes dreamless.

Hushed voices in the hallway wake me. I glance over at the window, where the waxing moon peeks through the curtains. I rub the hair from my eyes and wrap myself up in a blanket from the foot of the bed, then tiptoe close to the door so I can hear.

"Conall, listen. Figure this out or you're going to doom us all."

That's not Thorne's voice. The register is deeper, the accent is thicker.

Lord Conall groans, "I know."

Something hits my door softly. I hold my breath and clutch the blanket tightly around my body.

"I don't know what it is about her," Lord Conall says.

"Aye, but you can't see it through, can you?" The same voice from before whispers. I slide closer to the crack in the doorjamb and press my ear against the crevice.

"I know." Lord Conall snaps, a gruffness to his voice. I flush, my pulse quickening at the thought of him thinking about me.

He says something else, but his voice is too muffled for me to make out what it is.

"Get some rest, see this journey through, and don't do anything stupid. You'll be jeopardizing everything we've worked so hard to overcome."

"Sleep? You expect me to sleep?" Lord Conall whispers furiously. "Oh, don't look at me like that. I will risk nothing, believe me. This may kill me, but you know I'll see it through."

"Aye, and you've done worse things before." The nameless voice groans and a chair creaks as they stand up. "But I will say that you look awful. You need your rest if you're going to keep your wits about you."

"Remind me, again, why we're friends, Murry?" Lord Conall chuckles lightly, shifting in his seat.

A few footsteps tread lightly up the stairs and then the Fae named Murry whispers, "Grindel, my good fellow, what say you about this whole affair?"

"Och, you think I came up here to prattle? Our fears have come to pass, lads." Grindel says, his voice low and urgent.

"It couldn't be… It's too soon. We should've had another day, at least." A chair scrapes against the wood floor.

Lord Conall grunts as if he's stretching and then the sound of his chair creaks as he stands up. "I thought I scented them out there. Did you get the messages out, then?"

"Aye. But as I was heading back from the drop point, there were more of them arriving in the forest." Grindel's voice drops another octave. "You need to leave within the hour. They cannot find you here… This place…"

"Say no more, Grindel. I understand." Lord Conall whispers. After a beat, he says, "I'll just have to take her through my lands, then."

"Och, if you think that's wise." Murry interjects.

A heartbeat of silence and then someone growls.

Murray says, "Okay, it's your call. I'll go get Thorne. She has to be fit enough to ride."

"She will be," Lord Conall snaps. "She has to be."

A shuffling of feet, some murmurs of more plans that I can't hear, and then the hallway goes quiet as three sets of footsteps recede down the stairs.

There's no way I can get back to sleep now, as questions fill the space in the quiet they leave behind. I tiptoe to the bed and slide under the covers. When I reach up to my eye again, the swelling has gone completely, and I exhale. The tinctures Thorne has been administering have helped in my recovery.

A knock at the door cuts through my groggy thoughts.

Thorne whispers, "Princess?"

Thorne pops their head in. "Conall would like to leave in the next hour, since you're healing so well. He wants to get a head start before the sun comes up. I'm here to help you get your wound clean and get you dressed."

I sit up, asking, "Any reason we're leaving so soon?"

"They did not disclose it to me," Thorne says, brushing me off. Lighting the lamp on the dresser, Thorne walks to my clothes. "Now, to get you dressed. He wants you outfitted appropriately for your journey. I'll keep my eyes closed, if you like, but mind you, I've seen it all earlier." Thorne winks and tosses me the discarded shift that was sitting folded across the armchair. How it got there, I do not know.

Thorne busies about the room, grabbing tincture bottles and putting them into a folding leather case. They hand me one and I down it; the bitterness coating my tongue. There's a stack of clean bandages by the washbasin that they also grab and tuck away, along with the remaining cream. The bandages certainly weren't there before I fell asleep.

"Strange things happen in the land of the Fae, Princess," Thorne says, following my look of confusion around the impeccably tidy room. "You'd be wise to remember that little eyes and ears are everywhere."

Smiling at me, Thorne places a bit of honey and bread on the windowsill.

"Oh! For the — what are they called — brownies?" I almost leap from the bed with excitement. "They're real? I mean, I've read as much, but to know that they're the ones keeping this place so tidy? That's incredible! They really exist!"

I hurry to find something else to leave them, but all my possessions are gone. Turning around the room, I pick up the flowers from breakfast and hold them out to Thorne.

"Is this gift all right? They mended my clothes so beautifully." I say, twisting the stem between my fingers.

"I think the flowers will do just fine. Gifts for the brownies are always welcome," Thorne says. They smile and bow their head slightly as they exchange the flowers for my clothes. They turn their back to me, giving me privacy to change. I watch as they place the flowers on the windowsill with a serene reverence.

I slide on my shirt and tuck the hagstone under the collar. It settles against my skin, warming almost instantly. I breathe a sigh of relief, as if a piece of armor is sliding into place, and wrap my fingers around it through the linen. It pulsates with warmth.

Are there brownies in the room right now? Would I be able to see them? I tug the hagstone back out from beneath the shirt and bring it up to my eye.

In a flash, Thorne's hand reaches for mine, their face inches away. They cradle my hand in theirs, closing the hagstone in my palm and wrapping my fingers around it. They whisper solemnly, "I don't think you want to do that right now."

"Is it because they're shy creatures?" I whisper back.

Thorne looks down at me, their eyes a cloudy purple-grey. "So innocent, Princess. There's a bit more to it, but I would advise strongly against using a hagstone in the land of Fae unless your life is in danger. There are creatures here who would rather be invisible to the human eye until you are a trusted being. Other creatures wear a glamour, keeping your human sensitivities in mind, so as not to scare you. Mind, Princess, that a hagstone given as a gift is as powerful as the intent of the gift giver behind it. Use its power wisely."

"Well, that certainly sounds rather ominous." As the hagstone grows cold in my hands, the starbursts I saw earlier dim slightly.

Curious.

Thorne hands me my clothes and my riding leathers slide on easily. I strap my daggers on next, readjusting a few times because I keep forgetting we're riding horses from here on out. Instead of securing them to my legs, I put two in each boot and then my longer one along my waist, leaving my thighs free to grip the saddle comfortably. Thorne walks over with a thin woolen sweater and then a long wool coat, tailored perfectly for me, with a generous slit up the back to allow for the saddle. The detail and thought put into these items is remarkable, and I can't help but touch the buttons and stitching fondly, hoping that it was the brownies who tailored such thoughtful work.

Before we leave the room, I glance backward one last time. The flowers, honey, and bread we left on the windowsill are already gone.

We descend into the bar of the inn. Lord Conall's hushed tones fill the quiet tavern as his head is bent in discussion with another Fae. He must be a regular patron of this inn, for I haven't seen him have this ease of posture. The usual stock-straight back is now hunched over the edge of the bar, one foot casually crossed over the other, and his backside…

I bite my lip and then immediately blush, thankful that it's dimly lit in this part of the inn. I assume that the Faerie he is talking to must be the owner, but he doesn't have the pointed ears or the physique of the other Fae that I am used to. This one is shorter, rounder, and has a long beard that shadows a broad smile full of teeth. This Fae could easily be someone's grandfather back in the human world. At the sound of our approach, their voices grow hushed and stop altogether, causing me to glance over at Thorne, who shrugs.

"Ah, Sorcha. This is Grindel, the purveyor of this fine establishment." The Lord of the Borderlands introduces him with a warm smile and turns to me, expectant. My eyes dip quickly down the front of Lord Conall's body and back up to his face. He catches my gaze and quirks an eyebrow, eyes twinkling in the dim.

I clear my throat and smile warmly, turning to the owner. Hoping I sound regal enough, I say, "Thank you, Grindel, for the delicious food and the most comfortable bed I had the pleasure of resting in. Your hospitality was most kind, and I will tell others of your excellent service."

Grindel's face registers a sense of awe, and he bows low behind the counter. "My future queen, many thanks. My mate and I... this is our lifeblood since a mining accident decades ago rendered us useless to the rest of the dwarves. To hear you shower us with such kind words... it leaves me humbled." He brings his palm to his chest, over his heart, and bows again. "I really hate to push you out before you're healed, but you really should be on your way. The night wanes and there are—"

"Thank you, Grindel." Lord Conall interjects, shoving a purse full of coin his way. Grindel snaps his jaw shut and takes the bulging leather purse gratefully, sliding it into his front apron pocket.

A dwarf!

Realization dawns as I turn in a circle to see all the other little details in the inn that were tailored for the owners: ladders that slide against rails so they can reach the highest shelves of liquor, two sets of handles on the doors, rope tied to the chandeliers so they can move them up and down with ease. And a few steps leading up to the area behind the bar where there is a raised platform for him to stand on.

"Are you ready, Princess?" Lord Conall asks and, without waiting for a reply, he turns on his heels and leads the way through a side entrance, where the horses must be waiting. Grindel, head down and avoiding my eyes, hurries to the back of the tavern and dips into a bow once more before disappearing behind the kitchen doors.

The smell of hay reaches my nose once I step through the door, sending me back to the royal stables at home where beautiful thoroughbreds pawed at the ground, all saddled up and waiting for the hunt. My foot was already in the stirrup of one of the black horses when Father's booming voice came from behind me. Launching myself into the saddle before he had a chance to keep me grounded. My hands tightening on the pommel, my thighs instantly gripping the saddle so he would have to pry me off. His eyes were stormy and furious. His voice was low, barely above a whisper, as I sullenly slid off the saddle in front of the entire group of guests. My head hanging low as I skulked back into the shadows, yearning to be riding free in the hills. The craving to be free, always just at the tip of my fingertips, even as I got older. The predicament of having your fate already figured out for you.

Lord Conall clears his throat and I jump. His vibrant green eyes meet mine and, though he says something, I've blocked him out for over his shoulder are two beautiful dapple-grey horses. The darker of the two shakes its head and looks me in the eye. Humming, I reach out my hand for the dark horse to sniff. Saddled up and bags already secured, she's chomping at her bit, restless.

"Ahh, an equestrian at heart," Conall lilts, reaching out to grab her reins. He steps closer, petting her coat, and our hands dance around each other. "This one's Gealaich, named after the moon. She's got a soft mouth and is easy to ride. We thought you'd like her since she has an easy gait and is the smaller of the two horses. In Fae," he explains, gently, "we're not used to outfitting horses for humans or those smaller than us as dwarves don't care to travel on these animals. Hopefully, you'll find her easy to maneuver during your journey."

Myriad of colors in her coat shimmer in the torchlight, from dark midnight blue to silver, grey, and white. Running my hands under her mane and down along her jaw, I trace bursts of white markings that cluster together - starbursts that lead to a perfectly round silvery white circle in the center of her forehead, like a full moon.

"She's *beautiful*. Aren't you, Gealaich?" She snuffs out a breath and shifts on her hooves. One of her big beautiful grey eyes searches mine. "Oh, I think we'll get on nicely, eh, good girl?" She hangs her head over my shoulder, and I lean in, inhaling the smell of hay and horsehair, a familiar bolt of homesickness passing through my body.

"Conall, Princess," a voice from the shadows says. I spin around to face another Fae hovering in the shadows. Straw-colored hair pulled into two thick braids that hang low over his shoulders, pointed ears that poke out through the plaiting, and his face is a smattering of freckles. Besides the pointed ears, he looks so similar to Father a pain snags at my heart, and I blink my eyes against tears that threaten.

Pull yourself together, Sorcha.

Clearing my throat, I ask, "You are?"

"Murdock, Princess." He dips his head and bows. His black cloak falls forward, shrouding him in partial darkness. His voice sounds almost reverent as he adds, "I acquired the horses for your journey. Gealaich is a special creature."

"Thank you, Murdock, for your assistance. She's perfect." I say, patting her neck again as she nuzzles me.

I reach my hands up to grasp the pommel and reins, but my foot barely reaches the stirrup. The strain causes my head to pound again, and I lean my head against her saddle, closing my eyes.

"May I?" Lord Conall asks, his hands hovering near my ribs. Our eyes meet and even in the darkness outside, his eyes seem to glow, vines of dark green swirling around his pupils that fade into a bright, vibrant jade on the outer edges. I nod, slowly, and he lifts me up into the saddle with an ease that belies how strong of a Fae he really is.

"Thank you, Lord Conall. I fear my head is still…" I drift off as spots cloud my vision. Swaying slightly in the saddle, Lord Conall's hand rests on my leg.

"Breathe through it, Princess. We have a way to go before you're able to rest again," he lilts. He squeezes my thigh so lightly, my eyes fly to his. He looks away and drops his hand.

"Thank you. But can someone tell me why we're leaving in the dead of night like thieves?" I rock with the movement of the saddle, Gealaich stomping impatiently as Lord Conall adjusts the girth and my stirrups.

"Does this not suit, Your Highness?" Lord Conall asks, but I swear there's a hint of mockery behind his question.

I stare him down, bristling, and narrow my eyes. "That wasn't an answer."

The stables grow quiet. Murry turns to look at me and nudges Thorne, who coughs back a laugh and says, "She's learning quickly, Conall."

Lord Conall rubs his jaw and sighs, "Well, there are some—"

"*Dissidents.*" Murdock interjects, nodding subtly at Lord Conall.

"Yes, *dissidents* that are camping out in the forest just south of the Inn. I have it on good authority that they have been gathering their numbers for a proper search party." Lord Conall says.

"They think I'm somewhere in the forest, then." Instinctively, I touch the hilt of my dagger at my waist.

Lord Conall's eyes flick to the movement under my coat, and his mouth quirks with approval. "Yes, and we don't want to be at a disadvantage when they realize you've been here for the past two days with a minimal entourage to guard you. Now, if it pleases you, Your Highness, we must be on our way if we're going to get you out of here alive." He turns to Murdock and whispers something in his ear. The blond-haired Fae bows once in my direction and secures the hood of his cloak low over his profile. He slips into the dark of night.

Thorne, who is hovering by the doorway, shakes out their robes, a snow-white feather falling to the ground. "Don't fret, Princess. You're in excellent hands with Lord Tight—"

"Thorne!" Lord Conall admonishes. He walks his horse next to mine and takes one last long look at me before he swings himself up with an ease that makes me jealous. "Keep up," he says, a curtness to his words that has my spine tingling. Then, over his shoulder to Thorne, he clips, "See you at our first rendezvous."

With a click of his tongue, he's trotting off into the darkness, Gealaich and I trailing behind.

6

We ride in silence, the cool night air swirling around my shoulders, breath dewy in front of my face. The autumnal equinox draws ever closer, the light of the moon peering through the thick forest canopy.

Rounding a large evergreen tree, its craggy roots covered in moss, lights shine through the bracken in the distance. Lord Conall slows his horse and draws up close to me, whispering, "We will skirt by their encampment, traveling south first and then westward. I don't think I need to tell you to stay close."

I nod, fear tightening around my chest, strangling the breath from any words I might have said.

"Let's go," he says. He nudges his horse through a winding, overgrown game trail and I have to dip my head to keep the branches from snapping at my stitches.

We ride in silence, the weight of the past few days pushing down on me like a heavy cloak. My chest tightens, recalling the horned Fae in the forest, and each misstep from Gealaich has me flinching.

A white bird flies overhead, circling in front of Lord Conall's horse, swooping down onto the trail in front of us. Its wings graze a large fern from under which a muted squeaking sounds.

Lord Conall slows and pulls his horse to a stop in the middle of the path. He slides off his saddle, shooing away the bird of prey, and gets on his hands and knees to look under the leaves.

Pulling up beside his horse, I stumble, getting off of Gealaich, foot catching in the stirrup. Finally freeing myself, I crouch down under the bush that Lord Conall has somehow wedged himself under. The squeaking turns into a whimpering the closer he gets to the creature.

Under the fronds, a little Fae lies just out of Conall's reach, trembling and bloodied. Lord Conall's low voice shushes in the dark, coaxing the injured creature toward him. In the dim light of the moon, tiny legs and arms crawl into the waiting hand whose long fingers it clasps onto desperately as Lord Conall pulls it from its hiding place.

"An injured pixie," Lord Conall's voice vibrates with anger. His fingers stroke the damaged wings, and he pulls the pixie close to his face, noting the injuries. It whimpers and cowers under his gentle inspection.

Stepping quietly behind Lord Conall's shoulder, I peer over at the poor Fae huddled in his hand.

"What do you think happened?" I whisper, and Conall shakes his head. At the sound of my voice, the air around the pixie warbles and their skin changes from a light pink to a bright, scaly green, their eyes turn solid black, tiny claws and sharp teeth take the place of what was once human-like features. I look up at Conall, confused.

"Their glamour…" He explains, "They are too injured to use their magic to glamour themselves from you."

"Oh," I sigh and my heart clenches.

Lord Conall walks over to the horses and pulls out a flagon of water. He holds it up to the little Fae, cocking his head in question. The pixie nods slowly and Lord Conall grips the cork in his mouth, freeing it from the spout, and pours a gentle stream over the body of the Fae. As the blood washes away, I watch, transfixed, as the skin around the injuries slowly knits back together.

Leaning over his shoulder, I catch that scent of pine and rain-soaked fir again, inhaling deeply.

"Did you just smell me?" Lord Conall scoffs.

I stiffen and move back a half-step. "Don't flatter yourself."

He scoffs and pets the pixie with his forefinger. Cleaning away the blood from their wings as carefully as he can, Lord Conall turns to me, "I don't have pockets deep enough to hold her as she continues to heal," — he looks me up and down, nudging his chin at one of my pockets in my coat —"But..."

"Me?" I ask, thrusting my hands in my pockets, hiking my shoulders up to my ears. "You want me to hold a Fae in my pocket?"

"Just until she heals enough to fly," Lord Conall looks down at the pixie, who looks at me with her big, pitch black eyes.

"No." I shake my head.

"She won't hurt you." Lord Conall steps closer, holding his hands out.

My breath catches as I look into his eyes. I stutter, "I... I'm worried I'll hurt her."

"Or are you worried she'll hurt you?" Lord Conall's green eyes flick to the pixie's pointed teeth and then back up at me.

I swallow and nod.

"She won't. She's too injured. Just let her rest in your pocket until she can fly again." Lord Conall steps closer.

Reluctantly, I hold out my hands, cupping them together, hoping that my shaking isn't noticeable. Lord Conall gingerly hands her over, our fingers overlapping and lightening zaps up my arms at his tender touch. The pixie whimpers and curls into a tighter ball as I place her in my pocket, making sure she fits comfortably. Scooping up the bottom of my coat, I cushion her from my jerky movements as we make our way back to the horses.

"Just give her some time for her magic to work and she'll fly as soon as she's able," he replies.

"I just meant that —"

"Sorcha, things don't work here like they do in the human

realm. She knows you're doing her a favor. Just give her the time she needs to heal. If we hadn't gotten here, though..." he trails off, staring into the distance, rubbing his chin.

"What do you think happened to her?" I ask. Peeking into the pocket, her tiny body is curled tight, but her wings shimmer in the darkness.

"I think I have an idea..." Lord Conall says, looking over his shoulder. Susurrant noises filter through the forest as we mount our horses. We ride further into the trees, giant and ancient, with branches so thick they could support several full-grown men on their boughs. Old man's beard grabs at my clothes and hair as we pass underneath. Moss and mushrooms of every color and shape climb up the trunks, creating miniature forests of their own.

We ascend up an embankment of an old creek bed. Lord Conall slows us to a crawl as the undergrowth thickens at the crest of the hill. Orange light flutters between the trees down below and casts long shadows in the night as we travel above the edge of the dissident's encampment.

In the distance, someone picks up a fiddle to play a melody. The wordless lullaby filters through the trees, a light breeze rustling the leaves, and it reminds me of the lullaby that Geannie used to sing to me before bed. Lord Conall disappears around a large evergreen, so I nudge Gealaich a little closer to the edge of the hill, leaning in to listen to the soothing music. The forest melts away as the music of the lullaby intensifies with the fiddler's deft fingers, the hallways of my childhood taking shape behind my closed eyes.

Her voice carries the tune and there is Geannie, giving me a sneaky smile as she hands over a stolen cinnamon swirled pastry from the kitchens. She is humming into my ear the same lullaby as she holds my five-year-old body close during a thunderstorm. She sings the wordless melody as she ices my hands after my instructor smacked me with a wooden rod for talking back too many times. Geannie sings it again as she rubs my back during my first moon-bleeding.

"Princess!" Lord Conall's harsh whisper brings me back to

the present. My eyes flying open, alertness snapping my spine to attention. The pixie's tiny body shivers uncontrollably in my pocket despite my hand absently stroking the outside.

I sit atop Gealaich, fully bathed in the orange glow on the precipitous edge of the cliff side. The music has stopped and the entire forest has gone quiet as I meet the eyes of a Fae fiddler through the thin tree line. A slow, evil smile tugs at the musician's lips as he lowers his instrument.

My eyes fly to Lord Conall's. Fury laces his green eyes that glow in the dark, and he growls, "Go."

Without a second thought, I yank hard on Gealaich's reins and we're off at a gallop. Shouts claw at my back from behind us as the encampment scrambles to catch up to us. The pixie squeaks, shifting in my pocket, and I hold her tightly against my hip so she doesn't jumble around too much.

We ride hard between trees and overgrown shrubs, following a game trail next to a small stream toward the rising sun.

"This way!" He shouts over his shoulder and he kicks his horse harder. Disappearing between the large trees, he flits in and out of my vision in the darkness.

My head throbs dully, but I lean down against Gealaich's neck and kick her hard to keep up.

A few wolves howl behind us and she surges forward at the sound. The sun rises slowly in the east, periwinkle light filtering through the dark, ancient forest. A screech sounds from overhead and I spot a white falcon circling above Lord Conall before diving into the darkness ahead. Lord Conall turns sharply, taking us directly east toward the sun.

He loops back around, falling in behind me, as we race westward. The game trail widens and we ride neck-in-neck as the shouts of the Fae behind us escalate. He snatches at my reins, and he yanks us hard to the right as we crash through the understory, coming to rest beneath a large tree. He holds a finger up to his lips, shushing me, though the horses breathe heavily, still.

I watch in awe as his hands shimmer with green and the tree folds its boughs down, bending slightly forward, covering us in its camouflage. The air bends around us, blanketing us in a bubble of quiet. Within moments, torchlight skirts by us. A mob of angry Fae clamors through the trees, narrowly missing the tree within which we hide. I cringe, worried the Fae will see us, but they rush past and head south, completely unaware of our hiding spot.

I look at Lord Conall, confused, and he smiles. His hands spread wide, held in front of him, his fingers shining effervescently in the night, the tips matching the color of his eyes. A few moments pass, and the air shifts again, the boughs lifting and the sounds of the forest rush back.

Easing our horses from beneath the tree, Lord Conall pauses in the middle of the trail, tilting his head, sniffing the air before he nudges his horse forward. A quick look over his shoulder to check that I'm following, and he guides his horse down onto a mossy, overgrown path.

Lord Conall pulls his horse up short as two giant standing stones stand sentry before us. I pull Gealaich to a halt, staring at the looming stones that flit in and out at the edge of the forest. Whorls and swirls cover their grey bodies and I swear I see the engravings moving.

"We cross here," Lord Conall says, from my left. He brings his horse closer to mine and says, "My lands lay beyond, warded only to those with my blood. You'll be safe."

"Safe," I exhale. Is anywhere safe in Fae for a human princess?

Out of the corner of my eye, the rolling hills and the fields of home peeking through the southern border of the forest. Pulling Gealaich around in a circle, I could easily head south, leave the land of Fae behind, riding Gealaich to one of the port towns.

Sensing my hesitation, Lord Conall walks his horse in front of mine, the lavender hue of early morning casting his face in a soft glow. The forest grows still, waiting with bated breath for my decision.

He takes me in, his eyes scraping over my face, a deep understanding behind his inquisitive look. "The choice is ultimately yours, Sorcha."

The way he says my name has the hair on the back of my neck standing on end, shivers cascading down my spine. I turn Gealaich in a circle, pointing her nose south. To home. To freedom.

"If you go south, I can't guarantee that Fae won't attack your lands." Lord Conall says, softly. "You leave, and you're free. But…"

"But my people…" My heart sinks. I can't leave them with a possibility of war. Horse's whinny behind us and my eyes snap to Conall's.

"So be it," I concede, swallowing the dread threatening to overcome me. "Lead the way."

Conall rides through the stones first, the whorls flaring into bright, multicolored shimmers. I stare, transfixed, watching as the air between the stones quavers when he passes through, contracting and expanding with his passage.

This is wholly dissimilar to when I passed through the Border a few days ago. All I felt was the air pushing from my lungs as we passed an invisible barrier. Nothing like this. These wards must be much stronger.

I nudge Gealaich forward and I can feel her brace herself as she prepares to follow the lord's horse through the stones, putting her head down slightly. Instinctively, I tighten my grip on her pommel and squeeze my legs, securing myself in the saddle. At the last minute, I glance up as we hit what feels like a wall of thick, moisture laden air. We pass through and the stones fade in the morning light, disappearing behind us as if they were never there.

Gealaich comes to a stop on the other side and the sun is so blindingly bright after the dense, dark forest that I have to raise my hand to my eyes. I squint against the bright sun, flinching when my fingertips graze my stitches.

We've come out at the top of a bluff, and from this view, I can see that below us stretches a vast, wildflower-filled grassy meadow. A brook gurgles from the edge of the forest we just left and pours over the ridge, down large river rocks that create cascading, miniature waterfalls. The early morning light catches in the mist and throws rainbows in the air above several small pools that are surrounded by overgrown wild roses.

This is what I imagined the land of Fae would look like. This is absolute beauty.

My jaw must have dropped open because I hear Lord Conall chuckling next to me. He pulls his horse up to my flank and says, "It's a beautiful scene, isn't it? I always love coming home this way."

"It's... gorgeous." My eyes can't seem to take in all the beauty, admiration blooming in the center of my chest. I point to the stream, "But..."

"The water." Lord Conall interjects. He nods and his eyes flick over my face, registering my admiration for the scene in front of us. "It's an underground spring that comes from up north and turns into this stream. It just so happens that the wards prevent people from seeing - or hearing - what's really on this side."

I frown a little and look back, noting that the large warding stones have indeed disappeared and the forest beyond looks nothing like the one we traveled through. "Huh. That's a fancy trick."

Lord Conall chuckles again. "No, Sorcha. It's magic."

He slides off the saddle, stretches languidly, and my eyes linger over his lithe muscles.

The pixie climbs out of my pocket, shaking her wings free, and hovers in the air level with my face. Her body shimmers and I watch as her glamour unfurls before me, her green skin turning a light pink, her black eyes turning bright green, her tiny sharp teeth smoothing out. Her wings, however, remain delicately translucent, fluttering furiously in the cool air to keep her body in front of me.

"You look better," Lord Conall says, nodding at the creature.

She nods, flying over to land on Conall's shoulder, whispering something in his ear.

He chuckles, "Yes, that's her."

The pixie turns to me, eyes wide and bows deeply. She looks questioningly between me and Conall before he says, "Yes, you can take your leave. Just try to keep hidden these days, Plum."

"Her name's Plum, like the fruit?" I ask, watching her flit into the crown of a nearby tree.

"Most elemental pixies choose their names when they go through their Rites." Lord Conall says, dismissively, walking down to the stream.

"Rites?" I ask.

Lord Conall ignores my question, grabbing his horse by the reins, leading her down the hillside to drink.

I watch, feeling ever the voyeur, as Lord Conall crouches next to the stream, running his hands through the falling water. He glances up at me, but I can't seem to pull my eyes from his, noting that the green in his eyes almost matches the green in the meadows. The sun glints off his hair, and I realize that his black hair isn't just one color. In the bright light of the midday sun, there are streaks of deep auburn throughout and a few strands of silver that pepper his hairline around his temples and travel to the slight curls at his pointed ears. He turns and kneels down, rolling his sleeves up, and dips a cupped hand into the water, splashing it on his face.

My eyes roam up from his temples to his ears and then down his neck, to his broad shoulders, and then down again as he flexes his forearms. Openly admiring his strong back, I watch his muscles work underneath his shirt as he scoops up some water to drink.

"Let me know if you need help to dismount off of Gealaich," he says, before he splashes more water on his face, drenching his shirt.

Heat pools deep down in my core, and I shiver ever so slightly.

"See something you like, Sorcha?" he asks, and I drag my eyes up his chiseled body to meet his dead-pan stare.

I look away, heat flooding my face, as I stammer out, "I'll be over here…"

I practically fall off my horse, legs numb from gripping the saddle for so long, and I lead Gealaich over to the stream while I strip off my wool coat and sweater, tossing them onto a rock. Turning from the water, I hobble down the side of the hill, along the border of the forest and the meadowlands. My hand trails along the tips of the tall grass.

A breeze filters through the meadow, a soft symphony of "shush-shush" as the grass stalks dance with each other. The vibrant morning sun burns away the chill from the evening, warming the land in a way that is reserved for only late summer days. Pulling my hair back, I tie it into a low knot, willing the sweat to cool against my skin as droplets drip down between my breasts. I meander through the field of wildflowers, my hands touching the delicate petals as I pass, and find a little spot to lie back and rest for a few moments. Inhaling the sweet smell of crushed grass, I lower myself down on my back to twist my hips and stretch. Groaning, I splay out on the ground, an arm under my head as the other swings the hagstone on its chain, the pendulum matching the beating of my heart. Thorne's warning has me considering putting the hagstone back under my shirt just as Lord Conall comes up behind me and stands in my sun.

"Tempting, isn't it?" He asks, his lilting voice soft and inquisitive. I squint and look up into his shadowy face. His hair is loose and blows behind him in the breeze.

Begrudgingly, I sit up. Dusting grass off of my shoulders, I adjust my position as nonchalantly as I can when he sits down next to me.

"What's tempting?" I ask. *He's not saying what you think he's saying, Sorcha.*

"Looking through that hagstone of yours," he says, pointing with his chin toward the still-swinging stone. He looks casual, his arms resting on his knees, but his back is straight and he tilts his head upwind, ever at the ready.

"Oh... yes. Thorne gave me a fair warning back at the inn, and I intend to honor that."

"Very noble, Princess, but you've already seen a pixie without their glamour." Lord Conall reaches out his hand and twirls a wildflower between his fingers.

"Yes, but she was injured, was she not? Unable to glamour, like you said. Do all Fae wear a glamour?"

"Most, not all. Especially when there are beings around that they are not used to…" Lord Conall says, gesturing toward a cluster of wildflowers buzzing with bees.

"Are you wearing a glamour?" I ask.

"No," He exhales, "I'm not." He looks at me from the corner of his eye.

"Oh." Good.

"Thorne didn't think it'd be wise for any of us to wear a glamour around you," He offers.

"So you don't have horns like…?"

Lord Conall shifts, facing me directly, and shakes his head slowly, "No. I do not."

I nod, peeling my eyes from his face and looking into the field of wildflowers, watching them sway in the light breeze. "You were so gentle with that pixie earlier…"

"And why wouldn't I be?" Lord Conall asks.

My mouth opens and shuts, words refusing to form.

"We're not all as bad as you think, Princess," he scoffs.

"That's not…" I struggle, fumbling over the right thing to say. "What I mean to say is… Given my first introductions to the Fae, you'll forgive me if I thought…"

"We're not all of us bloodthirsty, warmongering creatures."

"I…" My hand drifts to the hagstone again. The weight is comfortable in my palm, the black surface sliding easily underneath the pad of my thumb as I stroke it absently. Geannie's scream echoes in my head and I shudder, recalling the feel of the horned Fae's hands on my legs.

Lord Conall's voice cuts through my haze. "That hagstone of yours is very rare, Sorcha."

I look at him, confused at his use of my first name. "It is? Thorne mentioned in the inn that the hagstone… is powerful. The intent behind it is even more so."

"Mmm," he nods. "They were right. Hagstones are some of the only tools humans can use against the Fae."

"What do you mean?" I ask.

"The hagstone is a way of seeing the Fae clearly. It sees through…" He clears his throat. "It'll help you see past a glamour that is around the surroundings or the being."

"Oh," I breathe, looking out into the meadow. "I didn't know that the Fae needed to resort to such methods."

"Not all of us do. Here in this meadow, these are merely elemental sprites. I don't think they'd mind too much." Lord Conall says, gesturing to the hagstone in my hand.

"You mean?" I ask, holding the hagstone up so the jet-black stone catches the sun. A twelve-pointed golden star flares in its curves as I lift the chain.

Lord Conall nods, "Go ahead, the sprites are shy creatures and their glamour gives them that added protection from the only human they've seen in a hundred years."

Looking through the hole in the center of the stone, tiny little bodies flit here and there, alighting on the edges of flower petals and the tips of the grass. The sprites are everywhere, with flower petals for wings and grass stalks for hair. Some even look like bees with their gold and black stripes. I take the hagstone away, and I am looking at what appears to be ordinary bunches of flowers full of bees again. My jaw drops and it takes everything I have not to squeal with sheer delight.

Chuckling, Lord Conall remarks, "Not everything is as it seems here, is it, Sorcha?"

He holds the wildflower in front of my face and I put the hagstone in front of my eye again. A delicate little flower sprite sits atop a blade of grass, their purple dress and wings glinting the sun.

"Oh!" I exclaim.

Lord Conall chuckles, holding his hand out for the sprite to sit. "Not all sprites are flowers — only a few. These sprites, in particular, prefer the spring and the proximity to the other elemental water sprites. They're big flirts."

"They are darling!"

"Yes," Lord Conall says, his voice wistful, "Until they were captured and kept in homes for entertaining humans."

I turn to him, curious. The sprite cowers in his hand, looking up at me curiously.

"I've never heard such tales…" I whisper. Of all the folktales and rumors Geannie had told me, I had never heard of sprites being kept in homes before.

"Not anymore, no, I wouldn't think the sprites could have lived long in the conditions the humans kept them in."

"Are they not immortal like all Fae?" I ask.

"There is a lot you still don't know, princess," he says.

The air around the sprite shimmers as the glamour fades from the creature.

"Of that, I am sure. I have so many questions…"

"I could answer a few." Lord Conall says, rubbing his jaw. "If you're comfortable asking me," he adds, a soft smile gracing his lips, as he shrugs and reaches for more grass.

The flower sprite alights from his hand, flitting off into the meadow. He twirls the blades of grass between his fingers, deftly tying them into knots. To be that blade of grass and feel his fingertips against my skin…

He clears his throat and my eyes snap up to his.

"Okay," I say, trying to ignore my thoughts. I hold up my fingers to count the myriad questions I have. "How many kinds of Fae are there? Are they all glamoured? Do they all have magical abilities? When will they let me see them without their glamour? Does glamour do more than protect them from human sight? If I'm trusted through your wards, why do they still use their glamour? How do wards work?"

He groans, running a hand over his stubbly chin. Turning to me, eyes alight with humor, he says, "I said a *few*, Princess."

The wind weaves through the grasses and picks up a few strands of my hair that caress Conall's back. He takes a deep breath, shuddering slightly. The air between us goes taut, tension building as I wait for him to talk. I nervously gather my hair and start twisting it into a plait while I wait for him to collect his thoughts.

He closes his eyes, frowning.

"Let's start with the most pressing, I suppose. There are many different kinds of Faeries. You have the more humanoid ones,"—he gestures up and down his body with both hands—"like the higher Fae and dwarves. And then you have the more wildling, lesser types of Fae like sprites and pixies, brownies, gnomes, trolls. And, yes, most of the Faeries have some sort of magic. Fae magic originates from an element like air, water, earth, and fire. Glamour extends from those intrinsic magical abilities. What I used back in the forest stems from my element of earth magic. There are also Fae that have very specific abilities within certain elements, like shifters."

"What is shifter magic?" I ask, turning to the field with the sprites again. I let the hagstone hang from my neck, wanting to see if I can pick out the pixies from the flowers from this distance.

"The shifter Fae all have their base elemental magic that they come from. So, for instance, Thorne is a shifter and they're an air elemental, so, their shifter animal is one of the air." His lilting voice wraps around the base of my spine and crawls its way into my head.

"Oh! That would explain the white feather," I muse, recalling the feather that floated out of Thorne's robes. "What kind of bird are they?"

"That isn't something I should disclose so freely," Lord Conall shifts a little farther away from me, and I wilt slightly as the tiny space between us yawns like a chasm. "In fact, I may have shared too much. Shifter Fae keep their animals to themselves as a means of protection."

Catching the hint, I change the subject. "Right. So, this elemental magic means, what, exactly? Is it like the class system in the human world?"

"Yes, and no? It's complicated." Lord Conall says quickly, standing up. He rubs the scruff of his face and then reaches his arms skyward, stretching. My eyes follow the long lines of his legs up to the curve of his hip as his shirt lifts with his movements. I watch as he swings his arms and rolls his neck, the muscles in his jaw tightening and lengthening. Then he looks down at me, meeting my eyes, raising an eyebrow at my blatant objectification. He says coldly, "Best to let your betrothed fill you in."

I twirl a blade of grass in between my fingers, opening my mouth to say something else when Lord Conall speaks before I say anything.

"It's not you, Princess. Some things I can't discuss yet. We need to keep going. I'd like to make camp before dark." He reaches out a hand and I take it, letting him haul me up to standing. His powerful grip encloses my entire hand, and I can feel a few callouses on his palms.

"Camp?" I ask, trying to pull my hand from his as my heart rate increases and sweat lines my palm.

"Yes, camp." He chuckles a little, still holding my hand. He pulls me a little closer and asks softly, "You have camped before, haven't you?"

I shake my head, and he releases me, looking me up and down curiously.

"That's a shame, Princess," he says, but offers nothing in the way of explanation.

He gestures through the meadow, back the way we came. I slide past his outstretched arm, catching his scent of pine and fir, my stomach flipping as I graze him with my shoulder. The cluster of glamoured pixies has shifted a few yards closer to the stream where more flowers cluster together. Reluctantly, I tuck the hagstone back under my shirt and twist my braid into a low knot at the nape of my sweat-lined neck as we walk back to our horses. I can feel his eyes boring into my back and I glance over my shoulder to see him staring through me. His eyes are clouded and a slight frown has formed in the center of his forehead.

My eyes drop a little lower, taking in his shoulders and forearms when I stumble, tripping on a dip in the path. His hand shoots out to catch me, quick as lightning. My palm connects with his forearm and a jolt of lightning travels up my arm where our skin meets. He rights me, holding my elbows gently as I get my feet untangled, but I can't take my eyes off his exposed forearms and the haphazard fold of his sleeves.

"See something you like, Sorcha?" He deadpans, and I sweep my eyes up the rest of his body. His mouth twists into a crooked grin as his piercing gaze meets mine.

"You flatter yourself, Lord Conall," I say and shake the loose strands of my hair from my face. Dropping my hand reluctantly from his arm, I turn my head and lift my chin, trying my best to redeem some self-preservation. My hand still tingles from where I grabbed him, and I clench it into a fist against my chest as we near the stream.

Our horses' ears perk up as we get near, but they continue eating the luscious grass. Gealaich meanders my way, picking her way through the grass. I rub her neck and coo as I get ready to mount her again, groaning as I struggle to get into the saddle. My short human legs, unable to get enough height to reach the stirrup, I grunt a few times, head pounding with the strain.

"May I?" Lord Conall's lilting voice sounds from behind my shoulder. He bends over, holding his hand out as he boosts me up and over the saddle, his free hand resting against my knee as I seat myself. Our eyes meet and he drops his hand immediately, fiddling with his shirt sleeve as he walks over to his horse. His forearms flex slightly, muscles and veins twitching. He reaches into one of his packs, shuffling around, and returns to hand me a flagon of water and a packet of dried fruit and meat.

His hand lingers on the pommel of the saddle and he says, "You should probably have something to eat and drink before we continue. We'll be in the sun for most of the day, passing through the meadowlands near the Border. We don't want you passing out."

"Thank you," I say. I turn the jerky around in my hand, the texture too closely resembling the skin of the horned Fae I bit. I put it back in the sack and gingerly pick through the dried fruit, putting a few in my mouth. His eyes flick to my fingers against my lips before he huffs and walks away.

7

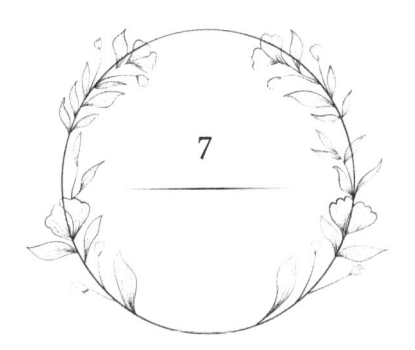

We travel east, both of us lost in our own thoughts. I'm thankful for the quiet ride, save for the gurgling stream we follow for another few hours. Leaving the wildflower meadows behind, we climb higher in elevation toward a small range of valleys and ridges. Scraggly oak and tall, thin pine mottle the encroaching hills, chilling the air as the sun dips lower in the sky, the soft glow of afternoon grabbing at the low-hanging branches on the trees.

My legs are jelly from sitting in the saddle for so long, and I am more than eager for the day to be done when we come upon a small glade of oak trees nestled into a rocky hillside.

"This is our campsite for the evening. Thorne should have been here by now… but…" Conall trails off, circling his horse around the perimeter and scanning the trees. He frowns to himself and dismounts, a distracted look in his eye, as he comes and grabs Gealaich's reins.

"But?" I lean down a little, trying to catch his eye. He leads us over to a tree and ties her up.

Lord Conall looks up at me, eyes still clouded.

I cough.

Awareness snaps back into his eyes and he says, "I just thought Thorne would be here tonight. Most likely they'll meet up with us tomorrow. They like to pretend they don't have their own agenda. May I?" He reaches up to help me off the saddle and I nod.

His firm hands grip under my arms, and he lifts me with such ease that has my heart fluttering. My hands rest on his broad shoulders and for a moment, the entire world goes silent. I blush at the thought of him lifting me up for other reasons, for I am not a light woman.

Casually leaning against the tree, the only strength I have in my legs evaporates as soon as I straighten. His arms box me in and, try as I might, I can't look away from his radiant gaze. My heart beats furiously against my ribs. A lock of his black hair falls into his face and my hand instinctively rises to brush it away.

He grabs my hand mid-air, enveloping it in his, an anguished look flashing behind his eyes. My heart drops as he turns quickly, letting go of my hand. Over his shoulder, he says, "I'll take care of the horses and then we need to set up camp."

Exhaustion overcomes me, and I sag heavily against the tree. I rub my face, trying to revitalize myself enough to move. My legs shake with each step and I sigh, "What a joy a bed would be. A bed and a hot bath."

Lord Conall barks out a laugh. He slings a few packs over his shoulders. "Unfortunately, I forgot to pack a wash basin. Would you prefer a dip in the river? Cold, but it'll do the trick."

"Oh. Thank you. No. I'll be *fine*," I say, snidely. Then, under my breath, I huff, "Would've been nice to have been consulted on this adventure, though."

"You know, Sorcha, the Fae have exceptional hearing. There is something to be said for keeping one's own counsel in these lands," he says. The packs drop to the ground with a thud on a patch of grass and he unbuckles the bundles, laying out furs for his bed.

I cringe and trudge slowly, achingly, behind him. Grabbing a pack, trying to be helpful, I open it and find his clothing inside, his scent filling the air. Before I think, I take a deep breath in, inhaling the woodsy scent that emanates from his clothing. Realizing my mistake, I close the pack quickly, but not quickly enough.

Lord Conall's mouth quirks into a tight line. "Here," he says, tossing me another pack. "I think you'll find your things in this one instead."

I catch the bundle of bed rolls and set his pack aside, face flaming red. "Are we going to be camping every night until we get to the castle?"

He nods, looking at me inquisitively. "Yes, will that be an issue?"

I don't answer, instead fumbling with the buckle on the pack, the intricate knots a tangle to my untrained hands.

"Ah," He nods, realization crossing his face. He sits back on his heels and pushes some of his dark strands out of the way. Somehow, even in the dusk light, his eyes find mine and pierce right through me. "It's a novel experience. Sleeping on the hard ground, under the stars, connected to the earth, wind, moon. It's good for the soul." He takes a deep breath and looks up at the sky.

I follow his lead and tilt my chin. The early evening sky is a cascade of blush and tangerine colors that melt away into the periwinkle twilight. A few stars shimmer in the soft hues of the darkening sky.

"Don't worry, Sorcha," he says, "you're safe in my lands."

I nod, apprehension still clawing at my throat. "And what do I do if…?" I trail off, cheeks flaming again, eyes askance, not used to asking about such intimate things.

His eyes take me in and then he motions to a thicket of trees with his chin as he continues to unroll his bedding. "There's a nice little area over there where some shrubs provide enough cover for your needs," he says. He continues to set up camp, so casually it is as if me asking him about relieving myself was a non-issue. I should feel relief, and yet, I feel a little silly for being so inexperienced.

Lord Conall grabs another bag, unpacking our flasks, a kettle, and a pot. He holds them up and asks, "Would you care to come with me?"

"No, thank you." I grunt a little as I fumble with another strap. He cocks his head to the side, watching for a minute as I struggle to unroll the bedding. I can feel his eyes boring into my back. Frustrated, I stand and smack my hands against my knees to dust off my pants.

"Fine. I've changed my mind. I'd like to join you," I say.

Chuckling, he hands me a pot, and together we walk deeper into the forest. A few bats fly overhead, already swooping for their dinner in the dusk. We walk past the shrubs and trees Conall mentioned earlier, and he jerks his thumb off to the side, not needing to say any more.

Through the trees, a few boulders loom between craggy pines as the sound of a large waterfall looms before us. Clearing the thicket of trees, we stop at the mossy edge of an enormous pool at the base of the most magnificent river I have ever seen. The roaring fills my ears as water rushes over an enormous, mossy cliff face, settling into a glassy, dark pool at its base. Ferns sprout from the banks and bright purple flowers adorn the mosses that cling to the river rocks. There are several flat stones protruding from the water, making this a perfect spot for bathing, if one could stand the cold.

Conall turns to me and says something. I shake my head, frowning, unable to hear him over the roar of the water.

He leans in close, his warm breath on my neck and his lips almost brushing my ear as he says loudly, "This is a sacred place, home to a water nymph. I need to make an offering first before we can take her water. Wait by the trees. I'll come get you when I've finished."

I nod and turn back to the tree line as Conall walks down to the river's edge. Leaning against a tree, I watch carefully as he puts the kettle down and reaches for something at his hip. My free hand trails up to the ear Conall whispered into and plays with my lobe.

The water at the edge of the river gurgles, lapping at Conall's boots, swallowing his feet in the froth. My hagstone warms under my shirt and my hands clasp around it, just as a water nymph completely emerges from the deep pool at the base of the largest waterfall. Crawling out from between the rocks, she is lithe and naked, the early evening light shining off of her jet-black hair and blue-tinged pearlescent skin.

She walks up to Conall, reaching out her hands as he drops something into her palms. Her sapphire blue eyes search his person, noting the containers of water, his boots, riding trousers, ears. The river swirls at the feet of the nymph, cascading around her in a torrent of foam and bubbles. Her skin gleams in the growing moonlight as she cradles the gift that Conall offered her. Jet-black hair billows around her body as if it were still in the water, twirling around their bodies, caressing his skin, and a jolt of jealousy whips around my heart. They stand there, talking for a few moments, as the hagstone flares so hot against my skin that I take it from underneath my shirt. It swings from the chain, the pendulum beating in time with my heartbeat. Carefully, slowly, I bring the hagstone up to my eye, curious to know if underneath the glamour, this nymph is the seductress the folktales have made them out to be.

Through the hole in the hagstone, green iridescent scales cover her legs, and fins adorn her hips. Her webbed fingers clutch whatever gift Conall has offered her, and she has more gills along her ribcage. My eyes move slowly up toward her face when her now jet-black eyes snap to mine, shock registering on her scaly face.

She screams, a blood-curdling cry that tears down my spine, and tiny rows of sharp teeth flash in the moonlight. She drops the offering from Lord Conall, points her webbed finger at me, then dives back into the water. I drop the hagstone, hands trembling, and meet his furious scowl.

Lord Conall gathers up the empty containers, stalking over to me, seething. He grinds out, "You insolent, arrogant human."

"I'm sorry, I didn't..." I stammer, hands shaking.

"Don't give me that," he growls, and stalks past me. "You knew *exactly* what you were doing."

"Conall—" I plead, trying to keep up as he walks back to the camp.

"It's *Lord* Conall, Your Highness," he snaps.

"I don't... I'm... Can you just wait?" I yell at his back.

He stops in his tracks, anger shuddering through his body, as he slowly turns around to face me. His usual vibrant green eyes are hard as he stares right through me.

"I'm sorry. Truly. I don't know what came over me..." I begin. He scoffs and rolls his eyes. "It was the hagstone. I thought with you around that I could... And... It got so hot so I pulled it out... and then..."

"And then curiosity got the better of you? You couldn't help yourself? You threw caution to the wind and decided that you had to see for yourself what an ancient water nymph looked like. You couldn't simply pass up the opportunity to break a promise. You thought that since you looked through the hagstone with me in the meadow that it was ok to do it again. Is that it? Is that what you wanted to say?" he asks, full of mockery.

"I just... I'm so sorry." I stammer, again. Lord Conall shakes his head and turns from me, walking back to the camp, leaving me alone with my shame. I whisper into the air, "I can fix this."

<hr />

I jolt awake, gasping, clawing at the ghostly hands on my body, evil laughter in my ears. The nightmare fades into the oblivion of my waking conscious, and I roll over, swaddled in thick furs on the grass. Pushing myself up to sitting and rest my chin on my knees, mist forming in front of my face as my nose drips from the chill. I swat the hair from my face, plaiting it into a thick braid that I toss over my shoulder. The embers of the fire burn with a soft glow, their dying light casting long shadows into the oak trees in the glade. Lord Conall is asleep, his back turned to me, and I watch quietly as his shoulders lift and fall with the even breath of a deep sleep.

Slipping on my boots with quiet resolve, I grab a dagger and make my way silently back to the river, determined to make things right with the water nymph. The sound of the rushing waterfall pierces the night air, numbing my thoughts with the din. The clearing by the pool, however, is eerily still, as if the entire river itself is asleep. Gingerly, I place one foot in front of the other, until my toes are touching the spongy, water-soaked moss at the edge of the pool. Sinking to my knees, I close my eyes and wait for the water nymph to sense my presence.

The smell of fish and moss fill the air and my eyes fly open. Bright blue eyes of the water nymph stare back at me, her face mere inches from my own.

She says nothing, just tilts her head and combs her hair with long, thin fingers as she regards me cooly.

The river swells around her, churning and propelling her forward, keeping her body partially submerged within its cool depths. She regards me closely, leaning so close our noses almost touch, as her eyes roam over me, calculating. A lump forms in my throat and, though I want to move away, I force myself to stay grounded and meet her gaze head-on.

"You are far from home, Princess," she says at last.

I exhale deeply. When did I stop breathing? How does she know I'm a princess?

"Yes, yes I am," I say, looking forlornly downstream to the South, and meet her eyes again.

"So, princess…" she says, walking around me in a slow circle. "What did you see through your hagstone?"

I hesitate, my eyes scanning her face for a hint of emotion. She stares back at me, placid and calculating, the very image of the Fae in the folktales. Best to keep my answers short. The less I tell her, the better. I say, "I saw you."

"And, pray tell, what *am* I?" she asks, her impersonal voice echoing against the roar of the waterfall.

"A magnificent creature of the water, unlike anything I have ever seen before," I say, bowing my head as she circles around me.

"Clever child," she croons, her feet gliding over the moss and rocks with ease.

I open my mouth to protest the moniker, but she extends a finger under my chin and closes it forcefully.

"Ah, ah, ah, you are still a child to one as ancient as myself," she says. Her nail digs into the delicate skin at the top of my throat. "Why did you disturb my ancient waters this night, child?"

"I came here to ask forgiveness," I say, quietly. Flinching when her fingernail presses further into my skin.

"Forgiveness? For looking at me through that?" She jerks her chin at the chain around my neck.

"Yes."

"And what do you think will earn your forgiveness for seeing me in my true form?" She asks, her nail slices into my skin. I swallow against the sting and a shiver runs down my body as a warm droplet of blood runs down my neck. Her pupils dilate as she watches it cascade over my skin.

"A gift." I hold the dagger up, palm open, and refuse to look away as her blue eyes flicker to take in the blade.

A laugh escapes her lips, pouring over me like water running over stones. I fight against pulling away, afraid her nail will open my neck further. She drops her finger and my hand instinctively reaches up to the cut. Relief floods my system as my fingers trace the small puncture.

She looks longingly at the dagger and touches it warily. Her eyes, a deep blue now, lock onto mine as she slowly takes the knife and turns it around in her hands. She touches the point and gasps, a thin smile forming on her lips, showing a glimpse of tiny, pointed teeth.

"This blade is not the offering I require to make amends,"

THE BORDERLANDS PRINCESS

she says, looking up at me through thick green lashes. Her lips curve into a slow smile.

My heart drops. I am wholly unprepared to offer anything else. "What... what kind of offering do you require so that I may right my wrongs?" I whisper, "I can offer you a debt, a promise from your future queen?"

"Ah," she croons, walking around me again. "A promise from the future queen. Yes. Yes, a promise and a blood offering. This should suffice," she says, flippantly. The moonlight glints off the edge of the blade as she holds it steady in her hand, angled at my throat.

My heartbeat rushes to my ears but my fingers move on their own and reach up to my neck, swiping at some of the fresh blood. I hold my fingers up to her.

"I offer you my debt and this blood freely, nymph, to make right the wrongs," I hear myself say. The rush of the waterfall fills my ears and I watch, dazed, as she takes my fingers in her hand and draws them into her mouth. Her eyes, gleaming, lock onto mine as she licks them clean and then bites down on the tips, piercing my skin with her many sharp teeth. I gasp and try to pull my hand away, awareness snapping back into my bones at the pain. Her grip tightens, and she keeps my hand in hers until she has her fill of my blood.

She releases my hand, throwing it to my chest. I clutch it tightly, searching for signs of punctures, but my fingers are whole. I look up at her, amazed, as she licks her lips. She throws the dagger over her shoulder and it lands without a sound in the pool behind her, swallowed up by the water.

"Consider your offering fulfilled," she says, her voice cascading around me, quieting the rushing of the water. Flinging her hands out to her side, her palms lift to the midnight sky as the river slows to a crawl, creeping over the cliff in slow motion. Her eyes, now pitch black, find mine as she says, "*I see you*, child. Ancient histories sing beneath the waters, from the roots of the trees and through the stones. We know what you aren't ready to hear yet." She pauses. The river bubbles around her, encasing her naked body in a swath of liquid silk. She lowers her head and leans down, her eyes black pools reflecting my kneeling figure. She sighs, her breath cold against my skin, as her deep voice reverberates in my head. "*We* know who you really are. Your story, Princess Sorcha Salonen, is only just beginning."

8

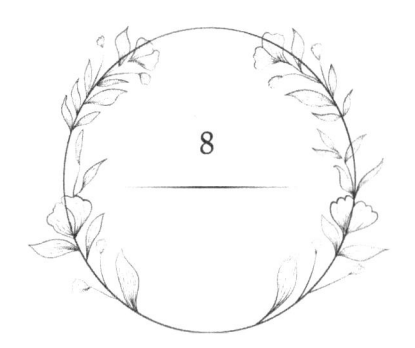

I blink and I'm alone.

The water in the pool shows no signs of the water nymph and my clothing is damp from the waterfall mist, soaking into my skin and chilling me to the bone. Violet hues of the early morning blanket the sky as the sound of the water rushes back, filling my ears with a deafening sound. I stand, slowly, my knees muddy, feet tingly from sitting for so long.

I look at my fingers, whole and unblemished, and stare into the depths of the pool before me as the nymph's words echo in my head.

Heading back towards camp, I stop and quickly relieve myself in the thicket of trees, hoping no pixies or sprites are near. The smell of burning pine and cooking bacon wafts from the campsite, beckoning me to quicken my steps so I can eat.

Lord Conall has already packed up the site, bedrolls and furs strapped securely to the horses. Impatience emanates from him, rolling off of his body in waves. I walk over to where he is angrily tightening the girths under Gealaich.

"Lord Conall, I—" I start, but he cuts me off.

"I left out some bacon for you. It's by the fire ring." He clips, jutting his chin over his shoulder.

"I just wanted to…" I try again, but find the words refuse to leave my mouth. Did the nymph tie my tongue?

"We need to get moving. Eat and then we ride." He says, walking away to get his horse ready.

I roll my eyes at his juvenile behavior. If he refuses to even hear an apology, then I won't be the one to give one.

We head north, following the sacred river upstream for several hours. Invisible eyes rake over my back, the water nymph watching me from her watery home the entire journey. We find a shallow place to cross, water splashing up under our horses' bellies, onto our legs. Try as I might, I see no trace of the ancient river spirit, though her cold water soaks into my pants and shoes, a chilly reminder of the offerings I made this morning.

Coasting up and down, we crest hills and saunter down into valleys, up and back down, up and down. The land, not so different from the meadows of home, eases me into a sense of comfort, flashes of riding horses as a child back home. My young, scrawny legs kicking the flanks of one of my father's horses as I raced Geannie across the meadows. Her laughter catching on the wind, egging me on as we took off through the fields. Father's admonishment when we finally made it back at dusk, having missed dinner. Geannie shooing me off to my rooms alone, as Father chided her for keeping me out past a reasonable hour. The echoes of her stunted arguments carrying down the stone hallways as I skulked away.

The sun signals late afternoon and a chill sweeps through the higher we climb. The foothills of the looming mountains cast long shadows across our path and I shiver, trying to reach back into a pack for my cloak that I packed away this morning, but I can't seem to get the right angle.

Gealaich's hooves slip a few times on the loose slate when we come upon a tiny mountain stream carving down the mountainside, bright green grass and vibrant purple flowers sprouting around the banks. Conall pulls his horse to a stop, sliding off, letting his horse eat and drink its fill.

Gealaichs stops, too, bending her head to drink and I hop awkwardly off the saddle, foot getting stuck in the stirrup again at an unseemly angle.

He comes over to my aide and asks, "May I?"

I nod. His warms hands untangling my foot, and he helps me stand.

"Thank you," I say, and turn to get my coat.

He nods curtly, returning to his horse and reaches into his pack. He pulls out some dried fruit and tosses it to me without saying a word.

"Lord Conall?" I ask, hoping to make amends and finally tell him about my time with the water nymph, "I wanted to—"

Cutting me off, Lord Conall says curtly, "We've got a little way to go until we're done for the night." He stalks off to a small outcropping of rock, gnawing on some jerky.

"Right," I say, tartly, to his back, fumbling with the sachet of food. Frustration wells in my throat and tears threaten. Determined to get him to hear me, I stomp over to where he stands with his arms crossed, strands of hair pulled about by the crisp mountain breeze.

I reach up to tap on his shoulder when he turns to me suddenly and says, "Sorcha."

"Oh!" I jump back, startled.

His brows furrow as he looks me up and down. "Did you forget we have exceptional hearing?"

"Yes," I stutter, shoving my hands in my pockets. Rushing through the next words, lest he interrupts me again, I say, "I just wanted to tell you I made things right with the nymph. I've been trying to tell you all day, but you haven't given me the chance."

"Ah," he muses, rubbing his stubble. His green eyes search my face and I shift under his scrutiny.

I straighten and lift my chin. "I could've saved you all this time brooding had you stopped interrupting me every time I spoke."

"I suppose you could have," he lilts. After a pause, he says, "Thank you for making it right."

I nod and step past him, staring out at the view before me. The Land of Fae stretches out in front of us, offering an unobstructed view shed from being so high.

"That must be the forest I can see from home," I remark, pointing to the rolling green hills that cascade into honey-colored fields, eventually melting into a thick border of forest to the South.

"Yes, in a way. Just like the wards from the other day, there is an illusory magic that creates the Border to the human lands," Conall says, stepping up close behind me. I could touch his chest if I leaned back a fraction. He raises his hand, tracing an invisible line with his finger across the entire landscape that we can see from up here. He leans down into my ear, his breath tickling my neck, and says, "You can almost see the thicker part of the forest, due west. That's the road that we were taking to the king's castle. And here,"—he pivots, his other hand rests on my shoulder and we pivot together as he points along the southern border and almost directly east—"is the Border that lines my land. It goes to the sea, creating an almost natural barrier on the East coast."

"Are your lands part of the barrier formed after the war?" I ask, our bodies having drifted even closer together. His arm wraps around my shoulder as we look at the expanse of his land. My shoulder rests against his ribs, and I have to fight the urge to lean my head against his shoulder.

"Initially, yes, that was the purpose of our title and position in the High King's court," he says. I turn my head towards his face and catch a flash of something cross his face, so imperceptible that I can't tell if he's insulted or sad. He takes a step away, dropping his hands, and the space between us pulls taut like the string of a bow.

"Initially? What is your position in the court now?" My breath leaves little puffs of air after each word. I turn to face him, the late afternoon sun dipping behind the last crest of the mountain.

"Simply, Lord of the Borderlands," he says curtly, and his eyes darken as he turns and heads back to the horses. He waits by Gealaich, watching me walk up to her. Only the flexing of his fingers indicates that whatever I said upset him. He holds out a hand for a boost. "Are you ready? We need to continue before it gets too dark."

I nod, reaching up to grab the pommel to hoist myself up into the saddle.

"Conall, I—earlier, I didn't mean to offend…" I start, but when he glances back at me from his horse, a deep sadness sits behind his eyes.

"I know." He says, then he clears his throat, taking his reins in his hands. "Stay close, these woods at night are unforgiving to a mortal if we get separated." He says over his shoulder, turning his horse westward up the mountains.

We steer our horses into an alpine forest and a thousand invisible eyes focus on us, peering out from the depths of the boughs. Taking a deep breath, I watch as a white and grey falcon flies straight into the darkened wood, its shape disappearing into the dark. It looks eerily similar to the bird from the previous forest and, though I should panic, a part of me relaxes at the familiarity of this bird.

Time slows as I watch Lord Conall ride into the shadows, swallowing him until all that's left is the beginning of a small trail. My hands tighten on the reins and Gealaich shakes her head with frustration, stomping her hooves. Conall nudges his horse forward, as he watches me from underneath an ancient oak tree. His calmness washes away some of my hesitation, so I take a deep breath, and click my tongue, turning Gealaich to enter the ancient wood.

The small path takes us through trees that tower skyward so high that I can't see the canopy. Similar to the Borderlands forest, this wood is dark and overgrown, but these trees feel more alive than the southern woods filled with the lively noises of birds and squirrels that titter and call to each other. I worry that we'll get turned around and several times I almost call out to Conall, but something about this forest stops me. We meander around large roots and through bushes full of tempting, juicy berries. Conall's remark from the other day echoes in the back of my head, 'Not everything is as it seems, in the land of the Fae,' so I keep my hands tight on the reins.

Wending our way along the base of towering mountain peaks, the trees thin out as we near towering cliffs that are chalk white. They glow bright orange with the fading light of day and I barely make out shapes flying in and out of caves on the cliff side. A part of me wishes they were dragons and not the lissome winged creatures instead. The falcon from earlier flies up into the tops of the trees and then comes back down, circling, its sharp eyes watching the forest below. Looking over my shoulder, I can't make out the trail anymore and the forest shrinks in on itself with the encroaching darkness. Gealaich's hoof prints disappear in the trail behind us, the sand shifting with an invisible wind.

Gealaich snorts, and the hair on the back of my neck stands on end, goose flesh covering my arms. I face forward, slowly. Conall is gone, nowhere to be found, and I turn us around in a tight circle, trying to find which way he went. I pull on the reins, bringing her up to a complete halt as she shakes her head. Before us is a large grey wolf, coat shining in the moonlight.

My mouth falls open and one of my hands goes instinctively to the hilt of the dagger at my waist.

Its coat is thick and luscious, and the eyes are practically glowing. It cocks its head, regarding me with a quiet curiosity. Gealaich shifts on her hooves, but nothing else about her raises an alarm. My hands shake but I grip the saddle with my thighs, readying myself for Goddess knows what. But I have nothing to fear because as quickly as it appeared, the wolf turns around and leaps back into the forest.

Holy Goddess.

I can't see where the wolf has gone, though my eyes continue to scan the underbrush, its dark grey coat blending into the shadows of the forest. Unnerved, I click my tongue and try to get Gealaich to keep moving, but she shakes her head and paws the ground, refusing to move. A wolf howls in the distance. A few yips from other wolves return the call, echoing around us. My spine goes rigid with fear as my hand flies up to the hagstone, gripping it tightly.

The world around me flashes bright white.

My hands strike out, I scramble and grapple at fallen branches, trying to find purchase without success. Branches whip at my face and pull my hair as I tumble down into an old creek bed, landing on my stomach with a breath-stealing THUMP.

I lay still in the mud, tangled in the forest debris, trying to find my breath. My cheeks sting where the branches snagged and I definitely have a sprained ankle. Getting my hands underneath my shoulders, I push myself up to sitting.

The bottom of the creek bed is dry, overgrown with ferns, and I peek my head over the fronds. The fog hasn't reached this part of the forest… yet.

Good, I have time.

Not much, but hopefully enough to make it to the stones. Limping and exhausted, I crawl over slick rocks and fallen trees, still hopeful that I'm heading toward the standing stones.

A wolf howls again at the top of the gully. I peer up and can barely make out a shadowy figure running against the trees. I look behind me, my vision swimming, and my breath coming in heaving gasps.

Get moving, Sorcha. Faster. You can make it.

Picking up my feet, I hesitate to put any weight on my sprained ankle, but I can hear horses behind me, their riders yelling into the depths of the forest. Determined to make it to the stones in any state, I wince with each step as searing pain travels up my leg. Branches snap as I hear more wolves coming up behind me, their yips herding me toward the stones.

The fog crawls up the creek bed towards me. I'm struggling to make it over the mossy undergrowth. Scramble. Limp. Scramble. Limp. I look up to my left. There's a small game trail leading up to the other side of the forest. Reaching, I grab onto slick tree roots and haul myself up the muddy embankment. The trail meanders through the rest of the woods towards the standing stones and —

9

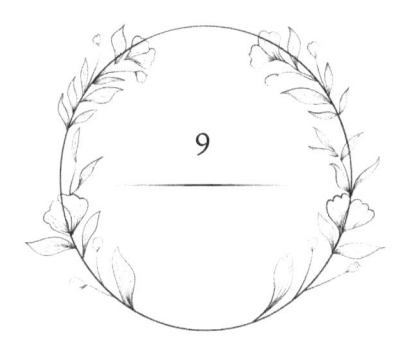

"Sorcha!" Conall's voice breaks the trance. Even in the shadows, his eyes still find mine, vibrant and sharp. "I thought I told you to stay close?" His mouth forms a tight line, his brow furrowing.

"Oh! Conall. There was… there… there was a…" I stutter. Adrenaline pumps through my veins, recalling the vision and the wolves howling.

"Whoa, hey, I'm here." He holds out a hand and grabs Gealaich's reins from atop his horse. His calm voice radiates into my bones. "We're almost there. Let's go." His voice is soothing as he brings his horse around, staying ahead of Gealaich's nose.

It feels like ages, but it couldn't have been more than a few paces when we find ourselves between two large trees as the forest ends abruptly. A glen greets us with a peaceful little stream running north to south. The waxing moon highlights a small bridge crossing the stream and leads up to a hunting cabin nestled into the tall grass. Dark and age-worn, it looks like it has gone a while without visitors. A heavy slate roof rests on top of sagging logs that push the entire building into the earth. It's a miracle that thing is still standing.

A light rain falls (or has it been raining this whole time?) as we enter the clearing and head towards the cabin through the grassy, water-logged field. We cross over a rickety stone bridge, passing a small, overgrown garden and a ramshackle little stable. The cabin looks even smaller as we get closer, and I cast a glance at Conall to see if this is a joke. By the time we've made it to the front, we are soaked and muddy and Conall leads us over to the dilapidated stable.

I hop off, taking Gealaich to a stall. "Sorry, girl, there isn't much hay here for you. But at least I can take your saddle off."

"She should be fine in the meadow for tonight." Conall's voice sounds from right behind me, and I startle. He reaches around me to hang up his horse's blanket on the railing. "It's more the tiny human that I'm worried about being out tonight after dark. We're getting closer to the full moon, and in Fae, that can be host to many problems."

"Oh. Well, I should..." I heft her saddle off and set it on a wooden rail. I take her wet blanket off and, unable to find a place to hang it up to dry, I hold it awkwardly in my arms. Conall reaches out and takes the blanket from me with ease. Reaching up high to hang the blanket in the rafters of the stable, his shirt comes slightly untucked from his pants. I have to force myself to look away.

"Thank you for your help." I clear my throat, giving Gealaich a light pat on her rump, sending her into the field for the evening. Tromping through the mud, I tell myself that at least tonight there will be a floor to sleep on and a roof over my head. Turning the handle, the front door creaks open with a touch of my finger and my jaw drops. Inside, the cabin is huge, with an ornately furnished interior.

Blinking, I ask, "What in the heavens am I actually witnessing?"

"It's glamoured." I jump as Conall answers from behind me.

"You shouldn't do that," I say. His chest radiating warmth into my back though we're feet apart.

"Do what?" he asks.

"Sneak up behind me like that," I retort.

"Oh. Right. Tiny human ears. I'll make sure I yell from at least three feet away next time." A glint shines in his eyes as he smiles crookedly down at me.

"Please do," I say curtly and push the door open further. A wave of heat washes over me from an enormous fireplace.

"Well, hello, you two," Thorne says, popping their head from behind a cupboard in the kitchen.

"Thorne! Weren't you supposed to join us last night?" I ask as I take my muddy boots off at the door and walk towards the fire in the back of the cabin, aching to get myself dried off and warm. I hold my hands out to the fire, and Thorne walks over and throws a few more logs on.

"Long journey, I take it?" They look between me and Conall, then back to me again.

"Avoiding my question, Thorne?" I ask. Thorne smiles at me, a mask of calm, but their purple eyes sparkle with glee.

"Get used to it, Princess. They're a closed book," Conall remarks, taking off his boots by the door.

"You're just jealous. If you just closed your mouth, Conall, you, too, can be mysterious," Thorne jabs.

Shrugging off my soaking wet coat, I hang it up on a hook near the mantle. The cabin is spotless and decadently decorated. "Is this a hunting cabin or a country manor? The outside is very deceptive."

Conall grunts and sidles up beside me, hanging his dripping wet cloak next to mine. I can smell his scent of pine and cedar coming off his clothing in waves. My head swims with want and I am thankful that the heat from the fire hides the flushing in my cheeks.

"It's a glamoured home in a magicked wood." Conall explains, "It's been here for centuries in my family, and the only outsiders who know of its existence are you and Thorne. I'd like to keep it that way."

"Understood," I say and glance around the cabin, noting a few doors on one side of the enormous fireplace. The kitchen nestles next to the fireplace on the opposite wall. Whoever built this place, constructed several ovens into the rock of the fireplace mantle, enough to feed a large party. The thought of food makes my stomach grumble.

"I don't know about anyone else, but I'm famished. Is the kitchen stocked with food? Might I be able to make some bread and tea?" Not waiting for an answer, I make myself at home, moving into the kitchen area, and rummage through the cupboards. It is indeed well stocked with dry goods, so I pull out some flour and leavening agent. I find a kettle for the fireplace to fill for tea and grab a large cast-iron skillet in which to make some quick bread for the evening. I look expectantly at Thorne and Conall to see if they had anything else planned for food.

They both look at me, awestruck.

"Who knew the princess could cook?" Conall remarks dryly. He elbows Thorne, who looks at me with a knowing twinkle in their eye.

"Just because I'm a princess doesn't mean I didn't spend time in the kitchens. I'm thirty years old. Isolated life in the castle can be extremely boring. I can't promise the bread will be edible; however, I *think* I know what I'm doing, even without a recipe." I shrug and roll up my sleeves, refusing to meet Conall's gaze.

"Oh, really?" Conall chuckles.

"Yes, really." I retort, rolling my eyes, "I'm not as one-sided as you may think. I have *lived*. If only in my human world, you know."

"A princess she may be, but you are still an oaf." Thorne hits Conall on the back, cackling, shaking their head and walking away.

Conall flushes a deep pink, clearing his throat. "I—Uh, what can I do to help?"

I look at him and ask, deadpan, "You think I need help?"

"No—I—Just thought…" He rubs his cheek, grimacing. "I'll leave you to it."

"Please." I say, meticulously measuring out the leavening agent. He walks toward the front door, grabbing an axe on his way out. Thorne chuckles from the other side of the cabin, and I smile to myself. "It feels good to have you here, Thorne."

"Oh?" They look up, eyebrow cocked and a knowing smile spreading across their entire face.

"Yes, I like your quips." I beam up at them, happy to know I have a friend in this vast world.

"My quips... Well, I am known for having a quick tongue and a preternatural ability to heal people from the burns of my words." Thorne winks, piling more wood into the fire.

I laugh and lean against the counter, waiting for the bread to bake. It would be easy to slip into a life like this. Casual moments with friends, tucked away in a cabin in the woods filled with laughter and good food.

The door opens and Conall strides in, his arms full of chopped wood. His wet shirt clings to his body and he must have felt me staring, for his eyes find mine. I shake my head, turning to check on the bread in the oven next to the fire, practically shoving my face into the heat to hide my flush.

The smell of fresh baked bread fills the manor and I am instantly reminded of Geannie, the times we'd spent in the kitchen with the cooks kneading and shaping suns and butterflies out of sticky dough for the winter solstice. I would watch little breads bake as I impatiently sat on a stool in front of the oven, eagerly waiting to pack them into a little basket for a picnic in the library.

The golden brown of the crust cracks and I slide a wooden paddle underneath the hot ceramic dish. Thorne, in the meantime, has somehow procured butter. Conall has taken it upon himself to find a jug of spirits, some dried fruit, and has unwrapped a cheese wedge from his pack.

We sit together at the long table by the fire, all of us at one end while nine other seats remain vacant on the other end of the large table. It's a simple spread but divine in my empty stomach, and I'm happy I could remember a recipe from the kitchens back home.

Thorne and Conall's voices fade to the background while I

take in the lavish decorations and furniture. Nibbling away at my bread and cheese sandwich, shadows dart and scatter near the floor by a wardrobe. Tearing a chunk of bread off, I keep my peripheral vision locked on the place where the shadows move, and regard the finer details of the cabin I missed earlier. The living area is cozy but large, and I can see how twelve people could easily commune in here and not feel crowded. They arranged several armchairs for conversation, and two doors on the far wall lead to what I hope are bedrooms.

Another shadow darts between the armchairs and the wardrobe. It definitely isn't a mouse because this creature has wings! I sit up a little straighter and try to track its movements with just my eyes, trying not to give away my excitement. Could this be the elusive house brownie?

"Sorcha, what do you think?" Thorne looks at me at an angle, trying to catch my attention.

"Huh?" I say, mouthful of bread. Tearing my eyes from the shadows, my indecorous behavior earning looks from my companions. Conall, wearing a crooked smile, and Thorne, who leans back in their chair, wait for my response. I swallow, the food traveling down my throat in a large lump. "I... Could you repeat that, please?"

"We were talking about the shift of the seasons, discussing the best ways to honor the Goddess, and we were wondering how you humans celebrate," Thorne explains.

"Apparently, trying to spy on our little house brownies must be more invigorating than our boring conversation," Conall says.

"No, no! I saw some shadows moving, and I got hopeful that maybe I could see one of them," I explain. "What's this talk of the equinox and the Goddess?"

"I was curious what customs you humans had on the other side of the Border to honor the shift in the seasons." Thorne recounts, "The Goddess used to be quite prevalent within these lands and, through the passing of time, our celebrations have gotten less... celebratory. Shrines are left unattended, and sacred places are forgotten, swallowed up by the forests."

"Sadly, that sounds similar to what has happened on the human side as well. The only celebrations I can think of are weddings and the shifting of the seasons that you mentioned earlier. We have feasts, special breads we make, and tables laden with food that represents the season." I hum a little to myself at the memories unfolding from my childhood again. "For spring, we make these delightfully folded pastries filled with honey and chocolate. Midsummer and the solstice, we make sun bread and pastries with fresh fruits. The Autumnal Equinox, which is close to my birthday, we have huge harvest feasts. It is easily my favorite time of year, when you can feel the summer heat during the day and the cool of autumn in the evenings." I sigh contentedly to myself, thinking of Geannie sneaking back pastries for me from the towns' celebrations. And then a crushing wave of heartache swallows me as I realize that my birthday and, subsequently, the day of my wedding, is coming up rather quickly and she won't be there to celebrate either. I am reminded, again, that I am entirely alone on this journey. Alone and woefully uneducated about my future subjects.

Seeing my chance to learn more about the Fae, I ask, "How do the Fae celebrate the Goddess? I was told that your kind was closer to her because of the gifts of magic she gave the Fae."

Thorne talks as they ready some tea. "Bestowed gifts by her and her generosity, yes, but… closer?" They shrug. "We used to give offerings at every shifting of the season and every midpoint. As Fae, we felt it important to recognize the Earth, the Mother, the Goddess, for her significance in the life and death cycle. We also knew that we needed to honor her for giving us some of her natural powers. To keep her influence going strong, we'd offer small but meaningful tokens of our dedication, feeding her the life-force that she gave us—"

Conall cuts them off, jerking his chin towards Thorne and adds dryly, "What they're trying to say is a blood offering."

My mouth drops open and I say, "Sorry, what? A blood offering?"

Thorne grimaces, walking back to the table with freshly

brewed tea. "It's not as gruesome as you think, usually just a prick of a thumb or—"

"Don't lie," Conall cuts in again, looking at me directly now. "The Ancients used sacrifices. Until someone realized that just a few drops are enough to rekindle our commitment."

Thorne scratches their neck, then cringes. "Blood carries a lot of potential for good and for bad. But if used when honoring the Goddess, it is the quickest way to send your energy into her and receive the energy she gives."

I rub the tips of my fingers together, remembering the sharp prick of the water nymphs' teeth. "You said you've stopped celebrating? Why?" I ask, leaning back across the chair to stretch my back.

"Well," Conall cuts in, his eyes flicking over my chest as I straighten. "I think it had to do with a lot of different factors. The Border Wars certainly took up a lot more time and energy. Fae politics are tricky."

"Yes," adds Thorne, "but that is a story for another time, I think. There are more pressing matters you need to know about, Sorcha." They look sharply at Conall, who shrugs and leans back in his chair.

"More pressing matters…?" A flash of movement from the corner of my eye and I whip my head around, searching again for the brownies. "Sorry. I thought I saw…"

"Aye, Sorcha, it's okay for you to look for them. Just know that they will show themselves once they know you better." Conall says.

"Oh, yes! Right," I cut in. "When they're comfortable, they'll choose to be seen. Does that mean they're comfortable with me being here if I can see their shadows?" I lean forward eagerly, taking the chair with me, and try to see around Conall's shoulders to peer underneath an armchair where I swear I saw one dart underneath.

He moves to block my view and catches my eye. "Yes, but stop forcing it," he says seriously, looking at me sternly.

A flush spread across my face at the reprimand, and I settle back down in my seat. "Apologies. I keep letting my excitement run away with me here."

"I think, Sorcha, that the more time you spend in Fae, not just at the castle, but *in* Fae, you'll see that we aren't as different to humans as you've been made to believe," Conall adds, his green eyes finding mine with an earnestness I haven't seen before. "In fact, the more readily you find commonalities, the easier it will be for you to lead our people with empathy."

"Yes," Thorne adds. "Our commonalities will be what wins you over to the more hesitant of our kind. It takes a great deal of empathy to see past differences and find common ground. But it takes a great deal of skill to turn that empathy into change."

"Point well made, Thorne." Conall looks at his glass, twirling it between his fingers.

"Empathy." I catch Conall's eye. How can his eyes look so vibrant in such a dark room?

"Yes," His voice goes low. My heart flutters in my chest, and his eyes dip down to the chain around my neck. "It is the one thing the Fae lack. The Rites help with that."

"Rites?" I force myself to look at Thorne. "What are the rites?"

"The Rites are the time in any Fae's life when their magic has matured. They prove their skills worthy in front of the other High Fae. If they pass and we deem their magic strong enough - true enough - they are gifted immortal life and control over their elemental magic."

"It's also the time in any Fae's life when they find their fated mate."

"Oh." I murmur. "Do I want to know what a fated mate is?"

Thorne's eyes flick to Conall and they say, "It varies from Fae to Fae."

"Right. Well," I find myself suddenly thirsty, drinking down the tea in my cup quickly. Thorne leans over and refills it, the heady scent of the leaves permeating the air. "If fated mates mean what I think it means, how does a Fae know when it happens?"

"Ahhh, that may be something we should save for another time." Conall says. He regards me behind hooded lids, one of his hands rubbing his stubbly chin. "Sorcha, you're the first human we've had here in over a hundred years. You can't expect us to give up everything in one night."

I nod, twisting the empty teacup in my hands, and refuse to meet their eyes. "And as the first human over the Border in a hundred years, how do you think I'm doing?"

"Why do you think you need our approval?" Conall asks, tilting his head to study my face.

Our gazes meet, the low candlelight flickering between us, casting shadows behind his shoulders. My eyes travel up to his pointed ears and the small curls that wrap themselves around his lobes. I want to tuck those unruly strands behind his pointed ear…

"Sorcha?" Conall's voice cuts through my thoughts.

The way he rolls the 'r' in my name causes gooseflesh to travel up and down my spine with the memory of his lips so close to my ear at the sacred waterfall. I clear my throat, and say, "I don't need your approval, I just want to know what you think about having a human princess as your Queen."

"How do *you* feel about it?" Conall asks. He rubs his jaw and pulls at his lower lip. Cataloguing all of his quirks, I store them away in my little mind-library.

"To be honest, I don't really know." I sit back, playing with the end of my braid. Thorne hums, nodding slowly. Neither of them speaks, so I continue, "I wish I did, but my history with the Fae isn't…"

"The attack wouldn't have happened if—" Conall starts, but Thorne cuts him off.

"You're not talking about the attack, are you, Princess?" They ask, a frown fluttering across their brow. Conall leans forward, concern etched into his features, his green eyes questioning, but he says nothing.

I shift in my seat, uncomfortable with their silence. But they wait patiently until I collect my thoughts and squeak out, "No. I'm not."

I take a deep breath, steeling my nerves, and begin recounting the moments leading up to Geannie's death. As my story unfolds, Conall's concern turns into quiet fury. He seethes in his seat, arms crossed, brows furrowed, and occasionally exhales and snorts. When I recall my father's curt words about Geannie, his loud snort and eye rolling stops me.

"What?" I snap.

"It seems to me like Geannie meant more to *everyone* than just a ladies' maid." He scoffs. "Doesn't seem fair that your feelings were dismissed so quickly."

"Yes," I say quietly, "she was very special. She was my only friend. After she died, I…" I push my hair from my face and wipe away a few tears that have escaped.

Conall and Thorne regard me thoughtfully from their places at the table. They are both quiet, Conall rubbing his jaw, Thorne sipping delicately from their teacup.

"If it helps, I think all of Fae may have underestimated what kind of queen you can be, Sorcha." Conall's gravelly voice pierces me to my belly, spreading a warmth up my spine. His chin rests in his palm and his eyes shine with admiration.

"That sounds like a good thing," I say, slowly, worried I've shared too much, showed too much.

"Yes." Conall answers without hesitation. "You'll need a fair amount of honesty and spirit if you wish to unite an immortal species like the Fae. We all need to be reminded once in a while how fleeting life can be and how life could be if we just lived a little. As immortals, we get bored with the concept of time passing and some of us have forgotten the consequences of the Border Wars."

Thorne sips their tea, eyes a vibrant purple, and looks from me to Conall. "Some Fae feel like they have unfinished business with the humans."

"The opposition…?" I deflate, sighing heavily.

Conall rubs his face. "It's a wee bit more complicated than that."

"How so?"

"Well, there are several factions at the moment and they're all thoroughly convinced they're right." Thorne chimes in, sipping at their tea.

"Aye, this is something we've all been dealing with for well over a century. The High King's father made it his mission to unite Fae under one crown. Abdicating and forcing Achill to take up the mantle. Now, King Achill thinks that he's done it, but there are Fae who don't want to be ruled under one solitary royal seat. They want to go back to elemental rule. Then, there are Fae who remember fighting in the Border Wars and will do anything they can to keep their families safe from human weapons. Even if that means killing you. And then there are Fae who believe that the only option we have as a species is to coexist together with the humans and move forward, honoring the treatise, the new Queen, and hoping that your marriage will bring about peace between the two races."

I sit back, my mind reeling from this information. "What side are you two on?"

Thorne tilts their head, studying my face before saying, "I am a healer. I remain impartial. It does no one any favor if those who heal take sides where people can die."

Nodding, I turn to Conall. "What about you?"

He shrugs, "I'm Lord of the Borderlands."

As if that was all I needed for an answer. I roll my braid in between my fingers and then rub my face, resting my head on my palms. I mumble more to myself than the entire table, "Perhaps my education was more lacking than my father initially thought."

"Possibly..." Throne says. "But that doesn't mean you stop learning."

"Yes, but until then, I don't even have the faintest idea of where to begin. My entire life, I was told I would be the savior of the two races by just marrying the Fae king and uniting our kingdoms. After they killed Geannie, I have dreaded this day even more. The pressure I feel from all sides is… I just wish I could stay here, bake bread, hide away from my life for a while." I groan into my hands again and rub my temples.

Something tugs on my breeches underneath the table. My eyes pop open. I drop my hands from my face and freeze, looking wildly at Thorne, who's smiling behind their cup of tea, and then at Conall, whose sly smile means they both know what just happened. Conall nods his head, and I slowly lean down and peek at what just tugged on my pants leg.

Staring up at me with large brown eyes, a mouse-like nose with whiskers, large ears, and a toothy grin is a small, winged house brownie. I glance up at Conall and mouth, "*Oh my goddess!*" and try not to squeal with absolute joy.

As calmly as I can muster, I say, "Hi there. Would you like some bread and butter?"

Nodding, the little brownie scurries up my pant leg and climbs up onto the table, their wings fluttering just enough to help them reach the distance. Their little belly is squeezed into ill-fitting pants and a shirt, held together by tattered pieces of string. Their knobby knees poke out from holes in their trousers, and bare feet with long toenails kick and swing off the table as they nibble a piece of bread with their tiny hands. Those large brown eyes focus on mine, and I hand them more bread and butter.

"Do you have a name?"

It nods, looking over at Conall.

"His name is Tufts," Conall says, chin resting in his hand as he takes in the entire encounter. His sharp angles have softened, and his voice has lost that gravelly edge. I meet his intense gaze and smile even wider.

"Tufts," I say, offering my pinky for the creature to shake. "It's very nice to meet you. I'm Sorcha."

Tufts nods and reaches for more bread and butter, their little tail twitching back and forth. I stretch my hand out slightly, wanting to pet the back of his head with my finger, but I hesitate.

"Go ahead; they don't mind physical affection, unlike some of the other lesser Fae." Conall motions to me, and I scoop up Tufts into my hands and stroke the back of his head. He almost purrs with satisfaction and snuggles into my hands like he's trying to burrow. His fur is soft and downy, varying from a light shade of brown on his head to a deep black around his ears and the tip of his nose.

I lean down and whisper, "If I could put you in my pocket and keep you forever, I would. You are the *sweetest* thing."

He finishes his bread, dusting off the crumbs with the bottom of his shirt, and looks up at me with eyes that could melt snow. His wings twitch, catching the light of the candles. "I've come completely undone. Are all brownies this heartbreakingly adorable?"

Conall chuckles, and I finally look up, noticing that Thorne has left the room and the door to the attic is slightly ajar. "No, no, they aren't. If they aren't taken care of properly—given a house to clean and left gifts in return—their hearts break slowly and then they turn into what we call *boggarts;* greedy, mischievous, possessive, neglected brownies. It takes a work of potent magic to fix a boggart's broken heart."

"Oh, how terribly sad. Who could ever neglect a cutie like you?" I nuzzle Tufts with my nose and kiss him on the head. He squeaks and swishes his tail, jumping down from my hands and quickly disappearing underneath the table again.

Conall leans back in his chair, surveying me. Fidgeting in my seat, I reach for the kettle of tea that Thorne left on the table, pouring myself a steaming cup. The earthy and floral aroma hits my nose, and I bring it to my lips, increasingly more aware of a piercing green-eyed stare.

"What?" I ask.

"Hmm," he shrugs.

I blow on my tea and raise an eyebrow.

"It would've been much easier if you'd been a less complicated human to escort to the castle," he says.

"I'm complicated? I know that getting attacked by a horned Fae wasn't the most ideal. And I really am sorry for looking at the nymph through the hagstone. But... complicated? You jest." I scoff and take a sip of the tea. Its warmth trails down into my belly, making my eyes grow heavy and muscles relaxed.

"No, Sorcha, I don't jest. You're complicated. I thought for sure that you'd—er, forget it." He grimaces and runs a hand through his hair, looking away.

"Please, speak freely. I feel like we've earned that right," I say.

"Well, I was going to say that I think we were all expecting someone a little more entitled. Not someone who was so interested in our customs," he says.

"That's awfully pessimistic." I pour more tea into my cup and offer some to Conall, too.

Nodding, he holds his cup out. "It's not pessimistic, just realistic. As much as we thought we knew humans to be cold, ruthless, power-hungry, magic-less but yet somehow still able to kill us, you are anything but...? So it's proven to be quite an interesting journey so far."

"You sound like Father when he comes back from trips abroad. Constantly assessing the threat, trying to find their weakness." I lean back, calculating his reaction.

"I mean no disrespect; it just comes as a shock." He spreads his hands wide and places them on the table. "I grew up having to think about strategy and learning to fight young."

"Just... how old are you?"

"I'm older than you think, Sorcha."

"Can I guess?"

He nods.

"Okay, so if you were raised to think of strategy and learn how to fight, you have to be over a hundred years old, at least, because of the Border Wars. So... venture a guess that you're going on 135 years old. Though you don't look a year over thirty…"

"Is that your answer?" He looks smugly at me, green eyes catching in the table candlelight. The chandeliers in the rest of the cabin have snuffed out, burnt down to the bottom.

"Hmm, no. I've changed my mind. Wait, no. Yes, I'm keeping 135 as my answer."

"You're sure?"

"Yes, definitely." I nod emphatically.

"245 years old."

My jaw drops and I take a sip of tea, swirling the cup and looking at the leaves settle. "Really? That's incredible, actually. What a life you must've lived until now, what with being an escort for a complicated human princess."

"I never said complicated was a bad thing." His voice is soft and cuts through my sarcasm. I look up from my cup and find his eyes immediately, his hooded stare cutting right through the candles, searing into my soul.

I lean forward now, resting my chin in my hand, and casually trail my eyes over his stubble and jawline, taking in the way his hair curls a little around his pointed ears. A lock of my hair comes free from my braid and falls over my shoulder, and now it's his turn to stare. His eyes pull up from my hip, burning their way up my arm and to my shoulder, stopping at my neck and then finally landing on my eyes. His scent fills my head as my core heats and I lean forward. Crossing my legs to clench my thighs against the want. The chair creaks, and he looks away, the spell breaking and the quiet of the cabin suddenly too quiet.

I drink the rest of my tea, push back my chair, and start gathering up the dishes. I leave out a few pieces of buttered bread and some honey on the windowsill by the kitchen sink and turn around to get ready for bed.

I bump right into Conall's chest.

"Oh! Oh." He's so close. The scent of fir and cedar fills my nose, making my head feel cloudy. My hands rest on his broad chest and I tilt my chin up to stare into his eyes, which have turned a very dark forest green. I whisper, "You've got to stop doing that."

He toys with that strand of my hair, his voice husky and low. "Sneaking up on you? Mm-hmm, I forgot what tiny human ears you have." His fingers twirl around the strand of hair, fingertips brushing against my ear.

I stand up on my tiptoes, slowly, afraid to scare him away. I raise my chin. He lowers his face. Our lips hover just out of touch. He steps forward, pushing me against the counter, pressing into my body. My hands slide up against his chest, fingertips brush underneath his collar. He exhales with a growl, rumbling deep in his chest, and braces his hands on either side of my hips. Our gazes lock and I watch as his pupils dilate as I reach my hand up behind his neck and slide the other hand down over his stomach.

A door creaks open and footsteps travel down a ladder. Thorne.

Conall's arm drops as I sidestep, moving out of his reach. He grabs a glass of water, slamming it down and cursing under his breath as he leans into the kitchen counter. His shoulders scrunch up to his ears and his hair has come undone, covering his face.

"Well, it's awfully dim in here," Thorne says nonchalantly. "I came down because I could see the horses in the field from my perch. I was going to go out and get them in—" They stop short and look from me to Conall.

"I'll go get them," Conall says gruffly, throwing his coat on as he exits out of the front door. A few heartbeats later, he reaches an arm back inside and grabs his shoes.

Thorne looks at me warily, and says, "Let me show you to your room."

10

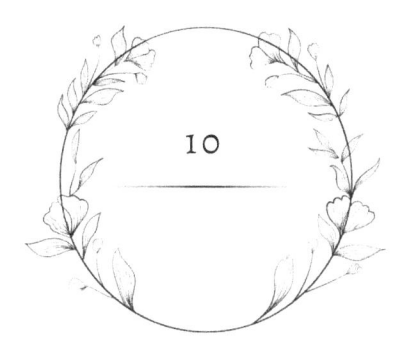

"He's been practicing since before dawn," Thorne says, staring out of the kitchen window the next morning. They wear a blanket of solemnity like a heavy woolen cloak.

Cradling a hot cup of tea, I pad over to the kitchen where Conall runs through fighting drills with a piece of wood. We stand there, shoulder to shoulder, looking out at Conall for a few moments. His movements look similar to the drills Father's guards would run through with Fergus, our weapons master. But, where the guards always looked jerky and abrupt, Conall looks lithe and fluid, moving with ease from one position to the next, over and over as his shirtless body beads with sweat despite the cool early morning. Tendrils of steam curl from his shoulders and his hair is plastered to his face.

"The same routine, the same moves, over and over. That poor—Ah, forgive me, Princess. Did you sleep well? You haven't eaten yet!"

Thorne turns, opening up a cupboard and pulling out some of the leftover bread from last night.

"I'm fine, Thorne, thank you." I grab their arm, stopping their bustling movements. "Are you all right?"

"Hmm?" They stop, eyes clouded over with thoughts I wish I knew.

"You just looked so forlorn watching Conall out there..." I jut my chin toward the window.

"He needs to know when to quit, that boy." Thorne waves a hand dismissively in the air, their robes stirring around them. Another feather falls to the floor.

I scoop it up and twist the feather in my fingertips, noting the light grey speckles on the ends. "Thorne?" I ask, staring at the feather. "What kind of shifter are you?"

"A bird, princess." Thorne answers, looking at me twirling the feather like I'm an idiot.

They walk past me with a plate laden with food and their powdery lavender scent follows. I sit with them at the table, pulling the feather through my fingers. They reach across and pluck the feather from my grasp, tucking it into the folds of their robes. "Speaking of shifting, I will be traveling the rest of the way in my shifter form, until we pass through Conall's lands. Before I go, however, I wanted to see about your stitches."

"Right, yes, I've practically forgotten they were there." My hand reaches up to graze my eyebrow.

"You're healing remarkably well. The scarring should be minimal, at best. Would you like me to remove the stitches now?" They reach down and withdraw a small leather kit from somewhere in their robes.

"Can I get a drink first?" I shift uncomfortably, twisting my hands in my lap.

"I promise you won't even feel me removing them." They gently take my face in their hands, tilting my head this way and that. "I think you should lie down, though."

I move to the floor by the table and lie down.

"Are you comfortable there, Princess?" Thorne looks down at me, raising their eyebrows.

"I'm ready whenever you are." They nod, joining me on the floor, and put my head in their lap. Thorne strokes the hair from my forehead for a few moments before I feel the *tug-tug-tug* of the stitches being pulled out. It doesn't take long until tears trickle down my face at the gentleness they show me.

Thorne stops. "I'm not hurting you, am I? I admit I'm more used to working on Fae that heal fast and not humans—"

"It's not you, Thorne. You're exceptionally gentle. Thank you," I sniffle.

"What is it, Princess?" They stroke my head again, tugging at the stitches with their other hand.

"I—" My voice sticks on the way out and I have to clear my throat. "It's nothing."

"There. All done. I daresay that was one of the best stitching jobs I've ever done. Certainly helped that you were out cold while I worked." They smile down at me and touch the healed skin lightly with the lavender scented cream from the inn, adding, "I don't know how much of a scar you will have, but hopefully it'll continue to heal well."

"Thank you, Thorne." They get up, busying themselves by putting their items away. I lay on the floor for a little longer, remembering the feeling of lying on Father's floor while I read. I spent most of my nights laying on the floor of his study after Geannie's murder, the scent of wood smoke and tobacco wafting from every one of his books on the shelves. The tears start up again and I turn to my side, closing my eyes. I feel a furry little body trying to snuggle underneath my elbow and peel one eye open slowly to see a blurry little Tufts looking down at me. His tiny hand brushes the hair by my ear, and his big brown eyes look at me.

"Oh, Tufts." And the tears come freely now. He snuggles in under my chin and starts purring like a cat. I cradle my hands around his tiny body and just cry. Over everything that has happened, over the past few days. Getting attacked, surviving, ripping someone's neck away, waking up in strange places, meeting strange Fae, pining after someone I shouldn't, marrying a stranger, leaving my life behind.

"I don't know if this will get easier or not, but I am already so exhausted." I whisper.

Tufts chirps a little in return, nudging my chin with his head. His downy, soft fur warms my skin and his tiny little hands wipe away my tears.

"I know a few things that could help," a lilting voice comes from behind my head, and I tilt my head back to find Conall staring down at me. I wipe my face quickly with my sleeve and sit up, trying to hide my running nose and puffy eyes. It's no use. I was obviously crying.

Tufts squeaks and chitters, curling up on my shoulder, holding on to my hair, dabbing at my face with the tiniest square of a handkerchief.

"Oh?" My voice cracks. Tufts pats my head and scurries away under an armchair. I smile after his quickly disappearing body, making a mental note to leave more gifts for him before we leave.

"Sleep would be one." He crouches down to my level, tilting his head, a few strands of hair slipping out from his leather strap. His shirt is open at the top, and I observe a few beads of sweat that travel from his neck down below his collar. "Talking about it is another. And then, my favorite, which is sparring." He holds his hand out to me, and I take it. His hand swallows mine, calluses line his fingers and palms and I flush as he pulls me up effortlessly.

Conall heads for the door, and I follow, putting on my socks and boots. He paces me as we walk towards a meadow and says, "I figure you're familiar with at least some sparring, considering you always have your daggers strapped to you." His eyes travel down my legs and back up again. He looks away quickly. The crisp air outside is a welcome rush of calmness, and I inhale a deep lungful. He turns to me when we reach the meadow and winks, handing me a dagger. I slide it into the holster in my boot.

"Oh, you think so?" I ask, dryly. "What kind of sparring are we talking about here?"

He unties his hair, shakes it out, and pulls it up into a topknot. Tucking in his shirt, I can't help but let my eyes drift up and down, taking him in. Conall catches me staring and pulls out two daggers from Goddess-knows-where on his person and lunges. I dart back and dip, taking the dagger from my boot and palming it, crouching low.

"Good," he says. He moves again, sweeping down and around, pushing me into another defensive position. I roll away, stand, and flip the dagger to point down. It's my turn to lunge, and I go low, slashing for his legs. I miss and roll with the momentum, popping up behind him.

"Better," he says, turning to me, tossing one of his blades in the air. "Stay close. Put them on the defensive." I'm distracted, watching what his hand is doing when he takes the next offensive move and I'm forced to lean backwards as his blade almost catches my shirt.

This time I lunge, adding more strength. I feign a low swipe to his left leg but come up swinging, just missing his face with my other fist. I spin back around, and we circle each other. My shirt is sticky with sweat, clinging in places where I can feel his eyes linger. He peels off his shirt, wet with sweat too, and tosses it onto the fence.

Oh, dear, sweet Goddess Above. My mouth drops open as I come face to face with the taut, lean muscles of a trained Fae warrior. Silvery scars pepper his body and beads of sweat travel down his stomach, dipping below his waistband. I swallow thickly.

He takes advantage of my distraction and lunges, feigning a swipe to my head that I dodge clumsily. He kicks my feet out from underneath me, knocking the air from my lungs. I'm pinned under his muscular legs, one of his hands holding both of my wrists above my head. His other hand holds a dagger edge against my throat.

I am *insanely* turned on right now, struggling against his hand, but it's no use. He is infinitely stronger than I could have ever imagined.

"You're distracted." He leans over, whispering into my ear.

I inhale his scent of sweat and cedar, turning my head into

the crook of his neck. Wetness pools between my legs. I stutter, "I—"

He shifts, blocking the sun, and I stare directly into the eyes of an immortal weapon. My chest rises and falls with labored breathing, my heart pounding. His eyes dip down to my chest, watching as the hagstone slides further from its hiding place, backwards toward my neck. I blurt out, "Conall, I gave the water nymph my blood."

Conall sucks in a breath and goes still. "You what?"

"I wanted to make it up to her and I—"

His grip tightens against my wrists, and I wiggle a little to keep my hands from going numb. He leans down in my face. "Did you promise her anything?"

I go still and say nothing.

He leans back, releasing my hands. Tilting his head to the sky, he sighs, "Goddess Above, Sorcha. You have so much to learn."

He rolls off of me, snatches his shirt from the fence, and walks back to the cabin, leaving me laying there in the grass, breathless and flustered.

The sun rests high in the sky when Thorne departs, leaving in their wake an unsteady quiet between Conall and me. It doesn't help that as we're packing up, all I can think about is being pinned beneath him and I get jittery all over again. Each time our eyes meet, my heart catches and my stomach does flips, and I swear he's reading my mind. Though I'm always the last one to look away, I catch him out of the corner of my eye, watching me as I pack up my bags and ready Gealaich. If there had ever been a bad idea, I should have never indulged sparring with Conall. I keep reliving watching him take off his shirt and seeing his bare chest sweaty and covered in small scars. His green eyes and lilting voice, searing into my brain, sending chills down my spine, as he leaned over and whispered into my ear, the knife held at my throat.

I brush Gealaich's mane out quickly and give her a once-over before I put on her blanket and saddle. Conall is there, ready to lend his hand again and boost me up. He lingers a little, checking my stirrups and packs, his hands resting on my ankle a little longer than necessary. His eyes flicker to mine and he clears his throat.

"Ready?" he asks, dropping his hands and stepping back.

I don't trust my mouth, so I just nod, slowly, once. He's already up in his saddle, steering us over to the forest. The magicked woods part before Conall as we make our way to another game trail. I take one last look at the cabin behind us, the rickety glamoured building showing nothing of the grand manor on the inside.

Deep in this ancient forest, Gealaich matches Conall's pace, and I ease myself back to observe the earth magic happening before my own eyes. I can now see, clearly, that the trees move almost imperceptibly out of the way. Their roots shift underneath the soil, trunks swaying a little with the movement, and the trail opens up ahead of us and closes as we pass. The soil shifts, covering up the trail we just left, and the hoofprints disappear.

The deeper we go, the quieter the forest gets. There aren't any squirrels or birds chirping. Even the horses' hooves seem quieter, and I feel like my breathing is the loudest sound around. Every now and again, I can hear a groaning and creaking as a tree moves out of the way. Conall pulls back and stops, allowing me to come up next to him.

"You need to learn more about the Fae," he says. Conall reaches down to pat his horse's neck, looking up at me underneath a curtain of black hair that's come undone from his topknot. "Ready for your next lesson?"

"Yes," I answer.

"You're sure?" he whispers conspiratorially, leaning close, green eyes glinting with mischief.

"Yes, definitely," I whisper back.

"Right, then." He straightens back in the saddle, all seriousness again. "I'll tell you a bit about the wood nymphs and the forest spirits that inhabit forests like these." He leans back, looking up toward the tops of the trees, inhaling deeply, a quiet smile spreading across his face. His voice becomes reverent as he asks, "Did you feel the shift in the energy back there?"

I nod slowly, and the forest grows still. I shudder a little in my saddle, and a chill wind shakes the leaves.

"Good." He nods, eyes alight with appreciation, "That feeling you have, when you can feel the shift, is the deep earth magic cocooning us within its power, letting us know ancient spirits live within these magnificent trees. Forest nymphs, dryads, gnomes, all creatures are welcome in these magical places. It is their home and what may look like a tree…"

"Not everything is as it seems in Fae," I interject, using his phrase.

Conall looks at me appreciatively and continues nodding. "Precisely. Moving through forests like this is nearly impossible unless you've been gifted way of passage. In order to pass through a magicked wood like this one, you have to be deemed worthy by the spirits that inhabit the trees and the creatures whose home you travel through. Usually, asking for a blessing or permission should suffice. You can travel through with me because you're traveling with someone who has eternal permission to be here."

"Right. Okay, so, say please and stick with you. I think I can manage that." I quirk a playful smile.

"Can you?" He snickers, and I squint at him. "If you ask for permission or wish to pass through with a blessing, you must give something to the woods in return for their continued favor."

I piece together what he's saying, "Like the water nymph at the falls the other night."

"Precisely." He nods again, smiling brightly at me this time. "The tree roots go deep into the earth. Their memories are long. They remember everything and they talk; with the wind, with the water, with the dirt, with other creatures. Every forest on this planet used to be like these sacred ones in Fae; magical, knowledgeable, powerful."

I shudder, remembering the water nymph's words, *"Ancient histories sing beneath the waters, from the roots of the trees and through the stones."*

Conall's jaw drops, "Yes. Exactly. Where did you hear that, Sorcha?"

"The water nymph," I shrug.

"Right." Conall frowns slightly, shaking his head subtly, "As I was saying, all forests on this planet used to be magical, ancient, sacred places. Shrines to the Goddess where the ley lines connect, stone circles constructed to help harness the Goddess's connection."

"What happened?" I ask.

He looks at me and then averts his gaze, swallowing slowly. "Humans."

"Ah. I see." I say. Just another reminder of just how unwelcome I am in this place. "So, if I wanted to travel in one of these ancient forests, what would I have to give?"

"If you want to never get lost? Some of your blood." He looks at me again, and the frankness in his expression has me shrinking in the saddle. "Something you should be familiar with."

"Oh."

"As a Fae with long life spans, these kinds of blood vows help us through the centuries, so we're not constantly having to remember to give little gifts each time we want to pass through. These ancient forests require a permanent connection with you, so you can pass through their magic unharmed. It's the forest's way of knowing *you* when you need to pass through and remembering that through the ages." He circles his horse around me, reaching out to place a hand on the trunk of a tree. A faint green glow shines around his hand and when he pulls away, it's gone.

"Wait, wait, I have a question. What happens if you come across a wood nymph? Are they similar to water nymphs?"

Conall pulls his horse back, raises an eyebrow, and looks at me. "How do you mean?"

"In that I'd have to give blood to them, too?"

He barks out a laugh, "No, Sorcha. You didn't even need to give your blood to the water nymph. She just knew you didn't know what you were doing."

"What?" I shake my head, blushing with frustration. "You mean the dagger I offered would have served its purpose?"

"Yes, she saw an innocent human and knew exactly how to get what she wanted. Are you ready?" He adjusts a little in his saddle.

"I can't believe I fell for it." I say, stunned at my naivety.

Conall chuckles, and I watch as he rolls up his sleeves, forearms flexing as he ties his hair back for the rest of the ride.

"See something you like, Sorcha?" Conall asks, dropping his arms and looking at me askance.

"Hmm?" I ask, picking off invisible lint from my coat. I add, as dismissively as I can muster, "You flatter yourself, Conall."

A soft chuckle comes from deep within his chest and lands right in my stomach, spreading warmth down to my toes and my cheeks to bloom pink. I'm grateful the forest is shady enough to hide my reticence.

Conall clicks his tongue and leads us through the rest of the ancient forest. We ride until the sun hangs low in the sky, dusk pulling its pink and periwinkle hues through the boughs. We weave our way between large trees and roots that slide out of our way. The trail inclines as we make our way farther down the mountain foothills, the energy shifting again. The feeling of being watched, the blanket of quietness, recedes the farther we go downhill. Boulders punctuate the sparse woods and the trail turns rocky as we leave the ancient forest behind. Some boulders we pass are enormous, frozen like sleeping giants underneath thick blankets of moss and lichen. Trees grow from the craggy rock faces, clinging to life on the edge.

Conall slows his horse, waiting for me to catch up. He says,

"These rocks were all once trolls. Caught in the morning light, they turned into boulders. They have been there for centuries."

"Centuries?" I ask, trying to find the faces in the stones.

"Yes, but that's another story for another time," Conall calls back.

An eerie chill settles into my spine when I pass underneath what looks like a stone troll, their arm thrown back ready to club an unsuspecting assailant. I click my tongue to get Gealaich to catch up to Conall.

We crest a ridge, as the sun sets and the waxing moon rises. A wolf howls in the distance. Gealaich's ears twitch, and I grip the pommel tightly. Conall pulls his horse off the trail, and we pop out into a clearing with a small campfire ring and a grassy meadow surrounded by a small cluster of oak and pine trees.

"This is where we make our last camp before we head to the castle tomorrow." He turns to me, a flash of sadness in his eyes.

My heart drops when I realize that this is my last night of true freedom before I'm married to a man I don't know, in a land I still don't know, to be queen to creatures I have yet to understand.

This might be the worst night of the trip yet.

11

Conall grabs Gealaich's reins and leads her to a tree near the clearing.

"May I?" He asks, waiting for me to nod, and then reaches up to help me off the horse. My hands on his shoulders, he sweeps me off Gealaich's back with such ease that I now understand why courtiers swoon.

Conall removes the tack from the horses and sets them free. Pointing his chin to some downed trees at the edge of the clearing, he says, "Let's get a fire going so the horses will stay close tonight. Not like they'd go far with the wolves out."

I hum a lullaby as I scour the forest floor for fallen twigs, picking at the rotting wood for little chips of bark. The nameless tune weaves itself into the night, the simple melody caressing the night sky as I bend and stoop. Filling my arms with wood, I hear a baritone filtering through the trees, lending lyrics to my wordless song.

> "The stones overflow,
> With the magic in our souls.
> When the flowers bud,
> Bestow your blood,

> Underneath the moonlight,
> Beneath the Goddess' sight,
> The forest sings in our bones…
> Can you hear the magic stones?"

Walking back to the center of the meadow, Conall has lit a fire with a pot and a kettle already cooking. He finishes singing the first few verses, leaning back against a log he must've dragged over to use as a seat, and looks up at me as I drop my armful down next to the fire.

He stretches, clasping his hands behind his head. "I haven't heard that tune in decades, Sorcha. It used to be my mother's favorite."

"Geannie used to sing it to me as a child before bed, but I never knew it had lyrics," I say.

"Strange, the things that pass through time and borders," he muses, rubbing his stubble. "It's a shifter song. It tells of the magic needed by certain Fae to shift."

"It's beautiful." I say, remembering the stormy nights when Geannie would sing me to sleep as a child. "What's in the pot? Dinner, I hope?" I waggle my eyebrows and smile, sitting down on the other end of the log.

"Yes, Princess. Dinner. It's nothing too grand, but it should do until you can eat like a queen tomorrow."

"I'd rather eat like this every night than never be able to eat how I want ever again." I say.

He looks away, leaning forward to stir the food in the pot, the delicious smell of lamb wafting up into the night. My stomach growls and I'm thankful for the roar of the fire drowning out the grumbly noises of my hunger. The chill of the night air sweeps around us, and I shiver. Almost like he can read my mind, Conall hands me a tin cup and fills it up with hot tea from the kettle. The cold recedes from my fingertips, and the earthy smell permeates the surrounding air. I sip slowly, savoring the warmth that floods my body.

"All the tea over here is just exquisite," I muse.

"Funny you should mention... this tea is from your kingdom." He smirks a little, poking at the fire and watching the flames lick up the side of the pot.

"No! I've never had tea that tastes *this* good back home." I say. *Home.* Not anymore.

"Yes, I thought it too risky to introduce you to Fae food *and* the land of Fae all at the same time." He smiles, running a hand through his hair that hangs loose near his shoulders.

"Well, that's—"

"Practical. Yes. Not having been around a human for a hundred years, I didn't know how your mortal body would react to such intense change all at once." He gets up and tends to the fire again, throwing more logs underneath the stew pot.

"Can I be frank?" I ask, looking at him as he stirs. He nods, his face earnest. "When we first met, you were so... you were..."

"Aloof?" He gets up, walking over to the pile of wood, picking up a few more logs.

"Moody," I laugh, watching as his forearms flex as he holds the wood in his arms. "But, in reality, I guess you were just analyzing the *complicated* princess. Assessing the threat, if you will." I throw his words back at him, waiting for them to land their mark.

He cringes a little.

"Yeah, well, you..." He trails off, busying himself instead of facing me. If he turned, he'd be met with my raised eyebrow. "We knew nothing about you. No one had any idea what to expect. It was all very much... a surprise. I meant what I said at the cabin: complicated isn't a bad thing." He's facing me now, his gaze soft and luscious.

"So..." I clear my throat, trying to not fall into the depths of that green-eyed gaze. "How is it possible that I haven't had any Fae food to eat?"

"You've had some... but I've carried most of the food with me. It's simple stuff like cured meats, dried fruit, dried tea, and cheese. Nothing too complex."

"Oh, my Goddess. That burnt bacon—was it burnt on

purpose? And that bread from the cabin. I thought there was something too divine about that bread, because it definitely wasn't my cooking."

Conall laughs. "Yes, the bread was Fae. And, no, I didn't ask for them to burn that bacon on purpose."

"If you say so," I look at him skeptically, then ask, "Do you have any Fae food with you now?"

"I do."

"Can I have some?"

"I don't think it's a good idea." Conall hesitates, standing with his arms crossed as he squints at me over the fire.

"Why not?"

"Well, it's... not really... food."

"Ooh!" I clap, feeling giddy. "Now my interest is definitely piqued. You have to tell me what it is."

"I don't *have* to do anything, Princess."

"Future queen," I say, pointedly.

"Fine, Future Queen, but I can tell you that once you have a sip of this, you won't want anything else called 'wine' ever again."

"Okay, Conall, really. I have to know what this is."

"Have you heard of 'mead'?"

"Honey wine? Oh, Goddess above. Yes." I snort, adding, "That stuff is so sickly sweet and causes the absolute *worst* hangovers. All things considered, I prefer a glass of throat-burning, ash-tasting whisky to that stuff."

"You've never had *Fae* mead before. It's not sweet, it doesn't burn, it's... just something you have to try." He shrugs, his lips pulling into an ear-splitting smile.

"Okay, then hand it over." I stand up, challenging him. I jut out my chin and cross my arms.

He shakes his head and some of his hair falls in front of his eyes. I want to reach over and tuck it behind his pointed ears, thread my fingers through that black hair.

"Oh-ho-ho-no. No, no, no." He crosses his arms, widening his stance. "You will have none of this."

Rude.

"All right. Well, if you will not get it for me... I'll find it myself." I head over to his packs.

"Sorcha, it's not a good idea..." But that doesn't stop him from walking over to his horse ahead of me and rummaging around in some of his packs. He withdraws a woven sling with a small ceramic jug inside. He comes over to me, close enough so I can feel his breath, as he says, "One sip is all. That's all you get. I'm serious."

"You *sound* serious," I whisper, not breaking his stare.

"I am. I know the human lore about eating or drinking from the land of Fae. They aren't true. But they aren't altogether false. You will not be stuck here for eternity if you taste our food, but just a sip of this and then Fae drink and Fae food is all you'll ever want ever again. So you won't ever want to return home because it's just too delicious, especially for a human." His eyes linger on my rounded ears, and gooseflesh spreads from the base of my neck down my spine.

The firelight dances in his eyes, and I watch as they follow my tongue as I lick my lips. My nipples tingle at the thought of his lips on mine. I wrap my hand around the mouth of the jug and step back, breaking the tantalizing position. I take a tentative sniff and my nose catches strawberries and honeysuckle, a slightly golden hint of apple blossom and pear. My eyes go wide, and I catch Conall smiling smugly at me.

"Can you smell it? The scent of spring turning into summer?" he asks.

"Yes! Yes, I can! It's..." I wave the mouth of the jug under my nose a few more times. "It's remarkable. This smells nothing like the mead back home."

The words echo in my head and I stare into the fire, watching the flames lash against the logs. Back home? Do I even have a home anymore?

"Try a small sip." His voice is low, and he leans down, catching my gaze and drawing my eyes back up.

I bring the jug up to my mouth, taking a slow drink,

watching him watch me the entire time. The honey wine meets my lips, and then fresh bursts of sweet fruits collide in my mouth, the flavor of summer on my tongue. I swallow. Lick my lips again. Look down at the jug, then back up at Conall, whose smile has gone wide, like he's finally shared the biggest secret of his life.

"Pretty amazing, isn't it?" He reaches for the jug, but I snatch it back. He frowns, taking a step closer. I slide back playfully. Keeping the mead out of his reach, I know that if he really wanted to take the jug, he could.

"Is there even any alcohol in this? I find it so hard to believe that something that tastes *this* good can make anyone drunk." I look at the jug skeptically, raising it back up to my mouth to drink a little more.

"Oh, careful, Sorcha," This time, he actually snatches the jug from my grasp before I drink again. He takes a deep swallow, and I watch as his throat moves in the firelight.

I want to tear his clothes away and run my hands up those amazing muscles, find every scar. I want to lick my way up that neck.

Oh. Maybe it *does* have some alcohol in it.

I sit down by the woodpile, throwing a few more logs onto the fire. Sparks catch and fly into the sky like exiled stars reaching for their home in the heavens, sputtering out before they make it.

Conall sits down next to me, taking another drink from the jug, and sighing. I nick the jug from him, turning away from him as I take another drink.

"Sorcha!" he scolds, but he doesn't reach for me.

"Really, Conall, you should know better than to dangle the delightfulness of Fae drink in front of a human. It's like you expect them to have some kind of self-control?" I laugh. "You really know nothing about human nature, do you?"

He sighs and rubs his jaw, pulling at his lower lip absently.

I take another sip, delighting in the layers of peaches and apple that come through this time. "Do the flavors change every time you drink it?"

"Sometimes, yes..." He looks at me underneath his hooded gaze.

"Interesting... Then I guess I'll have to take another drink to find out what comes through *this* time."

"If you're going to imbibe, you need to pace yourself. At least chase it with some water," he says, tossing me his flagon of water, and I catch it with my other hand, slinging the strap over my shoulder.

"Fine." I drink from the jug again, this time surprised peach and strawberry flavors coat my tongue. "Peaches *and* strawberries! This is absolutely mind-boggling!"

He laughs, an exuberant laugh from deep in his belly. It tingles up my spine and I beam back at him. What I would give to hear that laugh again.

"What?" He asks, smiling.

I shake my head and walk back around to his side of the fire, handing him the water and wine, and sit down. His scent of pine and cedar mixes with the wood smoke, making my head swim with yearning. I grab a stick and poke at the logs; the stew bubbling in the tiny pot.

"Time to eat?" Conall ladles stew in each of our bowls.

"This smells divine." I take a deep inhale of the steam, stirring my spoon around and watching the carrots mix with the chunks of meat. "Too bad we don't have any warm bread to go with this."

"Soon enough. I figured another with some campfire food couldn't hurt your constitution too much." He smiles slyly and dives in. "I still can't get over how bland human food is, though. If this had been Fae, the savoriness of the meat would be unbeatable. The sweetness of the carrots and onions would taste like the freshest vegetables you've ever picked from the garden." He scrunches his nose a little as he continues to eat, like the food itself has perhaps turned bad.

"I think it tastes delicious. But, then again, after a long day and traveling by horseback, I feel like anything would taste delicious. After all, a girl likes to eat."

"Just wait until you get to the castle and try the food from the kitchens there," Conall remarks sullenly and pokes at the fire.

"Thanks for the reminder." Bitterness coats my tongue as I chew on the tender meat.

"You're going to make an excellent Queen," he says, frowning at me, wiping at the corner of his mouth.

"Mm." I mumble, mouthful of carrot. Compared to the mead, the stew is insipid. And so is my mood.

"Sorcha, you're not the first person to marry someone sight unseen. It happens regularly in the Fae world…" Conall looks up at me, slowly putting his stew down. He picks up one of his daggers and a whetting stone. Taking a sip of the mead, he sharpens his blade.

"Understandably, but you also have fated mates, which, I assume, makes the whole 'pairing up for eternity' a little easier. Since I *was* born into royalty, it's never like my life was ever going to be mine, anyway." I remark.

"Surely, that's—" Conall says dismissively. He looks down at his dagger, sharpening away as if it's the most fascinating thing he's ever done.

"What, that's not true? Of course it is. I don't know why I would ever think it'd be different. My life was never my own. First, I was born into royalty, and then the treaty - dangling over my head like the executioner's blade. It is just something I have to be okay with. I've had several chances to change my future, but I love my people, Conall." He looks up, meeting my gaze with a sincerity I haven't seen before. I continue, "I do. I have a duty to them and to my kingdom. Restore peace and live in harmony. But, for the first time in my life, *in my life*, I have been making my own choices—some not so great, I admit, though meeting a nymph was pretty exciting." I flash a sly smile towards Conall and pass him the jug. "But this feeling of freedom is just… It's like nothing else I've ever felt. I have *friends* in creatures I once feared! *Friends*. I've never had friends before. Everyone back at home was just so placating and pitying towards me."

I close my eyes against the flood of memories that threaten to overtake me, tears well up behind my lids. A vision of me as a young girl, running through the halls, down to the stables, trying to get the stable hands to go riding with me. Completely unaware that they were not my equals. It took me months to realize that they were told specifically to not interact with me. When Father finally told me I couldn't play with them, I was crestfallen. I cried for hours. Geannie had to carry me back to my rooms. It was the first time I realized they only saw me as a war-prize. That my life wasn't ever going to be normal, that my life was never my own.

"You can't really mean that. Someone like you—" He takes a long swallow of the honey wine and corrects himself, "Someone of your station, I mean, had to have ladies-in-waiting and many people to keep you company."

"Yes. And, no. Father felt that, since I was leaving anyway, what was the point of having any 'emotional investment' in other humans? I think others felt the same, since they always kept themselves at arm's length. The only person I ever got 'close' to? My lady's maid, Geannie. After her murder, I have been well and truly alone for most of my life."

"Well, this all sounds incredibly shortsighted and cruel for your father to do." Conall cocks an eyebrow at me and throws more wood on the fire.

"No. No, *you* don't get to judge him. He thought he was doing his best. He had to send away his daughter, *his only child*, to marry a stranger for a political alliance that was set in motion before I was even born. I can't imagine what that must've felt like, knowing that your child was just a promise to keep a treaty going. And, after being widowed, I'm sure it made the reality of our situation more depressing. I'm a glorified sacrifice." I stand up abruptly and walk to the edge of the firelight, shivering a little as I leave its warmth. A quiet fury building in my chest as I fight tears that want to fall. I add quietly to myself, "It would've been nice to have been fought for, though."

Conall walks over to me, hovering behind my back, and lays a blanket around my shoulders, squeezing them lightly. "It's hard to know what really happened with the treaty if you weren't there. My father was one of the few Fae present at the signing and, even then, he was always tightlipped about the whole thing." I turn around, staring into his eyes, and he shrugs, walking back to his place by the campfire.

"Well, that's new…"

"What?" He sits back down, motioning for me to sit with him.

"You've mentioned no one in your life before… What was he like, your father?"

"He was brilliant, a master at his magic." He pauses and contemplates the stars in the night sky. "Compassionate. Kind. Curious. But he was so aloof. Gone on long trips, always disappearing to the human side any chance he could get before the wards got stronger. The King commissioned him as one of the High Fae to help enforce the magic at the Border. He so strongly opposed the idea that it practically killed him. Death was a sweet release for him."

"Is that how he passed?" I sit back down and adjust the surrounding blankets, cocooning myself into their warmth. They smell of cedar, fir, and rain. They smell like Conall.

"No, not really, but I think it was the catalyst. He was never quite the same afterward. His magic came sparingly… and, after, he stayed in his wing of the house more frequently. Our relationship splintered after that. The only person who could talk to him was my mother and, once she died, he practically withered away."

"How do you mean?"

"I keep forgetting that you don't know that much about the Fae." He laughs tightly, running his hands through his hair, and he ties it back again.

Oh, but it was so pretty when it was down.

"Remember, we mentioned the fated mate? Well, it's the one person who matches your soul, balances you out, cradles your love so close in their heart. Sometimes, fated mates meet in this lifetime, and they blissfully get to spend their long lives together. Other times, you wait several lifetimes to meet. But once you mate, that's all there ever is for you. Especially in our family, like with my father and mother. Once she died, there was nothing else left for him to live for." Conall takes a pull from the jug and passes it to me. "Not even his children."

"How heartbreaking." I take a long pull from the jug, looking sideways at Conall. "So, you have siblings, then?"

"Yes, I do," he says curtly. "You should tread carefully with that wine, Sorcha. Humans aren't equipped to drink at the rate we Fae do." He holds his hand out for the jug, and I look him in the eyes, defiantly taking another long swallow. "I'm serious, Sorcha. It's going to go to your head really fast."

"Eh, so be it. If this is my last night of full freedom, I'd like it to be memorable and make some really awful choices. This being one of them." Kissing Conall being another as I shake the jug in the air and take another swallow. "You were saying, about fated mates... How do you know when it happens? Do all Fae have them?"

"Yes, and no; some Fae are open to it, and others try to deny it as long as possible. Sometimes, denying your fated mate or not recognizing the connection you have with them can drive someone mad."

"Mad?"

"If both parties don't acknowledge the link, or if one refuses to accept the mating bond, then madness can set in."

"What's the mating bond?"

"Uh," Conall looks at me sidelong and if the light of the fire wasn't casting shadows on his face, I would swear he was blushing. "A bite."

"A bite?"

"Yes, a very physical claiming... on the neck." He coughs.

"Oh." I say, shocked.

"Yes, it's a way for the mates to mark the other. Permanently. For the rest of Fae to see." Conall says, refusing to meet my eyes.

"Sounds... primal." Something deep in my belly flutters. His eyes flash to mine and I clench my thighs against the desire that pools in my center.

Conall clears his throat and starts sharpening his blade again. He says, "Some Fae can hold off the madness for centuries, others for only months before insanity takes them." He looks up at the stars winking in the sky. "And then they return to the ether for the cycle to start all over again. There are few things that can actually kill a Fae without serious injury. Not mating is one of them."

"I had no idea," I whisper into the flames.

"It's not something we like to talk about." He takes another swig from the jug and hands it back to me. "Because it rarely happens. The lesser Fae, the wildlings, don't have mates. It's just the High Fae. We're the ones with the magic strong enough to recognize it."

He gets up to grab another log and throw it on the fire. I run my fingers against my lips, swaying a little as the flames of the fire swirl higher into the night. I tilt to the side to straighten the crooked campfire. "Ohhhhh, thas inters'ing."

Did I just slur?

I sit up a little straighter and look around slowly. The world shouldn't be spinning this fast.

Conall continues, "Some Fae know right away, and for others, it takes a while. But when the connection is close to being recognized by both parties, it's said that weird things happen. Thoughts are shared, emotions are shared, life paths can even become similar." Conall spreads his hands wide and looks up at the stars.

"D'you have fated mate?" I try to whisper, but it comes out a little louder than I wanted, and I cringe.

Too loud! Wishper more quiet.

And then I hiccup.

Oh dear.

"I have yet to experience those things." He looks at me, his eyes boring into my soul. They're sooo greeeen! I lean forward, searching for his searing gaze, trying to get the fire to stop spinning so I can stare harder, and I almost fall forward.

"Are all Fae this stupid gorgeous? Did I say that out loud?" My cheeks flame red and I snap my mouth shut.

Conall laughs and watches me closely.

I stand up, and the blankets fall from my shoulders. I need to get some space from the heat of the fire, his piercing stare, and the smell of him coming from the blankets.

The world spins and my hands shoot out to steady me.

No, no, I'm tilting!

"Careful, Sorcha." And he's suddenly next to me, holding my arms, and I'm staring even deeper into those intoxicating eyes.

"Mm-hmm," I have forgotten all semblance of language.

His hands move from my forearms up to my elbows, I grip his arms like a lifeline, his body anchoring me lest I fall flat on my face. Everywhere his fingers touch pulls me closer to him until my chest smashes up against his. His hands splay across the small of my back and I have to tilt my head so far back the world spins.

I hiccup and sway.

One of his hands cups my face. "Let's get you some water."

"Okay," I whisper, completely frozen in place, waiting for his hands to leave my body.

They don't.

"I'll go get it," He says, staring into my eyes, but his hands somehow pull me even closer up against him.

"Okay," I whisper again, his fingertips light my skin on fire.

Neither of us move, however, except my head that tilts upwards towards his mouth. He's so tall!

"Sorcha…" He whispers a warning, lips hovering above mine. His eyes burn a hole into my soul.

"Conall…" I mimic his tone. And then his mouth is on mine. His scruff chafes my chin, leaving a raw, rugged burning and I couldn't care less. My fingers are in his hair, and his tongue slides into my mouth effortlessly as I open to him. His hands slide down and grab my backside as my knees go weak. I moan when he presses me closer and I can feel his growing hardness against my stomach.

"Goddess, Sorcha," He breathes into my mouth, but he doesn't stop. "This is such a bad idea."

"It is?" I ask, struggling to find my footing, my chest heaving with anticipation. I pull him closer, wanting to absorb his body into mine, but these damn clothes are getting in the way.

His mouth consumes my skin as he makes his way down my neck, leaving a trail of fire in his wake. He goes lower, one hand opening the top of my shirt as he kisses the tops of my breasts.

"Oh." I shudder.

"I want you. I do," He says, his fingers hook into my waistband and I grow wet. "But…"

"But?" I breathe, fingers twining in his hair as he continues to worship my skin.

"Sorcha," He stops, taking my face in his hands, "I don't want to—"

"Conall," I say, cutting him off before he says something I don't want to hear. "This is my last night of freedom before I'm married to a man I don't even know. If I didn't want this, you'd know."

He drops his hands. The night air kisses my flushed cheeks. For a moment, I feel like I've said the wrong thing, but then his hand slides down my arm and he grabs my hand. We walk over to the makeshift bed of furs.

"Your tiny human ears." He pulls me into him again, tucking a loose strand of hair behind my ears, tracing the lobe. "You're sure?"

"Yes, definitely," I whisper, gooseflesh traveling down my spine. His thumb traces my jawline, my bottom lip.

"Then lie down," He says, getting on his knees at the end of the furs, "My Queen."

He undoes my shoes, pulling them off one by one with utmost care. My pants go next and I lift my hips to help him as he tugs them down over my thighs.

"Goddess, I love your body." He breathes reverently, placing kisses on my soft stomach, trailing his lips over my hips and along the tops of my thighs. He traces the stretch marks with his fingertips. Within moments, the only thing I'm wearing is my shirt and I shiver a little from the cool air.

"You're cold." He says, concern flashing over his face.

"A little, but I'll be fine." I say, slurring my words in haste.

"I can fix that." He slides up next to me, wrapping me in his arms, and then it's a tangle of hands on bodies, mouths crashing into each other. I reach up and grab his hair at the nape of his neck and he growls into my mouth with pleasure, setting me alight once more. He trails a hand over my hips and cups my bare backside. My bones liquify everywhere he touches. I open my legs and his hand slides down my thigh, fingers trailing lower. I'm grasping, desperate to pull him into me.

He slides a finger inside and I moan into his mouth, his tongue plunging deep. He growls and adds another finger, pushing up against me as he strokes me deeply.

I shudder, moaning, throwing a leg over his hip, opening my legs wider to get his fingers deeper. "Oh, Goddess..."

"Sorcha, you're... so..."

I arch my back, pressing my chest into him. He sucks at the curve of my neck and I reach down, trying to undo his pants. He growls into my skin, his arm tightening around my back as I free him from his pants.

My hand wraps around his hardness and he curses, stilling against me as I stroke him slowly, watching as his pupils dilate when I twist my hand. I nod slowly. He shimmies out of his trousers. My hands grab at his shirt and pull it over his head, tugging it free from his body. The campfire light casts shadows on every muscular curve of his body. His olive skin looks darker in the low light as I run my hands down over his chest, my nails catching lightly at the scars that pepper his skin. He shivers and grabs some furs, flipping me onto my back, enveloping us in the warmth.

I wrap my legs around his waist, eager to take him in when he says, "Sorcha, there's no going back after this."

"I'm okay with that," I say, infusing my eager consent into the words.

"You're sure?" His voice is low and soft, comforting. His thumb traces my bottom lip and then I take it into my mouth, sucking on it, and smile as his eyes go wide.

Releasing this thumb, I nod, "Yes, definitely."

He settles himself then pushes inside me with reverence and I gasp as he fills me. He seats himself, stilling against the deepest part of me, and I can feel him pulsing. I wiggle a little, wrapping my legs around his waist, and he inhales sharply.

"Don't. Move." He says, gruffly.

"You can't be ready yet, can you?" I giggle, squeezing a few times. He shudders. "Oh! Oh, you're really fighting it, aren't you?"

"Just give me a minute," He pleads. "You feel... Goddess, you feel amazing."

"Show me." I wiggle again, bucking my hips against his. "Show me how good I feel."

"As you wish, Your Highness," he growls into my ear. Weaving his fingers in my hair, he pulls my head back as he withdraws slowly. I cry out as he thrusts inside, over and over, his muscles tensing under my hands. I claw at his back, lifting myself higher while his hips drive into me. We peak together, our bodies shuddering, breathless, desperate but far from satisfied because within moments, we are devouring each other again as the stars above watch on.

12

Morning comes too soon, too bright, too early. Whispered voices sound behind my head.

"I told you it was a bad idea to take her this way." Thorne whispers.

"How else was I supposed to keep her safe?"

"Conall, you can't prolong the inevitable." Thorne admonishes, then adds, "It reeks of sex, you know."

Conall harrumphs in response, takes a few steps towards me, and says, "Come on, Sorcha. It's time to get up and finish the last few hours of our journey."

I stretch and inhale the lingering scent of him on the furs. Cracking my eyes open, the world spins precipitously.

"I honestly don't think I can move. I've never felt more horrid in my entire life," I groan.

"Ahhh, yes. The lovely after-effects of Fae wine," Thorne says, their calming voice filtering through the air.

My head pounds, and my dry tongue sits like a weight in my sandy mouth. Dry, cracked lips are on the verge of bleeding. I kneel on the ground and hang my head. My hair falls in a tousled mess over my eyes. Whimpering, I rub the sleep from my eyes and sit back on my heels. I most likely snored last night.

"You snored pretty heavily last night," Conall says nonchalantly over his shoulder as he finishes packing up the horses. He tosses me a wad of clothing. "You might want to put these on if you're thinking of standing up."

"Oh, the day keeps getting better." I roll my eyes skyward and immediately regret the searing sunlight that burns into them. Standing up too fast, bile burns in the back of my throat.

"I don't want to hear it," I point a finger at him as I tromp past the tree line to relieve myself, pants tucked under my arm, hoping to the Goddess above that the woodland creatures and forest spirits have averted their eyes for their own sake.

"I really don't know if I can ride today. Can you just magic me to the castle?" I say, walking back into the clearing, fully dressed.

"Sorry, Princess, it doesn't work like that," Thorne says, appearing from the opposite side of the forest from where I had just relieved myself.

"We have to enter on foot. The castle has been warded for centuries to prevent magical arrivals from occurring within the grounds. The only person who can magic themselves in or out is an heir to the throne," Conall adds.

"Oh. So there *are* better ways to travel through Fae than just constantly riding a horse or walking? Why am I just now hearing of this?" I raise an eyebrow and stare at both of them.

Thorne laughs and looks at Conall. "Should I tell her?"

"What? What am I missing? What don't I know?" I look between Thorne and Conall.

"It's not something you would've known, Princess. Only if you're a High Fae, you can use portal magic to transport yourself to places," Conall says.

"I'm sorry? Portal magic?" I am incredulous. Reaching into a pack on Gealaich's rump, I pull out a satchel of dried fruit.

"Portal magic works like this: Think of a mirror, opening up into another part of the world. You can step through, but it only works for mere moments because it requires a great deal of concentration and magic in order to tear a rift big enough for you to pass through. It takes even greater magic to travel somewhere you have never visited before," Thorne explains.

"But you can't portal me into the castle, then?" I ask, gnawing on the fruit. The nausea abates slightly with the sweetness of the dried apple.

Conall packs up the rest of the campsite, refusing to look me in the eye, deftly avoiding getting anywhere close to me. And all I can think of is falling asleep in his arms last night, the warmth of his body pulling me under, the feeling of him inside me.

Thorne coughs and I shove the memory down.

They continue, "Typically, portal magic works best if you have an anchor you can use to pull yourself through the rift and transport yourself safely. Water is one of those anchors, and so are memories of certain places. Emotional connection works really well. But what works best, and what most Fae choose to do, is to leave small tokens wherever they go in order to portal back and forth to places quickly. The castle, like Conall said, has been warded against this kind of magic to protect the crown."

"Wards are powerful enchantments, Sorcha," Conall says, finally. "My father and mother warded our lands before her passing, and it took the rest of my father's magic with my mother's combined to create unbreakable wards that would last longer than their lifetime."

Conall walks over to the edge of the forest where two large standing stones now rest. He places his hand on one and leans against it, almost patting it lovingly like he does his horse.

How did I not see them before?

"These stones mark barriers of our land that allow for travel into and out of our lands. They appear when one who shares my blood gets close. Otherwise, it's almost like our lands don't exist in Fae. We are the protectors of the Border for a reason. It's hard enough to pass through Fae on your own, but trying to pass through our lands, whether you are human or Fae, is nigh impossible unless you have me or one of my siblings to escort you. It's what made these lands so safe for you to travel through, Princess."

"So, wait a minute." I pinch the bridge of my nose and frown. "There's 'portal magic,' there's a magic called 'warding,' and it now sounds like land can be magicked, too?"

"Yes..." Conall hesitates.

"Are there any limits on Fae magic?" I ask.

Thorne interrupts the moment. "The lesser Fae, like we mentioned before, have more elemental magic. Pixies and gnomes, water sprites, sylphs, all have some kind of power over their elements, whether it's helping to control parts of the weather, grow plants, herbs, or crops. High Fae have the magic for things like portals, wards, and controlling stronger elemental magic. Does that make sense? Our magic is limited in what we can do. We can't be more powerful than the Goddess. We can't be more powerful than Earth herself, for she is the one who gave us these gifts."

I walk to the edge of the forest, looking at the standing stones, mulling over this new information. This time, upon closer inspection, I notice that the stones have swirls and whorls carved into them, creating deep rivulets all over. The stones have deeply embedded flecks of light and color into their carvings, giant stone snakes that slither and bask in the sun.

"The carvings move when they're being called upon to open," Conall says from behind me, startling me again.

"You have to stop sneaking up on me like that." I glance up at him and frown, then turn back to muse at the carvings.

"Remember that not everything is at it seems here, Sorcha." He sounds so serious that I shudder.

And yet, I reach my hand forward, watching the swirling snakes on the stone as they glimmer in the sun, and I hear the most beautiful humming coming from the forest.

Or is it coming from the stones?

Conall's hand reaches over mine and clasps it.

A flash of light and I'm thrown forward into a deep darkness.

I can feel the hum of the magic pulling me closer. Through the trees in the distance, the standing stones glow in the moon's light, beckoning me to come touch them. *The wind tickles my ear and I swear I hear it say, "Come home." My fingers tingle and the tips of my nails turn a light shimmering green with the budding magic recognizing familiar kin. The limp in my ankle fades to a dull ache with every step I take closer to the clearing.*

Looking down at my feet, the fog creeps through the forest again, wrapping its icy fingers around my ankles, thicker this time. The fog blankets the forest once more, advancing deeper into the undergrowth, climbing up my legs. My steps slow and I drag my feet through what feels like knee-deep mud as the fog pulls me back.

I'm... so... tired. I just.. need to... catch my breath... I have time for that... don't I?

The fog pulls at me, clouding my senses, filling me with fatigue. I lean against a tree and slump against the rough bark. The tree itself groans and a sleeping face forms in the trunk next to my hand. Should this bother me? I'm too tired to care.

The wind shifts, carrying with it the warm scent of vetiver mixed with lemon. I breathe deeply and—

My eyes fly open, and I gasp. I'm thrown backwards into Conall's chest, my hand clasped to my hagstone, his hand still covering my other one.

"You almost touched the stones." He holds me steady, his grip gentle and his presence soothing. I lean into him, my head wanting to rest against his shoulder, when he drops my hand immediately and takes a few steps back.

I stumble backward, stunned at the sudden change in his behavior. "I just—"

"We need to get going, Princess," Conall says, turning to the horses. He swings himself effortlessly into his saddle and I'm sure my face turns green with jealousy.

Thorne nods to me, their amethyst eyes shining brightly before they shift in a puff of smoke. A grey and white falcon soars through the wards that shimmer and pulse.

"Thorne!" I gasp, recognizing the familiar bird from the beginning of our journey. "They've been here this entire time, haven't they? Do you think they...?"

"Oh, I'm pretty positive they got an eyeful last night." Conall says and mumbles something else under his breath.

"What?" I ask.

"Nothing," he says, looking down at me from his horse. "Do you need help today getting on Gealaich?"

"No…? I think I can manage. Thank you." He doesn't meet my eyes when I look at him, confused at his change in behavior. I hop, skip, and somehow scramble enough to get myself in the saddle, which now sits crooked on Gealaich's back. I shift, playing with my weight in the saddle, trying to straighten it.

"Onward then," he says as he gestures his arm at the standing stones.

The whorls flare to life, swirling, shimmering colorful snakes in the bright light of morning. Gealaich walks us through and again the air contracts, squeezing my lungs as I pass through. The clearing behind us vanishes, the campfire ring, the packed grass where we lay last night, and with it my feelings of freedom. A weight settles on my shoulders as I face forward, saying a silent goodbye to the woman who felt agency for the first time in her life. Conall passes through next, a whooshing of air at my back, and I inhale his scent of rain-soaked pine and cedar. I look to the sky, but I don't see Thorne's falcon anywhere.

We crest a mossy hill, emerging from the woods to an incredible view of the land below. Craggy, sharp outcroppings that point skyward give way to thick pockets of ancient forests and grassy meadows further down the mountainside. Thick storm clouds gather in the distance, covering the land with intermittent dark shadows, the sun illuminating the vibrant green land below in a patchwork of light.

Conall pulls his horse around to my back and I can feel his gaze boring into me as I wait for him to break the silence first.

I snap, "What is it, Conall?"

"Sorry, what?" he asks, bewildered.

"Your whole thing…" I turn in the saddle, waving my arm at him vaguely, "You've been curt all morning. So, what is it?"

He harrumphs, nudging his horse toward the start of a

downhill trail. Mere inches apart, his legs almost brush mine as he passes.

"Good answer," I sneer at his back.

"What do you want me to say, Sorcha? I told you everything would change after last night," he says.

My mouth drops open in shock. I stutter, "I—I guess nothing, then. And I guess I'm nothing to you, too. Which is fine. I'd rather that be the case than be a part of something I can't have, I suppose."

"Sorcha, stop. That's not what I—" He scoffs, pulling on his reins and turning to face me.

"No. No, this is exactly what needs to happen. But you can't tell me that there's nothing between us. That nothing is here," — I gesture to the space between us and his eyes flick to me briefly —"especially after last night? And the conversation I overheard this morning… and then at the Inn."

"What do you think you heard?" Conall rebuffs, his voice gruff.

"Oh, don't patronize me. Not now. Not after everything we've just gone through." I pause, plaiting my hair and throwing it over my shoulder. Sighing, I say, "Forget it. I must be reading into things a little too much. Let's just move on. Pretend like we didn't just have a fantastic night together under the stars. Pretend like there is absolutely no chemistry here between us. I mean, why am I even entertaining anything at all? I know your job is done as soon as I'm delivered like a delicate little parcel to the king. This is absolute nonsense."

"Sorcha, I—" He starts.

Cutting him off, I spit out, "I said, let's drop it. I'm sorry I brought anything up at all. Besides, I'm the human princess promised to the Fae king, and Goddess only knows the path my life will take. Perhaps I *am* the fated mate of the king and then, heavens! This marriage won't be one that I'm dreading, and we'll make tons of babies, and you'll forget about this little adventure with your *complicated princess* and keeping me from trouble, and you'll live your long life with your fated mate, and we will all live happily ever after with tiny little halfling babies running around everywhere." I take a deep breath and realize that his posture has changed. He's shifted in his saddle and looks at me with his mouth open.

He takes a deep breath and grinds out, "How do I even answer rambling like that? I swear to the Goddess, Sorcha, sometimes you just—! You do not know the amount—"

"The amount of *what*?" I gesture wide, shaking my arms out. "What, Conall? Get it out while you still have the chance."

He rubs his jaw and tugs roughly at his lower lip. After an eternity, he finally says, "You do not know the amount of stress you cause everyone else, do you? All your talk of wanting freedom, trying to do the right thing for your people, and yet you don't even know what life has been like over here. What the creatures of this land have gone through over the centuries, what we have done. No. You just blow through here with your 'I'm a princess' and 'I love brownies!' and your horrible decision making and those lofty ideas." His grip tightens on the reins and he nudges his horse onto a small trail.

"Where do you think you're going?" I snap at his back.

"To get you to the King, I'm done with this discussion."

"You're *done? You're* done?" I scoff, kicking at Gealaich, riding close enough to force him off the trail. He pulls on his reins and looks through me as casually as if I wasn't there. I raise my voice, "Lofty ideas! If I remember correctly, you and Thorne both said that I need empathy and honesty to make it in a world like this. What's so lofty about trying my best? What's so lofty about me being open about my feelings and desires? I have so much weight on my shoulders, Conall, to do the right thing, marry this king, bring peace to both kingdoms, be a metaphorical and physical bridge. Everyone wants something from me! So forgive me for feeling like I could shirk responsibilities and live a little for a few days with you back there. But I also can't pretend that it didn't happen!"

"We need to get going. The king is expecting you." He says, woodenly.

"Oh, is he? Maybe it had something to do with you wanting to keep me out of his reach for a few days, bed me, and then forget about me like the noble lord you are." I spit out, riding past him.

"Sorcha, Goddess Damnit!" Conall calls at my back, but I ignore him.

Kicking Gealaich into a gallop, I ride hard and fast, savoring the fresh air that whips at my face, drying the tears that wet my cheeks. I wipe my nose on my shoulder, then lean against Gealaich's neck as I push her harder. The clouds roll in, blocking out the sun, and we ride through the edges of a burnt forest. Charred tree trunks stand like silent giants around us, black dust billowing behind as we fly through the scorched land.

The smell of rain builds, lightning cracks overhead, as we ride into the greener understory. Gealaich slows as we enter the part of the forest that escaped the burn just as the clouds come crashing together overhead. A sheet of rain releases from the skies, shrouding us in daytime darkness, and I'm soaked in minutes. The trail, now thick black mud, heads downhill, further into the thicker part of the woods. Gealaich slips a few times, my heart catching in my throat. We slow to a crawl, her tentative steps taking us around enormous trees.

I pull hard on her reins, halting immediately. Directly in front of us on the trail is the exposed back of a very large, hideous creature. They've stopped in the middle of the trail, facing away from us, but in seconds they turn and —

My jaw drops open and I immediately pull Gealaich backward, whose hooves slip in the mud.

I have never seen something this monstrous before.

The rain slows to a drizzle, and now I see the creature is holding a large metal mallet in one of their overly large hands, thick liquid dripping from the end.

Blood?

"Hungry. Tiny human," the great bellowing voice rumbles through the trees. The beast turns slowly and an icy shiver passes down my spine. It raises the dripping mallet and points at me, sniffing the air. They look at me with hungry, yellow eyes, and grin, showing an enormous jaw full of sharp teeth.

That's definitely blood. And some skin.

"I'm not a h-h-human," I sputter, and then say louder, with as much confidence as I can muster, "Let me pass and you can finish your other meal in peace."

"No." Easily five times larger than a human, their whole body heaves with the effort to breathe through a small pig-like nose. It looks at me again and smiles. "Smell fear. Smell tasty."

They rock back and forth, like they're deciding whether to launch themselves at me or wait until I make the first move.

Then everything happens so fast.

The ogre bellows, and he throws the bloodied mallet forward, slamming into a nearby tree, splitting it in half and knocking the top off. It crashes down in front of Gealaich and I scream. She rears back, neighs loudly, and bucks me off. Gealaich takes off at lightning speed through the thickest part of the forest, leaving me lying prone on the ground. I cough, breathless, and tears form in my eyes. There's a pain in my side as I try to get some air and a slight ringing in my ears, but I can hear the ogre lifting its mallet once more with a grunt.

I claw at the mud, rolling over onto my stomach, holding my burning ribs. Stars float in my vision while I breathe painfully. The mallet comes slamming down next to my face in the mud, and I scream, again.

"SORCHA!" Conall yells from a distance, but he's too far to reach me in time.

The ogre roars and swings his mallet back, but it lodges between the trunks of two enormous trees. He tugs, and yanks, grunting and I don't waste another second. I scramble to my feet and I run. He opens his enormous mouth and roars after me and I don't hesitate another second as I run into a thicket of trees, holding my ribs tightly, fighting against my labored breathing and screaming from pain at the same time.

I swerve, darting around trees, keeping to the path that Gealaich crashed through, her hooves making deep imprints in the mud. My ribs hurt with every breath, and I lean against a tree for a brief respite. The rain turns from a drizzle to a downpour again, making the forest floor slick and dangerous, washing away Gealaich's prints with ease. Over the rush of the rainfall, I hear the ogre roar again, the sound of tree limbs snapping, Conall yelling, and his horse neighing.

I keep running, pushing through the ferns and understory. Slipping in the mud, I land hard on a sharp stone and cry out as it cuts through my pants and slices into my knee. Thunder crashes overhead, and lightning strikes a tree several yards away.

The ogre bellows again in the distance. I grimace as I get up slowly, holding my rib. Blood trails down my pants, that are now soaked and covered in mud. I hear the answering call of another ogre… and another. Three different ogres are now calling from three different directions.

Panic builds in my throat, and I turn in a circle, carefully listening for the sounds of the ogres. The only direction I think is safe is downhill and I hear a snuffling noise, thinking it's Gealaich. But as I round a large grouping of trees, I see an ogre lumbering their way through the forest. I freeze and crouch down low, the cut on my knee stinging as it touches the muddy forest floor, biting back a scream as my ribs protest as the jerky motion.

The wind gusts and through the sheets of pouring rain, I can vaguely make out another shape clambering up the hillside. The second ogre walks up and over gigantic fallen trees like its nothing, pulling themselves up by the trunks and hefting its huge body uphill. They roar, waiting for the answering call of an ogre, and head off in the direction I just came from.

I wait a beat and crawl through the undergrowth, careful to keep my ears open and my movements quiet. My ribs burn every time I move, each stuttering breath a stifled cry of pain.

I make it midway down the hill when I hear more crashing through the forest behind me. An ogre roars above me and I flatten my back against a tree, feet sliding precariously down the muddy embankment.

Seconds later, a large, gnarled hand grabs the trunk just

above my head. The ogre roars, so close I can smell their rotting breath, and at that moment my feet give way and I slip, tripping, rolling, and falling down the hill. I land hard on the side of a fallen log and come to a sudden stop, tears escaping my eyes, my breath coming in heaving gasps.

I sit up slowly, listening for the ogre's crushing footsteps, but all I hear is the sound of rain and thunder. Perched on a steep incline, the only thing stopping me from tumbling further down the hillside is the rotting tree trunk. Reaching, I grapple at some foliage uphill when the log beneath me snaps and breaks, shooting me down the mountainside.

Screaming, I slide feet first down a large mudflow, snatching at anything as I'm swept away. I fly over the edge of a cliff and splash feet first into the depths of a cold, enormous lake. The wet wool of my coat weighs me down, and I swear I can feel cold, slimy fingers trying to grab at my ankles. Flailing, I claw at my buttons, trying to remove my coat as it drags me under. My hands are cold and stiff, and I realize I'm sinking lower when I hear another splash from up above. A strong, familiar hand reaches down, grasping at my clothing, slipping, missing my fingers.

I reach up frantically toward Conall's swimming figure.

"Conall!" I scream into the water.

I kick hard one last time as his hand clasps around my forearm and he wrestles against the weight of the coat that drags me downward. My ribs scream in pain. My lungs burn. I cry out once more and the last few bubbles of air escape my mouth, releasing in the water.

He hauls us upward, kicking furiously, and, at the last minute, we break the surface.

I gasp and cough and gasp, taking in deep lungfuls of air despite my broken ribs. His arm wraps around my chest, and I bite my lip to keep from crying out at the pain as he swims us to shore. My feet drag behind, along with my coattails, but soon we're touching the rocks at the bottom and then the mud on the banks and then I'm crawling to shore, heaving in deep,

THE BORDERLANDS PRINCESS

painful lungfuls of air, the heavy wool trailing behind me in the water.

"Here." Conall reaches around, grabs his dagger, and cuts the buttons away. I shirk out of the coat, Conall tugging it free from my arms, letting the gentle waves claim it into the depths. He wraps his arm tightly around my chest, lifting me up, and I cry out. "You're injured!"

I cough, breathing deep and wincing again.

"Can I see?" he asks, worry lining his face as his hands reach for my shirt. He looks at me, waiting, and I nod. Sliding the fabric up, the cool air chills my skin, and I shiver as his fingers graze my lower ribs. He moves around me, his fingers brushing my back near my spine.

"Ahh!" I cry out again, though his touch is featherlight.

"You're okay. There's nothing breaking the skin, though I think you have a few broken ribs from getting bucked off... and then tossed down the mountain... and then crashing into a lake."

I nod solemnly, clutching my ribs with each pained breath.

He pulls me close to him. I lean a little into his arms, thankful for his strength, and rest my head on his chest.

He lets me lean into him a little longer and then says, "I'd like to bind your chest to give your ribs a bit more stability for the rest of the ride. The jostling on the horse will hurt, but we're only a few hours away." He looks at me, a pained expression on his face, and runs a hand through his wet hair. "I just need to get back to my horse and we can head out."

"Do you"—I wince again, cradling my ribs—"know... where..?"

"I don't, Sorcha. I'm really sorry. It's just you, me, and my horse for the rest of the trip. I'm hopeful Gealaich will turn up. I can send a scout or two to keep an eye out for her, though. Stay here. I'll be but a moment. I promise." When he sees the panic in my eyes, he continues, soothingly, "I have dealt with the ogres; you're safe."

I shake and whimper. He squeezes my hand a little before he

walks back up to the cliff to get his horse. I watch the muddy water turn green again as the sediment settles, my wool coat lost to its depths.

The wind sends shivers down my spine, every tiny movement hurting. I look skyward; the clouds blowing in a gentle breeze, giving nothing away that they were once a terrifying storm.

Conall comes back, pulling his horse behind him, and somehow he looks even more handsome while he's soaking wet, bloody from the ogre fight, and trudging through the mud. He ties off his horse and comes over to me, a dirty white shirt and a sweater in his hand.

"I'll need you to take off your shirt, Sorcha, if this is going to be done tight enough to last the rest of the trip."

I nod and grimace, slowly unwrapping my arms and pull them through my sleeves. The effort is slow going as every time I breathe, I cringe, and every time I move my arms up, I cringe.

"May I?" Conall asks, holding out a dagger.

I nod.

He comes around to my back, taking hold of the collar, and slices through the seams. The shirt falls to the ground, shredded in two. Though I am shivering, the bright midday sun warms my skin and I wrap my arms around my chest. The hagstone rests between my breasts, cold from the lake water, the sunlight gleaming off of its shiny black surface.

"You're bruising already," he says. His fingertips kiss my back lightly. Warmth sprouts from beneath his featherlight touch, gooseflesh traveling in its wake. He shakes his head and says, "Let's get you wrapped up quickly. If only Thorne were here with their tinctures..."

He shreds both shirts into strips, placing them on top of the rocks, next to the sweater, to keep them out of the mud. Reaching around my rib cage, Conall looks me in the eye the entire time. Never once do his eyes dip lower and stray as he carefully lays the bandages against my skin. His hand grazes the hagstone, nearly missing the bottom curve of my breasts, setting it swinging. I shudder at the missed contact.

"I know you're cold. I know it hurts," he says, smiling softly down at me as he continues to wrap me up. "I'll try to be quick, but I want these to hold. Broken ribs while riding a horse down a mountain aren't any fun. Trust me."

"Even though you heal quickly?" I stammer. His hair falls into his face and I almost reach up to tuck some strands behind his pointed ear but think better of it.

He nods. His eyes never leave mine as he continues dutifully stretching his arms around my back. His head comes close as he ties off a strip, and I lean ever so slightly into his neck, smelling his skin. Even after he swam in the lake, his scent comes through, pervading all of my senses, calming my rapid heart rate, and easing a sense of peace deep into my bones. He reaches back, straightens, reaches back, and straightens again. Tighter and tighter he goes, the pain slowly receding as he secures the strips in layers, and I can finally breathe a little easier.

The sun dries our clothing and hair as we stand on the banks of the lake, looking at each other. How I wish we had longer than just a few hours until the castle. My eyes travel over the stubble on his chin and the curve of his jaw. A few deep cuts have made their mark along his brow and as I continue to inventory his injuries, I look down and see that his arms are healing already; the bleeding having slowed significantly.

I hover a finger over the deepest cut. "One look at you and you wouldn't think you just fought off enormous ogres." I smile crookedly at him, my eyes roaming over his features again. The stubble on his chin, the way the light catches in his hair, strands of dark red and a few small streaks of silver at his pointed ears.

Would he stop me if I ran my fingers through his hair right now? I raise my hand from his forearm, reaching upward, fingers outstretched.

Conall clasps my hand, stopping me mid-reach. He plants a kiss on my palm. Our eyes lock and something in my body snaps to attention. Readying myself to kiss him back, he pushes my hand back down instead. His eyes have turned a darker green, and he takes a deep breath, trailing small circles in the center of my palm.

His horse whinnies, Conall drops my hand, and my heart goes with it, sinking down into the muddy banks.

A small crease forms in his brow. He tilts his head to the side and whispers, "We should get going, Sorcha. The king is expecting you today."

He picks up the sweater, his fingers gently help me pull it up and over, sliding it onto my body carefully. A few sizes too big, the scent of pine and rain lingers on this collar, and I flush, secretly thrilled to be wearing his sweater.

"Wait here," he says, bringing his horse over. He cups his hands for a boost, and I grimace at the effort of trying to get into his saddle, but he lifts me up with ease.

"Are you okay?" He asks. From this height, Conall has to lift his chin to look up at me, worry written evidently all over his face. But all I see is how the sun hits the light in his green eyes, highlighting tiny flecks of gold that sparkle back at me.

I force myself to look away and answer curtly, "I'll be fine."

He says, "All right. I'm riding behind you. Ready?" And without waiting for my answer, he lifts himself up into the saddle, settling behind me.

Conall adjusts himself, his thighs pressing against mine. He clicks his tongue and turns us southwest.

The jostling of the horse sends pain shooting around my ribs. My breath is shallow as each step forces air from my lungs. I feel faint, black spots forming in my vision, and I'm about to pass out when Conall speaks.

"Can you try to relax a little?" Conall asks in my ear, his breath cooling my neck.

"I... can't... breathe..." Each jostle pushes more air out of my battered lungs.

"Can I try something?" he says, and I can feel his voice reverberate between our bodies.

I grimace and exhale, painfully, stuttering, "Y-y-yes."

One of his brawny arms snakes around my front and holds

me to him, caging me against his broad chest. His other arm drapes casually over our legs as he holds the reins, fingers dangerously close to my center. I heat immediately, a warmth growing deep from my belly up to my ears.

"Oh…" I exhale.

The sharp, jabbing pain subsides slightly and my body relaxes into his chest, molding easily into his supportive form. His forearm flexes slightly, adding more pressure to my ribs.

"Better?" His voice is husky, and he dips his head a little, so much so that I can feel his breath on my ear. His thumb strokes under my arm, my skin burning where he touches so lazily. It takes all the fortitude I have to not shift, so his hand cups my breast.

"Yes, thank you. I can actually breathe." I want to turn my head, but I know that if I do…

"Good," he says, clearing his throat, breaking the moment. "Let's get you to your betrothed." His fingers stop moving and he lifts his arm off my leg.

We clear the forest and follow a small stream from the lake down the remaining foothills of the mountains. Out of the corner of my eye, I see a little grotto with what looks to be a marble statue.

"Is that a shrine to the Goddess?" I pull on the reins, bringing his horse to a stop, and try to get down, but the pain in my ribs and his arm around my chest keep me in the saddle.

"What?" His breath tingles against my neck. "What are you doing?"

"I… uh… I think I see a shrine over in that grotto. Can you help me get off, please?"

"You want to give the Goddess an offering even though you broke your ribs?" He scoffs but dismounts anyway, reaching up to help me off. I walk over, slowly, and realize that I have little in the way of offerings since my packs fled on the back of Gealaich.

Sinking to my knees next to the statue of the Goddess, I bend my head.

Whispering in stunted breaths to her battered form, I begin,

"Goddess above, I don't know if I'm doing this right, but someone told me that this might work, so here goes."

I reach down for the only dagger I have left, pulling it out of my boot sheath and prick my thumb. Swiping it across her forehead, I squeeze a few more droplets into the bowl she holds with arms outstretched. Faltering for the right words, I finish with a simple prayer we used to say during the seasonal celebrations: "May this appease your watchful eyes, open heart, and compassionate grace."

I try to stand up but stumble, grabbing my ribs. Conall runs to my aid, supporting me under my arms.

"Oh, Princess," Conall says, squeezing my hand. "Are you ready now?"

Nodding hesitantly, I look back at the mountains that we came down and pretend I can still see the glamoured cabin that is tucked away back in that ancient, magical forest. A longing fills my bones, a deep desire to return to the ease of the last few days.

"You're sure?" He frowns down at me, stopping us in front of his horse. The wind kicks up, and I wish it would blow me away, like a seed traveling across the earth, waiting to grow its roots elsewhere.

"Yes, definitely." I choke a little at the last part.

Conall nods briskly and helps me back up into the saddle. He swings up behind me, reaching around again to brace my ribs with his arm. Each minute movement of the muscles in his arm causes my heart to sputter and yearn for his intimate touch again. It takes all the energy I have to not push his hand down between my legs, yearning to feel a relief from the pain of my battered body. He strokes me under the arm absentmindedly as he steers his horse back onto the trail, and I am grateful that he can't hear my thoughts.

We ride quietly for the rest of the journey toward the castle. The land is now pockmarked with farmland and orchards, their fragrant fields wafting through the air. Structures pepper the landscape, growing closer together as we near the castle. Another forested area covers the land on the north side of the butte where the castle sits, looking over the valleys below. The thick stone walls shore up a side of the butte that looks like it will crumble with a strong wind. Conall steers us toward the forested area, away from the main roads and buildings.

"Sorcha—" He says and my heart hitches with anticipation, "I need to let go now."

I deflate.

"Okay," I reply, woodenly.

He slides his arm from my chest slowly, his fingers lingering at my hip. My breathing stunts immediately with the loss of the pressure.

"We'll be inside the gates in about five minutes. I just wanted to say—" Conall starts, rubbing his leg, his thumb almost grazing my lower back.

"No, don't. It's okay. Thank you for getting me here safely." I force myself to look straight ahead, wrapping my arm around my chest to help with the pain. The air chills as we enter the shadow of the castle and turn, heading up a small cliff-side trail.

"Of course, Your Highness." Formality bleeds into his tone. Then, in a low, barely there whisper, he says, "Remember, not everything..."

Is as it seems in Fae. The rest of his warning echoes in the back of my mind, and I shudder as his warm breath trails over my neck. I nod slightly.

"Thank you, Lord Conall. For seeing me safely to the castle so I can meet my betrothed," I intone, as regally as I can, even though the movement of the horse jostles my lungs again. My heart collapses, knowing that this is as close as I will ever get to him again.

We grow silent, a yawning chasm of unsaid things growing between us. He guides us to a small side gate with only one guard post. Conall's body goes rigid against mine and he hops down stiffly and with none of the grace I have gotten used to seeing over the past few days. He takes his horse by the reins and leads us over to the gate, nodding briefly to the soldier stationed there, and the gate creaks open.

"He's waiting in the throne room for you, milord." The soldier salutes as we pass through the walls of the castle, but the guard doesn't even look in my direction.

Thick stone, at least three people wide, encircles the entire castle complex, and this place feels like a remnant of a bygone era. The courtyard that we've entered is void of any creatures or plants, and the grey cobblestone is clean. Feeling very dirty, even though I slide down a mudslide, swam, drowned, and almost died in a lake, I tug my hair back into a low knot, trying my best to smooth the sides and tidy myself.

"Impressive, isn't it, Your Highness?" he says woodenly, his voice carrying in the echo of the empty courtyard.

"It is an excellent example of Fae architecture." I exhale, painfully, but feign interest because I remember what Thorne said back at the inn about tiny ears and eyes watching. My hands tremble, so I wrap both of my arms around my ribs, feigning cold, because I will not look weak.

Not today.

Today, I will enter this castle as a future queen, and meet the king with as much grace as I can muster.

Conall leads us to the stables and looks at me sidelong. He mouths, "You're okay," and I so badly want to believe him, but I can't help but feel like my life is slipping slowly from between my fingertips.

With the help of a stable hand, I am down quickly, and we make our way through the courtyard and into the castle ahead.

13

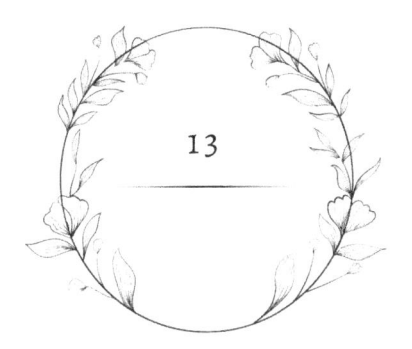

The doors to the throne room are impressively large, gilded with gold, studded with jewels of all kinds. Two guards are on either side, and a page that stands before them looks smaller than me, but the closer we get, the more I can see just how impressive these doors are. I feel minuscule, even next to the gangly looking page, who seems to grow with self-importance as we stop in front of him.

Conall intones, "Princess Sorcha Salonen, here to meet her betrothed, the High King of Fae, Achill. Show us in." He waves his hand, dismissing the royal page, and again I am reminded of his status as Lord of the Borderlands.

Scrunching his nose, the page looks me up and down slowly, and scoffs as the guards open the doors. The page slips between the crack in the doors and the guards follow, leaving us to wait outside. I take this moment to smooth my hair back into a tighter knot as quickly as possible and straighten my coat. I sidle up next to Conall and thread my fingers through his.

Whispering as quietly as I dare, I say, "I know we didn't leave on good terms, but may I still call you a friend before I fully give my fate to the king?"

Conall stiffens but gently squeezes my hand back. "If only it were that simple…"

The doors swing open and I release Conall's hand, my palm cool from the lack of his warmth. My knee, thankfully, has stopped bleeding, and I can only hope that meeting the king in this state of disarray will not dissuade him from finding me at least somewhat tolerable.

Courage, Sorcha, courage.

Drawing in a deep, painful breath, I take a slightly limping step forward as the page announces my arrival to the king.

"Your Highness, may I present Princess Sorcha Salonen of the Human Lands," he says, and leads the way in with his arms behind his back.

"Come," intones a deep baritone from where I see the top of a throne at the end of the room.

The page walks forward, blocking my view of anything in front except his back. His gait is a little lopsided and his shoulders seem tense, like he's carrying the weight of disappointment. The throne room is massive, with arched columns that stretch to the elaborately carved ceilings. Stained-glass windows line the sides, allowing for a rainbow of light to come through, and I can't help but let my eyes soak in the intense beauty depicted in the tall ceilings. Carved and brightly painted images of the Hunt cover gold-veined marble. The decadence of this place is so overwhelming that my breath catches in my throat, and I turn back to where Conall should have been behind me.

But he isn't there. He's hovering at the threshold of the room, in the shadows, and his eyes are downcast, not even meeting mine.

My heart sinks, but I force myself to look forward. The page steps to the side of the throne, and I lock eyes with the most immensely gorgeous Fae.

"Finally," says the king, his voice echoing against the stone. "I have waited a hundred years for this moment."

"Your Highness," I curtsy low, the knot in my hair coming undone, the matted mess falling forward into my face. I breathe, shallow but controlled, through the pain in my ribs and the spots that dance in my vision.

"You may rise, Princess. This will soon be your home, and you are to be my wife. The curtsy is entirely unnecessary anymore," he says, his voice a soothing bass.

I rise, meeting his glacial blue eyes as he assesses my appearance. He takes a few steps down from the dais and, with a wave of his hand, dismisses the page. He saunters up to me, reaching for my hair. Our eyes lock again, and my breath catches as a familiar scent of vetiver and lemon rolls off of him.

His piercing gaze sweeps over my face, stopping at my forehead. His pupils dilate ever-so-slightly at the sight of my wounds. He reaches up and tucks some strands of my hair behind my ear. The king wears his white hair in a thick plait down his back. A small golden crown rests on his head and a brilliant red ruby rests in the center of the diadem. His jaw is clean shaven, and I can see the muscles in his neck work as he swallows. I almost reach out to touch his velvet jacket to trace the finely threaded gold embroidery.

Quite the contrast to my woolen coat and torn breeches. I cringe a little at what I must look like standing here before him.

"Pardon my appearance, Your Highness. Our route has been—"

He waves his hand dismissively, saying, "You needn't apologize to me, Princess. I quite admire the tenacity it takes to make your way to me. I have requested a bath, and some food taken to your rooms as I'm sure you're exhausted after your harrowing journey through the wilds of Fae." He leans in a little closer, and I'm overwhelmed by the sheer strength behind his pose and have to tilt my head back to look into his eyes. Without taking his eyes from mine, he intones deeply, "Conall, thank you for your service to the crown, you are excused."

The doors to the throne room close, the clicking of the handles echoing into the chamber. It takes every ounce of sheer will to not turn around and glimpse Conall as we finally part ways. The king drops his fingers from my hair and walks slowly around me, stopping behind my back. I can feel his eyes roaming over my figure and I shudder slightly, feeling very exposed despite the thick wool sweater I'm wearing.

"Forgive me; you must be cold from traveling through the mountains." He snaps his fingers, and a little pixie comes flying from who knows where.

"Yes, milord?" they ask.

"Prepare the princess's rooms, just like we discussed earlier. And make sure you send in a seamstress to take her measurements. I want her fitted in Fae attire fitting her status here in her new home."

"Of course, milord." They bow and fly off into the dark shadows.

"Now." He walks around to face me, still hovering close enough that I can feel the warmth radiating from his chest. His hand gently cups my chin as he lifts my face and tilts it toward the sunlight streaming through the windows. "Tell me, how did you come by this cut?" His fingers hover, trailing the path of my healed cut in the air, and I close my eyes as I recall images of the forest attack.

"Someone ambushed us as soon as we crossed the Border, Your Highness. A large horned Fae attacked me. I'm told he didn't survive the night." My eyes snap open to his intense glacial stare.

He bristles and drops his fingers, grabbing my hands in his. "What a welcome my own creatures gave you. The first human to cross the Border in a century, and this is how you were greeted?" He stares into my eyes, and worry lines crease his forehead.

"It was quite a shock, but I didn't mean to cause unnecessary worry."

"What's another week added to a hundred-year-long wait? Let's get you settled in, and then you can tell me the rest of your journey tomorrow." He squeezes my hands again before releasing me, stepping back and walking up the dais to the throne. He sits down, snaps his fingers, and another page comes forward. They talk in hushed tones, ignoring my presence, and I feel more like an intruder than a fiancée. Closing my eyes, I take a shuddering breath and try not to wince outwardly. I hear a soft whirring next to my ear, and a small pixie with shock-red hair hovers in the air above my shoulder.

"Princess, if you'll follow me, I'll show you to your rooms." She pips, curtsies, and flies toward a side door that I hadn't noticed before. I look around the throne room again. The soft light has shifted ever so slightly, catching the veins of gold in the marble.

I follow mutely behind the pixie, through a winding hallway with windows along one side of the hall and large, vibrant tapestries lining the stone on the other side. The lighting is dim compared to the light in the throne room, and by the time we make it up to my rooms, late afternoon has turned into dusk. The pixie, quiet and reserved, delivers me to my rooms with a knock and curtsies before flying hurriedly to the other end of the hallway to leave.

The door creaks open slowly, and a dwarf woman pops her head out. When she sees me standing in the hallway, she grins and opens the door with a curtsy. The Fae comes up to about my shoulders, and her portly figure exudes a calmness I haven't felt since Geannie. She braided her scraggly red beard into her hair, creating an elaborate hairpiece, and wears a large, beaming smile as she opens the door wider.

"Your Highness, welcome. I'm Fern, your lady's maid. We've been waiting and preparing your rooms whilst you've been traveling. Hopefully, you'll find it all to your liking. If it isn't, however, we are more than happy to rearrange some. Come in and I'll show you around." She rushes through her introduction, sounding breathless, and ushers me inside just as quickly.

Chandeliers adorn the ceiling, lending bright light to a very warm and welcoming sitting room. A glass door sits alongside a wall of windows that leads to a balcony, overgrown with roses and some honeysuckle vines, with a view of towering trees that reach up and over the castle walls. Velvet curtains drape the edges of floor-to-ceiling picture windows and the colors of the sunset stream through, crawling across the floor. A fireplace, without logs, roars in the wall opposite the doors, surrounded by armchairs and a chaise.

I twirl around, looking up at the chandeliers again, noticing that there aren't any candles, and look back at Fern.

"How…?"

"Ah, yes, well. The king," she gestures up to the lighting and the fireplace.

"Oh, his element must be fire, then?"

"Yes, that is correct, milady." A look of appreciation registers on her face. "His family has magicked most of the castle to have light and warmth without the need to burn anything."

"That's impressive."

"Aye, it is and very useful, too. Would you like to see the rest of your rooms?" She walks over to a door to my left.

"Please." She takes me into a short hallway that leads to a spiral staircase. We wind our way up smooth stone steps that open up into a spacious bedroom. A four-poster bed sits on the far wall between floor-to-ceiling windows. Several bookshelves, already filled with some of my books, and a small desk decorated with some of my possessions from home, line another wall.

"My belongings?" I ask, curious how they got here.

"Ah, well, when word of the attack came to the king, he sent an entourage to retrieve what items were salvageable," Fern says.

I smile appreciatively.

Underneath a bright stained-glass window is an oversized armchair with a rolling teacart. A double-sided fireplace leads into the bathing rooms, and it is already lit. I can see a large free-standing tub through the other side, and I hope it's already filled with warm water.

"Milady," Fern dips. "Are you cold?" She tilts her head slightly and looks at my arms, that are wrapped tightly around my ribs.

"Oh, no, I just…" I trail off. What do I say? I'm having trouble breathing because I have broken ribs?

"Is that a bath?" I grind out as carefully as possible, trying not to sound winded from the walk up the stairs and my labored breathing.

"Oh! Milady, yer injured! Would you care for me to send for a healer?"

"That won't be necessary, Fern." I take a few shallow breaths. "Unless the healer is Thorne, perhaps?"

"I can inquire…" She turns to leave, and I grab her hand quickly.

"Quietly, please. I don't want this to get back to the king."

"As you wish. Would you like help into the bath before I leave?"

"No, thank you, Fern." I take a few more shallow breaths and try to talk through the pain. "I'd like… a few moments alone to get acquainted with my new rooms. Everything looks lovely." I give her a slight smile and sit down on the edge of the bed as she shuts the door.

I look dejectedly down at my laces and grimace as I try to bend over and untie them. After struggling for a few moments, I decide that it's probably best to just cut the laces off instead of trying to loosen them. I struggle a little with my dagger, but the blade is long enough to slice down with minimal bending, and they slide off. I wiggle out of my pants, shimmying to get them down the rest of the way, while I squeeze my ribs together. The sweater is easy enough to get off, and as I'm lifting it over my head, I catch a faint scent of Conall along the collar and inhale deeply. I stash it under my pillow as I make my way over to the bathing room.

Sliding into the tub, bandages still wrapped around my chest, the hot water melts away the stress of riding, the pain of my broken ribs, and the cuts on my knee. I lose track of how long I stay in the water since it doesn't seem to get colder and I hear a knock on the door. Fern's voice echoes into the room and then she pops her head in.

"I could not locate the healer you requested. It seems as you'll just have to do with me, milady. If you will allow it." She shuffles into the bathroom with her arms full of clean bandages and a few jars of creams. "As a wee lass, I used to help mend the miners when they left the caves with injuries. I know my way around a smaller body, but forgive me if I'm a wee bit rough. Humans are a fair bit more dainty than even I have done."

"Yes, thank you, Fern. I would like that very much. This bath has been one of the few reprieves I've felt all day." I say, trying not to think of someone's muscular arms around my chest.

"Well, let's take a look at you, then," she says. Fern helps me out of the tub with a strength and steadiness that I relish. She comes behind me and unwinds the wet bandages. The hagstone comes free, swinging, and I reach up, wrapping my hand around it, finding strength in its presence. I turn in the mirror and glimpse my ribs in the mirror behind the washbasin. My skin is already turning a deep purple and blue. Fern's countenance doesn't change at all, however, as she turns me around all the way to see the extent of the bruising.

"Aye, I've seen worse," she says, throwing the rags into the fireplace.

Fern glances down at the hagstone in my hand, looks at me, and nods, then turns to the counter and opens up a few creams. She mixes some of them together into a large bowl, a thick white paste forming on the end of a spatula, and slathers my back with the mixture and wraps me up in clean bandages. I tuck the hagstone in between my breasts and take a few slow, deep breaths, testing the pressure, and smile when I find a little more relief.

"Oh! That's lovely. Thank you so much, Fern. But…!" My skin gets hot and then turns cold, gooseflesh traveling up and down my arms at the unfamiliar sensation. I look up at Fern with wide eyes.

"Aye, a simple anti-inflammatory and some topical painkiller should see you through the night so you can get some rest." She nods her head a little as she cleans up. As she reaches the door, she turns and says, "That hagstone on your neck… radiates a power that only some Fae can detect. Guard it carefully."

My hand reaches up reflexively, the smooth stone cool to the touch. "Thank you, I will. It was a gift…"

"Ah, then. Even more powerful." She nods and heads downstairs, closing the door and leaving me sitting on the edge of the bed. I look down at the glinting stone, light refracting off of its curves and flaring with mini starbursts in the firelight. The rest of the lights in my room slowly fade and go out as I snuggle in. The fire burns low but still warms the room significantly and I crawl, bandaged and swathed in a robe, under the covers. My fingers reach beneath the pillow, grazing Conall's sweater before I slip easily into sleep.

14

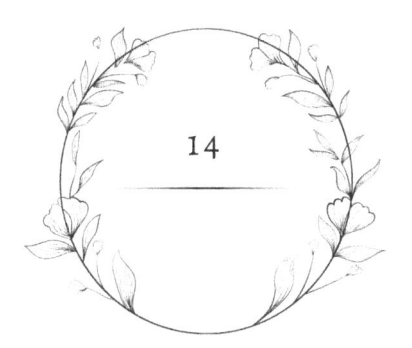

The silk dress shines in the sunlight, falling around my body effortlessly, cool and liquid against my skin. Fine silver embroidery in the shape of leaves and vines lines the edges of the neckline, catching the sun from the window as Fern escorts me through the castle to meet the king. My bandaged ribs already feel better after Fern put the same healing cream on them as yesterday. I relish in taking deeper breaths.

We walk down the same long hallway as yesterday with the windows and tapestries, Fern's voice echoing off the stone as she describes the scenes of the Hunt woven throughout the fabric. Four riders lead a charge through a misty forest, each with different colored eyes. The Fae at the front wields a staff and points it toward something in the distance that has faded from centuries in the sun. A raised mound of earth sits in the background with a stone circle on top, cocooned in a swirl of mist.

The tapestries end, the story of the hunt remains unfinished, when we round a corner where several guards stand sentry in front of a doorway that leads into the King's wing.

One guard opens the door for us, but neither of them addresses me or even acknowledges my presence. A swift closing of the doors as soon as I'm through, though, has me grabbing my dress quickly to keep it from getting caught.

Rude.

"They're all a little rough around the edges, Your Highness. Soldiers, you know, who can't fight are forever looking for a fight they *can* win — no matter how little or dangerous." She shakes her head and glances up at me, a knowing gleam in her eye.

We enter another hallway, all brightly lit from massive windows and large marble arches that draw the light upwards to the white ceiling, where magicked candles are lit. A guard opens the doors at the very end, and we come to a stop in a shorter hallway with two doors.

Fern turns to me and says in a soft voice, "The door to our left leads to the King's Chambers, and the door straight ahead leads to the Morning Room, where he takes his breakfast and sometimes luncheon when he's in the castle… or in a mood." She whispers that last part a bit more conspiratorially.

"Thank you, Fern," I say with as much confidence as I can muster.

"At your service, Your Highness." She curtsies and leaves me before an imposingly large Fae guard.

He opens the door to a bright room with tall windows and glass doors that are thrown open to a balcony outside. A light breeze blows white, gauzy curtains around, the scent of jasmine and honeysuckle floating from outside. There is a small table with a few chairs that sit to my right, next to a fireplace that's roaring. A few small bookshelves and a large map of the continent hang on the wall opposite the fireplace and I take a few steps closer to peer at the map. The land drawn below the Border looks like someone has taken a cloth and swiped across the paint as it was drying. Hardly any land demarcations come through, except for a clear path directly south to my family's castle.

"Princess," the king's deep voice resonates through my bones. "I see you found the new dress."

I turn slowly, meeting his gaze as he comes through the doors from the balcony. I curtsy quickly, dipping my head, and reply, "Yes, thank you, Your Highness. The workmanship is remarkable."

He saunters over, long strides making his movements graceful. In the morning light, his hair practically glows. It hangs loose this morning, and wisps of white hair frame his angular jaw, drawing my eyes up to his dark brows and his eyes that are the color of the sky at noon.

"I thought you'd like to take a tour of the castle gardens. They are especially pleasant in the early morning hours." His finger reaches under my chin and tilts my head up again, pulling the rest of my body up with it. He looks down into my eyes and whispers, "I have waited so long for you to join me in this castle… It almost feels like the hundred-year wait was worth it." His lips curve into a smile and his eyes roam over my face and down to my lips.

Could I love him?

He holds out his arm, and I place my hand in the crook of his elbow tentatively. His other hand covers mine.

"A tour sounds delightful, Your Highness." My eyes never leave his, and he smiles down at me, guiding us over to the balcony.

"These gardens were my mother's pride and joy, centuries ago," he explains.

He leads us down a grand staircase, and from this vantage point, I can see a gorgeous conservatory in the middle of a labyrinth of hedges, the glass and metal work shining in the sun like a beacon.

He tracks my gaze and comments, "The conservatory. It was her life's dream. A place for the plants and fruits to grow during the winter. Her retreat, if you will. We used to host lavish parties when I was a young chap. I'd sneak out just to see the costumes the other High Fae would wear for the Hunt celebrations."

We wind our way around one of many fountains, a faun spouting water into a wine jug, lily pads floating above a school of small orange and yellow fish.

"It's gorgeous." I lean my hand down into the water, and the fish scatter when my fingers create ripples, trailing behind me in the water. "We have nothing like that in the human lands. Smaller structures, yes. But nothing to compare to the size of your conservatory."

"I would imagine it'd be hard to have something like that without the use of magic and wards to keep things from falling apart over the years." He looks smugly down at me, turning us down another set of stone stairs.

"I would imagine, Your Highness."

"Please, call me Achill. Formalities between us are now unnecessary," he says with a wave of his hand. Achill looks down at me. A soft smile touches his lips, and he squeezes my hand against his arm.

"Then you may call me Sorcha," I pause, adding, "*Achill*."

He nods, turning us down another pathway. A cascading waterfall of fountains follows us as we travel down the stairs and a gentle breeze stirs, cooling the air as we walk between more hedges. He pulls me closer, and I can feel his warmth radiating between us. Turning again, we come upon a lake with a small temple made of white marble sitting serenely on a grass-covered hill in the middle of an expanse of water. He stops us at the banks near a tiny boat and turns to me with a bright smile.

"Would you care to join me?" He holds his hand out, expectantly, with one foot in the boat and the other on the bank.

"If it pleases you, Achill." I smile demurely and take his hand. He helps me into the small boat, but its rocking causes me to lose my footing and sends me lurching forward. His arm snatches out and catches me around the waist, preventing me from falling into the water. He braces me against his chest, his hand flexes around my waist, and I try not to wince as my tender ribs throb.

He chuckles, a deep rumbling in his chest reverberating into my back, "Let's try that again, shall we?" he breathes in my ear and gooseflesh travels up my spine.

I clear my throat. "Yes, well, this is my first time on the water…"

"You don't say?" He smiles down at me, blue eyes catching the water and glinting with mischief. He helps me to sit on a bench on one side and settles himself on the bench opposite. The boat smoothly casts off, and I look up at him with wonder. "Ah, yes, the wonders of Fae. It's a magicked dory. There is no need to row, since it'll only take us to the temple and back."

"What a marvel!" I lean over slightly, peering into the water below. A few fish swim among the reeds, and a turtle darts around them, its shell green with algae. The light glints off the ripples, and I watch as my distorted face peers back at me from the water. A crown rests on the top of my head, faint lines show near my eyes. My hair flows freely behind me, a few streaks of grey at the temples. Leaning over the bow of the boat, I can see one of my hands clutches a staff covered in ivy with a glowing green stone in the center. The queenly apparition smiles back at me, I reach my hand out to touch Older Sorcha and—

"I wouldn't do that if I were you," Achill's voice startles me from my thoughts. "There are water nymphs below. They don't take too kindly to anyone disturbing their habitat."

I open my mouth to tell him I'm familiar with at least one water nymph, but the boat reaches land and jerks as it comes to a stop. He leaps out of the boat and onto the grassy banks, leaning over to help me out. I wobble a little, and before my feet can touch the water, he lifts me under the arms and places me gingerly on the stone steps leading up to the temple. I look back over my shoulder, and the lake has grown to twice its size.

"Oh! Is this magicked, too? It didn't look like we went that far, but…"

"Not everything is as it seems, Sorcha," Conall's voice echoes in my head.

"Yes, it's glamoured. As is mostly everything here," he says loftily, sweeping his arm across the air, gesturing to the entire garden and castle grounds. He walks to a table laden with fruit, fresh bread, a carafe of honey wine, and two glasses. He pours some mead into each glass.

"This mead," he begins, "comes from the base of this butte. An ancient vintner tends the land with elemental Fae of all kinds." He raises a silent toast, bringing the drink to his lips, and I follow. The mead tastes delicious, but this time, the flavor of blackberry and honey swirl in my mouth, tiny bubbles fizzing on the way down. I can't help but smile at the sensation and just how different this wine tastes to the one I shared with Conall.

"Do you like it?" he asks, soaking in the expressions on my face as I take another drink.

I nod, choosing my words carefully. "It is delicious. Are there bubbles, or is that my imagination?"

"Mm-hmm," he says, his voice deep and husky. He takes our glasses and pours us more to drink. Grabbing a few berries, too, he says, "You should try a bite of this blackberry and then drink. Tell me what you taste."

I open my mouth, and he feeds me the blackberry, his finger lingering on my bottom lip. I flush at his brazenness and take a sip of the wine. Bursts of honey seep through the fizz, drawing out the delicate sweetness.

My eyes grow wide and I gasp, "That's incredible! It's as if I was the bee, making the honey, from the blossom of the blackberry bush."

He smiles knowingly and walks toward the center of the temple, settling himself down in the middle of a heap of floor cushions. Achill lounges back with ease, clasping his hands behind his neck, and watches me with hooded eyes. A harp sits in the corner and, when he waves his hand, the strings pluck a simple melody. The music echoes over the lake and the sun shimmers against the lapping waves, flicking golden light across the ceiling of the temple.

Achill's eyes never leave my figure and my stomach somersaults at being assessed by my future husband. Will I live up to his expectations?

I swish my skirts, knowing the sun will catch and shine

through the fabric, and his eyes roam slowly over the shadowy silhouette under my dress. Feeling like the lamb sent to slaughter, I swallow thickly as he licks his lips and sits up, leaning forward, arms on his knees, cocking his head.

"Come here." His husky voice carries across the distance, sending shivers down my spine.

My palms grow sweaty and I take a few small steps forward. He smiles and his eyes drop to the crest of my breasts, rising and falling, my breath coming in ever-quickening beats. The wind billows the skirt around my legs. He gets up from the furs, his powerful body sliding up against mine as he snakes an arm around my back, holding me close against his form.

His free hand comes up to cup my face and tilts my head back, thumb tracing the fresh scar on my temple. Achill lowers his head slowly and places a gentle kiss there and then lower, at the corner of my eye. He flexes his arm, holding me a little tighter, and I try not to cringe as my ribs feel the pressure, my breath hitching a little from the pain. He smiles, not knowing that my ribs are flaring against his strength, and kisses me on the mouth. His tongue sweeps inside, against my tongue, and I freeze a little. Panic sets in at the intimacy, but the only thing I can think is why isn't this Conall?

I shove the thought down as I reach up and stand on my tiptoes, twining my hands in his hair at the base of his head, pushing myself back into him. He groans into my mouth and releases me slightly as he kisses down the side of my neck. He pushes my back against the wall of the temple and shifts, then pushes against the fabric of his pants and against my core. I heat, wetness growing, and his nostrils flare. He buries his head into my chest, kissing my breasts and licking up the side of my neck.

"Oh, Sorcha…" He groans, hands roaming down my backside.

"Yes…?" I answer. I know I can forget those green eyes…

"You're driving me crazy." Hungrily consuming my exposed flesh with his mouth, his tongue and teeth nip at my décolletage. His scent of vetiver and lemon swirl around me, licking at the edges of my mind, and a feeling of panic claws its way up my spine. He squeezes my backside, rocking himself against me, and the wall crushes into my back, pain searing across my ribs. I cringe, breathing roughly, and he stops. "Are you okay?"

"Umm—"

He smiles down at me, "Good."

He returns his mouth to mine and plunges his tongue inside deeply. The pain in my ribs recedes as he leans back, shifting his weight so he can look at me while he reaches between us. He groans and his hand travels slowly up my inner thigh, stroking closer and closer to my apex.

Instinctively, my hand clasps his wrist, stopping his movements. His eyes flash to mine and he looks at me with a frown.

I pant. "Sorry, I'm just… I'm not there yet."

"Oh." He exhales, forehead resting on mine. "I thought…" His grip loosens, and he drops his hand from my thigh.

"I just… I think I need a little more time. We hardly know each other…" I sputter, now feeling flushed and exposed. I slide my legs down from his waist, pulling my skirts back down over my legs and adjusting the neckline of my gown. I swallow thickly, wishing I had some water to drink instead of honey wine.

He clears his throat and steps away, clasping his hands behind his back. "I understand," he says gruffly. "I thought a nice day out would warm you up to my… unusualness… the pointed ears—"

"No, no, Achill. It's not that. At all." I rush over and grab his arm, hoping he'll turn to face me. "I didn't mean to offend you. I just… I think I just need a little more time."

He nods, face bowed away from me.

I drop my hand and walk around, facing him. "Really, just give me some time." I smile faintly, trying to hide the crushing feeling of guilt.

"As you wish, Sorcha. Let's return shall we?" He asks. I nod and place my hand on his arm. Covering my hand with his own, he asks, "Would you care for a ride this afternoon through the country?"

"It would be my pleasure," I say, smiling as genuinely as I can. The thought of getting outside the castle and back on a horse sends a thrill down my spine.

He smiles back, but the light doesn't reach his eyes, and now I regret having said anything at all, worried I've offended him. He walks us back to the boat, which sways calmly on the water, and as we near, something dips below the surface and a shadow crosses Achill's face. I almost reach up to touch the hagstone, but fight my instinct as a feeling of foreboding settles deep within my bones.

Achill's hand squeezes mine as he helps me into the boat, settling down on the bench more gracefully than last time. I hear another splash and look behind me at something dark passing by the steps of the temple in the rushes.

What else is hiding in plain sight?

15

After a brief respite in my rooms, a change of clothes and a quick bite to eat, a page collects me to escort me down the winding hallways towards the stables. The freedom from the past few days with Conall still sings in my bones and I find myself eager to get back on a horse and ride. Grabbing the hagstone through my shirt, I regret not strapping any daggers on my person. The thought of riding through Fae again with no sort of protection worries me. But before I change my mind, we have arrived at the stables.

The smell of hay and horse manure reminds me of home again, and a reverberating feeling of loss sings in my heart. I walk past the many stalls, each filled with enormous horses. All of them with different markings and colorings, all much larger than Gealaich by at least a few hands. It isn't until I reach the end of the stalls that I see a smaller bay colored horse. It shies away from my smell at first as I reach my open palm toward its nose.

The horse snorts and stomps its foot, but then, slowly, nudges closer. I smile and coo a little, making soothing sounds as my hand meets its velvety soft muzzle. It breathes in my scent and I run my hand up its face and over its forehead.

"I see you've found the runt of the batch." King Achill's deep voice echoes in the stalls. A few horses stomp their feet and whinny, knowing their master is here.

I look over my shoulder, not wanting to break this moment with the gentle creature, and say, "Yes, I think we'll get along nicely."

"She's an interesting choice, certainly one I wouldn't have picked for you." Achill strides into the stables, tugging at his cuffs, slowly pulling on his riding gloves. Outfitter in snug leather pants, Achill walks with the ease of a practiced equestrian. He wears shining leather riding boots with a plain wool coat that is tailored extremely well but without adornments or colors.

I can feel his eyes on me, assessing my stature and clothing choice. He intones, "You have dressed well and Doone should indeed be a good fit. We Fae are so much taller than humans. Her runt size will do nicely. Tristan!" He barks, causing me to jump.

I withdraw my hand from Doone. She snorts and steps even closer to the gate, eyeing me with her intelligent brown eyes.

The king walks away as a stable hand walks through the doors. "Tristan! Excellent, see that Doone is in proper tack for the princess. If you have anything for young Fae in storage, any of those options should suit."

"Yes, Your Highness." Tristan dips his head quickly, then dares a glance my way before adding, "Cole is ready, as are the guard's horses."

"Excellent. We will wait for you by the gates." The king nods once and, without looking back, heads out of the stable.

I realize I am supposed to follow, giving Tristan a brief nod as I hasten past the stalls, trying to keep up with the king's long gait as he makes his way to the front of the citadel courtyard.

I reach down to pat Doone's mane, crooning Geannie's lullaby quietly into her ears to soothe her. Tristan walks around us, checking the straps and then adjusts the stirrups.

In a low voice, he says, "Careful, Princess. Doone needs a wide berth while riding, she is only familiar with one other horse here."

I nod curtly, fully aware that eyes and ears are on me. "Thank you for the adjustment, Tristan."

He nods and backs away, walking back to the stables. Two of the king's guards in plain clothing saddle up, their swords the only indication that they are here for our protection.

The king sits, adjusting in his saddle. "I keep forgetting how uncomfortable it is to ride a horse."

"Oh?" I ask, almost adding that I know about portal magic, but I think better of it and keep my mouth shut.

"Yes, we Fae have other means of travel." He says. "Though it will feel nice to get out of the grounds."

"It is a beautiful day," I add, and then ask innocently, "What other means of travel do the Fae have, Your Highness?"

"Ah, well. Perhaps it is something I should show you one day. It might be too much of a shock since you have never seen magic in practice before."

"Very wise, sir." One of his guards pipes in, eyeing me as he brings his horse up to mine.

"I don't recall asking for your opinion, Rhys."

The guard nods, "Apologies, Your Highness."

"Fall in," The King orders to guards and he clicks his tongue, leading his horse through the gates.

I kick Doone and follow in the king's path. We wend our way through parts of the Northern Forest; the king adding commentary to certain place markers as we canter under towering trees and criss-cross over small streams. We turn southward, exiting the woods and start descending along a narrow path cut into the bluff. Though I keep expecting Doone to spook since we are between the king and the guards, she navigates us downhill with ease, and I wonder if Tristan knows horses as well as he thinks he does.

I glance up a few times, awestruck at the view from this height. Patchwork farmlands, clusters of homes, and minor roads webbing between them. Pastoral calm permeates my vision and I take a deep breath, feeling only a slight pain in my ribs. How can there be violent Fae with a life like this?

We switchback down the bluff, nearing the end and I dare a glance up, shocked that we rode down such a steep trail in such a short time. The castle walls tower above, a looming fortress to any who reach the bottom of this cliff.

The king waits until Doone pulls up to his flank. He turns to me, asking, "Impressive, isn't it?"

"Very much so, Your Highness. The views from up there, though, are absolutely incredible."

He nods. "I'm pleased you know how to ride. My sister used to love to ride in the afternoons through the countryside. She'd say it has the best light for..." His voice fades, eyes clouding over as he looks in the distance.

"Achill?" I ask, his eyes flicking to mine, "Is your sister—?"

"Dead, several centuries passed." Bitterness coats his words and he turns his horse around, calling over his shoulder, "We head this way."

Achill kicks his horse, and we set off at a canter through the countryside. The winds whip my hair around my face and I didn't realize how badly I craved this feeling again, being on a horse, riding through the country, and my heart soars. I imagine myself as a bird, flying over the land, freedom beneath my wings. Freedom. The word tastes sweet on my tongue. Even though I am riding with guards and my future husband, it's enough to make me feel alive.

We near a little settlement of houses and a larger manor, vineyards lining the road as we get closer. The wind stirs, kicking up dust from the horses' hooves. Doone snorts, shaking her head, and I pull back on her reins slightly, easing her into a light trot. The king, however, doesn't slow, and he keeps riding toward the manor house. One guard, Rhys, kicks his horse, following the king, but the other guard stays close to my flank. His presence lends me a little reassurance at being in such a new place with no weapons of my own. My heart beats a little faster when Doone refuses to budge, shaking her head a few times, her ears twitching. My palms sweat and my eyes dart around, trying to figure out if there's an actual threat or if it's just Doone being touchy. The wind picks up again…

Hands grab at my ankles, pulling me backward through the forest…

A hand lands on my shoulder, shaking me from the recollection, and I yelp.

"Princess, I'm sorry. I tried calling out to you, but you didn't answer." The other guard looks genuinely concerned.

"Y-yes, I'm sorry," I say, shaking my head. "I'm fine."

"We should really keep up with His Highness." He looks me up and down and then juts his chin forward. The king has stopped his horse, and it stomps impatiently. I can't see the king's face, but I can detect annoyance seeping from his posture.

"Of course," I say, nudging Doone with my thighs, patting her neck soothingly. She snorts and picks her hooves up, making our way laboriously toward the king.

"Horse trouble?" The king looks at me as we are near. Then he turns to his guard, raising an eyebrow.

I open my mouth to respond but the guard interjects before I have a chance, "Apologies, Your Highness. Her horse got spooked."

"Noted, Neil. You'll keep to her flank in case it happens again." The king says, and he leads us through a small cluster of homes near some farmland.

Ramshackle houses line the small street. Built smashed together, their topsy-turvy frames barely supporting thatched roofs that have flowers, mushrooms, and moss growing in the eaves. Clusters of trees all weave around each other, their branches creating natural bridges that lead to smaller houses up in the canopies.

We make our way down the simple street as shadowy figures

gather on the road up ahead. Achill pulls his horse back, reaching over to grab my reins as we come up short. There are roughly a dozen Fae armed with farmer's tools.

"Whoa, whoa," the king says out loud, but whether it's to the horses or his subjects, I do not know.

Neil guards my flank and Rhys rides ahead, shouting orders to move out of the way of the High King. The group of Fae murmur, clustering tightly together, unsure about what to do.

The king holds my reins as our horses walk toward the group.

Rhys has corralled most of the Fae off the road, and they all watch me with weary eyes.

One Fae creature pipes up, their horned face looking eerily similar. "Oy! Human! I hear you were the one who killed my brother and drank his blood."

King Achill looks from the horned Fae back to me. My eyes grow wide with shock at the accusation. I shake my head at Achill and he frowns.

Achill turns to the accusing Fae and lets out a slow, menacing laugh, "You mean to tell me that my bride, my soon-to-be-wife, is a murderer? Of Fae? The very Fae that she will rule one day?"

"'Tis true, milord! She drank his blood and left his body to the crows!" the horned Fae shouts. He looks around at the other gatherers. The crowd gasps, murmuring again, and they all turn their eyes back on me. The horned Fae gives me a contemptuous look, jabbing at the air between us with a pitchfork.

Instinctively, I pull Doone back a few steps, putting space between me and the crowd that has somehow grown in size to a few dozen. Neil comes up to my flank, a buffer between the group. My hand drifts to my waist, but no dagger rests there.

"Now, now, billy goat," Achill growls, "You'd best lash that tongue of yours before I take it." He leans forward in his saddle, flicking one of his hands forward, flames licking against his fingertips.

"Your Highness, with all due respect, I request retribution." The horned Fae stands straighter, sneering at me.

"Little billy, I suggest if you want to keep your hide, that you run on home. That goes for everyone here! Otherwise…" He waggles his fingers in the air, the flames at his fingers growing, wrapping around his hand.

I shudder, not only from the might of the king's authority, but from the shock at seeing fire magic so close. The crowd shrinks back, some gatherers looking warily at each other. Slowly, the crowd disperses, the wisest of them keeping their distance from the horned Fae.

Achill clicks his tongue, looking back at me, and nodding to follow. I nod, swallowing thickly, nudging my horse down the road, Neil falling in close behind me.

At the last moment, the horned Fae hovers at the edge of the road, pure malice behind his eyes, and shouts, "I'll get vengeance for my brother, human. Best to sleep with one eye open!"

"Pay him no heed, Sorcha. He knows better than to mess with the Fire King." Achill calls over his shoulders.

It isn't until I ride right by him that the horned Fae hisses under his breath, "human bitch."

He spits, and it lands on my boot. I flinch.

"What did you call her?" Achill has turned his horse around and heads back to me. I'm frozen in place, watching as the horned Fae laughs at my shock.

"I called her a *human bitch*. I thought…" The last words out of his mouth replaced by bloodcurdling screams as flames engulf the creature mid-sentence. He screams and writhes on the ground as he burns alive. Clawing at his skin, rolling around, Achill watches calmly from the seat of the horse as his magic flames lick across . It doesn't take long for the creature to die. A burned shell of him lays crumpled by the side of the road. Any of the stragglers from earlier have long since departed. It is eerily quiet but my heart throbs in my ears and I can barely make out what the king is saying to me as I stare at the lifeless, terrified body laying in the ditch below surrounded by grass that didn't burn.

"Sorcha." The king's voice barely cuts through the noise in my head. "Sorcha, you're safe now."

16

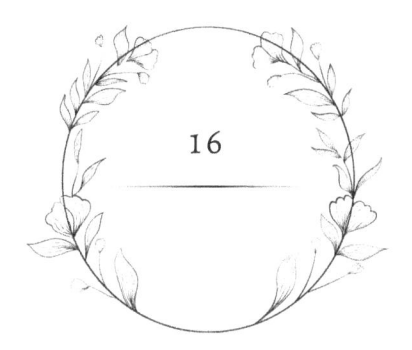

The walk back from the stables limps along like an eternity as I wander through the castle halls, my boots dragging on the floor behind me. The spit stain on my shoe winks at me with every other step and I cannot wait until I am back at my rooms and I can shuck the shoes in the corner. I can still hear the screaming Fae as he slowly burned to death by the side of the road - the king's face impassive while the Fae writhed on the grass trying to obliterate the magical flames that consumed him. And then how oddly cold the king's hand felt, even though he had flames dancing on his fingertips moments before.

Nothing is as it seems in Fae, I remind myself.

By the time I make it back to my rooms, the light has shifted and a warm tangerine glow pours through the windows.

"Aye, milady, you look exhausted." Fern rushes over to my side, helping me take off my boots.

"Yes, it was an eventful day." I sigh, shoving my leaden body off of the door and walking toward a table full of food.

The fireplace is roaring, and the smell of freshly baked bread warms my soul. Leaning my head back against the wood, it takes every ounce of strength I have to not crawl to the table. I sit down in a chair closest to the fire; the warmth seeping into my aching body.

"This came for you while you were out." Fern withdraws a letter from a pocket in her dress. My heart jumps at the familiar scrawl scribbled on the front.

"My father?" I flip over the folded parchment, sliding my finger underneath the family seal. I tear it open, my eyes scanning the letter, though tears cloud my vision.

> *Sorcha,*
>
> *I heard they ambushed you on your way to meet your betrothed. Though by now I am sure you are in excellent hands; I hope this letter finds you well, in good health, and finally able to enjoy your new home. Hopefully, you won't let one terrible misfortune taint your impression of the Fae. A queen must remember that you are the product of your subjects, no matter rich or poor, kind or evil. You are their Queen, so long as they are your subjects.*
>
> *You are dearly missed here. The entire castle feels lifeless without your vibrant spirit here to grace us.*
>
> *I am interminably looking forward to your ceremony when I get to see you again and rejoice in the unification of our lands. You are a beacon of hope for our people. It has been a long time coming. I can almost taste the sweetness of everlasting peace.*
>
> *Yours,*
> *Father*

I crush the letter to my chest, his scent of tobacco and aged leather wafting from the parchment. Fern pats my shoulder and sets a heaping plate of food in front of me, watching as I clutch onto the letter like a lifeline.

I sniffle, trying my best to compose myself, and rationalize away my tears, "It has been a long few days, that's all."

Fern tilts her head, resting a hand on my shoulder. Her thoughtful eyes search my puffy ones. She says, "Eat. It'll help. Every one feels better once they eat Beatrice's meals."

"Beatrice?" I sniffle again, wiping away the straggling tears.

"Aye, the cook. Her talent knows no bounds." Fern leans in, pouring me some fruity, herbal tea, and whispers, "It's said that one cinnamon roll from her can melt even the coldest of hearts."

"Would you like to join me tonight? I fear that once I'm alone, the tears won't stop falling and…" I look around at the table, smiling up at her, "I can't possibly finish this myself."

"Your Highness, I must decline. I have a few more duties to see to before the night is done. With your permission, of course," she stutters, rubbing her hands on her apron and backs away to the servants' doors.

I nod, dismissing her, and continue to poke at my food through the tears.

"Excuse me," a quiet voice whispers from the floor.

Sniffling and dabbing at my eyes, I peer down to see a tiny figure clutching the leg of the table. "Yes?"

"Might I join you, Your Highness?" Her little voice trembles with trepidation.

"Oh! Of course, here," I reach down and she climbs easily into my hand. Her golden hair glints in the firelight, long braids trailing down the center of her back.

She scurries easily onto the top of the table, sitting at the edge of my plate, looking at me with large green-gold eyes.

"I'm Sorcha," I offer, "What would like to eat first? Some bread with butter? Fruit?"

I grab a saucer and put a few bites of various foods onto a plate for her, her hands reaching out delicately to accept the food.

"Thank you, Your Highness. I'm Hazel," she says, stuffing her mouth full. "Goddess, I love Beatrice's food. I usually get the scraps, though. It's much better when the bread is warm."

"The scraps? Are you not allowed to eat hot food?" I ask, confused and offended at the same time that this tiny Fae would have to eat leftovers.

"Well, I'm not really supposed to be alive, technically, so

Beatrice does her best and sets out food for me at night and in the morning."

I stare, trying my hardest to keep my mouth closed from shock. "I'm sorry?"

"Well, her food is great whether it's hot or cold, really, it's just nice to have the company. I hate being alone all the time." She shoves more food in her mouth, this time helping herself to the platter.

"Well, you're welcome at my table any time, Hazel. I, too, love the company," I smile at her and bite into my food, forgetting the feeling of homesickness with the ease of a friendly conversation.

"I've been watching you, you know," she says, crumbs flying from her full mouth.

"Oh? I assumed there were many creatures here who have been watching me."

"Yes, the brownies. And me."

"And what have you noticed, Hazel?"

"Seeing as how you're the first human I've ever laid eyes on, you're definitely shorter and softer than the High Fae." She pauses and looks at me, wide-eyed. "I didn't mean that in a bad way. My previous experience has only been with the High Fae in this castle and they are all so… sharp."

"Well," I chuckle, "I'm not offended. I enjoy the honesty."

"I can tell," she says, sitting back and crossing her arms over her chest. "But how much honesty is too much?"

"Can I tell you something?" I whisper conspiratorially, leaning toward her. She nods enthusiastically. "I think I can handle it."

She shakes her head. "Not yet, you can't."

"Well, then I'll leave it up to you to tell me what you think I need to know. May I ask you a question, Hazel?"

She nods, her mouth full of food.

"How do you get around?" I ask. Her face closes in, eyes clouding over. Worried I've said the wrong thing, I add, "I just mean that you're rather small and I know that some brownies have wings and..."

"I shouldn't be here, I should go," she says, her eyes withdrawn and vacant.

"Hazel, I'm so sorry if I've offended you, that was not my intent," I reach out toward her but she shirks away. She gets up to leave and at the last moment, I see large scars on her back near her shoulder blades.

"Hazel," I say, she stops mid-step. I ask, softly, "Did you used to have wings?"

She nods, refusing to turn around to face me.

"Do you want to tell me what happened?"

She shakes her head, still facing the other way.

"Okay, well, when you're ready, I'll be here."

She nods and whispers, "Just please don't tell anyone I was here."

"I promise," I say.

She slides down the table leg at the far end and I drop my head underneath to see where she goes. She is already gone.

Sliding into the bath, I lean my head back against the rim of the tub. Bright morning sunlight streams into the bathing room behind my closed eyes. The warm water licks at my skin, and my hand drifts below the surface of the water. I skim my fingers between my legs, slipping a finger inside. To be wanted by two gorgeous High Fae within the span of a few days is proving intoxicating. My thoughts swirl with the heated exchange I had with Conall that last night and the eagerness with which Achill devoured my skin in the temple.

My eyes fly open at the knocking on my bedroom door.

Sitting up, I call out, "Come in!" Splashing some water on my face and covering my chest in shame.

"Milady, the king sent this over this morning," Fern says, peeking her head into the bathing room.

I reach a dripping wet hand over and take a carefully folded letter from her hand. Opening it slowly, I read the practiced lettering of the High King's script.

I fear yesterday may have been too taxing for you. My sincerest apologies that I won't be able to show you more of the castle grounds today, as I have business requiring my immediate attention. I've left instructions to set up a table off of the Morning Room balcony for your breakfast. It would delight me immensely if you would join me for dinner tonight.

"Fern?" I ask. "Perhaps I could have breakfast in the gardens today? I find I am craving sunlight and flowers today."

Fern beams a bright smile. "Seems Beatrice's food did a turn for the better, eh?"

"Do you know if she has any of her... famed cinnamon rolls this morning?"

"Aye. She makes them every morning." A shadow flashes across Fern's face, so quick that I think nothing of it. She grabs a towel, helping me out of the hot water, and scrubs my body dry.

Glancing at the windowsill as we make our way into the bedroom, only a few crumbs remain from the offering I placed to the brownies last night. I smile contently to myself, hoping I've made yet another friend in this place.

Fern helps me get dressed in another elaborately decorated dress. Dark ruby red, woven with fine gold thread this time, and it settles easily against my skin. I put on a pair of slippers and we head out to have breakfast in the gardens.

Gold veins swirl in the marble walls of the hallways, lit up by the morning light streaming through the windows. Every corner of this castle emanates with Fae power and magic. And I have the whole day today to explore and I finally let all the details sink in. Turning the corner, the guards open the doors to the Morning Room and my jaw drops. Vases of florals abound and the doors to the balcony are open, allowing the fresh morning air to flow freely throughout the room. The trees outside are vibrant green, billowing back and forth in the breeze that carries the scent of rose petals on its cool fingers. A simple glass table sits underneath a trellis climbing with deep purple wisteria. They set the table just for me, complete with tea, fresh fruit platters, and flaky pastries. And, sitting by itself, is a single, solitary cinnamon pastry, steam rising from its middle. The scent reaches my nose and my stomach grumbles, and it takes everything in my power to not lunge at the table and shove it into my mouth.

Before I head outside, I walk over to the smaller bookshelves and grab a title from its shelves that looks interesting, *Magic in Lesser Fae*. Hopeful that this book can give me more information on the different Fae I will rule soon, I bring the book outside with me and sit down to eat some of this divine food.

With the first bites of the cinnamon roll, I'm lost to the sweet flavor of the pastry and I devour it within moments. The scent reminds me vaguely of Geannie, a soothing comfort settling in my heart. Popping a plump, juicy grape in my mouth, the flavors burst, and this tastes nothing like the grapes back home. The same with the cantaloupe, the blackberries, the apples, all taste infinitely better than anything I could have imagined.

I sigh as I finish up breakfast, my stomach content, tastebuds delighted, and sit back, opening the book.

"… You could have at least told me, Rhys."

Rhys? The guard from yesterday?

Footsteps crunch on the gravel below. I'm tempted to lean over and say something, but, knowing the cool manner with which Rhys interacted with me yesterday, I think better of it and stay seated.

"Why? He wanted it to be believable." Rhys replies. "Come on, Neil. If he had told you…"

I shift in my seat, and the chair creaks against the stone, cutting Rhys off.

It's dead quiet and I clear my throat and decide to say, quite louder than necessary, "Is someone there?"

"Ah, Your Highness." Neil's voice sounds from around a

hedge. Their footsteps resume as they find a side staircase emerging from the garden and onto the balcony. They both face me, bowing, and Neil asks, "Are you well after yesterday?"

Rhys' face twitches as he avoids sneering. "Yes, His Majesty mentioned you left the stables quickly."

"I did—" I say, curious about where this conversation is going.

"Luckily, he is a powerful Fire Fae." Rhys interrupts, and I look at him with a raised brow. "Apologies, Your Majesty."

Neil coughs, nudging Rhys. "We didn't mean to interrupt your morning. We best be getting on to our duties."

"Indeed." I nod my head briefly, feigning disinterest in them by raising the book a little higher and pretending to read. As they take their leave, my head swirls with what I overheard of their conversation. A sinking feeling fills my gut.

He wanted it believable? Are they talking about the King?

Gathering up the book, clutching it to myself, I quietly leave the garden and follow them. Their voices echo from the hallway and I creep along the floor of the Morning Room as quietly as I can. Thankful to have worn slippers today instead of my boots, my footfalls are soft as I slide around the door and out into the hallway, Rhys and Neil's figures disappearing around the corner. Clutching the book to my chest, I walk with purpose down the end of the hall and peer my head around the corner. They open a large stone door and I hurry to catch it before it closes.

I peek my head through the crack in the door. A dark stone lines the hallway and no magicked candles light the way, no windows let in sunlight. The guards walk through the only door at the end of the hallway and disappear, their voices disappearing with them.

I wait a few moments until I step all the way in when my foot goes out from underneath me, a searing pain shooting up my leg. Biting my lip, I slide down against the wall and stare at my foot. Nothing is there. No cuts, no blood. I pull out the hagstone and look around, finding nothing. No magic, nothing that would suggest I stepped on anything painful.

I get back up, shaking my head in disbelief, and continue down the hallway, smelling a tinge of smoke through the door at the end. I creep closer, the smell of smoke gets stronger, when I hear a loud bellow come from behind the door. Stopping in my tracks, I wait, and then I scream in pain as my other foot feels as if it is on fire.

Dropping to the floor, my foot throbbing, I crawl on my hands and knees towards the exit, terrified of a magic I cannot see. I shake violently, spots clouding my vision, both feet stinging from an imaginary burn. Ripping off my slippers, I run my hand over the soles of my feet, but again, nothing is there. The sensation abates, a coolness seeping up from the cold floor and into my skin that still feels tingly.

Standing, slippers in one hand, I realize I have dropped the book in the hallway behind me. As I stand there, debating going back to get it, I double over, feeling like someone has punched the air out of me. I fall forward onto my knees, struggling to get air. A terrible fear courses through my veins and I feel like I am going to die, choking to get enough air in my lungs, when, suddenly, the pressure releases and I can take heaping breaths again.

The hagstone burns against my skin, and I take it out, putting it up to my eye. Nothing is here, no magic, no invisible creatures.

And then the phantom pain happens again. A man's screaming escapes through the cracks in the door at the end of the hallway and I, too, cry out so loudly my voice echoes down the hallway. A horrible pain radiates from my left arm, as if something has snapped it in half. My breath comes in great heaving gasps. I cradle my arm to my chest, but it's not broken. It's perfectly fine other than the intense, throbbing pain. I barely have enough clarity to reach the doorway, nudging the stone door open with my back, hurriedly exiting to the other hallway.

More pain radiates through my body as my feet burn again. I go down on my knees, tears flowing from my eyes as I cry with an invisible pain that tears through my entire being. The door open behind me and a voice shouts orders. I swallow thickly, trying to see through my tears, but I scream again as pain sears through my other arm. Two sets of hands catch me as the world fades to black.

17

I scream awake, calling out for Conall, groping the sheets in the dark of night for someone that isn't there. Drenched in a cold sweat, my head pounds and my mouth feels full of sand. I lay still for a few heartbeats, moving my feet and my arms and when nothing feels out of sorts, I sigh, relief flooding my system. Whatever happened yesterday didn't leave any physical damage.

Throwing off the sheets, I slide out of bed and change into my simple riding clothes. Then I grab a pair of slippers and slide quietly out the door. I am determined to get my mind off of a certain green-eyed Fae and the phantom pains from yesterday as I make my way through the castle.

Furious at myself for trying to hold on to someone who isn't here, furious at myself that I can't seem to just let him go as easily as he did me, and puzzled at the odd series of events from yesterday, I rush through the halls, lost in thought. But the fact that my thoughts keep returning to the strong arms I want to wake up in infuriates me to no end and I throw my arms up, exasperated. I take a turn through the hallway that leads to the Morning Room and bump right into Achill's back.

"Oh! Goddess!" I curtsy clumsily, regaining my balance. My

hair falls into my face, curtaining me from view as I flush a deep red.

"Sorcha, good morning. You're up early," He says, his deep voice resonant in the hallway. He leans over, pulling the curtain of hair from my face.

"Good morning, Your Highness. I... couldn't sleep." I say, straightening.

He looks me over, his blue eyes alight even in the dim candlelight. Tucking some of my hair behind my ears, he says gently, "Your hair... you should wear it down more often. It suits you." His fingers linger on my lobe.

I smile, "Thank you, I will."

He nods, clasping his hands behind his back. We walk a few paces down the hallway together, when he says, "You couldn't sleep?"

"No. I..." I swallow, curious if he knows about what happened to me yesterday.

"Neither could I. I was worried about you. My guards said they found you, fainted, on the way back to your rooms," he turns to me, head tilted, eyes searching my face.

"Yes, I was on my way back to my rooms." I start. "I saw a stone door left ajar. It led to a hallway I hadn't seen yet, but as soon as I went inside, that's when I heard..."

"You really shouldn't worry about such things," he brushes me off. Achill straightens, adjusting his collar, and says, "I was just heading to the gardens. I often walk the grounds when sleep escapes me. Would you care to join me?" He holds his arm out and, though I had wanted some time to be alone with my thoughts, I take it.

"Thank you. I think a walk through the gardens would be refreshing," I say.

"Mmm," he murmurs, "I have thought often of the morning in the temple with you."

I flush, looking away. "Oh?"

"Yes, I... Maybe this is too forward, but I have found myself rather lonely the past century. It was nice to see the gardens through a new set of eyes. I don't know what a life without magic is. Before the Border War, magic intermixed with everything. It wasn't uncommon to have brownies living with humans," He drifts off, his eyes unfocused and a look of sadness passes his face. Silence fills the hallways, our shoes echoing in our wake with the lack of conversation.

"I find magic enthralling," I offer, hoping to fill the awkward silence until we get to the gardens.

King Achill's eyes flick to my face and then over my hair as it falls around my shoulders, "I could see how it would."

"Would you ever…?" I start but hesitate, unsure if asking a Fae to show me their magic is uncouth or not. King Achill looks down at me, an openness in his face that I haven't seen before. I take a deep breath and try again. "Would you be willing to show me a little more of your fire magic?"

The king stops us in front of the Morning Room doors, his hand on the handle. He hangs his head briefly, but turns to me. "Did I frighten you?"

My eyes grow wide as I open my mouth to object.

He quirks a half-smile. "I thought so. If you're interested, yes, I could show you some of my magic."

He throws open the doors and the candles all flare to life. My breath hitches a little in my throat and I hesitate to step inside, dread creeping into my bones as I recall the phantom pain from yesterday. I close my eyes briefly and shove that fear away as best as I can, stepping inside and following King Achill into the room.

Through the balcony doors, the sun lights up the mountains and peeks through some spires of the castle, catching the tip of the conservatory. The wisteria sways in a light breeze, filling the room with their blossoms, and I notice that there are even more blooms on the vine than yesterday.

"You seem on edge, Sorcha." The king says, his arms casually resting against the railing. He watches me slowly, eyes traveling all over my face.

"Am I that obvious?" I smile. I can't meet his gaze, though it burns into me. Tilting my head, I close my eyes and listen to the birds in the gardens as they wake up.

"A little. You storming through the hallway with purpose was almost a dead giveaway. It seems like half of your head is always thinking about something else."

"Yes, I suppose so." I answer, walking under the shade of the wisteria. Gathering my hair in my hands, I plait it into a thick braid, throwing it over my shoulder, and walk inside.

"Oh?" Achill follows me, pushing off the stone railing, tucking his hands into his coat pockets. He walks back inside and stands by the fireplace. "Let me show you some of what my magic can do, then."

Gesturing to the open seats, he leads me over to the sitting area. I hesitate but find a seat in a comfortable armchair.

He frowns at the look on my face as I look from him to the unlit fireplace. "It's smoke magic, Sorcha, not fire."

"I thought you had fire magic?" I ask, confused.

"I do, but my strength lies in smoke magic. Watch this." His eyes glint with mischief as he brings his hands up and smoke tendrils unfurl around his fingers. The heady scent of vetiver swirls in the air as the smoke swirls around me. "Just breathe, Sorcha. Feel yourself get lighter."

I inhale, the smoke swirling around my arms, gently licking at my skin. Immediately a sense of peace and calm washes over me and I look up at Achill.

"This is the calmest I have felt in... Well, since I've left home," I sigh.

"Mm," he hums, voice low. He stands in front of me, cupping my chin in his fingers. "Let me see you back to your rooms."

I take his arm, his smoke magic still wrapping itself around me, caressing my skin. Breathing deeply, the smoke magic smells of fresh garden air, a hint of the King's vetiver and lemon, and vanilla. We walk slowly back and I feel like I'm floating on clouds. If his smoke magic can make me feel this way, what else can it do?

Turning to me, he reaches for my hands, squeezing them lightly. "Thank you for this morning, Sorcha."

"No, Achill," I say, squeezing back, "Thank you. This was the lightest I've felt in a while."

I watch as his smoke pulls back and my heart lurches a little, wishing the feeling of calm and peace would stay. It does and I look up at him, astonished.

"Maybe you just needed to be reminded what it felt like," he says, quirking a half-smile. The door opens, Fern's face greeting us with a knowing smile. He reaches up, fondling the ends of my braid in his fingers, combing out the plait piece by piece. His fingers twine in the loose hair at the nape of my neck, shaking it out so it falls behind me. He turns to leave, but stops, and says, "You really should leave your hair down."

Late afternoon light filters through the windows of my bedroom and I luxuriate in the post-nap, post-smoke magic grogginess. I stretch once more and notice that Fern has left a bouquet of fresh flowers on the nightstand along with a small gift box, and a brief note from the king:

"Made by the dwarves of the Northern Mountains centuries ago, this necklace is fit for a princess. Please do me the honor of joining me for dinner tonight."

I open the gift box, and a golden necklace sits nestled in the black velvet cushioning. Its delicate twisting chain comes to a point, a single blood-red ruby dangling from the end - a twin to the ruby that rests in Achill's coronet. I hesitate to pick it up, feeling like my hands are too clumsy to hold the fine intricate metalwork, so I close the lid and set it back on the small table.

Fern pops her head around the door. "Milady! You're awake!" She says with a bit more cheer than usual and then adds, "If you'll excuse the intrusion, the king has sent up a dress for you to wear."

"Another one?" Anticipation builds and, in my haste, I throw back the sheets and blankets, sliding quickly out of bed.

"Aye, another dress. This time, though, it seems as if we'll need some help. I brought some friends with me..." A few voices titter behind Fern's back in the stairwell, wings fluttering furiously.

"Of course! Please..." I gesture with my hand, welcoming them inside. "It'd be a delight to meet some...?"

"Pixies, milady," Fern offers. They grow silent as I walk closer, huddling together in the stairwell. "Ladies, out with you." She shoos them in front of her. Behind them floats a gorgeous silk dress glimmering in the dying light of day. An opalescent sheen of blue, pink, and purple highlights the curves and swooping neckline, inset lace, and high slits on either side. It looks six inches too long until I see Fern holding a pair of heels to match.

"Oh. I'm... to wear those? With that?" My mouth agape as I point to the shoes and then the dress. "I've worn nothing like this before." I turn to Fern, confusion clear on my face, and she cracks a smile.

"Ah, yes, well. Some may think them out of fashion now, but they were once very popular when the king was younger. They wrap up and around your legs, stopping at the upper thigh." Fern waggles her eyebrows a little as she motions for where they're supposed to stop. The pixies titter, their wings beating furiously.

"Oh! Oh..." I flush a little, too, but with embarrassment or anticipation, I can't quite decipher. "Well, it looks like we've got our work cut out for us, ladies."

What feels like days later, I emerge into the hallway outside of my rooms and walk, rather unsteadily, down the slick marble floor. Fern, at my elbow in case I need help, escorts me through the doors, and we turn left this time, my heels sending echoing clicks in our wake. The slits on either side of the dress leaves a part of the gown hanging between my legs that somehow tangles around my ankles with each step I take. I stumble a little, and I snatch Fern's arm, feeling small and helpless, an awkward human struggling to look like a gorgeous High Fae queen. My fingers reach up to where the hagstone should be; instead, the necklace the king gave me sits at my collar. I clutch the single ruby in my hand and will my stomach to calm, my legs to stop shaking as we stop in front of a large wooden door, carved with intricate scenes of books, Faeries, and fireplaces.

Two guards stand at attention outside, and Fern announces in a clear accent, "Her Royal Highness, Princess Sorcha, for dinner with His Highness, the High King."

They nod, opening both doors, and I'm awestruck at the intimacy of the room.

I take in the two large armchairs, cushions on the floor, furs strewn about. There are several bookshelves, some reaching ceiling height along a far wall with a few windows. Two fireplaces roar on either side of the room, heating the place to a comfortable temperature. The chill from the hallway clings to my back and I shiver in the thin dress.

Low candlelight flares brightly as I step inside. A small table sits in the corner next to the bookshelves, set up for an intimate dinner with two chairs across from one another. The king himself steps around a large bookshelf in the middle of the room. He's holding a tome half-open, a casual white dress shirt tucked into form-fitting pants. His eyes rake over me as he snaps the book shut, and I jump, feeling suddenly very naked underneath the sheen of the silk dress as it swishes against my skin.

"You look delicious." That deep voice of his rumbles low, sending shockwaves of pleasure up my skin.

"Your Highness," I say, still clutching on to the ruby like a lifeline.

"Welcome," he says, striding over to me, "to my private study."

Stepping forward, the dress tangles around my ankles again, rooting me to the floor lest I fall flat on my face in front of the king. I ask, "What is it you were reading this evening?"

"Ah." He waves his hand and sets the book down on another

shelf. "Nothing exciting. I didn't want to be distracted from you tonight. Do you like the dress?"

I let go of the ruby necklace and run my hands down the front, feeling self-conscious but meeting his direct gaze. "I've worn nothing quite like it before. Thank you, Your Highness."

"That necklace complements you." He strides over, his firm body radiating heat, and I'm swallowed in his shadow. His voice is low, breath grazing my cheek as he leans in and tucks a strand behind my ear. "You left your hair down, I see. Good."

Butterflies alight in my stomach, and his fingertips caress my neck before grabbing my hand. Dazed, I let him lead me to the table. A carafe of honey wine and possibly another one full of whisky sit surrounded by glasses in the center of the table. A large chandelier laden with candles hangs low over the table, casting shadows every which way.

He pours us a glass of mead, and I curiously bring the glass to my nose, sniffing to decipher if I can smell any of the fruit featured in tonight's drink. A comfortable position seems out of the question since the dress wants to cling to every single divot in my body, so I sit slightly angled, fully aware that my breasts are on display. My confidence shatters as I realize how much the silk gleams in the candlelight, the iridescence of the dress highlighting every curve of my body, leaving nothing to the imagination. Trying hard to not pull at the seams, I cross my legs and catch his eye gliding up from my foot to my thigh.

He finally looks up at me and raises his glass. "To an evening of getting to know one another."

"Slainte," I say.

We drink, the mead carrying warmth down to my belly, and bright, vibrant flavors of honey and nectarines filling my mouth. I smile a little at memories of running through the orchards back home as a child, plucking fresh fruit from the trees, reading under the shade of the carefully pruned limbs, scraping my knees as I climbed the rough bark.

"You can taste the stone fruit, can't you? This mead,"—he takes a deep sniff and swirls the liquid in his glass—"comes from the southern vines, closer to the Border. Nectarines thrive in the strong summer climes in that region." His eyes drop to my lips as I take another sip. "Forgive me. Are you feeling better? You seemed so out of sorts this morning."

"I am, thank you. Your magic was very helpful, Your Highness." I take another sip, swirling the mead in my mouth, tasting the nectarines. Images of Conall and the campfire dance in front of my vision with each sip of mead.

Achill places his glass down, the cup ring and shaking me from my reverie. His gaze drops to my breasts, dragging up the front of my bosom, landing on the necklace. I look away, self-conscious, and down more mead, my eyes studying the bookshelves that tower over me.

I clear my throat. "Your collection of literature is impressive. Have you read them all, Your Highness?"

The candles dim a little, some snuffing out, smoke trailing around me and then up to the ceiling. I inhale deeply, wondering if this is his smoke magic at work, but I can't detect his scent this time.

"Some," he says. "I find it difficult to read any of the collections that were taught to me when I was younger. It reminds me too much of being tutored. I have not read some volumes in ages; they decay as soon as you touch them. So, no. I have not read them all. I am at a loss for the literature that can keep me engaged these days. You are welcome to read whatever graces these shelves. I can only imagine how limited the human literature you must have had at your disposal." He smiles crookedly, a hint of smugness behind his comment.

"That is very kind, Your Highness, thank you," I say. I drink a bit more of the mead, savoring its coolness as it slides down my throat. "I have a few questions, though."

"You do? Pray, ask away." Achill gestures with his hand and leans back in his chair, regarding me with hooded eyes.

I take another sip of mead, frowning when I realize my glass is empty already. "Well, I have a few questions about the Border

Wars I was hoping you could help me understand. I take it you were alive back then and—"

Achill reaches over and refills my glass. His posture has grown tense, the languid movements from earlier are now clipped.

When he's finished, I raise my glass and continue, "The Fae that attacked me several days ago…"

"Those degenerates, you mean," His elbows perch on the edge of the table, chin resting in one hand, the other swirls mead in a glass. His back is rigid, his shoulders square. When I meet his gaze, his blue eyes find mine and they pierce my soul.

"Yes, well… About those Fae…" I hesitate, a knot in my stomach growing, dizziness from the mead overtaking my senses.

"You mustn't trouble yourself with these things yet, Sorcha. You've just arrived. Let's enjoy our time together and then… Then we can talk about such matters." His dismissive tone washes over me. And, though my questions are still unanswered, a calmness takes the place of my inquisitiveness.

A few more candles snuff out and the lights in the study dim further.

"Of course," I say, my voice sounding sultry and far away to my ears. Is he using his smoke magic on me again? "I have another question, though. About yesterday, when I thought I heard a man screaming, and I just wanted to know if everything was all right?"

"Of course it is," Achill says, waving his hand in the air dismissively. He leans back, downing his mead. "Perhaps tomorrow you'd like a tour of the royal library?"

"I would like that very much." I shift again, my breasts tight against the silken fabric and I watch as his lips curve into a lazy smile.

His crystal blue eyes drop to my throat as I drink the rest of my mead, and servants come in to serve us dinner. While we eat, Achill never takes his eyes off of me—whether it is my lips, my breasts, or my hands. He is constantly studying my form in the dimming light. As I make my way through our meal, I grow a little more comfortable being admired so openly.

Each bite I take is a sinful dive into the delightfulness of the food and I revel in this new experience. I down another glass of mead and follow Achill's gaze to my breasts.

"Can I show you more of my smoke magic? It's been ages since I have had someone admire it with fresh eyes," he croons, playing with his cuffs.

I nod, my head swimming from the mead. What did he just ask?

The air in the room turns thick with the smoke of snuffed-out candles. I look up and notice that even the chandeliers are dark and then the fireplaces flare up brightly to make up for the sudden darkness. Smoke curls around me, twining between my legs.

My eyelids grow heavy, my dress skin-tight, and I shift, shimmying a little to find some room to breathe. My breasts brush up against the silken fabric, and Achill's blue eyes travel from my fidgeting hands to my breasts, nipples now hard from the sensation of the sultry movement.

"Is this the smoke magic, Your Highness?" I cock my head and raise an eyebrow.

He coughs.

"I…" He smiles sheepishly, shrugging, drinking down more of his mead. Feeling dangerously courageous, I stand up, my head fuzzy, swaying a little in the heels. Achill raises his eyebrow and watches as I make my way over to him. He puts his silverware down, pushes his chair back, and opens his legs. I slide in between them, my chest level with his mouth.

My body moves as if on its own, and I watch myself twine my fingers in his white hair, pulling his head back. I kiss him gently, tongue playing with his soft lips. He wraps his hands around me, cupping my backside, and he squeezes, drawing me in farther, pressing me up against his body.

Emboldened, I kiss him deeply, then pull away, looking into his hooded eyes. His pupils dilate, and he shifts my stance, standing up suddenly, picking me up and wrapping my legs around his waist. He walks us backwards to the furs and armchairs, setting me down on the edge of the leather seat. I unwrap my legs, watching him as he sits down on his knees by my feet.

I take a deep breath as he looks over my body.

"You feel cold..." the king says, running his hands up and down my legs.

I'm too nervous to talk, so I just nod.

With a wave of his hand, the fireplace roars again. My skin beads with sweat, small droplets slipping between my breasts. Achill straightens and dips me backward, tugging on the hair at the nape of my neck. He traces kisses up and down my chest, licking the sweat up from between my breasts. His tongue flicks against the ruby droplet on the necklace, and he places a kiss in the hollow of my neck. His hands trail down my upper thigh, and he slowly unties the straps of my heels, fingers grazing the inside of my legs, letting the laces fall to the floor. I kick them off, stretching my toes in the furs beneath me, and I sigh, willing myself to relax into the moment. He settles himself in front of my core, lifting the edge of my dress, and places kisses along my inner thighs.

"Ohhhh..." I breathe. His lips close to my center. I grow wet and heady with desire. His fingers reach around the back of my thighs, and he slides me down the chair, spreading me out before him.

"I've been wanting to do this since the other day." He looks up at me, licking his lips and spreading me even farther, fingers tracing up my thigh, dipping into the wetness in my core.

"The other day..." I sigh, my head swimming. Smoke curls around my throat, licking at my skin, as he peppers kisses on my inner thighs, stroking me deeply, "Oh, yes. At the temple?"

"Mm," he hums, spreading my legs wider, pushing the tip of his tongue against me, and tracing a slow line up my slick, wet center.

"Ohhhh, Goddess," I shiver, shocked at the movement of his

tongue. I almost groan out Conall's name, so I slap a hand over my mouth and moan into my palm wordlessly instead.

He leans back, smiling, but holds my legs open. Exposed to his gaze, I have never felt more vulnerable. The fires die down and the candles go out, smoke filling the air, and my head swims again. My breathing becomes shallow, and my breasts strain in the dress that has somehow twisted itself around my body. One of his hands travels up and fondles my nipple through the silk, pinching it lightly while he slips two fingers inside me.

I spasm.

My fingers grab the edge of the chair. He chuckles as he slips his tongue over my clit, his fingers stroking deep inside. He groans into my wet core and my legs tremble. I breathe deep, trying to relax into the moment, and close my eyes as his fingers stroke and thrust inside of me. Images flash across the dark shutters of my eyelids—a dark-haired lord with emerald-green eyes and strong arms that held me secure, arms that kept me from drowning, arms that held me as I bled from a head wound, arms that held me after wild, uninhibited sex under the stars.

My eyes snap open, guilt consuming my thoughts, and I look down at the head between my legs. I realize, sadly, that this chalk-white hair doesn't belong to the person I want inside of me right now. Desire leaves my body quickly, and I quietly go stiff against the chair, suddenly unable to enjoy any more of the moment. Achill keeps going, fingers pumping inside of me, his mouth fixed on my clit. I watch him as he continues, not even noticing that my mood has changed.

A knock at the door makes me jump, and Achill stops suddenly, cursing. He pushes back, wiping his mouth, and sits back on his heels as he wipes his fingers on the rug. He looks me over, scrutinizing my exposed breast and the dress that has twisted itself around my middle. "You should cover yourself."

Flushing, I hurry to straighten my dress as I walk over to the table. Downing some more mead, my gut roils with shame for not being more excited about the evening.

"Come," Achill's deep voice intones, and the door cracks open.

A page sticks his head in. "Milord, you'll—"

"This had better be of utmost importance—we were in the middle of dinner," he snaps, turning his head slightly, his sharp profile outlined by the light of the fireplace.

"Y-Yes, milord," he stammers, looking from me to the king and then down at the floor. "Y-You'll want to know that His L—"

Achill holds up a hand, and the page's mouth snaps shut. "Enough. Sorcha, our evening has come to a close. I trust you can see yourself out. I'll call upon you tomorrow." He strides over to the door, yanking it open wide, and the page cowers, scurrying off down the hall. Achill follows the page down the hallway without so much as a glance backward and the doors slam shut behind him.

"Your Highness." I curtsy to the empty room, stunned. What could be so important that he had to leave?

Dessert lays forgotten on the table. I swipe a finger through the whipped cream, tempted to take some dessert back to the room for the brownies. Instead, I turn to get my shoes and lose my balance, bumping into a bookshelf. It wobbles a little, and I reach out suddenly to steady it as a thin volume falls from a shelf up high. I reach out and catch it, reading the title: *"Stone Circles and Their Magical Anomalies: A Study by Cariad Deoir."*

Without a second thought, I tuck the book against my chest and hurry out of the room, leaving the shoes forgotten on the floor. Opening the heavy wooden doors again, smoke billows out behind me, fading into the night. I notice the guards are gone and I brace myself against the doorjamb, taking in deep lungfuls of cold air, clearing my head.

The cold marble soothes my bare feet, and the more deeply I breathe, the better I feel. My head clearing quickly. I take a right down a hallway and stop at a small side door that is open to the gardens. Hovering on the threshold, the light of an almost-full

THE BORDERLANDS PRINCESS

moon cascades over my dress, making it shimmer with muted colors. I swish it around and let it fall, noticing how thin the fabric really is, and I grow self-conscious again, holding the book over my chest, though it's just me. Looking out, I can see the conservatory, its spires gleaming in the moonlight. A few will-o'-the-wisps flutter about, alighting on the tops of the hedges and around the spouting faun fountain. It's a gorgeous garden, and my hand drifts to where the hagstone should be, grazing the ruby necklace instead. I look down, twirling the teardrop jewel in my fingers and in the moonlight, noticing it looks like blood in the dim light.

The vine climbing up the doorway waves a little in a light breeze, honeysuckle flowers bending down to kiss my head. Inhaling their sweet scent, a few flowers fall free, landing in my hand. I hold them delicately, eager to leave them for the brownies.

Heading back to my rooms, honeysuckle flowers in one hand, the book in the other, my head swims with confusion over the evening. Why would the king leave so suddenly? Why couldn't I just relax and enjoy a gorgeous Fae between my legs? It had never been hard to enjoy that with human men, though they had never been that good at it, either. And here, a king was between my legs, and actually doing a fine job of it. If only I hadn't fixated on someone else.

The door to my rooms looms in front of me, looking far larger than before. I turn the handle and fall against its support, feeling exhausted from the mead and the evening spent on display for the king. I drag my feet behind me as I head up the endless stairs to my bedroom and place the honeysuckle flowers on the windowsill, saying a quiet gratitude to the house brownies. I push the dress down over my body, happy to be rid of the clingy fabric and toss it onto the armchair. Climbing into bed, I don't bother with taking off the ruby necklace or putting on a night shift.

My fingers slide under my pillow, finding the lump of Conall's woolen sweater and my hagstone tucked neatly within its folds. I clasp my fist around the stone and drift off to a welcome slumber.

I'm too tired to be scared anymore.

A wolf howls ahead of me on the trail.

I drag my eyes slowly away from the face in the tree and see a wolf dash between the trees, the grey coat looking like dusted starlight under the moon.

The wolf reaches the stones and turns, eyes boring into me that glow so brightly I can see them from yards away. He stretches his neck skyward, ears pressing back against his head, and then a lonely, sad howl escapes from his maw.

The sound is so mournful I feel an overwhelming urge to weep. Other wolves join in his call as he vanishes in the dark, the howls reverberating for a few beats.

It's only after the sound fades that I realize the rest of the forest has gone deadly quiet. No wind rustling, no more wolves howling. It's as if the entire forest is waiting with bated breath for something.

I take a deep breath, exhaustion filling my lungs, and then I smell vetiver. A niggling sensation blooms in the back of my mind, telling me I should know that smell...

How do I know that smell?

18

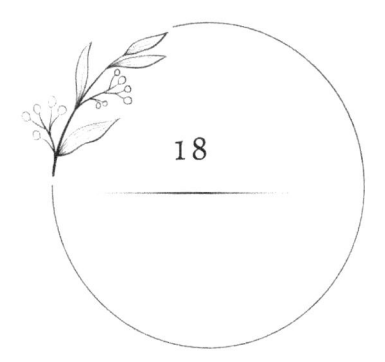

Day one-hundred and seventy-five. It isn't so bad, he thinks, as he runs his fingers through his matted hair then down his jaw, pulling on his lower lip.

The mossy, cold stone floor seeps into his bones. He flexes his right hand, holding the memory of her ribs pressed underneath them at the forefront of his mind. How he longs to hold her close to his chest again, arm encircling her, holding her tight enough he could feel her heart pounding through her back and into his chest.

If he had only dared bite her neck that night at the campsite and marked her, even just a little. Would she have responded to the heart-call, that deep pull he felt from the moment he first saw her? Do humans even feel the heart-call of a fated Fae mate?

His shoulder groans as he stretches, waking up his stiff muscles from sleeping on the ground. If only he could shift into his wolf form each night, it would have made sleeping so much more comfortable. But then, it wouldn't really be imprisonment if he could shift, would it? No. He shakes his head.

He grunts, folding his legs under him and pushing up into a plank to start his morning press-ups. Sweat collects between his shoulder blades, drips down his face as he tries furiously to stave off the feeling of containment. His mind drifts listlessly as he loses count of how many push-ups he has done so far, his thoughts pulling him back to Sorcha and those last few moments when they parted; how regal she looked, standing there, trying to breathe with her broken ribs.

Now, he understands why she never looked back, never gave him that last glance. Maybe she knew deep down that it would've been futile. It would have put so much more in jeopardy. He flips over to his back, rolling up to his knees and back down again, sweat rolling down his back, soaking his shirt. His stomach burns with hunger and exertion, and he finally stops, lying back down on the cold ground with his hands behind his head, panting heavily.

His eyes trail the moss that climbs up the walls, merging in the center of the ceiling where a slow drip falls onto the floor, creating an indentation in the stone that fills with stagnant water. Again, if he were in his wolf form, he could actually quench his thirst and drink that water and not get interminably sick. But here he is, stuck in his two-legged form, unable to get a good night of rest, unable to help her, unable to do *any*thing of use and, well, he could go mad.

Or, he could keep working out, keep his mind as sharp as possible, knowing that his immortal body may be weaker, but at least he's still alive, and if he's still alive, that means she must still be alive. But, if *any*thing has happened to her, well, he supposes he would have felt it again. It was only during those first several days when he felt her searing pain, as it radiated up into his shoulder, down his arm. He got a splitting headache, too, causing nausea so bad he dry-heaved until the pain abated. And it drove him mad. To be caged in while she suffered was unbearable as his trapped wolf struggled to come through. He fought to keep his claws in and his shifter from taking over, lest shifting kill him while he was under these wards. The agony of not being able to shift back into Fae form and be stuck in a cell, unable to reach her? Not a possibility.

So, he'll wait, biding his time, knowing that she's alive

because he can feel that enduring tug on his heart, so strong and so powerful, like a beacon trying to guide him home. But should that tugging snap, so taut and so quick, madness or death would be the only relief he would feel.

For now, all hope isn't lost.

He rolls back over and gets to his feet, sliding his arms through the bars. He leans against the door. The wall sconces aren't on today, which means, more than likely, no visit from *him*. Fine, all the more time to think about how in the Goddess above he can get himself out of this mess. He can't access his magic, given the place is warded against it and he can't shift, can't see the moon, can't get any fresh air or fresh food, which means he has to take his shot the next time the king visits, and who knows the next time that will happen, as he comes less and less lately. Really, the fewer visits, the better, he supposes, as that hopefully means he has some time to figure out a way to break through to Sorcha. He hums the tune he sang around the campfire on the last night they had together. The only other thing he can do that brings him comfort.

> "The stones overflow,
> With the magic in our souls.
> When the flowers bud,
> Bestow your blood,
> Underneath the moonlight,
> Beneath the Goddess' sight,
> The forest sings in our bones...
> Can you hear the magic stones?"

"Bravo." A slow clap echoes down the hall and long, languid steps follow the voice. "What a sweet little lullaby, Conall. I take it you didn't got little sleep in your sad little cell?"

The king rounds the bend and comes into full light, the wall sconces flaring to life before him.

Conall lifts his head and smirks. "I slept fine, as usual."

"No, 'Your Highness' this time? I'm disappointed."

"Last time we talked, you had me locked away in that silly little nightmare dungeon of yours as you burned my feet and broke almost every bone in my body out of sheer spite. So forgive me if I'm not feeling keen on having a pleasant discourse with you."

"Come now, don't hold a grudge. And you really didn't talk. If I recall, you screamed more than anything, especially when I used my smoke." Achill flicks his hands, smoke swirling from his fingertips, and smiles when Conall flinches. "Oh, stop, Conall. Fear doesn't suit you. Besides, thanks to your shifter blood, you healed easily enough. You won't have any… lasting damage. Which is good, since Sorcha…"

"Sorcha, what?" Conall's eagerness at hearing her name almost gives away his desperation.

"Oh," Achill waves his hand in the air, dismissively. "You don't know, do you? How could you? Being locked away, miles from her. She felt your pain, Conall. Every bone breaking, every scream, she felt it all."

Conall swallows, shoving his horror down deep, feigning nonchalance. The last thing he wants is to give Achill the satisfaction of knowing that her pain got to him. "Since I'm no longer your whipping post, how are you releasing all that tension? Circle jerks with your loyal guards?"

Achill laughs, leaning back against the wall opposite Conall's cell door. "Whatever happened to wolves being loyal to their masters? You disappoint me."

"I think you are confusing dogs with wolves. Wolf shifters don't give a fuck about having a master." Cocking his head to the side, he raises an eyebrow in challenge.

"Unfortunate. See, if you *had* been loyal, like your father, you wouldn't have forced my hand to violate the treaty. I wouldn't have broken a vow. You wouldn't be here. And that darling little human princess wouldn't be where she is now—"

Where she is now? Conall shakes his head, a mask slipping over his features once more. "Achill, you know as well as I that you can't change fate. Aerona—"

"Don't you DARE speak her name!" The king throws himself forward against the cell door, spittle landing on Conall's cheek.

"Relax, Fire King. I was just saying—" He slowly wipes the spit away, taking a slow step backward.

The king seethes, gripping the bars so hard his knuckles turn from white to red. "Don't you *ever* say her name again. Not while I still breathe."

They're both quiet, and after a moment Conall holds up his hands in surrender. "I know I do not know what you went through. But—"

"Tell me," the King starts, his eyes cold and his voice dripping with malice. He paces in front of the cell, hands clasped behind his back. "How long has it been since you've seen the moon, Conall?"

Conall sighs, rubbing his hand over his beard and twisting the ends around his fingers. To Conall, it feels like it's been an eternity, but he can't let the king know that, so he keeps his face blank and replies as calmly as possible, "Eh, by my calculations, 175 days…?"

"Yes, hmmm, that must be *so hard* for a wolf shifter."

"I know what you're doing, Achill, and it will not work."

"I'm merely pointing out that while you're in here, you really don't have any hope of ever getting out again while your fated mate still lives. Such a pity you were fated to a *human*. Their temporary life spans are so… useless." He waves his hand in the air, turning away and walking back up to fresh air. "You'll know the same madness soon enough." His cackling bounces off the stone walls, reverberating down the hallway, into Conall's spine.

He waits until the king's echoing ceases and the dungeon door locks closed before he leans his head against the cell bars and lets out a long, desperate howl.

19

Shaken from the dream, I find it nearly impossible to keep sleeping. The scent of vetiver and lemons clings to my skin and hair and I grimace. Mercifully, the brownies must have known, as the bathing tub is full of hot water and dried flower petals.

"Thank you, brownies," I say, sliding into the piping hot water. A little squeak from under the bed has me sliding down into the hot water with a grin plastered on my face.

The stone circle book rests on the chair next to the tub, and I open it up to read a few passages as I soak. Sketches of various stone circles pepper the pages as I flip through the book, getting a feel for the volume. With no table of contents, this looks more like a personal journal than a text. Turning back to the first page, a handwritten note addressed to no one in particular reads:

> *This is my attempt at an application for other Earth Fae that may not have as much experience with these stones as I do. I have tried to find ways in which these ancient stone circles, some here prior to the birth of my parents, have survived millennia buried deep in parts of Fae and scattered across our world. Some rituals work, some don't. Some rituals yield more magic, some rituals yield less. So, what exactly happens to our power within these stone*

circles, and why do these rituals produce such inconsistent results? Are the stone circles conduits for our power, or are they merely monuments to powers that once existed? I have made it my life's work to understand the answer to this very question, and I am still nowhere near understanding it...
　—*C. Deoir.*

A knock sounds at the door and I close the book quickly, placing it back on the chair as Fern's voice sounds from the top of the stairs.

"Milady?" she asks to the empty room, her footsteps echoing on the floor as she walks towards the bathroom. Fern's arms are full as she opens the bathing room door, curtsying quickly, "'Tis early, dearie. You aren't supposed to be up for another hour, at least. I brought you some fresh day clothes and the clothes that you came in, all washed and mended."

"Thank you, Fern. The king said he was going to take me to the library today. I think I'd like to wear my riding clothes again."

"Aye, would you like help to get out of your bath this morning?" She asks.

I shake my head.

"Then I'll be but a moment with your breakfast." She curtsies and turns, leaving the room quickly.

Stepping out of the bath, my skin pink and raw but luxuriously smooth, I wrap myself in a bathing robe and snag the book to hide it under my pillow.

A brownie chirps from under my bed, their shadowy outline following me over to where my clothing lies. A simple day dress accompanies my old riding clothes, along with a new half-boned stay. My riding boots shine, the spit stain from the horned Fae scrubbed clean.

"Oh, brownies," I breathe, "Thank you."

Muted sunlight comes in through my windows with a pattering of rain on the panes. A gentle rumble of thunder overhead shows no signs of letting up soon. Fern returns with a generous tray of tea and pastries. I eat while she helps me get dressed in my riding clothes, the pants and loose shirt, the perfect accompaniment to curling up in a chair to read while it rains. Last, I slip the hagstone over my head, its comforting weight settling against my skin.

I give the room a once-over as we head out for the day, remembering my promise to the brownies from earlier. I turn to Fern, asking, "Could you make sure that we give the brownies a sweet little treat today? They did such a lovely job with my shoes and my bath this morning."

Fern nods, and out of the corner of my eye, I can see a shadow underneath the day bed jump up and down. Warmth floods my chest and a smile spread across Fern's face.

Leaving my rooms, we make our way through the maze of the castle, taking several turns down new hallways and climbing up a few sets of stairs. The castle guards regard me with an air of impatience as we make our way through a new section of the castle. She turns once more, bringing me to a stop in front of a very large, very imposing set of carved wooden doors coated in a thin sheen of dust.

"These doors look like…" I start, trailing off as I look intently at the carvings in the wood. Fauns, sprites, and magical dryads dance around each other, a jubilant scene that fills the door's surface.

"The doors to His Highness's study, yes. We are a little early, but His Highness won't mind if you peek around beforehand." She reaches forward, tugging on the handles.

"Thank you," I say. My fingers itch to touch old books and, as she pulls the large doors open, I inhale deeply and smile. Dust motes fly, and the smell of ancient paper, leather, and mold wafts around me.

"Hello, lovelies," I say to the room. Before I can turn around to thank Fern, the doors click shut behind me.

Magicked candles flare to life as I step down into the center of the room. Nooks and crannies around the many towering, jam-packed bookshelves illuminate with flickering light. Craning my head to see how high the shelves go, and I can make out at least three levels, with a spiral staircase on each end reaching to the uppermost floors. Large floor-to-ceiling windows peek in between each shelf and each level, allowing in some of the muted light from the storm outside. It's both cozy and entirely overwhelming and I do not know where I even want to start.

Heading to the right, my fingers trailing behind me as I walk along the shelves, trying to read all the titles behind layers of dust. I grab a few random books off of the shelves, picking ones with titles that I can read. Lost in a daze of book heaven, arms heavy with tomes I have never read before, I hum the lullaby Geannie used to sing to me, quietly remembering the lyrics Conall put with them.

> "The stones overflow,
> With the magic in our souls.
> When the flowers bud,
> Bestow your blood,
> Underneath the moonlight,
> Beneath the Goddess' sight,
> The forest sings in our bones…
> Can you hear the magic stones?"

I make it up to the second-floor landing and look down into the main room, noticing that the floor is an inlaid map of Fae. The bookshelves cover parts of the map up, but I can see that there is no noticeable border between the human lands and what is now Fae territory. The woodland area that we crossed through during the first few days' travel over the Border is far more extensive on this map and, as I walk along the railing, I find it stretches for a lot longer, reaching to a depiction of a sea that forms the main entrance to the room. Walking to the far side of the library, the forest ends at an expanse of mountains that I didn't know existed when we had initially traveled east through Conall's lands.

Conall.

I stop and take a deep breath, my heart dropping to my feet

as I remember that last tense hour we shared. My hand aches with the memory of his large hand pulling me up from the depths of the lake, wrapping up my ribs, and never dropping his gaze from mine. I can imagine the warmth of his broad chest radiating in my back as he held me in his arms.

Meandering between a few more shelves until I find a large armchair by a window, I set down the books on a side table. Wiping off the layer of dust from the leather chair, I tuck my legs up to my chin and flip through a few pages of *A History of Baking with Magicked Flour*. Glancing out of the window at the rain traveling down the windowpanes, I follow a solitary drop that trickles down, gathering more speed as it makes its way to the bottom. It slides down the long window and my eyelids grow heavy. I rest my head against the wing of the chair and hum the lullaby as the library around me shudders, fading from view.

The moonlight shines bright and low, casting long shadows across the forest floor.

Tall standing stones form a circle with an altar stone that sits in the middle.

Overgrown vines encase the altar in a sea of foliage.

There is no wind, but my hair is blowing about my shoulders.

I stand in the middle of the stone circle, watching as the whorls and swirls on the stones shift like colorful snakes in the moonlight.

Reaching out, my fingertips graze the altar stone, leaving little blooms of moss and tiny purple flowers where my fingers touch.

I hear a shuffling and turn around.

A large black wolf walks between the large stones and enters the stone circle.

It sits on the other side of the table in the center of the stones, watching, waiting.

Its green eyes are luminous.

It tilts its head one way, and I copy it, tilting mine.

It yawns, and I yawn.

It licks its lips, and I do the same.

I reach out my hand slowly, itching to touch its fur.

It bows its head and leans into my palm, soft meeting soft.

I walk closer, wanting to nuzzle within its chest and hold it close.
I bring my forehead down and touch its head with mine.
"SORCHA."
A powerful growl echoes in my head, shaking the stones, and my head snaps up in shock as our gazes connect.

I wake to Hazel shaking my leg, and the book drops from my lap. She squeaks at the near miss and hides under the chair.

My heart beats in my ears and I blink a few times, the sound of my name reverberating in my head. I look at my hands, still feeling the fur of the wolf on them.

"Hazel?" I call, looking over my knees as I reach down and pick up the book. She pokes her head out from under the chair with a few other brownies. "I'm so sorry. Are you ok?"

She nods, taking my outstretched, and climbing to the arm of the chair. She says, "I was scared you wouldn't wake up. The King is on his way."

"Thank you." I smile and yawn.

"Are you ok? You shouted out a name before you woke..." Hazel tilts her head, frowning.

"Yes, I think so. It was a strange dream, that's all."

"Do you really know Lord Conall?"

I look at her, shocked. "Yes, how do you know that name?"

"Centuries ago, he used to frequent these halls." Hazel says, "With his brothers."

"Really? What was he like back then?" I try to hide my interest, but my heart beats fast, regardless.

"Lighthearted," she muses, "We all were. And then..."

A scuffling sound from the shelves above sounds as a book flies past me, landing with a large thud on the floor, sending dust flying and the brownies scurrying.

"Oh!" I reach down to pick it up, careful to keep it closed until I can see if the fall caused the ancient bindings to come loose. Cradling the ancient book in my hands, angling it to the light coming from the window, I trace the gold filigree that lines the spine, the title written in a language I don't know. Soft leather encases the pages, yellowed with age and only slightly chewed up by bookworms. A shimmer of the gold leaf remains on the fore edge and rubs off onto the tips of my fingers, leaving a light sheen of iridescence and glitter behind. The end sheets have a hand-drawn map on them, the ink so faded that it makes it hard to see anything other than the forests and mountains depicted.

"Well, then…" I exhale and add affectionately to Hazel who watches me curiously, "I don't think I've ever held something this old in my hands before."

"It's a beautiful book," she muses. "If you leave it here, the library brownies can bring it to your rooms."

"Oh! A delivery service! My, that's clever," I say, flipping through more of the pages. The book falls open to the middle, an entire section of the book devoted to the most beautiful illustrations of Fae creatures I have ever seen. Creatures with branches for arms and birds in their hair, some with wings adorning their backs and tails of all shapes and sizes and lengths, multiple hoofed feet, and mossy, silky beings climbing out of the water that resemble the water nymph I met. I keep flipping through, trying to burn these images into my memory, frustrated that I don't know the language.

"Your Highness," Hazel says, tiny voice trembling, "He nears. I don't want to be here when he arrives."

I look up from studying a beautiful water nymph. Hazel's eyes plead with mine, her hands fidgeting with her little tunic.

"Of course," I nod, frowning.

She disappears into the shadows, between the bookshelves and the walls, just as a door down below opens. Several long strides walk into the center of the library, and I quietly close the book in my lap, tucking it into the cushion of the chair.

"Sorcha," Achill's deep voice echoes, "are you enjoying yourself?"

I untangle myself from the chair, straighten my shirt, brushing out the wrinkles. Following his voice, I walk down a few aisles to where I heard him stop. I lean over the railing, my hair spilling over my shoulders, curtaining my face within. From within its shroud, I take a moment to study how imperial his presence really is. Broad shoulders trail down to a slim waist and long legs ending in low black boots. He's left his hair loose today, flowing freely underneath a simple crown. He tilts his face up to mine, sharp nose and jaw looking more severe in the flickering light of the library. A simple white shirt adorns his body, rolled up to his forearms, showing off lean lines of muscle.

"I was, yes, Your Highness." I smile brightly. "Would you care to join me? I've pulled a few thrilling books, one of which is about baking with magicked flour."

"No." He crinkles his nose and looks outside, dismissively adding, "It has gotten rather late, and when I inquired about your whereabouts, they informed me you were spending your leisure time in here. I thought maybe you had previewed the library without me."

"No." I pause, picking my words carefully, "I wanted to get here early, in case I ran into a book about magicked flour." I throw him a brilliant smile and walk to the stairs as slowly as I dare. I take one last look at the book nestled in the chair cushions, silently willing it to stay there until I can get back to it. The spiral stairs make me a little dizzy, and my foot misses the last step, sending me careening forward into Achill's arms.

His hands grasp my arms and he holds me close against his chest. "Careful there," he intones, helping me stand up.

I flush a deep red and look up into his eyes. "I'm not usually so clumsy."

"Perhaps it's the Fae architecture that has you tumbling about. We are taller than you humans," he says, raising an eyebrow. He pulls on his jacket, straightening the lapels where my hands had been. "I haven't been in here in quite some time, but I remember a great little corner in the back with some tantalizing titles."

He glances down at me, flashing me a smile, as he pulls me toward the dimly lit back corner. Achill twirls me around to face him, wrapping his arms around my waist, hands clasped at the base of my spine. Bending low, he murmurs, "Apologies for last night."

"Those kingly duties," I smile, the bookshelves pressing in around us.

"I don't plan on leaving you in the middle of our fun again." His lips form a sultry smile and he pulls me in closer, thumbs stroking my low back.

His smoke unfurls, wrapping around me, but I place my hand upon his chest. Leaning back, I look up into his blue eyes. Lightning flashes through the windows, highlighting his sharp features and Hazel's worries echo in my head. I push against him, protesting his advances, "Your smoke magic…"

"I thought you would like it," he leans down, but I turn my head slightly and his lips contact my cheekbone. Achill drops his hands from my waist and looks at me, confused. "We'll just have to make another night of it, then."

"Yes," I answer, dipping my head in a bow, and sliding past him back into the center of the well-lit library. He follows shortly after, straightening his crown. Thunder cracks overheard and the candles flare to light as the storm worsens outside.

The main doors creak open and a page pokes his head in. "Milord?"

"Yes," Achill's deep voice sounds from behind me and I jump. He places a hand on my shoulder, trailing it down my spine and hovering over my backside. I take a small step to the side, trying not to flush in front of the page.

"It concerns the…" The page's voice trembles. He hovers near the doors, not stepping fully inside.

"I'll be there momentarily," Achill snaps, sending the page scurrying back through the doors. "I would see you to your rooms but…"

"Kingly duties," I finish, bowing my head as he takes his leave. The heavy doors slam shut behind him in the rush.

I stand in the center of the room, on the boundary marker to Conall's lands, and out of the corner of my eye Hazel emerges from the shadows. She scurries across the open room, and I scoop her up into my hands.

"I think we should follow him, Hazel," I say, the hagstone warming my skin.

"If you must," she whispers, shivering.

"I just have this feeling..." I muse. Placing her on my shoulder, Hazel buries herself against my neck, covering herself in my hair.

As silently as I can, I heave open the doors and the library candles behind me snuff out. Achill's coat flutters behind him in a flurry of fabric at the end of the hallway, his deep voice barking something at the page.

I scurry down the hallway, sticking to the shadows, and poke my head around the corner Achill disappeared behind. The hallway is empty, save for the lingering trails of smoke that disappear behind a door at the end of the corridor.

Hazel tugs at my hair, whispering, "I don't think you should go in there..."

"Why not? I whisper back.

"It isn't a place you want to see." She says, curling up against my neck. I can feel her tiny body shaking with fear.

"Fine, you stay here or meet me back in my rooms," I whisper, taking her off my shoulder and placing her on a windowsill near a curtain. Tiptoeing, I edge closer to the door. Turning the handle slowly, I open the door a crack.

Muffled screams echo in this chamber and I almost miss Achill's coattails as he heads through a side door.

"What...?" I whisper.

The door at the other end of the corridor creaks open so I slip back into the shadows of the hallway behind me. Running, I head back towards the library just in time to open one of the large wooden doors, turn around, and pretend that I am leaving the room for the first time.

The page comes from around the corner at the same time Fern approaches from the other side. Both creatures look at me, but only Fern greets me. "Your Highness, I've come to see you back to your rooms."

The page flicks his eyes in my direction once more and sweat beads his brow. As he nears Fern, he picks up his pace, rushing through a side servant's door.

"Thank you, Fern," I say, tracking his hurried movements. I look around for Hazel, but she is long gone, scurrying in the shadows somewhere.

"Of course, milady." She dips her head, and we walk through the myriad hallways.

"Fern," I hedge, "What does the king do during his days here?"

"Aye, he is a busy man," she dodges the question seamlessly.

"Yes, I've noticed. I often feel like an unwelcome guest, truth be told."

"Och, don't worry about it too much. He is busy, but I know he tries to make himself available to you."

I nod, biting my lip, wondering if I should push Fern to answer more of my questions when we round the corner, the doors to my rooms visible at the end of the hall.

We enter the sitting room, and Fern takes her leave through the servants' door saying something as she departs, but I am distracted by the several stacks of books that lay on the table. I immediately make my way over and run my fingers across the spines. The titles are a few of the tomes I had picked out from the royal library intermixed with several others that I haven't seen before. Hazel pokes her head from behind the stack, climbing to the top of the books.

"Hello," she says, "did you find what you were looking for?"

I shake my head, tilting so I can read the titles a little easier:

> Fae Land History
> Pixies and Their Counterparts
> Fae Folklore and Myth
> Fae Ancestral Lines
> Elemental Magic and Mastery
> Too old to read...
> Too old to read...

> Something about Fae theater and their musical instruments…
> Baking with Magicked Flour
> Royal Fae Family Lines of the Last Five Hundred Years
> Human Folklore and Myth

I hover, uncertain which book I'd like to read first, when two of the brownies from upstairs chirp next to my feet, nudging me out of my trance.

"Oh!" I startle. "Brownies! Any books either of you'd recommend?" I ask, bending down and holding out my hand so the little creatures can join Hazel on top of the table. They squeak their confusion back at me. "Ah, yes, I see. You don't know how to read, then I take it."

All of them shake their heads at my question.

I smile broadly down at them as they clamber on top of the stacks. "I suppose we should start at the top of the pile, then. What about *Fae Land History*?" I point to the book. They shake their heads. I point to another, with a pixie on the cover, and they cover their eyes in fear. "Ah, that's a no, then. This one about *Fae Folklore*? Well, then… How about this one, *Fae Ancestral Lines*?" Their eager nodding has me lifting the ancient tome, and as I look at the cover, I realize it is the same one I had hidden in the library, but today I can actually read the title.

I gather the brownies up in my hands and let them crawl up my arm to rest on my shoulders as I walk over to an armchair by the balcony windows and curl up in the sunlight. Left alone with the brownies, my books, and my thoughts, I bring the book up to my nose and inhale the dust and leathery smells. The brownies looking at me curiously as I do.

"I just… really like the smell of old books." I shrug, and they titter, grabbing fistfuls of my clothes as they slide around on my shoulders.

I immediately open to the middle of the book, finding the delicate pictures of the different Fae. At the bottom of each picture, I can fully read the words that I didn't understand just moments before.

"Well, that's odd… I could have sworn I could not read this, but now…?" I look from one brownie to another, and they scurry away, underneath a bookshelf on the far wall, as Fern enters the room with a tray laden with food and hot tea.

Flipping to the first page of *Fae Ancestral Lines*, the writing shifts magically in front of my eyes—the ancestral text unveils as I read the opening lines. Entranced, I turn the pages slowly, watching the words unfurl across the parchment. My shock must be apparent, as Fern comes over and brings a blanket, tucking it around my shoulders. She also brings a plate of food over and a teapot.

"Must be a gripping read, milady." She looks sidelong at me as she pours me a cup of tea.

"I—I don't know what I'm witnessing here. Can I actually read Ancient Fae?"

She shrugs, turning back to the rest of the room. "It wouldn't surprise me if you were—"

"Huh." I sit back and pick up where I left off, sipping my hot tea. Names that I don't recognize are at the beginning; except for one, *Deoir*.

Deoir. Deoir. My fingers drum along the pages.

I slam my tea down on the table, spilling a little and dash up the stairs, clutching the ancient tome to my chest. Running over to my bed, I thrust a hand underneath my pillow and pull out the book about stone circles, laying it on my bed. I flip to the first page, my finger scanning down the pages until I see the name underneath that handwritten note: *C. Deoir*.

"Ha!" I open up the *Fae Ancestral Lines* book, back to the section of the book for the Deoir family, listed under the Earth Fae Ancestry. As I do, a previously empty page now contains a beautiful illustration of the tree of life. Color fills and paints the pages, and I watch as leaves spread across the page, names ancient and powerful forming the root. My eyes travel up the magical page, following the branches on the tree, watching with bated breath to see the name fill in: Cariad Deoir. But something else catches my eye, as my father's name unfurls underneath hers: Gareth Salonen. And then mine: Sorcha Salonen.

Holy Goddess.

My hands shake as I gather up the books and trudge down the stairs, eyes wide and mind whirring with all the possibilities.

"Milady, are you all right?" Fern reaches out to me, and I stare at her, jaw open, eyes wide, trembling slightly.

"I... don't... know?" She takes me back to the chair, tucking a blanket around my shoulders. I show her the book, pointing to the tree of life and where my name sits.

"Aye, so I see you finally figured it out." She smiles knowingly at me. "Well, that makes things a tad bit easier, eh?"

"What?" I look up at her, still awestricken, clutching the books tightly.

"Aye, Sorcha, dear. Have you been more clumsy of late?"

I nod slowly, as a frown forms on my face.

"Aye. Has the food stopped tasting *just so delicious* and a wee bit more normal?" Fern walks to the table, bringing over pastries and some hot tea.

I nod, again.

"Aye. Have you been having vivid dreams?"

I nod, chewing on my lip, thinking through the past few dreams I have been having lately with the wolves, the forest, and the feeling of Conall being so close and yet just out of reach. The stones in my dreams, that look like the warding stones on Conall's land, that are discussed in my grandmother's book, and their colorful whorls of shimmering light.

"So I thought. Have you also been conversing with, say, brownies when you haven't been able to before?" She places a few pastries on my plate and pours more tea into my cup.

I nod. "Yes, but I just thought it was because they were getting more comfortable with me—Oh my dear Goddess. They're more comfortable with me because I have Fae blood?"

Fern nods, a twinkle in her eye and a sly smile. "That seems about right."

"But... why now? What happened?"

"Well, milady, I can only imagine that the change started happening when you crossed over into the human lands. But for your Fae blood to come through *this* fast and *this* strong, I can only assume that something must have sped up the process for the land to have recognized kin."

I sit quietly for a few moments, staring outside at the trees waving in a gentle breeze, and then my head snaps back to Fern, face growing pale. "I performed a small blood sacrifice to an altar of the Goddess on my way here."

"Och. Aye, that'll be it, then."

"Well, this is unexpected." I get up, wrapping the blanket around my shoulders tightly. "How did you know I was part Fae?"

"Remember your broken ribs, milady? That poultice I used on you wouldn't have worked as quickly on a human. Your Fae blood practically jumped at the healing powers, and the poultice just amplified it."

"That makes... so much sense now." My fingers graze my ribs under my clothes and then my hand strays to touch the scar above my eyebrow. "I just thought it was because the poultices *were* magic."

Fern puffs up a little and asks haughtily, "Who said they weren't?"

Her indignation makes me laugh and the dam breaks. I laugh so hard tears form in the corners of my eyes. I have to brace myself against the back of the chair, bending over as I get a stitch in my side. Fern stands there, arms crossed, cheeks puffed out, and the indignation turns to concern as I keep laughing.

"This whole—" I wave my hands in the air, gesturing wildly to the entire room, the castle, the land, the events of the past few weeks, and wipe the tears from my eyes. "It's all utterly impossible. Why don't I have pointed ears? Why doesn't my father? What about magic? What about longer life spans, hmm? It makes little sense." Out of breath, heaving from laughing, I get furious, and the questions just won't stop, but I can only squeak out, "What happens now?"

Fern walks slowly over to where I stand, taking my hands in hers, and leads us to the glass doors. "Let's go get some fresh air and talk this through. I have a feeling that some of these books might help, but later. Right now, we have a right mess to sort out, and I think being in the fresh air might help."

We walk out onto the balcony, the fresh air pulling my hair from the blanket and whipping it around my shoulders. The trees bend in the breeze as if their sturdy branches are trying to reach out and shake my hand, welcoming me back home.

20

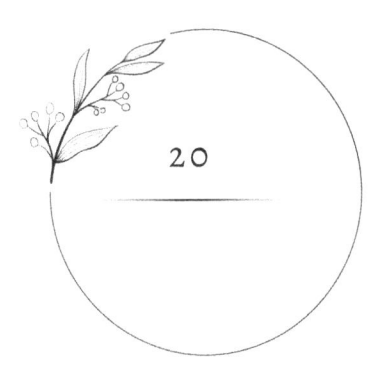

Day three hundred and, what, fifty? Or is it fifty-one? Like it even matters anymore. But that tug still pulls on his soul, so he knows it has to matter since Sorcha is still alive out there.

He thinks it might be the endless waiting that will eventually kill him, drive him mad; waiting to get out of here, waiting to get to Sorcha, waiting to seal the mating call. His wolf itches underneath his skin, getting restless as he paces the same path in his cell, over and over. His power dwindles every day, and he can hardly feel the tides of the moon anymore. He looks dejectedly at the stale bread and cold soup that sit in the corner of his cell, untouched since… when? He can't remember. He'd rather have to deal with a constant, gnawing hunger than touch something that tastes worse than human food.

How long has it been since the king has visited his cell? At least several months, give or take a few days. Maybe that was the whole point: he'd become forgotten, fade into Fae history, just like his father. He would descend further into madness and waste away alone until he died of a broken heart or he ended his own life. But what would happen to the Borderlands, *his* land, and the Fae he kept safe within its borders?

Why couldn't he have kept his stupid head down? He tried, but damn, being fated to that princess—that clumsy, naïve, foolhardy human princess. He can feel the madness setting in slowly. Almost a year without recognizing his fated mate and it has unraveled the edges of his heart and mind. His sleep has gotten worse as he relives the same dream every night. Watching Sorcha running through a forest, wolves herding her toward standing stones, the smoke creeping after her, and then the King. Standing there, waiting for her to come into his arms.

Why can't he even bring himself to finish the rest of the dream? He swears that when he dreams of her, Sorcha calls out to him. If only he could call back to her, if only he could sleep for longer than a scant few hours each night.

He continues pacing and kicks a singular stone out of the way. It ricochets off the walls and lands in the center of the pool of water, splashing water over the floor. He reaches into the pool of water, feeling around for the stone, and holds it in his hand. Sitting down, he stares into his reflection, his bearded figure waving back at him in the ripples, then coming into focus as the water calms its movements and grows still. A stranger stares back at him with gaunt cheeks, dull green eyes, a long black beard with white and red hair peppering his temples. He can't believe that this is it. He refuses to believe it.

His eyes grow heavy as he absentmindedly strokes the stone between his thumb and forefinger, rolling it over and over. His breath evens out and deepens, as his shoulders relax, and he nods off for a few more minutes, sitting there in the middle of his damp cell. He dreams of his heart calling out to a beautiful princess in a stone circle. Maybe this time he can reach her, maybe this time she can hear him.

21

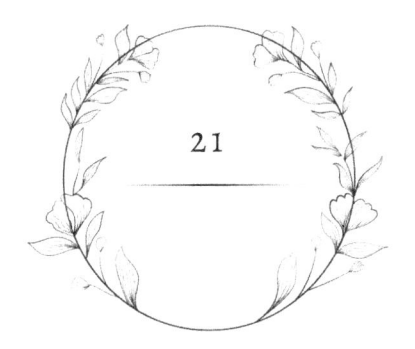

We sit outside for hours, digesting the news that I am part Fae. Fern patiently answers my questions about what to expect next, now that I am in the magical world.

"What I still don't quite understand is how I didn't know until now? It must mean that Father doesn't know that he's half Fae."

"Magic works differently on the human side of the world. When the Border was warded, even several hundred years before then, the human side was devoid of the strongest magic. Something in the earth weakened the Fae, and if your father was born on that side, then I can only guess that even his physical attributes like a long life and pointed ears haven't even had time to fully develop or his Fae side is being extremely suppressed."

"That makes a twisted sort of sense, I suppose. I just don't understand how I wouldn't have noticed if he had pointy ears or the fact that he's so much older than I thought? His beard doesn't have any grey in it… Ohhhh."

"Aye, if he is in his middle years and doesn't have any grey, perhaps he is aging a lot slower than you thought," Fern muses, turning to me. She stares at my face, and her hand reaches up to touch my ears. "You aged more like a human than a Fae on that side of the Border. Dearie, fate has other plans. Have you felt your ears lately?"

"What do you mean?" I reach up and feel my ears, noticing now that the ends are slightly more pointed than a few days ago. Conall's deep voice reverberates in my head again, but this time it's soothing and calms my swirling anxiety.

Nothing is as it seems...

"I have a few more questions..." I turn to Fern, but she's already heading toward the servants' quarters.

"Aye, I'm sure you do, milady. But let me go grab some dinner while you dive into more reading. Those books have answers that even I don't know." She says, dipping her head and closing the door behind her.

Hours later, as I've read through books on Fae history and ancestral lines, I have realized two things.

One is that my grandmother was Cariad Deoir, one of the most powerful Earth Fae to have existed, and her sister, Aerona, was one of the most powerful Water Fae. Both died, but only one, Cariad, left an heir. That heir was my father, who then had me. Whether I have any magical ability beyond healing quicker than a normal human is still unknown.

And two, that I am so deep into this unraveling mystery of my lineage and the Fae world that a lifelong imprisonment is sounding less and less daunting by the minute. I don't have enough time in the day to read as much as I want to about the intricate political power that once held the Fae kingdoms together. What used to exist as a harmonious republic of monarchs is now under one High King, and how that happened is still a puzzle I need to piece together.

I haven't seen Hazel in a while, though, but a part of me can sense her lurking about in the shadows with the brownies. As eager as I am to tell her all the things I have discovered, I feel like she already knows.

Fern knocks a few times, opening the door carrying a tray laden with an enormous roast, and behind her are two new pixies I haven't seen before that help carry a spread of food large enough for four people. Their translucent wings catch the light of dusk and the candles and their hair cascades down their backs in multitudes of long braids, bits of feathers, and petals woven throughout. Their tiny bodies hefting large trays of food portrays that there is more strength to them than meets the eye.

"Fern, I can't possibly eat all of this by myself." Standing up amongst the spread-out books on the floor, I walk over to the table. Delightful aromas fill the room, and I finally register the growling coming from my stomach is hunger.

"Nonsense, dearie, you look wan and you've been reading all day."

"Then, please, I insist everyone sit and enjoy this with me. You, too, brownies!" I call out to my bedroom upstairs where I can hear them tittering. I sit down and look up at the women, intent on getting them to share a meal with me.

The pixies look at each other and then at Fern, who then looks at me, a little baffled. "If… if you insist…"

"Yes, of course. I've been wanting to know more about all of you, anyway." I say, hopeful that they can tell me more about the High King and the politics of Fae.

The brownies, who have told me they are called Hush, Scruff, and Puff, rush downstairs, alight from their little wings, and scurry up to the table, sitting next to my plate. Hazel is still noticeably absent, so I make a note to save some food for her for later.

The pixies hover, uncertain about joining, but eventually fold their wings in and sit timidly next to Fern. The brownies dive right into the fruits and bread and begin dipping their hands into a small pot of honey. They chitter gleefully to each other as they smear their sticky hands all over their faces and lick their fingers clean, only to dive back into the pot once more.

Heaping our plates full of food, I wait until everyone has taken their first bites before I jump right into conversation. "So, I have a few questions about Fae that I was hoping you could all answer for me." Looking around at the guests, no one objects. I continue, "From what I understand, pixies are air elementals, dwarves are earth, but brownies are a mix of air and earth?"

They all nod their heads. One pixie with dark purple hair opens her mouth to talk but gets nudged in the side by her red-haired companion's elbow. My eyes meet the purple-haired pixie's eyes. "No, it's okay, you may speak. What is it you wanted to say?" I try my best to maintain an open face, remaining neutral so they know that in here they can speak freely.

The words rush out of her mouth, "Earth elementals sometimes take the pixies in if they don't have their wings anymore."

"Oh, I didn't know that you could switch elements? I thought you were born with that magic?"

"You—you are, sort of. Sometimes. But, when a pixie loses their wings, they're grounded and no longer in favor of the air element. Some earth elementals, especially shifters and brownies, take in grounded pixies and start teaching them how to use their lack of air element." She blushes a little, sitting back in her chair, and takes a deep breath, almost like she had spoken little in front of anyone for a while.

Her red-haired companion, who had been eyeing my reaction this entire time, takes a big bite out of her apple and rolls her eyes. With a mouthful of food, she begins, "You forgot to mention—"

"I think it best if you finish your mouthful of food there, Cherry, before you choke in front of the princess," Fern admonishes as she heaps her plate full of more roast and vegetables.

Cherry bristles, her wings flexing behind her back, but swallows her mouthful and continues, "What Lily forgot to mention is that usually pixies lose their wings when their service to the king is no longer needed. It falls on the earth elementals to bring them in and show them how to live afterward. All pixies have ever known is the freedom of flight. One slight transgression and you're snipped. The king, he… clips their wings and tosses them out like last week's rubbish. He can go back to whatever hole he climbed out of. Pardon my frankness, Your Highness, but it had to be said."

My jaw drops. "I'm sorry, he… what? He clips pixie wings? Is this a common practice?"

Fern shakes her head slowly, sighing. "'Tis a practice his father, King Brant, put in place centuries ago and it seems to have stuck." She lowers her voice. "We all had high hopes after his father died, but…"

"The bastard took up the mantle ruthlessly, if you ask me." Cherry interjects. "I mean, if you could only see Hazel or the cook…" Lily elbows Cherry roughly in the side.

I swallow my food, trying not to choke at hearing Hazel's name.

"That's not your story to tell, Cherry." Lily snaps. "Leave them out of it."

I look at Fern. "Is this true?"

Fern shrugs, saying, "Lily's right. It isn't our story to tell. But, then again… I suppose Beatrice wouldn't mind if I shared with you. She can't speak for herself. After all, her voice ceased decades ago. We all thought the King was going to kill her when he found out that she was working with the humans to get extra provisions for the castle at the beginning of the war. But he stole her voice instead. Rendering her silent and forever indentured to work for him. And she can't leave the castle. Anytime she travels too far, his magic fills her throat, ensuring that she has to stay within the perimeters or she'll suffocate to death. It's a cruel punishment. One she never deserved."

The brownies nod their heads solemnly. Lily sulks, crossing her arms and staring at the ceiling.

Cherry pushes her food around her plate slowly, picking at the remnants. She says, "Don't forget about Hazel. He ripped her wings from her back and left her to die in the gardens. Right next to the lake that—"

Fern cuts her off, "Now *that* is a transgression, Cherry."

Cherry sits back, sulking, and Lily reaches over to pat her back.

I sit back as I mull over what I just learned. As much as I wish it to not be true, I say, "I don't *want* to believe all of you, but I do."

Everyone at the table looks at me; the pixies stare skeptically, Fern smiles knowingly as she continues to eat her food, and the brownies nod their sticky little heads.

"I have had these weird premonitions," I say, carefully choosing my next words, "and I have been so curious about the King's business. I can never get a straight answer from him."

"Aye," Fern says, "he can be evasive."

"Evasive," I muse, "but why?"

Cherry and Lily look at each other and shake out their wings. Lily says, "Thank you for dinner, Your Highness, but we best be getting back to our duties this evening."

"Of course, and please, come tell me about anything you think I need to hear. I would like to know what is going on in the kingdom I am to rule." They nod and curtsy, wings beating in rapid succession behind them as they leave out the servants' door.

Fern says, "Well, Your Highness, I don't know about you, but I sure love Beatrice's roasts."

22

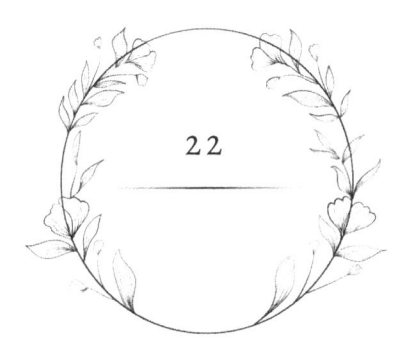

The next morning, I struggle to get dressed as all of my clothes have stopped fitting and I can barely pull my riding pants up over my thighs. The shirt sleeves are shorter, too, which leaves Conall's sweater as the only thing that can fit me still. I opt for my dressing gown instead and head downstairs to dive back into reading.

Plagued with thoughts of stone circles, wolves who say my name, and evil kings, I plait my hair, twisting the ends around my fingers. A niggling feeling in my mind that sits just out of reach from everything I've learned about my heritage, the way the King treats his subjects and staff, his treatment of Beatrice and Hazel, the Fae he burnt to death.

Am I to marry a dictator?

I open the door to the sitting room and find Fern setting up some tea and breakfast. She says, "'Tis an early morning for you, milady. Are you searching for more answers in those books?"

"In my grandmother's book, she talks of her ancestral lands and a stone circle that is on, what she thinks to be, an ancient ley line that dates back so far she thinks it's from when the Goddess first created this land. But the book itself is unfinished, and I can't seem to find any more information on where our ancestral lands are or even how to find them. I have this sinking feeling, however, that I need to get there. The answers lie within that circle."

"Aye. You'll find a way," Fern says, smiling softly.

"I hope so. There is this... feeling in the back of my head that makes me think I am missing something vital. I have these books on ancestral family lines, on magic, on folklore, and land history. I just wish I had something a little more personal to read about my family."

A squeak from the corner of the room has us both turning to look. Underneath a bookshelf, Scruff shuffles out, holding up one corner of worn leather and Puff holding up the other.

The journal?

"But it's blank." I say, walking over to take it from their hands. Bending down, I can just make out tiny little feet that don't belong to either of the brownies. I reach a finger out to touch Hazel's toes, but she scurries back into the shadows.

I sit down in an armchair by the fire and Fern peers over the wing of the chair, watching me flip through the blank pages.

"Hmmm..." she muses, stroking her beard again. "This isn't blank, milady. It's been magicked. Do you see the markings on the inside cover?" She reaches over my shoulder, gently flipping the pages back to the front, running her finger down the side of the end page. "These indicate a ward of some sort on the book itself." She flips through the first few pages, pointing to some indentations on the corners of the pages. "And these here are wards on each individual page of this book. Someone went to great lengths to ensure that only a certain set of eyes could read what's within these pages." She pats my shoulder and walks upstairs with an empty linen basket.

They set wards against whatever was written in this book and the stone circle book is unfinished, too. Reaching down, I grab the book about the stone circles and flip to the blank pages. No markings or wards on this one, then. Closing the book quickly, fed up with the dead ends, and having more questions than answers, I grab the journal next and flip through the pages once more while pacing the room. Tilting the book this way and that, I see if I can catch anything on the pages beyond the wards.

Nothing.

Pulling at the end of my braid, I pause and turn to the stack of books on the floor, remembering the book on *Elemental Magic and Mastery*. Laying it down on the table, I crack the spine and attempt to scour the contents to see if it lists anything on wards. Instead, the pages push my hands out of the way and fly open, moving on their own and landing on a section of the book about reclaiming elemental magic.

A passage immediately catches my eye:

Reclaiming your elemental magic requires a few items that pertain to the element that inherently exist in your blood. Using a stone circle with an altar stone is the most effective and enhances the potency of your spell work. Earth elementals will need several items of importance that come from the earth, such as (but not limited to) crystals, plants, and herbs. Water elemental reclamation does best when using fresh or moon water collected in an empty container, poured over the altar stone in the center of the stone circle. Air elementals should use items pertaining to the air, such as feathers, a jar of ether or fog. Fire elementals should pay attention to the color of candle they use when lighting their altar in the stone circle. See; candle colors and magical associations.

My head spins with the possibilities and I revel in the plausibility of being able to claim some earth magic from the Deoir bloodline. Twisting my hair around my fingers, I mull over what it might feel like to have magic for the first time in my life as the sun shines brighter, signaling midday.

I finally get up and stretch, opening up the balcony doors. My bare feet meet the cool stone and I take in deep lungfuls of clear, fresh air. The mountains to the North glow with the afternoon flaring off their white-tipped peaks. Peering into the forest beyond the castle walls, only the tips of the trees and vines curling up and over the walls are visible. The foliage is thick and green despite the changing of the seasons.

A chill in the air signals that autumn is on its way and I yearn to be back, watching the harvest festivals in the castle square. I used to love to listen to the street musicians from the balcony of the Great Hall. The laughter and cheering from below as farmers, entertainers, townsfolk, and their children all mingled together after a hard day in the sun. As a child, I'd long to sneak out with Geannie, hoping to see the vendors setting up their tables with their wares and fresh baked foods. Of course, I was never allowed into town, but Geannie would always come back with a basket that was heaped full of delicious breads, fresh pastries, and trinkets from faraway lands, and we'd stay up late into the night having a festival of our own on the balcony. She'd sneak me back through the servants' passages and into my room safely before Father would come in to kiss me good night.

Tears well up in my eyes, and I slide my back down the rough stone of the castle. Leaning my head back, I listen to the light breeze shake the leaves and wrap itself around the spires of the castle's towers.

"Fern?" I call, turning my head, my eyes closed against the sudden onslaught of tears. "Do you know anything about—eeek!" A rustling of feathers and a quick thrust of air brushes by my head. I duck instinctively and cover my head with my arms. "What in the—Oh my goddess. Thorne."

An injured and bloodied Thorne rests against the railing.

"Princess," they say, breathlessly, their voice laced with pain as they cradle a limp arm that drips blood onto the stone.

"Milady! Is everything all right?" Fern yells as I hear her tromping down the stone stairs inside. She rushes out, clutching her side and panting heavily. Her eyes meet Thorne's and immediately lowers herself into a reverent curtsy. "Minister Thorne."

"Up with you, Fernie." They wave their free hand dismissively but wince as they do so.

"Let's get you inside," I say, reaching out to help them inside, giving Fern a concerned look. "We can't have you bleeding willy-nilly, now can we?"

"Yes, I seem to be quiet, don't I?" Thorne smirks and hobbles a little closer. I loop my arm around their middle, letting them lean on me as we walk inside.

Fern heads back inside, bustling about, and cleaning up the books strewn about on the floor. She pulls the chaise close to the fire. "I'll be right back, dearies. I just need to get some supplies and an extra pair of hands."

"Thank you, Fern," I say, gently sitting Thorne down. "What… happened? What hurts?" I try looking at their arm, noting a couple of gashes and — "Is that a puncture?" A slow trickle of blood seeps onto the chaise as they painfully try to show me their wounded arm.

"Yes." They wince, looking up into my eyes with a pained expression. "I got caught in a crossfire. Someone shot at me in the air and I had to shift into Fae form to break the arrow enough to get my arm to heal, so I could shift again and fly. Fly directly to you. You have to know what's—"

Fern rushes in with her arms full of healing supplies and shouts into the room, "All right, dearies, I've got to get in there. Minister, if you'll allow it, of course." Thorne nods tightly as Cherry, the red-haired pixie, breathlessly follows behind her, with her arms full of bottles of tinctures. She almost drops her armful as she sees Thorne is the wounded one, and she shakes.

"You—Your Grace," Cherry sputters and dips into a curtsy in the air.

"I'm sorry, Minister? Your Grace?" I look at Thorne, scowling, folding my arms. "Here I thought you were some regular old healer not befitting a title of Minister… or Your Grace?"

"I can explain," they say, a painful wince as Fern lifts the arm where the arrowhead is still protruding. "It's, well, it's a long story. I didn't mean to mislead, but it was best if you didn't know exactly who I was…"

"Why, imagine that, Thorne being secretive. Let's get you taken care of, and then you can tell me what brought you here with an injured wing."

"Spoken like a queen," Thorne says, a smile quirking their

tight mouth as Fern slathers their arm in a greenish poultice and begins wrapping it up.

After an hour of checking over Thorne, Fern and Cherry, finished with their ministrations, clean up the bloody remnants as I pour some tea for everyone. "Thorne, I honestly can't even tell you how happy I am to see you—even though the circumstances that brought you here are less than joyous. How did you make it here with that wound in your arm bleeding so much?"

"Princess." And I can't help but smile at my title coming from my friend's mouth. "I honestly don't know myself, but I knew I had to get to you because I need to tell you something of the absolute utmost importance." Their face turns grave, and their free hand reaches out to mine, clasping it tightly. "The farmlands… Your father…"

My throat goes dry, and my stomach feels hollow. "What."

"King Achill, his army… laid siege on the outlying fields near the Border in the early morning hours."

"No."

"It was a small army of his most loyal guards…"

"No." The room spins and I sit down.

"It took them several days to get to the Border." They pause, waiting to see if I want to hear more. I stare at the flames in the fireplace as the room continues to tilt. "They lay in wait in the forest and attacked in the early morning hours. The fields were gone within mere moments. I tried to stay long enough to see if they'd burn the villages down, too, but I was spotted and had to flee."

"No. No. This can't be." My breathing turns shallow.

"Sorcha, I'm so, so sorry." Thorne sits next to me, wincing as they turn themselves to face me. They keep talking, but it's hard to hear over the thump-thumping of my heart in my ears. "I had been scouting for a few days, following the small troop through the forest. It wasn't until I flew too close to the village that I was noticed and… well. I'm not the only white falcon, but I am the only white falcon with purple eyes and, apparently, recognizable by other bird shifters who are not a part of the resistance."

"The resistance? You say things that sound like this had been his plan all along. Had they been planning to attack during harvest? Do you know how many people they killed? Oh, god. The children." Something in me snaps, my body heaving with sobs.

Fern walks over, handing me a kerchief. I sit up a little straighter, sniffling, and try my best to compose myself. Thorne, their face pained and purple eyes a soft lavender. A tear slips down their cheek, and they reach out a hand and cup my face.

"Thorne, I—" My voice cracks. Clearing my throat, I try again. "Thank you for your bravery and your dedication. I owe you—"

"Hush, Princess. You owe me nothing. My title as Minister of Health means that I am not above watching the world hurt, but it doesn't mean I feel nothing when it happens. Senseless violence can only cause senseless pain and hurt."

I nod, raising my chin a little, defiance settling on the tops of my shoulders. "This changes everything."

23

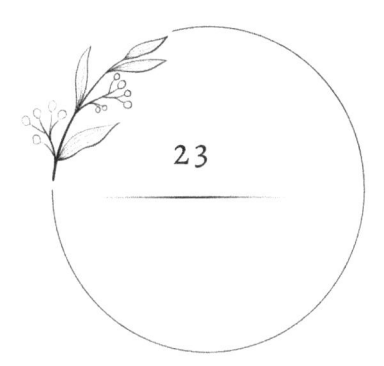

Three hundred and fifty-five days, probably, give or take, or something. Does it even matter anymore?

Conall swears loudly to himself as he gets up slowly from his reclined position against the wall. He should really stop counting, he thinks, as he splashes some cold water on his face. It's only making things worse, making him more frustrated, making him feel even more desperate. The heart-call didn't work last night; he was too exhausted and actually had his first night of dreamless sleep in twenty days.

A whistle echoes down the hall, followed by the creaking of a door closing.

Shit.

The king's back, and he didn't even prepare this time.

He rolls his neck on his shoulders, stretches his jaw, and wishes he could shift into his wolf form and just tear that Fae's head from his shoulders.

"Here, boy," the king calls, clapping his hands, voice dripping with venom. He rounds the bend and this time, Conall makes his face completely dull and unreadable. He can't let the king know that he's finally been able to make that heart-call with Sorcha, even if it is just in the dream world.

"Woof," Conall replies. He knows the game well enough by now.

"Good boy. I'll give you a treat if you behave." King Achill stops in front of the cell door, dangling some jerky from his fingers. Conall can't help it as his mouth salivates at the hope of having some meat instead of a cold, bland, liquid diet. "My, you look awful, Conall."

"What do you need, Your Highness?" He sighs and sits back against the wall, legs outstretched in front of him. The king waves his hands, candles flaring, lighting up the hallway and the cell. Conall shirks from the intense light, blinking to adjust his eyes.

"Well, this is a sorry sight for the son of the Borderlands Lord. What would your father think? Seeing you this way? Unwashed, weak, and powerless? You look as pathetic as the humans do." Achill pockets the jerky, watching Conall closely for a reaction.

Conall steels himself and maintains what he hopes is a perfectly neutral face as he shrugs. "Well, my father's dead now, so I'm sure he can see everything from wherever his souls lives. Goddess Above."

"How cute. Still praying to your Goddess. What I don't understand, Conall-boy, is how you are still holding on to your sanity?"

"How are you holding on to yours after Aerona died?"

The king's pupils dilate, nostrils flare, and he takes a deep breath in, whispering, "I've told you to never say her name while I still lived."

"Fine. I just want to know what makes you think she even ever wanted to be your mate? From what I know, she rejected you while she was living. What does it matter now that she's dead?" Conall tosses the stone up and down, watching for Achill's reaction from his hooded gaze.

"You. Insolent. Foolish. Dog." The light flares up, heating the cell, and Conall quietly relishes in the warming of his bones. The king seems almost sad, shoulders sagging slightly, when he continues, "Aerona was my *mate*. My *fated* mate. I was supposed to be with her forever. I would've waited for her forever."

"Oh, yeah? And how'd that work out for you?" Conall huffs and throws the stone against the opposite wall. It lands in the water as he stands up, dusts off, and leans against the wall, just out of reach of the door.

The king roars and grips the cell bars. "I could kill you."

Maybe that was a bit much, but Conall keeps poking. He won't get anywhere being nice, and if he has to suffer broken bones, then so be it. He needs more information about Sorcha and the humans and the rest of the outside world.

"You could, but you can't because, technically, you killing me kills Sorcha by proxy… so… looks like your hands are tied, Fire King." He shrugs, feigning cockiness, but his stomach drops to his feet. He'd better not hurt her, or he will rip out the king's throat with his own bare hands.

"Conall, you aren't even worth the time." The king stops mid-sentence and turns to listen as a guard calls out from down the hallway. "Besides, I have such a busy schedule. You know, lots of humans to conquer. Enjoy the next few months of solitude." He turns, waving off Conall like a pesky fly. Then, like an afterthought, the king reaches into his pocket and drops the jerky across the hallway, just slightly out of reach of Conall's cell door.

Well, fuck.

24

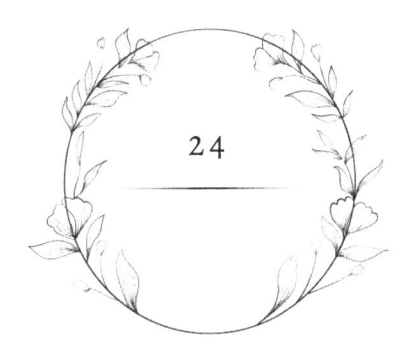

A deep sadness has wiggled its way underneath my skin, and with it, the tiny flame of doubt I have been harboring grows. The feeling increases as the evening wears on and turns into a restlessness that stokes my need to find the answers to my questions and fix all of this.

Thorne is the picture of perfect calm and has healed enough to use their arm in little ways. They drink their tea and watch me as I pace the room, muttering to myself as I mull over the books.

"Thorne, it is extremely unnerving how quiet you are. I don't know how you can just sit there and be so… calm after what you've just been through and witnessed." I say, turning to the fire to hide the tears.

"Princess, I have had centuries to practice the art of holding space for people in pain." They turn their purple eyes to me, watching me closely as I twist my hair around my fingers, plaiting the ends nervously.

"Right, well, I don't know if I have centuries to figure out who I am." I huff out a breath and sit on the floor. I pull over the warded journal, flipping through its blank pages again. Turning it over in my hands, the firelight shines through the vellum, and I can see some light indentations.

"What is that?" Thorne's chin lifts at the journal in my hands.

"Apparently, it's a warded book." I close the cover, setting it down on my lap, and ask, "Are you familiar with reclaiming elemental magic?"

"Hmmm, a little, yes. But only with reversing the effects on a Fae that has spent too long in the human lands." They unwrap their arm, and Fern slaps their hand away.

"Leave it be, Minister," she scolds. Thorne, not used to being the patient, holds their hand up in submission.

"Right. So, what if someone was part Fae? And they grew up in the human lands. But they came from a powerful Fae bloodline. Could they use a reclaiming spell to call that elemental magic back into their blood?"

"Well, if you're speaking hypothetically, then I think it is worth a chance." They look at me and their eyes sparkle with mischief. "What are you thinking, Princess?"

I smile, shrugging, then close up all the books and grab a blanket. "I'm going to go sit outside for a little while."

"I'll get dinner, milady, Your Grace." Fern curtsies and leaves but comes back for Cherry, who hasn't been able to take her wide eyes off of Thorne for the entire evening.

I sit with my back against the stone, the cold ground seeping into my bones, and stare up at the stars in the sky. Thorne quietly comes to sit next to me, holding his bloodied bandages in his hands. "She's going to give you a tongue lashing, you know," I say, nodding at the linen.

"Aye, but I'm almost healed, see? Besides, I want the scar. Living an almost eternal life shouldn't be without its lessons and reminders. This one I deserve," they say solemnly.

"Why do you deserve it?"

"Well,"—they turn to me slightly—"remember the ogres?"

I nod, waiting.

"Well, the king pulled me through a portal right after we crossed out of Conall's lands." They wince.

"Oh?"

"Yes, I was to report to the king regarding your whereabouts and any pertinent updates, but since we went through Conall's lands, I hadn't been in communication with His Highness for nigh almost a week. I knew he would inevitably pull me through, but I thought I'd have a little more time. Once I was through that portal, I knew, deep down, that he never had your best interests at heart. I could see his intentions behind his carefully placed mask. But what he didn't know was that I made an oath when I helped heal you after that attack in the forest. After all, you were my patient, and you told me things in confidence. It goes against my ministry to divulge any kind of information like that. But—" Their voice cracks a little. "But then he locked me in a room in the castle, in the hallway of nightmares. And I tried, Sorcha, I tried to hold steady, but when your worst fears are used against you… in ways… in ways that test…" They hang their head, sighing heavily.

I reach my hand out, stroking Thorne's back, letting silence fill the air.

"The only way I made it out of there was by telling him what he wanted to hear." They look at me, grief lining their face.

"And what was that?"

"That your heart belongs to another, and it wouldn't be easy to win you over."

"Ah, I see." Silence settles between us and the wheels click together in my head, churning, piecing everything from the past few weeks together. The stolen glances, the heated exchanges, that last night as we rode through Fae. His immediate change in behavior. Again, my thoughts go back to the feeling I have that he is constantly here with me, just out of reach.

"Sorcha," Thorne calls me back from my thoughts. "You know Conall's your fated mate, don't you?" Thorne says, touching my shoulder.

My eyes water and I look up at the evening sky, blinking back tears as I take in the constellations above. A soft wind rustles the vines and out of the corner of my eye, I swear they wave directly at me. My soul feels like it's finally found its calm after the upheaval from earlier today. I breathe deeply, inhaling the scent of fir and cedar and the honeysuckle vines. "Does Conall know that we're mates? I mean, that would explain why our last few minutes were so…"

"I would assume so. I know that on that first night when the Fae attacked, he raged. He fought with a fury I have never seen."

"You were there?" I frown, thinking back to the beginning of the journey, not recollecting any purple-eyed Fae.

Thorne smiles and says, "I stayed in my shifter form, keeping to the shadows during the fighting. It wasn't until Conall found you unconscious at the feet of the Fae that I shifted back. Keeping my identity relatively hidden was hard. The king can't know that I play both sides."

"So, you work for the resistance, then?" They nod. "And have you heard from Conall at all?"

"I… no. When I went through the portal, I wasn't able to contact anyone until the king no longer had use of me. Rest easy, Princess. I'm sure he's doing well. Besides, his lands are so strongly warded that I'm sure he's safe," Thorne says, nudging me with their shoulder.

"It's so… strange. I feel like I can sense him, deep in my bones. This tug that keeps me grounded. And I thought, all this time, that I was just pining for someone out of desperation. I didn't know that having a fated mate would feel… like this."

"And it will, forever. When you finally mate, that feeling will only get stronger if either of you have to part ways for any length of time. It's the heart-call, a tether from soul to soul, that keeps you connected and tied together. It's rare, and it's beautiful and you should cherish it as much as you can." Thorne's hand squeezes mine, and they head back inside.

I stand, leaning over the balcony, my hands twining with the vines that are still climbing and creeping up over the railing, despite the changing in the seasons. I play with a small, newly unfurled leaf, stroking its soft waxy surface when a green spark flies from the tip of my finger to the tip of the leaf. The vine grows suddenly, its tendrils reaching out and wrapping around

THE BORDERLANDS PRINCESS

my fingers. My jaw drops and I stand there, still, watching as the vine clambers over the railing, reaching for my feet and the rest of my body. It wraps itself around my foot, and I swear I can hear a whining sound coming from the plant.

"Princess?" Fern calls from inside, and the vine stops growing, letting go of my hand and foot, and sliding back into the shadows. I take a few steps backward, watching as the vine waves goodbye, as I close the balcony door behind me.

"The king has asked for you to attend a dinner with him this evening." She stands next to the door, the king's page hovering at the threshold. Her body gives nothing away as she inclines her head a little, waiting for my response.

"Indeed." I smooth the front of my dress down, glancing around the room and noticing that Thorne is nowhere to be seen, but the door to my bedroom upstairs is slightly ajar. Walking closer to the page, I smile calmly. "Please tell His Highness that I'd be delighted to join him."

The page nods quickly, turns to leave, and Fern closes the heavy door and looks at me sadly. She hands me another black velvet box. I open it slowly, noticing another delicate piece of jewelry.

"All will be well," I say confidently. "Hopefully, I can get some answers tonight about the attacks and we can come to some sort of understanding." My stomach fills with dread. "But first, I'd like to stop by the library. I have a few things I'd like to look for."

☽ ✿ ☾ ✿ ☽ ✿ ☾

Dressed to the nines, but without the necklace or the bracelet, Fern leads me down to the library. My hand instinctively reaches for the hagstone at the end of the chain, pulling it out and clutching it tightly as we take a shorter route through some of the servants' passages. We enter the library through a side door.

"What are we looking for, milady?" Fern whispers conspiratorially as we enter the dimly lit room. The candles must sense that we don't want to draw attention, as they only increase their light a fraction.

"A map of Fae that was made roughly one hundred years ago or older." I head to the left near the main doors where large wooden cabinets with long drawers rest. Pulling open the drawers, I see there are hundreds of sheets of sketches, some detailed plans of houses and others sketches of mountains. Fern opens a different cabinet drawer and starts rifling through what looks like detailed roadways in the human lands—some places I've never heard of before.

"Some of these maps are so old that these places are no longer spoken of," Fern says. I come to stand behind her shoulder as she points to some towns on the maps. "The Border War decimated most of the neighboring border communities of both human and the Fae. These drawings look like when trade routes were open."

"Are these what we're looking for, then?" I ask. She nods and starts sliding them out of the stacks and placing them on the floor. Laying them out together, they almost make a complete map of Fae some two hundred years ago.

"I think these will have to do. I can't tell what these landmarks are, though." She points to the edges, her finger trailing some dotted lines toward the interior. "No matter, I'll take these back to your rooms, and Thorne and I can start looking through them. We need to get going so we don't keep the king waiting, milady." Fern stacks each sheet carefully, working quickly to roll them up, tucking them under her arm. She leads me out a different side door of the library, down another servants' hall. We reach a small door, and she cracks it open, brushing aside a thick tapestry.

Silently, she signals for me to step out, and when I look back to see if she's coming with me, the tapestry flutters and Fern is long gone behind it. I push away from the wall, peering down the hallway between several marble columns, and when the coast looks clear, I stroll toward the king's study.

No guards are outside, which makes sense if they're all at the

Border, so I knock on the door myself. No answer. I am about to raise my hand again and knock once more, when the scent of vetiver and lemon wafts down the hallway. I turn, lowering my hand, and plaster a smile on my face as dread fills my gut. The king walks toward me, his lithe body tense.

Straightening my shoulders, I take a step toward him and bow my head. "Your Highness," I say.

His eyes roam over my body, stopping where the ruby necklace should have been, and a shadow crosses his features. "Sorcha, I sent my page to retrieve you, but you had already left. I figured you'd come here since our other evenings…" He smirks as his eyes trail down over my breasts and back up to my eyes. I shiver, but not from excitement. "Perhaps the formal dining room would be à propos for this evening. But if you've changed your mind, we can easily rearrange things."

He reaches around me, leaning in close, and opens the door. His study flares to light and I am instantly reminded of all the things that I *almost* did in there. I inhale slowly and turn to meet his gaze. Sultry, hooded lids look down at me, and this time, I feel nothing in return.

Play along. You can do this, and when the time is right, ask him what happened at the Border.

"As you wish, Your Highness," I say, smiling tightly as I take his arm. My feet feel leaden, but they follow him inside.

"Are you hungry?" he asks as he pours some whisky into two identical glasses and hands me one. He takes a long sip, watching me carefully as he sits down in a chair at the table.

"A little, yes, Your Highness." I clear my throat, wanting to reach up to the hagstone. Instead, I grip the whisky glass tighter and inhale the burning aroma. Making my way over to the armchairs, trying to put as much distance between us as I can, I sit on the edge and sip at the whisky.

The whisky burns on the way down and I try not to choke, but a cough escapes my mouth, anyway.

He scoffs as his eyes dart down to where the necklace should be. "Where is the jewelry I gifted you? Did it not suit?"

I run over what I want to say in my head one last time and ready myself to speak when a knock sounds on the door.

Achill huffs out an irritated sigh and says briskly, "Come in."

"Milord, I b-b-beg your pardon." Another nervous-looking page pops their head in, sweat already on their brow.

"I told you, we were not to be disturbed this evening," his voice growls, low and threatening, as his eyes turn a shade darker.

The page clears his throat. "Yes sir, but you'll w-w-want to know that the F-F-ae from the other night—"

"Excuse me," Achill grinds out and shoves the chair back, legs squealing against the floor. I flinch at the sound as he makes his way over to the armchairs, placing a hand on my shoulder. "I won't be but a moment, Sorcha."

The door closes against murmuring voices in the hallway, and I'm left alone in the study. Time ticks by, unease settling into every nook and cranny in the room. Sweat coats my palms, so I get up and walk over to the bookshelves. I grab one down about ancient Fae languages and begin flipping through while I walk around the room, then sit next to the window, lightning lighting up the sky in the distance. A storm builds and settles over the castle, thunder and rain starting simultaneously. I lean my head against the cold windowpane and look over the book. The gold filigree on the cover is newer than the other ancient texts I have been reading, and as I flip through, I come upon a chapter regarding the language I couldn't decipher the other day, before I realized I was part Fae.

Ancient Fae is a language descended from the Goddess's tongue. Often when we see it printed, we can ensure that—

"Again, I find you reading..." I jump up, closing the book, dust puffing up into my face, and I cough a little. Achill comes around to stand in front of me, his hands resting on my waist. "I scared you."

"Yes—no. No, I just didn't hear you come in." I try to step back, away from the touch that causes my insides to recoil. "Is everything all right?"

"Sorcha." He ignores my question, bringing me in closer, and leans down to whisper, lips brushing against my earlobe. "Let's *really* get to know each other."

He pulls his face away and cups my cheek with one of his hands. "I apologize for earlier. I just want for us to have a night alone since every other night we have been interrupted. When reports of your beauty first crossed our border—"

"Wait, wait, what do you mean *reports?*" I frown, taking his hand down from my cheek. My eyes scan his face, noting a muscle tic in his jaw.

"Yes, reports." He tilts his head a little. "I waited a hundred years for my betrothed. I had to know to whom I was going to marry."

"I—I thought Fae weren't even supposed to cross the Border until our marriage." I clutch the book to my chest and lean back against the cool window, twisting out of his arms and trying to put space between us.

"Well, technically, we can still cross, but with consequences like loss of our magic and—"

"Is that what happened to the Fae that came across the Border and killed Geannie?" I ask, fury rising in my throat like acid. I swallow more whisky down.

"Geannie? Who's Geannie?" He looks at me, confused.

"And what happened to the magic of the army you sent to burn down the fields?" I ask, anger lacing my words.

A flash of fury crosses his face, a split second of his mask slipping, and my heartbeat increases. But he steps forward, arms outstretched, and asks, "Sorcha, are you accusing me of harming your people?"

I swallow thickly, shaking, but force myself to meet his cold, hard gaze. "I heard that a small army attacked the outlying villages close to the Border. Why?"

"Why would a small army attack? I would assume it's because soldiers crave war." He waves his hand dismissively.

"You didn't answer my question."

"Who told you an army attacked?" He turns and walks to the table, pouring himself more whisky, and looks out the window.

"*Not everything is as it seems,*" Conall's voice whispers in the back of my head. I raise my hand to the hagstone that sits at my sternum. With as much confidence as I can muster, I say, "You still haven't answered *my* question."

"Fine. Why, why, indeed." He growls, a snarl forming on his lips, and downs the rest of the whisky. "Well, let me put this to you plainly. *Your* kind... *ruined*... my life!" He grips the glass so hard it shatters in his hands. He exhales, shaking the shards from his skin, sending blood flying. His head dips and his shoulders shake. For a moment, I worry he is crying but then realize suddenly that he isn't crying; he's laughing.

"I don't see what's so funny. You've killed dozens of humans, you've broken the treaty. This union,"—I gesture between us—"was supposed to end senseless killing. This union... can't happen. I came here to get some answers that would hopefully change my mind. Answers that could help endless suffering on both sides, but I can't go through with the treaty on these pretenses. I can't marry you. I can't wed someone who will so gladly start another senseless war." Picking up my skirts to leave, he snatches my elbow, blood smearing on my sleeves. Spinning me around to face him, he leers over me, his face contorted with anger.

In the back of my head, I hear Conall's voice. "*Not everything is as it seems...*" And I can feel the hagstone get warmer.

"That's not what *I* agreed to, *Princess*." He practically spits at the last word as he glowers down at me. "We Fae, we keep our word. I just had to find the right loopholes." His smile grows wide, but there is only malice behind it. His cold, calculating eyes stare back at me.

"Let. Go. Of. Me." I try to shake his hand, but he only tightens his grip, blood soaking through my sleeve. "Let go of me, now."

His grip clamps down harder, bruising my elbow, and I wince.

"Never." He yanks me closer to him. "I may not want this, and you may absolutely hate it, but I vowed to marry you. And marrying you is what I intend to do."

"Absolutely. Not." I step back and yank my elbow away from his hand. He inhales deeply, clenching his fists. "I'm leaving. Tonight. I expect a horse to be saddled and waiting for me within an hour. I will send for my things once I go back home."

"Home?" He laughs maniacally. "You think you have a home? *This* is your home now. *This* is your future!" The fireplaces roar to life, sending blazing heat into the room. The candles snuff out, vetiver and lemon smoke filling my lungs, and my eyelids grow heavy as the room spins.

"What…" I cough a little as the smoke trails around me, growing thicker and making me feel heady with lust. Why do I want to climb on top of him and ride him until I scream? I suppress a moan as wetness pools between my legs.

He steps away from me, chuckling menacingly. He looks over his shoulder at me as he pours more whisky into a fresh glass. His sharp, cold eyes cut through the fog in my head.

Not everything is as it seems…

"No… I… You need to stop your smoke magic," I put a hand out to brace myself against the bookshelves. My skin feels hot, too hot, and my clothes feel too tight. I tug at the laces, wanting to shed the layers just so I can breathe.

Achill walks closer, slowly, his eyes nearly glowing with the fire's reflection. "You're sure you don't want to stay and have some… fun?" His laugh is deep in his throat now and he downs more whisky, sidling up next to me, casually leaning on the bookshelf. His eyes roam over my skin, down my breasts, and back up to my face. He licks his lips.

My nipples ache with longing. I suppress another moan as I squeeze my legs together, and I almost bring my hand up to his neck to pull him in to kiss me. The heat of the room builds. I breathe heavily, lust filling my veins.

Something creaks and a cool breeze rushes in, along with the smell of rain and sounds of thunder. A window is open and a chill courses over my body. Achill's head snaps to the window and he curses loudly, walking over to close it as the rain comes in sideways, soaking the books and the floor.

"*Not everything is as it seems!*" Conall's voice yells even louder in my mind and my head clears so quickly that I snatch up the hagstone, its starbursts flaring brightly within. Raising the hagstone to my eye as quickly as I dare while Achill's back is to me, I cringe at the image that comes through the center of the stone. An ashy, misshapen figure, hunched over with a protruding, curving spine, balding head, shriveled-up hands, and long claws. The creature stands in front of the window as the rain pours in. I look around the room as quickly as I dare and notice a few scurrying little shadows slipping underneath the door and back out into the hall.

He curses loudly. I drop the hagstone, his glamour snapping back into place. I shove the stone back down in between my breasts and watch him as he reaches his glamoured hands up and slams the window shut. Steeling myself, hoping I can hide the shock on my face, I find I can't even reconcile that I almost willingly had sex with that… thing.

What *is* he?

He saunters back over to where we were, but my head has cleared enough from the fresh air and the discovery behind the hagstone that I smooth my hands down my dress.

"Again, Your Highness, I expect a horse to be saddled and ready for me in an hour," I state, clearly, calmly, though my heartbeat must give me away. "Consider our matrimonial commitment terminated. I release you from your obligations." I nod briskly and turn, walking away as unhurriedly as I can. Not looking back, I leave him standing there, fuming, in the middle of his study.

25

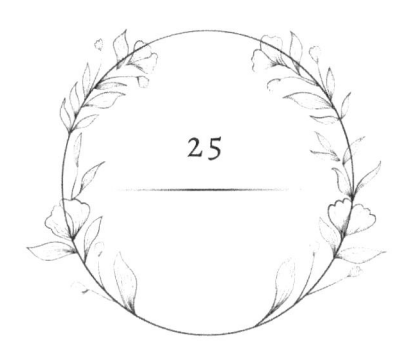

The door closes behind me and I take off running down the hallways, making it to my rooms breathless and shaking. I open the door to Fern tidying up the myriad books strewn across the floor.

Startled, she looks up at me. "You did it."

I nod, still trying to catch my breath. "Yes, I did. I broke off the engagement and I told him I wanted a horse ready within the hour so I could go back home. I need to pack the necessities and leave. Hopefully, he'll give me the hour and then come looking."

Thorne tiptoes down the stairs, peeking their head out. "Sorcha, what's going on?"

"Thorne, Fern," I say, "you both need to go. Now and quickly. Shift, hide, go somewhere safe. I don't know what the king will do next, but when he realizes that I'm not coming to get a horse, he will tear this room apart. I don't think he ever intended for me to leave this place."

They look at each other, Fern hesitating for the briefest of moments before she nods. "What do you need me to do?"

"I—I think just help me get a few things together." I pause, my hands trembling with anxiety. "Did either of you know… who… or, what, the King really looks like?"

Thorne winces a little. "What did you see?"

Unable to find the right words, I stutter out, "I saw... I saw a horribly misshapen figure. I don't even know if he's Fae or not. I used the hagstone, I had to," I shiver, thinking of the King without his glamour. And then it hits me, "Do you both look like him, too?"

"Oh! No. No, Princess. We do not." Thorne emphasizes. "I can assure you. You can pull out the hagstone right now and see for yourself, if it'll make you feel better."

Fern adds, "Absolutely never. I never once wore a glamour with you, milady. I promise."

I sigh, nodding, clutching my stomach that roils. "Okay. First things first, then. We have little time."

I grab the few items I think I'll need to make it to my ancestral lands—the book on stone circles and the empty, warded journal. While Fern busies about getting my things from upstairs, I write a hastily worded letter to my father, sealing is with wax and leaving it unlabeled. Thorne hovers by the fire, flexing their injured arm.

"Are you able to shift?" I ask.

"Yes, it has had enough time to heal, thanks to Fern's poultice." Thorne says.

"I need you to hold on to these for me, if you can," I tell Thorne, handing over the book and the journal. "Find a place to keep them safe. I know there's more to what's in their pages than meets the eye."

Thorne tucks the books into their sleeves, nodding.

Fern rushes back down the stairs with most of my necessities and immediately turns me around to strip me out of my dress. I scramble to slide the ill-fitting riding pants on, strap on my holsters, and put on my boots. My half-stay goes on over my shirt, and then I slip my cloak on. Fern is standing in the middle of the room, Conall's sweater in one hand, and a note I had written to my father in the other.

"Milady, what do you want me to do with...?" She holds

them up, and I take the sweater from her, bunching it up and inhaling Conall's scent one more time before giving it back.

"Please return this sweater to Conall. As for the letter, get it to my father. He needs to know that I had nothing to do with this, that I've broken off the engagement." I hold her arms, staring into Fern's eyes. "I plan to fix this."

Resolve settles deep in my bones as Fern and Thorne both nod. Then Thorne slips upstairs, and Fern opens the servants' door, sliding quietly into the dark hallway.

I make my way to the pile of maps, memorizing the familiar features. My eyes find the stone circle landmarks, matching them up to the ones in the book my grandmother wrote. I still don't know which stone circle belongs in my ancestral lands, but a cluster of them seem to be gathered northwest of the castle, heading to the sea. With one last look at the images, I throw them all on the fire, watching them burn to cinders. Cinching my cloak hood tight over my head, I leave a few pastries on the windowsill for the brownies and Hazel, thanking them silently for coming to my aid earlier this evening.

Opening the balcony doors, the vines have grown a little thicker, their stalks as thick as my forearm, as they creep their way over the stone baluster. I take a deep breath and swing my legs over, grabbing the lip of the balcony railing and lowering myself down, using the balustrades to brace myself around the thickest vines. Grasping the vines in both hands, I wrap my legs around and shimmy to the ground below. I land with a thud and fall back on my behind. Tiny scratches mar my palms, but otherwise, I'm fine. I look up at my balcony, pride soaring in my chest, when I hear a slow clap coming from the shadows.

"Brava, Princess." The king keeps clapping and pushes off of the castle wall, walking out of the shadows and into the light that shines down from my rooms. His glacial eyes glimmer and his mouth curves into a dangerous smile, showing his sharp canines. "You made it. What a strong, determined little human you are."

I lift my chin and swallow my fear. "It's one of my best traits, determination."

"Yes, I can see that now. Pray tell, where did you think you were going to go? Running into the dark like this?" He takes a few steps closer, and somehow his body seems bigger, though I know underneath his glamour his spine protrudes from his curved back.

"Not into your arms, those shriveled-up, clawed—" The back of his hand contacts my jaw and my head whips to the side.

I run my tongue along the corner of my mouth, tasting blood. The back of my hand wipes at the corner of my mouth. Trying to stand up straight, I look him right in the eyes as I reach down for one of my daggers as slowly as I can.

He grabs my wrist before I can reach the hilt and pulls me close. "You humans will never know when to quit, will you?" he derides.

Achill grabs me by the throat, lifting me up off the ground. My toes dangle freely and I clamp my hands over his wrists, trying to find purchase to keep from choking.

"Stupid mortal." He flings my body backward, and I go flying, landing roughly on the ground. The air leaves my body with a resounding crack, the sound of my ribs breaking again.

He stalks over to me and crouches in my face as I struggle to take in a breath. "What do you think will happen if you get out of this castle, hmm? You'll go run to your dear father and warn him of his impending doom? You'll go rally the resistance and magically end my plans?"

I roll over onto my side, wrapping an arm around my middle, trying to get in a deep breath. I look up into his eyes and reply, "That was part of the plan, yes."

He laughs and pulls out the letter I had given to Fern. My eyes go wide, and I panic.

"You mean this? This was going to be your saving grace?" He rolls his eyes and holds the letter between two fingers. I watch as flames crawl up the envelope and engulf the letter within seconds, burning it to ash and blowing away in the wind. "Fern was never on your side, *princess*. She told me everything."

Everything? My heart plummets. How?

"You know, you really should be more careful who you give your counterintelligence to." He stands up and turns to walk away. Thinking he's going to leave me there, I relax slightly, but he pivots at the last second and lands a solid kick to my stomach.

I heave and cry out, clutching my middle, as I curl into a ball.

"You humans are so pathetic. So trusting, so naïve. Get up," he says, waiting, and when I don't move, he yells, "I SAID GET UP!"

He leans down, grabbing me by my throat again, and lifts me off the ground by my neck.

I struggle, clasping his wrists as best as I can, trying to breathe through the pain in my ribs and stomach. I stare into his vacant eyes. He cackles and sets me down on my feet. I wobble a little, clutching my ribs, and decide that it is best if I don't stand up straight.

"There, there, little one. That wasn't so bad? Your future is about to be so much more fun now. At least... fun for me." And his fist meets my jaw, snapping it back and careening me down to my knees. The tang of copper fills my mouth as blood mixes with my spit. I tongue a loose tooth and more blood fills my mouth. He steps back, almost as if he's admiring his handiwork, and lands another blow. This time, his fist meets my left eye, one of his rings slicing open my eyebrow. The warm trickle of blood flows into my eye. I close it against the sting.

Sitting there, on my knees, my head bowed before him, he says, "I think I like you on your knees before me."

My breath comes in wheezes and blood drips from my mouth. Rain trickles from the sky, its cool drops touching my skin and stinging the open cuts. My fingers dig into the mud and grass, and my knees sink down into the wet earth, yearning for some support.

He walks a slow circle around me. "Now, you see, with the treaty, since I vowed it long ago and some details are still fuzzy, I agreed to not kill *you* specifically. But that doesn't mean I can't *hurt* you, either. So, here lies the fun for me. Since your family destroyed any hope I ever had of a future with my fated mate, I am going to destroy *yours*."

As he talks, the grass becomes thicker; the shrubs grow a little bushier, and the vines by my balcony unfurl their tendrils. Closing my eyes against the hallucinations, I say, "I don't know what my family did to you, but we could've made a difference. Together."

He chuckles, walking away from me with his hands clasped behind his back. "That's where your naivety is so quaint. You still think you had any power here? As if I would ever want a human for my queen, for my equal. Unfortunately, I am oath bound to uphold my side of the treaty, so we will deal with this after I return from your father's castle. Until then, I will keep you in the dungeon to live out the rest of your pathetic human life."

While he was talking, my hand reached down and palmed the hilt of my dagger, sliding it out as quietly as I could.

I whisper, "I'm not going with you. Anywhere."

"That's cute that you think you have a choice in this matter." He walks back, crouching back down in front of my face, placing a palm on my cheek that is already swollen from his blows. He pats it roughly, causing me to wince, and I grab his wrist with my other hand and drive the dagger down into his shoulder with my other. The motion causes me to cry out, my ribs digging into my lungs.

Achill sits back on his heels, looking at the dagger protruding from his shoulder. He looks at me, eyes never leaving mine, while he takes the hilt and pulls hard, sliding it out of his skin. The blade slices back through his skin and muscle with a suction. A sweeping chill covers my body and I ready myself for another attack.

Instead, he laughs, a dark, menacing baritone. Then he looks me in the eye.

"You can't kill me, human. You don't have it in you." He slowly touches the point of the knife with the tip of his finger, playing with it as it carves away at his fingertips, his blood dripping onto the ground. Flames erupt on the edge of the knife, and he presses it to his skin with a hiss. He grimaces a little, and the smell of burning flesh reaches my nose. It takes everything I have to not retch. He groans and gets up, tossing the blade underneath some shrubs against the castle wall.

"Don't tempt your fate," I say, my shaking voice giving away my nerves. I spit more blood onto the ground, tonguing my loose tooth.

"No, I *really* don't think you could do it. I think you're just a scared little human. You've failed so miserably at even the simplest task. All you had to do was give yourself over to me. We'd have been married within the week and your job would be done. You could have even lived your days out in the Tower, complacent, with all of those *books* to keep you company. But, no, even this you had to fuck up. Your daddy will be so proud when I tell him you've called off the engagement. I wonder, what will his last words be when he finds out that you've thrown it all away?"

"You can't." I shake uncontrollably now.

Grabbing my shoulders, he leans down to whisper, "Yes, yes, I think I can. The treaty never specified I couldn't kill the rest of your family. I just couldn't kill YOU." He stands up and grabs my hair by the handful and yanks me up off the ground. I scream, scrabbling to grab his hands to relieve the pressure on my head as my scalp burns.

"Pathetic," he says and throws me against the castle wall. I hear something crack in my shoulder, my arm twisting behind me. I slide down, cradling my left side, the pain searing through my body. Shaking uncontrollably, each little movement shoots daggers down my arm and into my ribs. Tears flow freely down my cheeks now. I hurt. Everywhere. Never did I ever think my life would come crumbling down like this. In this moment, so utterly, entirely alone…

A wolf howls in the trees beyond the castle walls. And, soon, another wolf joins. Then another. Their echoing sounds come from all over the grounds outside of the castle.

The king straightens his jacket as he stalks towards me again.

I mumble something so inaudible that even his ears can't pick it up.

"What was that, *Princess*?" He sneers, leaning down, so he's level with my face.

"I said, fuck you and your small, shriveled up dick." I smile, cradling my arm, and blow him a kiss.

"Welcome to the rest of your brief life, Sorcha." He pulls his hand back, slamming his fist into my face, breaking my nose. Blood pours forth as my head slams back against the castle wall, and everything fades to black.

26

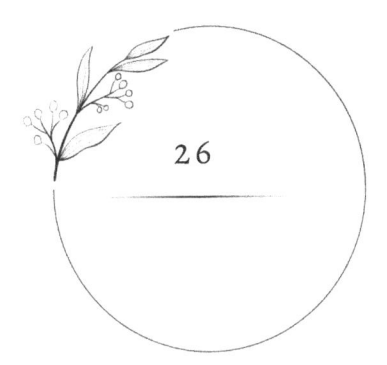

Three hundred and, Goddess above, fifty-nine days. Overhearing the guards talking about the upcoming equinox in a few days means that, maybe, he still has time?

A little less than a year in the dungeon, and he feels like he's closer to finding out what happened to Sorcha by using the heart-call. His days are restless, filled with constant pacing and worrying. He's started eating again, though the liquid diet they're feeding him can't really pass as food, trying to build up his energy stores for when he eventually gets out of here.

Because he will get out of here.

But he is still so damn weak. The one thing that isn't weak? That tether to Sorcha flaring bright and strong, connecting his soul to hers even when they sleep.

Especially when they sleep.

At first, he could only watch as she moved through her dreams, watching her explore and walk around the stone circles. Now he knows she can see him. She looks for him each time she's in the stone circle. His voice calls out and he can see her look up, look around, trying to find him, but she doesn't respond. She doesn't answer.

He will get through to her. He has to.

Conall throws the stone against the wall again, tossing it so it ricochets back into the pool of water, watching the ripples grow steadily. He settles himself back into a meditative state, sitting calmly on the floor, breathing deeply. His eyes close as he dives back in to try the heart-call again before the night is over, before she stops dreaming…

He sits there, at the altar stone, waiting for her. Calling to her heart from a place so deep in his bones that he swears he can feel her heart beating back faintly. Ba-dump, ba-dump. The waiting is agony, his tail thump-thumping impatiently on the ground, stirring up a little dust. He tries to settle in for the long wait until she can make it back to the stone circle, back to him. His mind wanders back to their last moments together. The terrifying worry as he killed that last ogre, turning around to find out she was nowhere to be seen. Following her path with his keen sense of smell, the blood on the ground, the limping footsteps, and then her fall down the mudslide. Half of the hill gone in an instant and Sorcha with it, panic settling into his bones as he slid down, peering into the water, watching her struggle. It took but a moment for him to dive off the cliff and down into the water, arms immediately reaching for hers. He tries to think of how beautiful her hair flowing in the water was even as the lake dragged her under. He remembers how determined he was to reach her white fingertips as they reached up instinctively to grasp at his arm. Those precious few moments when it felt like he wasn't strong enough to save her.

The wind shifts and he can smell her before he sees her, amber and rose floating on the illusory breeze. Sorcha appears in the stone circle, looking around at the stones in the moonlight. He can't see her face, not yet, so he sits in his wolf form, this time behind the altar. He lets out a large huff, trying in vain to catch her scent and imprint deeply into his memory, for when he wakes, that is the smell he wants to remember.

She turns around and looks at him curiously.

He tilts his head one way, and she mirrors his movement. He yawns, she yawns. He licks his lips; she licks hers. Her soft, voluptuous lips. He can't stop staring as her tongue touches the bottom lip. He wants to be her tongue, playing on her lips, tasting the air she breathes. She reaches out a hand, gingerly trying to touch his fur. He bows his head in submission, eager to have her move closer but unable to speak those four words he's dying to tell her.

"Sorcha." *Nothing. He leans against her head, her fingers stroking his fur and calming his panic. He tries once more, his voice feeling stuck in his throat. He closes his eyes as her forehead touches his.*

He tries one more time to open his mouth and...

He wakes with a start on his back, screaming her name out loud in the cell, his voice bouncing off the walls in the dungeon. His heart pounds in his ears, and he rubs his face, astonished that she could touch him this time. Every time in the dreams before, her hand would always stop right before his face, an invisible barrier preventing her from reaching him. This time was different. Tonight, he'll get even farther. Goddess knows he is running out of time to get it right.

He rolls over then, determination rousing him from his position, when he sees a crack in the doorway that lets in a sliver of light. He crawls a little closer to the cell door, peeling the door open as quietly as possible to listen. Nothing but subdued light in the dungeon hall greets his eyes. He stands up then and peers down the hallway. Empty. He sniffs the air, trying to see if he can scent anyone else. The coppery smell of blood rushes up to his nose.

He slides the door open farther, all of his systems on high alert as his hair raises on his arms and his ears perk up.

Conall slips through his cell door, keeping to the shadows. No sconces are lit and the rest of the cells are empty. As he creeps down the hallway, padding along on his bare feet as quickly as he can, he peers around a corner. The smell of blood gets stronger and then two headless bodies of Fae guards lie on the floor near the door, their blood running down the stairs and pooling near his feet. He steps around the stream of still-warm blood, placing his feet carefully on the cleanest stones he can find. The door at the top of the stairs is wide open, letting in a sliver of moonlight from the world outside. The soft light touches the feet of the dead guards, and Conall's skin itches, finally able to feel the power of the moon tides calling out to his wolf.

He stops at the top of the stairs, listening for any sign of fighting or life beyond his own breathing and heartbeat. Nothing. He slips back down into the shadows, grabbing a blade from one guard, and slides easily outside. He presses his body against the stone building, sliding deep into the shadows as he makes his way into the ancient forest beyond.

27

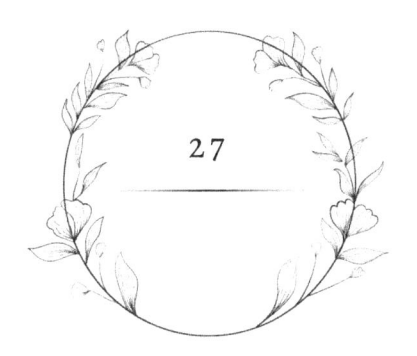

"Move her to the room," the king says. The scent of my blood, vetiver, and smoke fills my burning lungs.

"Aye, Your Highness. Until then?"

"Until then, she's yours to do with as you please." His scent fades with the squelching sounds of his footsteps in the mud. A door creaks open and slams shut.

A few moments pass, and I can hear my wheezing breath. I moan and try to lift my head. Blood still seeps from my nose and the cut above my eye, so I lay back down. Throbbing pain fills my body in waves, from my head down to my toes and back again.

Hands reach out and touch my cheek. I flinch, groaning, trying to scramble away. My shoulder screams and I whimper through a mouth full of blood.

"Shh, shh, Princess. It's Murdock. I swore an oath to Conall that he wouldn't take you, but I need to get you out of—"

"Oy! You there!"

"Lay still, Princess, we'll get you safe yet..." A whisper close to my ear. Then, louder, "Aye! She's in a bad way. We'll need the stretcher. We need to get the room ready, too."

Footsteps fade...

A cool breeze pushes my wet and bloodied hair out of my face, and several tiny, soft hands touch my cheek. The smell of honeysuckle, lilac, and fresh cut grass tickles my nose.

Groaning, I'm lifted and cradled in stalwart arms. I whimper from the pain as the shifting hurts my shoulder and my ribs.

The strong arms shift around me again, keeping me close against them, wrapping me up in their fragrant embrace.

A vibrational sound fills my ears, the rhythm sounding similar to the lilting lullaby Geannie used to sing.

I hum along some notes, noticing the tinge of copper in my mouth has subsided.

An effusion of warmth fills my body then, and golden orbs swarm behind my eyes that are still swollen shut. They swaddle my arm in close to my body, and my ribs feel supported and wrapped tightly, giving me enough reprieve for the pain to subside so I can find some relief. I succumb to fitful sleep.

The wolf is there again, pacing inside the stone circles

The entire meadow is covered in plants of every kind—vines, flowers, shrubs, bushes, grasses, trees.

The whole earth feels alive and I walk slowly around the circle, dragging my fingers behind me, flowers sprouting where I've touched the stones.

The wolf pads slowly around the circle with me, calmly waiting as I reorient myself to this sacred space.

I can almost see into the thick forest beyond, a few glittering eyes staring back at me.

I turn back to the wolf, but it's turned and starts walking out of the stone circle, down a path that leads into the depths of the trees.

I take a tentative step forward, leaving the stones, and walk soundlessly behind the wolf. Its tail twitches, and they look back over their shoulder, checking to see if I've followed.

Green eyes stare at me through the darkness, and I stop, my breath catching.

"Sorcha..." A howl-like call comes from the closed mouth of the wolf.

The wolf tilts its head.

I tilt mine back.

"Sorcha..." A little louder this time.

My heart beats faster.

I think I know those eyes.

The rain has moved on, leaving a chill to the air that carries the scent of freshly watered grass and wet earth. The light of the moon has shifted, casting darker shadows across the garden. My eyes open, head throbbing, shoulder pulsing with pain.

The evening's events come rushing back, and I snap to awareness knowing that Murdock has somehow infiltrated the king's guard. I don't have long until he returns with more Fae, who are most likely not working on both sides. I try to lift my head up from where I landed, but instead of lying on the ground, I'm suspended in the air. The vines from my balcony have crawled all over me, wrapping me up in their arms, cushioning my broken body with their leaves.

Shifting within the vines, I hear them sigh with relief as they unfurl slowly, gently placing my feet on the ground. Baffled, I move my body around. Offshoots of the vines have wrapped my arm against my body into a makeshift sling. Though it isn't fully healed, the support the vines provide feels immensely better.

This can't be possible? Can it?

My hand flies to my face, and I touch my left eye. It is less swollen, and the cut has scabbed over but is still tender. My shoulder feels sore but no longer screams in pain, and I take a few breaths to fill my lungs. My body has healed enough for me to move without wanting to cry out.

The vines shove me along the side of the castle under my balcony, their leaves like little hands nudging me over the grassy walkway, ushering me into the darkened corners of the garden. My boots and holsters are gone, but a glint of something underneath the shrubs opposite catches my eye. I glance left and right to make sure the coast is clear. I dart as quickly as I can to the castle wall and squeeze in between some shrubs. They shift and wiggle, moving their branches, magically giving me cover. I look down at my fingertips and they're dusted with green light at the ends. My mouth drops open, realizing that this must be earth magic.

Voices come from the courtyard, and I crouch further under the bush. Grappling around desperately through the mud, the hilt of my dagger grazes my fingertips. Snatching it up quickly, I slide it into the belt of my pants.

Looking over my shoulder, along the length of the castle wall, a few roots poke through the base. Their knotted tendrils crawl through a small hole between several large bottom stones. From my hiding place, it looks like small game animals have been using the hole to sneak in and out of the castle gardens for a while. I edge closer; the shrubs shifting their branches as I move, creating a small tunnel that I can crouch through. Clenching my hands closed, lest my shining fingertips give away my whereabouts, I scoot closer to the hole and peer through. The castle wall is easily three feet thick, and the hole seems to be about a foot and a half wide from this angle.

I stick my right arm down the hole as best as I can, inhaling a sharp breath as I twist. My left shoulder screams in pain at the movement and I bite my lip to keep quiet. I don't have time to make the hole bigger, especially with voices coming from the gardens.

Drooping boughs of a tree, possibly from the same one whose roots have broken through the wall, lean down over the top of the crenels. Reaching my hand up as high as I can, I will the tree to reach down far enough so I can grab on to the boughs, hopeful it will lift me up and over like the vines did.

The voices in the garden get louder and my body shakes with fear.

"Come on," I whisper to the tree as I stretch a little higher. "Please. I have to get out of here."

A breeze flows through the branches, the leaves grazing the tips of my fingers that glow a little brighter. They glimmer in the moonlight, and I cringe at the thought of my fingers acting like beacons to any of King Achill's guards. The roots of the tree creak and stretch, filling up the hole in the castle.

"No! I need to get *out* of here." Frustration builds, and sweat beads my brow, but I can't reach any higher and my left arm screams in pain.

The voices in the courtyard escalate, and I can hear their boots on the stones. The trees' roots shrink, pulling all the way through the wall, taking large chunks of stone with it. Without a second thought, I drop and slide onto my back, mud soaking my clothes, and snake my legs through first. I cringe at the angle, pain shooting up my arm and down my neck as I wiggle through. The vines, somehow still attached and wrapped around my shoulder, tighten their hold and cinch my arm close to my body. My legs slip into the crevice and I slide them through easily enough until I get to my thick thighs. A shard snags on my pants and tears along my side, creating a gash that runs from thigh to hip. I freeze, blood seeping into the ground, and bite my tongue to keep quiet as guards' armor clanks when they round the corner of the castle that leads to my balcony.

Turning almost completely on my stomach, I shimmy myself farther through the hole, bare feet meeting the slick tree roots on the other side of the wall. My leg throbs and the smell of my blood creeps up my nose. I shift farther, my calves and now my thighs, exiting into the forest on the other side. My wrapped elbow drags along the muddied earth underneath my body, and it takes everything I have to shuffle through the rest of the hole without crying or passing out from the pressure on my broken bones.

Delicate moss brushes against my stomach and I slide all the way through the tunnel, finally pulling my head out. The stars shine brighter and the air feels cleaner in ways I didn't think was possible. My free hand rests on the trunk of the tree, and I breathe heavily, covered in blood and mud.

"Thank you, friend." I sigh. I watch in awe as its roots fill up the hole again and cover up the tracks I left behind. Relief floods my system as I finally hear the guards' voices rise in alarm. I can't make out what they're saying, but their shouts tell me I have little time to get a head start.

Without my shoes and my free hand pressed to the gash in my leg, I hobble along on the mossy rocks and roots. Breathing deeply, I face the depths of the ancient forest, readying myself for the long journey to my ancestral home.

28

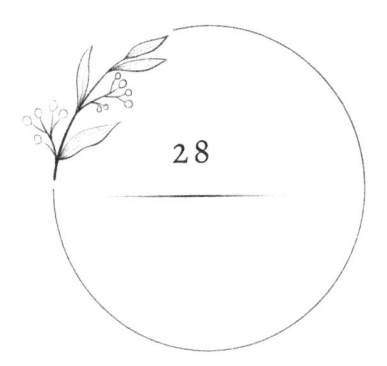

Day three hundred and sixty. Conall runs into the dark forest blindly. Without his full shifter available to him, his sense of smell is far more muted than what he is used to. He has to stop frequently, taking big heaving gasps of air, weak from almost a year in the dungeons. His feet are tender, too, used to the mossy stone floor and not walking over pine needles and fallen branches.

Captivity.

The very thought of being caged in again makes his skin crawl. How he longed to feel the forest floor underneath his feet all that time. His wolf smiles and he can almost feel his fur coming in, his nails getting longer and craving to dig into the soft dirt. He can't shift yet, though; he's still too weak.

That bastard king is going to pay.

First, he needs to find his brothers. All six of them. Someone is close, because he can scent the sea air coming through the forest. Only one of his people could still smell like the sea this far inland. He smiles as he sees the blonde-haired, slightly bloodied mer-shifter step from behind a tree.

"Murry," Conall says, smiling wide and opening his arms. "It is good to see your face."

"You look like shite," Murdock replies.

"Aye, it's good to see you, too, brother."

They clasp forearms and embrace. Conall pulls away and looks into Murdock's eyes, confusion on his face. "What have I missed?"

"Och, I really don't want to be the one to tell you this." Murdock grimaces, shrugging his shoulders up to his ears.

"Tell me what? Be straight with me, man. It's Sorcha, isn't it?"

"It's Sorcha… and then some. You should probably sit down for this. Come, I've set up a small camp back home near the inn." Murdock's arm waves in the air and a portal opens. Conall inhales as the smell of the meadows comes through. They step into the portal as it closes behind them, and he finally lets himself relax as he collapses to his knees by his favorite stream.

He crawls into the fresh water for the first time in what feels like forever and washes off the grime from the dungeon. He dunks his head under the small waterfall and strips off his old, tattered clothes, sitting bare-assed in the flowing water. In the sunlight, he can see his ribs and hip bones sticking out, his arms and legs far too gangly. Just as he thought; he's still too weak for his wolf, lacking the strength to shift back into Fae for a while yet. He keeps scrubbing, scooping up sand from the bottom of the stream to rub across his skin and clean it all off.

Pixies poke their heads out of the roses, tittering in that secretive way they do, already sending the gossip far and wide that the lord is back home. At least their talk won't leave his lands. He can't risk his escape threatening Sorcha right now. Rinsing one more time, he runs his hands through his long hair and shakes his head, flinging water from his beard. He climbs out of the cool stream and lies down on the grassy banks, letting the sun warm his pallid skin.

"Aye, Conall. You're going to blind someone." Murdock laughs and takes a seat next to him. Then he says more solemnly, "You've been missed. I'm sorry it took me so long to get to you."

Conall grunts. "I figured you had your reasons." He cracks

open an eye, peering up into the shadow of his friend, the sunlight searing his eyes. "Tell me, what news?"

"Well, it's all gone to shite. All of our plans. Everything," Murdock says. "I tried to get to her, to help her. She... Where do I even start?" He rubs a hand down his face, grimacing with the recollection of memories. "It's a long story, but she's relatively safe. She's been in a kind of stasis; there's a rumor that even the king can't wake her. And he wants to wake her. He needs to marry her to void the treaty. Until then, he can't outright do anything except attack small parties of humans and blame it on 'self-defense.' But the humans know something is amiss. An entire year with no news of a wedding celebration? An entire year without their princess? They're taking up arms. There have been talks of small bands of armies coming from offshore, too."

"Wait, what do you mean she's in a stasis?"

"The most I have been able to glean off my sources is that she has fallen under some kind of sleeping spell. No one has seen her since he captured her in the forest near her lands and brought her—sleeping, mind you—into the castle grounds. He keeps her locked in the conservatory, and no one—except Hazel—has gone inside. Hazel says she looks like she's made of stone."

"Stone?" Conall asks, pulling on his lower lip.

"Hazel doesn't know what to make of it, either. But she's alive, she has to be, because you're still here. Though you could look better, and your wits still seem to be about you, for now." Murdock looks at Conall, holding his hands up and shrugging. "That's all the intel I've been able to get."

Conall sits up, resting his arms on his knees and strokes his beard. "She's in the conservatory?"

"Aye," Murdock says softly.

They sit, shoulder to shoulder, the warm sun beating down on their backs as silence settles between them. Conall closes his eyes, breathing deeply the smell of the grass baking in the sun. He listens to the trickling water, an offshoot of the raging river upstream that now slices through the meadow. His heartbeat slows, his breathing evens out, and his mind taps into that heart-call.

It pulses, vibrates. He tugs on it a little, imagining a bell on the other end, giving it a little jiggle so it rings. Then he waits. There! He feels her tugging on the other end.

"She's there," Conall whispers.

"As it stands, we have little time," Murdock says, holding his hand out for Conall. "We need to get your energy up first. You could stand to put on some weight if we're going to go in there and get her."

"I appreciate the offer, but I need to do this on my own, Murry. You've already risked too much," Conall says. He reaches up and grips Murdock's extended hand and allows himself to be hauled to standing. They turn and head closer to the tree line, the ward stones glowing faintly at their approach. They set a small tent up in the shade of the trees, and Murdock holds up his hand for Conall to wait. He ducks in and returns with a pair of breeches and a shirt, tossing them to Conall.

"You'll want to cover yourself. I don't think anyone in there wants to see their lord in this state," Murdock says.

"It can't be *that* bad…" But he puts on the breeches and tucks his shirt into the waistband. Yes, he definitely needs to gain some weight. His hand holds the pants up as they walk into the tent.

The glamoured tent is far larger on the inside, of course, since it wouldn't fit nearly everyone if they had actually used a smaller tent. A war table sits in the center and several heads are bent over a map, in deep discussion. They don't even look up as Conall stands wide-legged with his arms crossed, scanning the interior, mentally noting all of his siblings that are there, blood and bond.

They're missing one.

"Where's Thorne?" Conall's gruff voice carries through the tent, disturbing the conversation happening over the table. Stunned silence. All heads turn and meet his scrutinizing gaze.

"They… We…" Channe, the youngest of his blood brothers, stutters.

Murdock cuts in. "I have not seen Thorne since he left the first battle."

"First battle?" Conall asks. "When was this?" He walks over to the war table, scanning the map and all the little red X's along the human side of the Border.

"The king's been hard at work." Murdock points to each little X that is marked along Conall's lands.

"Hmm, he's cutting off access to my lands from all points of Fae. The only entry he's left is by the sea or with portals," Conall remarks, stroking his beard. "It seems I have a lot of catching up to do."

"Aye, and not a lot of time." Murdock nods in agreement.

29

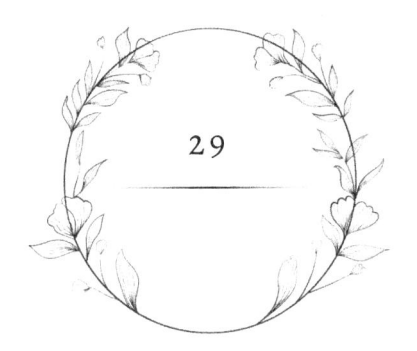

I slide down an embankment, groaning out loud as my shoulder burns and the gash at my hip continues to seep blood. It's slowed enough but keeps tearing open with each hurried step I take. I don't have time to stop the bleeding because I know the guards are going to mobilize a search party soon. One voice, that of Murdock's, was exceptionally loud moments ago. I send a silent prayer up to the Goddess that his voice carried over the wall so I could have a head start.

The moon sinks lower on the horizon, signaling daybreak soon, and I have to get as far away from the castle as possible. I can't help but think of Gealaich and wonder where she went because, Goddess, having her right now would be heavenly.

A horse neighs behind me, and I freeze. Gealaich? As skeptical as I am, I still turn, not fully believing that she'll be there.

She isn't.

A brown horse with a guard wearing the king's colors of blue and white stops. They have not seen yet me, since the horse is facing away from me, but the guard's head turns slowly, searching the forest, and it'll be mere seconds before I'm recognized.

A hand grabs the back of my shirt and another one clamps over my mouth, keeping my scream in as I'm yanked backward and into the brambles. A familiar voice whispers in my ear, "Shhh, Princess. Scream and they'll find us in a heartbeat."

I nod and hold up my free hand that's caked in my blood.

They release their hands, and I turn. Amethyst eyes find mine, shock white hair, and a kind face that cracks into a wide smile.

"*No, Thorne!*" I mouth. I gesture wildly with my arms, pointing at them, and make a flying motion.

They nod, holding a finger up to their mouth. Moments later, the rider and horse clomp through the forest loudly. We shrink farther back, the moss on the surrounding ground thickens, and the shrubs shift slightly, quietly, to cover us in the shadows.

Thorne looks at me wide-eyed, pointing to the ground and the shrubs. "*You?*" they mouth.

I shrug.

Their eyes catch my bloodied hand and finally take in my arm, the cut above my eye, and my broken nose. They close their eyes, sighing and shaking their head.

"*It's okay,*" I quietly whisper, "*I'll be okay.*"

They hold their finger up again, listening. Their sharp shifter eyes scan the forest for any movement. The shrubs must sense the coast is clear, as they release a little, shaking out the branches that had covered us.

We stand up, slowly, and Thorne reaches into their pockets, pulling out a tincture in a small purple bottle. They pop the cap off and hand it to me, and I down it in an instant. Its bitter taste is familiar but, this time, it warms my belly quickly, and my injuries tingle. I look down, noticing the green light shimmering above my hip as the gash slowly closes on its own.

My head snaps up and I stare at Thorne. "What in the Goddess?" I say, shocked.

"I think your part-Fae is really coming in stronger. We need to move as soon as your hip has healed fully. Which should be in... just a moment," Thorne says. They move a strand of my hair out of the way, noticing that my ears have gotten even sharper. They look at me, then down at my hip, then back up and jerk their head for me to follow as we make our way deeper into the forest and away from the castle.

We walk in silence for the rest of the evening, not daring to say anything as our footsteps already feel loud enough. A few times, Thorne shifts into their bird form to scout ahead, but always flies back and shifts to walk with me. The sky turns from indigo to periwinkle, and I finally have to stop. Hunger gnaws at my stomach, and exhaustion pulls me down as I sit hard on a fallen log. Thorne, graceful as ever, leans against a tree and watches me with closely with their healer eyes.

The vines loosen around my shoulder as I shift, grimacing as the pain climbs back up into my neck and shoots down my arm.

"Let me look," Thorne says softly, crouching down in front of me.

"I don't know, I—" I flinch a little at the thought of someone touching it.

"Sorcha, we can't keep going if I don't fix it."

"It's fine. I have a magical vine-sling," I say, gesturing to the vines that are already loosening the closer Thorne's hands move to my arm.

"Mm-hmm," they say. "Bite this." And then, before I can say no, they shove a wad of cloth into my mouth and take my forearm in theirs. They wrench it hard and fast and my shoulder pops. I scream and yank my arm back.

"What was that!" I yell, glowering at them. The vines have already started twisting back around my arm with less pressure, keeping the sling comfortable.

"Your shoulder was dislocated," Thorne says, patting my knee. "You did great; you're the perfect patient." They dust off their hands, holding one out for me. "We really need to keep moving if we're going to make it to your ancestral lands."

My glowering intensifies, which only causes Thorne to chuckle as we continue our trek northwest.

By the time we reach a small stream, the sun is full in the bright blue sky, and I'm parched. I kneel at the edge of trees, keeping to the shadows as I wiggle my way down to the banks.

Looking downstream, the castle stands on the bluff, imposing and stout. The mountains to the east that lead to Conall's lands have a light dusting of snow from last night's storm. The meadows are green and vibrant, the smell of rain hanging pungent in the air. My shoulder aches as I lean forward, scooping water with my free hand so I can drink. I dunk my head into the cool water in the grotto, swirling my hair around in the water, washing away as much of the mud and blood from my body as I can. Flipping my hair back, I look over my shoulder, trying to find Thorne, and instead make eye contact with a small shrine to the Goddess.

I crawl closer, staring at her profile. From this angle, her forehead is caked with dried blood and I smile to myself, pulling the dagger from my waistband.

"All right, Goddess." I laugh a little as I prick my thumb again, smearing more of my blood on her forehead. A few drops fall into the bowl that rests in her hands. "I don't know what your plans are, but please take this other blood offering as my way of saying 'I trust you. I trust in you. I trust your plan. I trust you know what you're doing.' I know I sure as hell don't. But I'm figuring it out. Thank you, Goddess above, for watching out for me."

I wipe my blade off in the moss, scooping another handful of water into my mouth, and head back to Thorne. They shift into their bird form and hop down to the water, drinking their fill and cleaning a few of their feathers. My eyes scan the forest, taking stock of the direction we need to head, recalling as much as I can about the maps from memory. They shift back and join me in the underbrush, grabbing a stick to draw what they've scouted from above.

"See these large boulders here? Almost due west..." Thorne says, making a few marks that look like enormous boulders and a large waterfall. "These are the places where we will need to be cautious, since it's the old border to the Earth Fae lands. Once we reach that border marker, your ancestral lands aren't but a half-hour walk from there, according to the maps you found.

Currently, we're about two days away from reaching those boulders—if we don't stop."

"So," I whimper, standing up, "we keep walking."

Thorne nods, tossing the stick into the undergrowth and shuffling their feet, wiping away evidence of our map. We make our way through the thicket of the forest, watchful for the king's guards, ogres, and any other Fae we may come across. With only my dagger as a weapon, I'm on high alert, keeping to the shadows and walking as closely as possible to the trees. My stomach growls, reminding me that, though I may be part Fae, I still have human tendencies, and that includes wanting to eat delicious bacon and drink piping hot tea. I would kill for a cup of hot tea right now.

The vines around my shoulder tighten slightly as I stumble around, exhaustion pulling at my limbs and my feet hurting from walking barefoot through the underbrush. I look down, and the tips of my fingers glow a shimmering green and I rub them together. They glow brighter and, as if in a silent answer to my aching, moss blooms underneath my feet, adding cushioning with each step I take.

I stop, dumbfounded, and stare as moss grows in a careful path through the forest, heading directly due west, keeping to the shadows and thickets. Thorne notices, too, stopping, and turns to look down at my feet, eyes traveling up to my fingers, and then meets my gaze.

They smile wide and say, "Looks like someone's magic is coming in. I remember those days. I had no control over my shifting. Every time I sneezed, I turned into a bird and back again. It would happen so quickly I'd get whiplash."

"Right, but I'm only part Fae. Is this… normal even for those that aren't full blooded?" I ask.

Thorne shrugs and keeps walking. "Who knows? The Mother Goddess works in mysterious ways."

"Huh. Well, then." I shake my head, skipping a little to keep up pace with Thorne.

Not everything is as it seems.

We stop for the night in an alcove of gnarled oak and yew trees, their thick trunks carving out enough space for me to crawl inside. The air here feels ancient and my soul sighs happily, feeling a deep sense of reverence for this copse of sacred trees. I can barely keep my eyes open as I sluggishly climb inside a yew tree root cluster, falling asleep almost immediately on the cold, hard dirt.

The stones sing this time, a low vibration, and I know I've heard that song before.

Try as I might, I can't seem to recall the words.

I hum along while I walk through the circle to the altar stone, hands outstretched, fingertips glowing green.

I walk closer to the altar stone, and the green light travels up my arms, veins of magic filling my body.

I tilt my head back, looking at the full moon on the horizon. No stars fill the sky.

The pond ripples as a light breeze kicks up, pulling my hair from its plaiting, lifting my skirts from my legs and tugging them behind my body.

The wind blows stronger, and I look over my shoulder, watching the leaves and the vines as they tremble in the wind.

The black wolf is standing there, green eyes glowing, fur gleaming in the moonlight.

I turn around slowly, willing myself to remain calm and walk closer to the creature.

My hands reach out, grabbing fistfuls of fur, my green fingers twining in its hackles.

Our foreheads touch, and a shockwave rocks my body.

I step back, gasping, my hands tightening in the fur.

The wolf smiles, cocking their head.

"*Sorcha?*" *he asks.*

I nod my head, still too shocked to speak.

"*Can you hear me?*"

I nod.

"You're sure?"

"Yes, definitely," I whisper, my fingers tightening in his fur.

"You'll need to wake up soon…"

"Wake up?" I ask, staring into his green eyes.

"Yes, Sorcha, I've been trying to call to you…"

The urgency behind his words leaves me gasping awake, shivering, sweat lining my brow. He's been trying to call to me? All this time?

The moon hangs low in the indigo sky, its silvery light casting shadows through the boughs, signaling the coming equinox and full moon. Grass has grown underneath my body, cradling me against the earth, and I have to shake my hand free of more vines that have crawled their way over the trees and around my body. I reach up to the hagstone, finding familiar comfort in its weight, clutching it tight in my fingers.

Conall.

My heart beats with longing. I close my eyes against the sting of oncoming tears, and then I hear large footsteps through the forest. My breath catches, and I roll over to find Thorne. He perches high in the tree above me, their purple eyes finding me. They tilt their bird head slightly, a signal, and I nod back, crawling deeper into the root system as they shake their wings and take off into the night.

Voices carry beyond the sound of their footsteps, boisterous, but in a language I don't understand.

Gigantic shadows lurch through the trees. Then the smell hits me.

Ogres.

I scramble farther into the tree, trying to squeeze my body as far back as possible as a group of four ogres comes stumbling into the alcove of trees. They drag behind them something wrapped in burlap, along with their weapons. My heart beats in my ears and I shake, hands growing cold. I twist and crouch among the roots, trying my best to keep myself hidden and quiet.

I swallow bile, flashing back to the first encounter of ogres with Conall. They sit down in a circle, setting up camp for what looks like the rest of the night. They drag over a tree, *a whole tree*, and light it on fire. The flames flare up into the canopy, singing the tips of these sacred trees.

Anger courses through my veins, and I can hear the sacred trees crying out in fear and pain. My fingers flare bright green, and I clamp them under my arms to hide their light from view.

"Hmmm," one of them groans in a deep, resounding baritone and turns to look behind them, sniffing the air with their pug nose. I shirk away, trying my best to sink into the depths of the roots, but my foot slips, knocking dirt and rocks skittering into the clearing.

The beady little eyes flare wide, following the trail of the rocks up to where my foot is now somehow stuck in the roots. I stop moving, hoping their eyesight is poor in this light, but I'm not that lucky.

The lumbering, nosy ogre pulls himself up. He stands, easily ten feet tall, and sidles over to my tree, dragging his hands behind him. He comes closer to my hiding spot, reaching his thick hand into the hollow. From this close, his stench is overwhelming—a mix of rotting meat and wet goat. I can see the pockmarks atop his balding head, pointed ears, and wart-covered skin. His teeth are far larger than the other ogre we encountered, and his breath is putrid as he sniffs around, shuffling his hand back and forth in the crevice.

"Human…?" he grunts into the roots. His fingers brush my foot, and I shudder, keeping in a scream as he locks down on my ankle and drags me from my hiding place.

30

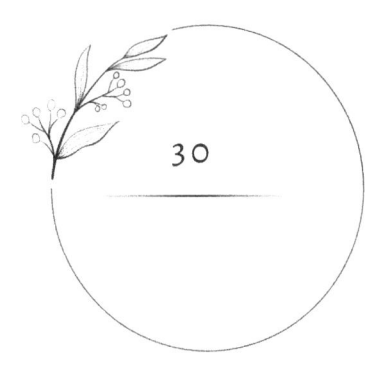

Day three hundred and sixty-two.

Conall's head spins as he pulls back from the heart-call.

She heard him that time. She *talked back* that time. Their connection must be getting stronger, which coincides with what his brothers mentioned about the upcoming equinox and the veil getting thinner.

He only has three days left until the autumnal Rites, and he needs to reach her by then. He needs a lot of things by then: to be strong enough to shift, to be strong enough to lift whatever curse is on her, to keep his wits about him while he breaks her out of the king's clutches. So much is riding on this perfect timing that the possibility of going back to sleep this morning escapes him. Rather, he lies there on his cot, quietly waiting for the morning to talk to Murdock. Surely, the king has figured out he's escaped by now. It'd be a stupid miracle if their distractions have actually kept the king busy enough to forget about that dungeon for a few more days. He strokes his beard as he finalizes the strategy he and his brothers have been working on for the past few days.

His thoughts drift, the quiet calm in the tent carrying him

back to those intelligent amber eyes, flecked with green and gold. Her nose, peppered with soft freckles, that crinkles when she smiles or gets frustrated. He closes his eyes and inhales deeply, imagining her scent, the amber and rose mingling together with a hint of cedar. It's earthy and floral and makes his cock flex with want. Conall stifles a groan as he gets hard, his thoughts drifting down to her mouth. How delicious she looked, lips wet from drinking mead that night... how delicious she tasted on his fingers. He chuckles softly to himself and then feels a pang of regret. He tried to warn her about drinking too much, too fast. But to be fair, he was also pretty drunk on both mead *and* want, so it's not like he tried very hard. He didn't feel too bad, however, taking her into the furs, sliding inside of her, wrapping his body around hers to keep her warm. And he smiles, remembering nuzzling her hair while she slept, her soft murmurs of comfort as she warmed underneath the furs with him, and the softness of her full hips settling against his harsher angles, the perfect balance of feminine to his masculine.

 Conall sighs and rolls over, scanning the cots full of his sleeping brethren. Maccon, the second eldest and beta in the pack, lies in his cot across the tent and curled up on his side, seemingly asleep but somehow still always ready to jump into action in a heartbeat. Felan, and now apparently Channe, asleep on the floor with their backs touching, are now the mid-ranks. Thank the Goddess for that development, because they have always needed each other to lean on; the two of them are completely inseparable, though Felan is older by a few decades. Rowland, still a pup in the shifter world, is asleep in the center of the room underneath the table in his wolf form. And, finally, Murdock, the mer-shifter asleep in the water outside. Though not his brother by blood, he easily could be with how deep his bond goes with Conall.

 Each of them accounted for, except for Thorne. Thorne, the peace-loving, highly magical Minister of Health. Formerly the daydreaming jokester heir to the Air Elemental Fae. Hopefully, they made it to the outer isles, biding their time in the healers' sanctuary. If not, well, Conall couldn't let himself mourn someone yet, not without knowing whether they actually died.

Light pokes through the tent, early morning light hitting the top of the tent, and everyone stirs. Conall is up in a flash and stalks outside, hoping to catch Murdock by the stream as he wakes. He needs a few moments with him alone or he'll be talked out of his plans by Maccon.

He stalks over to the water, toes curling against the chill of the frost-covered grass on the bottoms of his feet. He forgot what it felt like to have the pure earth beneath his feet. His wolf itches to get out from underneath his skin. He growls, suppressing it, and sees Murdock slide out of the stream with an ease that belies his shifter heritage.

"Murry, we need to talk again."

"Aye, I was wondering when you'd have another harebrained plan. A year in solitude really did a number on you, my friend." Murdock shivers a little and starts changing into dry clothes, already shaking out his head of hair. "At least you've got a mate waiting on the other side…"

"Always finding the silver lining, eh?" Conall says, running a hand through his hair and tying it back.

"Aye. Looks like you need a trim?" Murdock badgers, nudging Conall with his elbow.

"You know, I've always wanted it longer. It was my father who…" Conall stops himself, still choking up this many years later at his father's death. He strokes his beard, musing out loud, "You think she'd recognize me if I came to her looking like this?"

"We've all had a hard time adjusting to this new… you." Murdock frowns.

Conall nods, sighing, as he looks heavenward, his tone serious. "We need to talk about the upcoming equinox, Murry."

"What about it? Are you feeling the effects of the mating bond?"

"Yes," Conall rubs his chin, pulling at his lower lip. "At first, I thought I was going mad… But it gave me an idea."

"You mean a *harebrained idea*. Yes, yes, we've heard it all. Grand plans to rescue your fated mate. From the evil king. Restore balance and whatnot," Murdock replies dryly, waving a hand in the air.

"I mean it, though. It's an absolutely stupid idea, but I think it might work." He turns to Murdock again, open and pleading. Then he adds sheepishly, "I can reach her through the heart-call."

Murdock stares wordlessly at Conall, and his mouth hangs open.

"Yeah, I know, I shouldn't be able to, since we aren't technically mated," Conall says quickly. He paces in the meadow as words pour out of his mouth. "But I *can* do it. I had been working on it for the better part of the last few weeks. I think it has to coincide with the equinox. If I don't reach her in time, we lose more than just me and my sanity. We lose her, too."

"Och, mate," Murdock says, hands on his hips. He rocks back and forth, watching Conall closely for telltale signs of madness.

Conall continues, "But last night I actually reached her, broke through, and she talked back…"

"Conall, that's…" Murdock exhales, staring up at the morning sky.

"Don't say impossible, because obviously it's not. It has to be the Equinox and the autumnal Rites. The closer we get, the easier it is for me to reach her." He points at Murdock and continues. "Now, do you want to know what I've figured out or not?"

"You might as well. The rest of us are completely out of ideas. Even your brothers couldn't get to her—"

Conall growls, cutting Murdock off. "I'm aware."

"Och, mate, you can't fault them for trying to help even if it was—"

"An infringement on my future mating bond?" Conall kicks a stone into the stream. "I know their intentions were good, honorable even, but damn if any of them had gotten their scent on her…"

"Right, right, you would've torn them all asunder. Assuming you had gotten out. And compelled the mating bond with her. You never finished sealing it that night. You told us you couldn't bring yourself to bite her when you…" Murdock says, trailing off, gesturing with his hands. He walks toward the tent, saying over his shoulder, "You might as well talk about this idea of yours before we reach the others. I'm starved."

Conall smiles. "Right. So, here's what I'm thinking we do…"

31

The ogre yanks on my leg, twisting my body and wrenching me from the tree roots. I kick out, but his grip only tightens, and he tugs harder. The roots are too slippery, and I finally have to let go. He swings me out and hangs me upside down, my dagger and hagstone falling silently to the ground below as he brings my face parallel with his. He sniffs by my ear, and I repress a full-body shudder as his stunted little nose twitches and he grins wide. His mouth opens a little wider, and I can see the rotting food stuck in between his razor-sharp teeth. It takes all that I have to not retch and breathe normally. I know now that they can smell fear, so I do my best to remain calm and unbothered.

"Human?" He looks back at his companions, shrugs, sniffs again, and says, "Good food." They all grunt in agreement. He swings me over to the fire, setting me down with gusto, and my breath leaves my lungs in a huff as my back hits the ground.

My feet are then bound, and I'm hog-tied, somewhat quickly, given their thick, gnarled hands. The largest ogre walks up to me and drops me down by the burlap sack, which smells like meat that has been baking in the sun for a few days. One of them stokes the fire, the log burning from the inside, and I stare deeply into the flames. The log crackles and pops, and the king's eyes stare back at me. I startle. But his face is gone just as quickly as it appeared.

Was that really the king? I realize I don't want to wait around and find out. I pull and tug at the rope around my hands, tension knotting in my throat, and I twist my body, angling to bring my hands up to my mouth.

"No," an ogre chides, smaller hands grabbing me and hauling me up into their arms. I dare a glance up, staring into the face of the smallest ogre. She has two saggy little boobs that hang deflated against her chest, and she almost cradles me in her arms. Our eyes meet for a brief second, and she looks away, but in the depths of her eyes I could've sworn I saw a sort of sadness hovering there. She grips me a little tighter to her chest as she walks me over to a tree. Her hands are softer, not as rough as the other ogre, and she is almost gentle as she hangs me upside down from the limb of the oak tree. I swing on a low branch, like meat on a hook, as the rest of them prep for their meal. My hagstone lies hidden in the dirt and I watch as the female ogre shuffles her feet around on the ground, covering it up even more. She looks me in the eye once more before rushing back over to the fire, stoking the flames and pulling out cooking supplies.

I try not to pass out as the blood rushes to my head, watching the three other ogres sharpen their knives. The female throws some more wood onto the fire. The flames dance higher, burning the oak trees again, and I swear I can feel a part of my arm burning in tandem with the tree. I curl into myself, gritting my teeth against a scream, and then pass out.

I come to, still suspended from the tree, my head full of blood and my heart pounding in my ears. My arm feels burnt and throbs, and I can't see much under my shirt, but my forearm looks red and inflamed. My hands have turned purple, and I struggle against the bonds. The world swings slightly while I'm suspended upside down. Even from this uncomfortable position, I see that they have made quick work setting up their camp and have added another tree to the fire. The embers from the first tree have burned down enough for them to start a slow spit, set up with a grilling rack that they must have pulled from the burlap sack.

A few of their weapons are strewn about, including a bloodied club and a rusty axe. The female ogre bends over to pick up a machete, and her hip bumps the bag. It topples over, and dwarven body parts come pouring out—arms, legs, a foot. A head rolls and rolls, coming to a stop below me. The head is missing its eyes, pulled from the sockets. The cheeks have been peeled off, exposing the teeth and jawbone of the poor creature, the face locked in a permanent horrified scream.

Panic claws at my throat, my heart beats in my ears and it's only when I feel like I'm going to pass out again that the female ogre comes and lifts me back up off the tree. Sadness weighs her shoulders down as she tightens the rope, bringing my feet and hands together, burning the fibers into my wrists. I'm taken closer to the fire pit and notice slices of meat being placed on the coals, the skin simmering, fat melting and dripping off into the fire, flames licking and charring.

Bile rises in my throat, an empty threat as I try to remain calm and figure a way out of this. Where in the bloody hell is Thorne? That damn flighty-ass bird.

The large ogre barks out some kind of command to the female ogre, who hangs her head and grunts in reply. She trudges over to the machete and yanks the decapitated dwarf head up by the hair, carrying both over to the makeshift camp kitchen. She drops the head into a large pan that sits at the edge of the fire and then stands up, bumping into the large ogre, knocking the food from his hands and onto the ground.

He roars, spittle flying from his mouth, into her face. As she scrambles to pick up the meat from the dirt, he stands, gaining several feet of height on her. She cowers even as he raises his hand and pummels her with his fist. She curls into a tight ball, taking his beating, not even crying out, as he continues to beat her into unconsciousness.

I shake, fury building in my bones.

"Hey, Ogre!" I scream, still wiggling against the bonds of the rope, trying to free myself from this infernal situation.

The ogre continues to beat her into oblivion, blood spraying from her mouth. He reaches over to get the club, gripping it tightly, as he raises his hand. A vine whips out from the depths of the forest, wrapping around his wrist, tugging him backward, forcing him to drop the club.

"I SAID HEY, YOU UGLY FUCKING OGRE!"

I stand tall; the rope falling from my wrists and feet, while little flowers bloom against my skin where welts were forming. My hands and arms glow green, vines crawling up and out of the ground, wrapping around my legs. The trees above shiver, their leaves shaking with an imaginary wind.

The ogre stumbles back, shock on his face as he tries to free himself from my vines. They only multiply and tighten on all of his extremities. Veins in his neck bulge as he tries to free himself, struggling violently. The vines only grip tighter, grow thicker, wrapping around his body over and over.

The other two ogres rush in, one picking up the dropped machete, and rush to chop away the vines that continue to grow around the large ogre.

"No, no," I say, my voice low and threatening. "You can't save him now."

I stretch my arms out to my side, and the green light flares up my arms, filling the edges of my vision. The large ogre gets swallowed quickly by vines that crawl over his skin and down his throat as they choke him and cut off his screaming. The vines make quick work, tearing back down through his stomach, devouring him. His body tears asunder, as the sound of breaking bones and tearing ligaments fills the night. Vines grow out of his eye sockets and squeeze his head until an audible *pop* resounds as his head is burst like a ripe melon.

The other two ogres pale at the sight of their leader being ripped apart. The dumbest one stumbles into the mass of vines, trying to hack away and free the body. But he's far too slow, and the vines swallow him whole in no time—doing unto him what happened to his leader in half the time. The other turns on me, roars, and lunges, swinging his machete, slicing into the air in front of me. I step backward and stumble, throwing up my hands. He lifts his machete again and lurches forward, slicing right into my forearm. He strikes bone and pulls away as I cry out, blood flowing freely from a gash that runs from wrist to elbow.

"Fuck." I cry out, trying to hold my bleeding arm as the magic dissipates quickly, the vines retreating into the forest as fast as they appeared. My hands no longer glow green, and the ogre stands back, a self-satisfied smile on its grotesque face. He raises his arm to land another blow when an axe protrudes from his head. Blood trickles down his face as he stares lifelessly back at me, falling over. Heaving, bloodied, and bruised, the female ogre releases the axe and falls back on her behind to sit.

Both of us stare at each other across the downed body of the last male ogre, in a stunned, bloodied silence.

"Princess," Thorne says from the shadows, and I jump.

"What in the flying fucking Goddess, Thorne?" I whip my head around, meeting their purple-eyed gaze. "Where in the hell were you?"

"Waiting." They smile smugly, mischief twinkling in their eyes.

"And what, pray tell, were you waiting for?" I snap, hissing as my arm throbs, the blood flowing freely through my shirt. The female ogre sits there quietly as her swollen, bloodied eyes follow our conversation closely.

"Let me see." Thorne walks closer, leaning down, grabbing my hand, and peeling back the cuff of my shirt. My skin peels apart, and I gag as blood seeps from the slice and continues to drip profusely onto the dirt, soaking into the dry ground. Thorne makes quick work, pulling a tincture from their pocket, uncorking it with one hand and holding it out to me to drink, while their other hand holds the flaps of skin together as their hand glows purple. I down the drink, knowing the bitter taste well, not even cringing as it slides down my throat. The purple of their magic twines with the sinew of my exposed arm, weaving in and out of the muscles. A green glowing light pulses from deep within my bones, grabbing onto the purple tendrils of light, pulsing in time to Thorne's magic. The colors weave together, plaiting around my skin, pulling the wound tightly together and sealing up the injury.

I stare at Thorne, opening my mouth to speak, but they cut me off.

"Before you say anything, I need to explain two things. First, I needed to see what your magic would do when you were pushed. You're only part Fae and never had a magical rite, so we don't know what kind of magic you have, nor how much. Second, I would've come when you needed, but I wanted you to know that you could handle this on your own." They stand, holding out a hand to help me up.

Still pissed, I allow myself to be hauled up to standing, anyway. "I—I've still got questions." I glare at them, and they let out a low chuckle.

"I'm sure you do, Princess," Thorne says. "Now, who's our little friend?"

We both turn to the female ogre on the ground, focusing our attention on her. She cowers under our scrutiny. I walk slowly to her, my hands open and relaxed, hoping she understands that I'm not a threat.

Her body shakes, and she scoots backward, holding her stomach and cringing at the exertion. Though her skin is leathery and brown, I can see several bruises already forming.

"Hello," I say, softly. She tries to scoot back, her body caving from fear. I stop, crouching down to her level. "Hey, hey, it's okay," I say in as soothing a tone as I can. "I will not hurt you."

Her eyes go wide, though they're still swollen, and she swallows thickly as she wipes the blood and spittle from her mouth.

"I don't really understand your language, so you're going to have to help me a little. Do you understand what I'm saying?" I ask.

She nods her head slowly.

"Do you have a name?" I scoot a little closer and sit down on the ground, facing her.

She nods, pointing to her chest. "Rhol'bar."

"Okay." I look back at Thorne, who hands me a small bottle full of a thick, sludgy liquid. "I'm Sorcha. Thank you for what you did." I nod to the ogre, who lies dead a few feet away and pop off the cork of the bottle, holding it out to Rhol'bar. "I have a healing tincture here for you. It looks like you could use a little help."

She holds out her large hand tentatively, taking it carefully in her forefingers, and plucks the bottle from my hand. Rhol'bar's eyes go wide as she downs the liquid. She spasms, coughs a little, contorting her face, and then passes out.

I whip my head around to Thorne, who just stands there, hands folded in front of them. "What the fuck, Thorne? What did you give her?" I crawl over to her, feeling her wrist for a pulse. It's there, but faint. "Will she wake up? Is she okay?"

"Why do you care, Sorcha? She's an ogre." They shrug passively, watching me with those purple eyes closely.

"What do you mean, 'Why do I care?' She saved my life! What's gotten into you?" My head still spins, and the trees above stir, their leaves shaking with my pent-up anger. Moss sprouts underneath Rhol'bar, cushioning her body.

"She'll wake. When she's healed," Thorne says, coming to stand over my shoulder. Their head tilts as they take me in. The firelight is but embers now and casts long shadows across the trees. The air cools against my skin.

"Goddess above, Thorne. Is this you testing me, still?" I shiver.

They look at me with pity in their eyes. "Unfortunately, yes. Usually Rites last for days, weeks. And, usually, you'd have had more training in calling up your magic. But it all depends on the person and the magic they hold. We don't have time to do a real Rite, so I figured this was the best way to see what would happen. Better to beg forgiveness than ask permission in this case."

"I don't see you asking for forgiveness." I stand, crossing my arms, glaring.

They walk to the fire, saying slowly, "Sorcha, I am sorry. I knew you could handle—" They stop talking, going silent, and crouch down, reaching into the embers of the fire. They send a light breeze out from their fingers, blowing away some of the ash. "Did you see this?"

"What?" I walk over, leaning over their shoulder.

They point to a rune that is scratched into one of the tree trunks that had yet to burn to cinders. Thorne looks in my eyes, holding a finger up to their mouth. A wind picks up, billowing around the log and picking it up from the fire pit. Ash flies every which way. An invisible hand lifts the log higher than the trees above us and sends the log flying, landing quite a ways away in the forest.

"We need to move. That rune was a Kaunaz rune, the fire rune, capable of listening in to conversations and making it *much* easier to track you. The king will know by now where we are and where we're headed. We need to put this place far behind us, and quickly." Thorne stands, dusting their clothes off, and heads into the darkness.

"I can't leave her here, Thorne. She's vulnerable and killed one of her own kind. To save me." I hesitate, walking back over to where Rhol'bar sleeps. She's snoring now.

"You can try to wake her, but I can't promise that she'll move. If she doesn't wake in… two minutes… we leave her here." They look to the sky, noting the position of the moon and frowning into the darkness beyond.

Unease crawls over my skin and I shiver, worried that we've somehow outlasted our time here tonight. I sit down in the dirt and reach out to grab her gnarled hand. She has curled up into a tight ball, and a frown lines her leathery face. When she exhales, her lips open, and I can see that she is practically toothless. My eyes look over the rest of her body, and I notice things I hadn't before: bones poking out from underneath her skin, wrists and ankles rubbed raw from being restrained, scarring on her back from being whipped.

"Thorne, they held her against her will." And my heart breaks. I feel the wetness of tears slide down my face as I squeeze her hand. "Rhol'bar, you need to wake up now. We need to leave this place, and I don't want to leave you behind."

I squeeze her hand again, a little harder this time, and I feel an almost imperceptible squeeze back. I meet her eyes that slowly open, and I smile. "Would you like to come with us?" I ask.

"Sorcha, I don't think—" Thorne starts.

"Would you like to come with us?" I ask, cutting them off. "If you do, you need to come now. And you need to be quiet."

"I quiet. I soft. I good," Rhol'bar says, sitting up, rubbing her eyes. The cuts and swelling have noticeably healed. She stretches, rubs her arms and her stomach, and looks at Thorne with an appreciative wonder.

"Yes, though they're an outright *ass*, they certainly know what they're doing." I roll my eyes and smile, earning me a smile from her in return.

We all head into the darkness of the forest, quietly and quickly putting that alcove behind us, Thorne with his tinctures and self-righteous attitude, me with the machete from the last ogre, and Rhol'bar with her axe and a satchel filled with a few of the camp items. The moon sits low in the late-night sky, almost full in its monthly rotation, casting shadows through the forest. I can't help but feel skittish as we put the gruesome killing scene behind us.

32

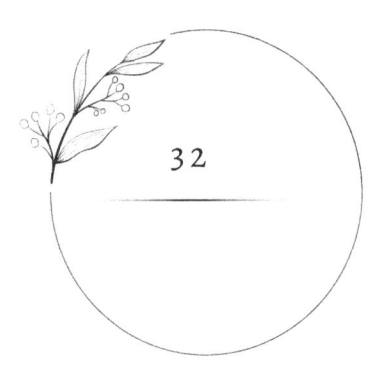

Day three hundred and sixty-three. Two days left until the Autumnal Equinox. Already he can feel the madness forming in his bones. He sees shadows out of the corners of his eyes, phantoms of his father that shouldn't be there.

He takes a few deep breaths, trying not to let the others know just how precarious his mental state is. Conall has talked over every single angle of this plan with his brothers, so he knows it will work. But with his mind already playing tricks on him already, he can't be too sure.

Murdock has long since left with Felan, both of them on horseback, riding through the northern border of his lands to meet up with him on the second day by nightfall. Murdock's parting words ring in his head, over and over, like a mantra. *"It may feel like forever, but it really is only a few days."*

He can wait a few more days. He can be smart about this. Right? Sure.

Conall watches his two other brothers stalk through the wards in their wolf forms, already on the prowl, hackles raised. Pulling on his old sweater, he prepares for the chill of the dark forest and catches a faint scent of Sorcha. He inhales the collar deeply, imprinting her in his soul once more. How he missed that scent. He smacks his face, trying to wake himself out of his mating stupor. He follows his brothers through the stones into the ancient forest. Putting one foot in front of the other, they head to the inn, his thoughts jumbled and clouding his focus.

All he wants is to hold her in his arms, nuzzle into her neck, inhale the scent of her skin. Not the faint traces from his sweater. He needs to fuse it to his own. He wants to lay her down and… Goddess above, he just wants to mate, sink his teeth into the soft skin of her neck, hear her scream his name. And it is going to drive him insane trying to rein that feeling back in, fighting with his wolf this whole time. He can't be thinking with his cock while this entire scheme plays out. It'll cost lives and compromise their whole rebellion. So he stuffs it down, conserving that desire for when he tries the heart-call again when he's at Grindel's.

They make their way quickly through the forest. Channe behind Conall, tailing him in the undergrowth while Maccon scouts ahead. The last time he traveled through here, he was on horseback, stuffing down his feelings yet again. Trying not to glance back over his shoulder at Sorcha whenever she yawned or groaned, causing his cock to flex in an immediate carnal response to the noises coming from her mouth. That perfect mouth—Goddess above.

He walks right into a branch and stumbles. Channe snorts behind him and he whips his head around, glaring at his brother and the twinkle there in the wolf's eyes. He really needs to think about something else, rubbing his face where the pine needles smacked him.

In only a few brief hours, they arrive at the Land's End Inn. Midday, the place is quiet, with the smell of stew and fresh baked bread coming from the kitchen. A few horses are in the stalls, calmly chewing on hay, all of them unsaddled and looking freshly rested. He nods to Channe and Maccon before they exit the forest, and the brother's shift quickly, straightening their clothes and hair. They all fan out, each taking a cardinal direction. Channe climbs up and over the east side of the building, easily slipping into the open window Grindel leaves cracked for the resistance fighters. Maccon enters through the front and, finally, it's Conall's turn to enter through the kitchens. He waits a few minutes, unease growing in his stomach as he crouches in the forest's darkness, listening for any sounds of fighting. A shadow dances in his vision and he shakes his head, willing it away. His stomach drops, palms growing wet with sweat, and he swallows tightly. He's waited too long.

A noise from the kitchens causes him to snap his head up. A chicken runs free from the back door that was flung open, Channe running after it laughing, and Grindel's mate, Lyra, comes rushing out behind him, pan raised.

He lets out a breath, leaning against the tree, then takes another deep breath and heads toward the kitchens. Stepping out into the bright daylight, he squints a little, his eyes still not used to the bright sunshine after being underground for almost a year. He much prefers the dark these days.

The chicken runs in a weaving line toward him, and he lunges out, not as fast as he would've a year ago, but still fast enough to clamp his hand down around the chicken's neck. He gives it a quick shake and snaps its neck, flips it over, holding it by the legs, and walks over to Lyra.

"Looks like my idiot brother let the chickens out again." He smiles as Lyra takes the chicken under her arm.

"He was supposed to help me cut its head off and start plucking." She eyes Channe, shaking her pan in his direction again. "Thank you, Conall. It is good to see your face, my lord." She turns and heads back inside the kitchen door.

Conall gives Channe a withering stare, as he reaches his arm out, grabbing the pup by the neck and giving him a slight shake.

"Hey! I've shifted back," Channe grumbles, trying to pull away.

"Oh, you did you?" Conall shakes his brother by the neck again, drawing him in under his arm. He says more seriously, "Then behave. We're not playing at this, pup."

Channe rolls his eyes and scurries away as quickly as he can, grabbing an apple on his way up the back staircase. Lyra sets the chicken down and promptly chops off the head, letting the blood drain into a bucket.

"We thought we'd never see you again, milord." She bustles about the kitchen, stirring the soup with one hand, pulling down a few drying herbs with her other. Conall reaches up and helps her take down a few sprigs of dried rosemary and thyme, their fragrance filling his nose, reminding him of his many rough nights in their tavern as a younger man.

"Aye," he says, solemnly, grabbing a knife and helping to chop up the myriad vegetables lying around.

"Your brothers and their silly little schemes. If it hadn't been for Murdock and Felan pulling them together…" She clears her throat and glances at Conall sidelong. "Anyway, what's up your sleeve this time, eh?"

"A lot of things. And they all have to work perfectly," he quips, not wanting to give Lyra any damaging information.

"Right, very secretive stuff. I get it. I'd better not catch you thinking with your head up your ass, Conall. We lose you, we lose many more." She points a butcher knife at his nose.

He smiles, pushing the blade away and holding his hand to his heart. "Point taken."

"Right, well, add those into the stew and then, when you're done with that, get to plucking that chicken. I want it in the oven soon."

They're in the stone circle again. She looks different tonight. Her eyes have more green in them and look clearer than they have since he first started calling to her.

She walks over to him, immediately curling her hands into his fur. She nuzzles her face into his neck, and he leans his head over her shoulder. He breathes her in.

She sighs.

"Sorcha," he says, his dream-voice reverberating against the stones.

"I've missed you," she breathes, nuzzling against him.

"I don't have long. But you need to be ready. I'm coming to get you."

"Where am I?"

"You don't remember?" he asks.

"I escaped the castle. I'm running with Thorne."

"No, Sorcha, no. You're in the conservatory. Wherever we are, together, here, this is where you are. This is real."

"What do you mean?" she asks, "Real?"

"I need you to be ready. When the time is right, I need you to—"

"When the time is right?"

"Trust me, Sorcha. I'm coming for you."

She pulls back, looking deep into my eyes. "I can't be without you anymore. It hurts too much."

"Be ready," he says again. "I'm coming for you."

"I will." She nods quickly.

"You're sure?" he asks, nudging her nose with his.

"Yes, definitely."

He gasps awake, drenched in sweat, heart beating ten times too fast. He lies there for a moment, catching his breath. A stupid smile spreads across his face, her scent still in his nose as if he were right there with her.

Shouts from the woods and torchlight flares up outside his window, casting dappled shadows into the room. He rolls out of bed, grabbing his boots in one hand and his daggers in the other. He wakes his brothers quickly and quietly. Channe yawns and stretches, unaware of the threat looming outside, but Maccon sits upright immediately and launches himself over to the trapdoor in the floor, yanking it open. They all scurry in just as Lyra throws down several bags of potatoes, covering their tracks, closing the door slowly and spilling chicken blood on the floor to cover up their scent.

Conall whispers a quick, "*Thank you, Lyra,*" and they wend their way through the shallow tunnel underneath the inn, Channe and Maccon both in wolf form, Conall on his hands and knees. They crawl through cobwebs and over stones that cut his knees until the tunnel widens into three more branches. Conall sits back, keeping his head low, and nods to each of his brothers as they head down their own tunnels to the middle and the right.

Conall, meanwhile, heads left, toward the castle.

33

I want to stay in the dream, in the in-between, so I can relish in the feeling of Conall's fur in my hands. His words echo in my head; be ready. The feeling of urgency presses around me, squeezing the air from my lungs. I sit up in the honey-colored meadow, uncurling my fists slowly, feeling empty. That same niggling feeling sits between my shoulder blades, and it irritates me, like a mouse scratching inside a wall.

The midday sun beats down on my skin. Beads of sweat form on my brow, and I swipe my arm across my face, the sleeve crusty with dried blood. Rhol'bar is curled up into a tight ball again, shivering while she naps. Thorne's shadow passes overhead, swooping down in large arcs as they scout out our route. We cleared the forest long ago and, according to Throne's calculations, are only a day away from the old Earth Fae boundary markers.

I crawl over to Rhol'bar and gently stroke her hand, rubbing the back of it until she wakes. Her eyes are slow to open, though once she remembers where we are and who is holding her hand, her eyes lighten considerably and her face cracks into what I can only assume to be a toothless smile.

She sits up, holding her hand out for me to wait, as she delicately passes me my hagstone.

"Thank you," I whisper, smiling widely. "I thought I'd lost it."

Rhol'bar nods and picks up her things, and we're on the move yet again. We've fallen into a familiar pattern on our journey—Thorne flying in front, me in the middle, and Rhol'bar bringing up the rear. Now that we're in the open meadows, she and I walk side by side, and Thorne scouts as they catch the air currents on their wings. My feet ache, shoeless as I am, and the dust from the forest floor has etched its way into my skin. I laugh a little at the irony and how badly I wanted to be barefoot as a kid back home, running across the gardens, bare feet slapping on the stone, calluses thick and "un-princess-like," as Father used to say. Now that I am barefoot, I long for shoes to give me a cushion.

This meadow feels so familiar that I pause, Rhol'bar looking at me uncertainly as she stops with me.

"Everything okay, Princess?" Thorne says, shifting their form midair and walking over to me.

"Yes, it... it's fine." I look around slowly, trying to figure out why this feeling of unease and this strange sense of urgency presses me forward. Conall said I needed to be ready, but for what?

They both nod, Thorne shifting back, and Rhol'bar shifting from side to side as I slowly shake my head and continue on. This far north in Fae and it still feels like autumn isn't just a day away. Sweat soaks my shirt, and I peel off the half-stay, throwing it over my shoulder and letting my body feel the breeze through the thin cotton. We trudge on, hunger gnawing on my stomach, and I keep looking to Thorne and Rhol'bar as they keep pressing without so much as needing to stop.

Do they just not need sustenance since their lives are longer?

The stone circle felt more real in my last dream than it has in the past, and the sense of urgency stays with me well into the rest of the day. By the time evening approaches, we reach a fairly small river that heads directly west, and I collapse near the banks, soaking my feet in the icy mountain water. Splashing some water on my face I relish in the freshness. Rhol'bar, with her leathery skin, climbs in up to her thighs and just sits in the middle of the river. She sighs heavily and almost purrs, pulling a laugh from both me and Thorne.

"It feels good, doesn't it?" I ask her.

She nods, slowly, almost like she, too, revels in feeling clean and cool and surrounded by water.

"Rhol'bar, do you mind if I ask you some questions about ogres?"

She shakes her head, turning a little to me and wiggling her body down into the water to drink big mouthfuls of water.

"I don't want to pry, but I know little about, well… any of the Fae… and I was hoping you could teach me."

"Yup, yup," she says, her eyes lighting up.

I clear my throat, trying to keep my questions as neutral as possible. "Okay, well, are all ogres like the ones from the other night?"

She shirks a little and nods.

"But you're not like other ogres."

She shakes her head.

"Do you like being alone?" I ask.

She shrugs, slinking down into the water some more.

"I'm sorry. If you don't want to answer, you don't have to. I'm just trying to understand why you're different from the other ogres I've encountered."

She dips into the cold water so only her head is above the water level. She smiles and slides down farther. I get up to help her if need be, but she holds up a hand and gestures for me to stay there. She's almost fully submerged in the water and then I notice her eyes are a pitch black, reminding me of the water nymph from Conall's lands. I sit on the banks, ready to get up and help her in a flash, but I continue to watch her with awe as her skin gets less leathery and her patchy hair becomes a little thicker.

"Thorne," I say as calmly as possible, "are you seeing this?"

They hop over to my side, still in their bird form, ruffling their feathers.

"Rhol'bar," I ask, tentatively, "are you...?"

She nods, rising from the water, looking less like an ogre and more like a water nymph with long flowing hair, softer features, and blue-tinged opalescent skin instead of leathery green. Rhol'bar still looks part ogre, but she looks healthier, and her scarring, though not gone, is less significant. She smiles and sighs, her teeth actually having come back in.

Thorne sits next to me. "I thought so," they say.

"How did you know?" I tilt my head.

"Well..." They hold out their hand, counting on each finger. "She was small for an ogre. Her comprehension of our conversations was not typical of those kinds of Fae. She killed the other ogre instead of killing you and eating you. And, like you said, they had held her against her will. The ogres only ever treat their own kind like that if they're half-breeds." They shrug and smile at Rhol'bar. "I take it your name isn't even Rhol'bar?"

"It isn't," a soft voice sounds like water rushing over rocks. Both Thorne and I jump and look upstream. "Her name is Opal."

A water nymph sits casually on the rocks upstream, combing her long black hair with her fingers, taking both Thorne and me in with those unusually large black eyes.

"Opal," I say. "It's very nice to meet you, officially."

Opal smiles back and snatches her hand out, grabbing a fish and tearing into it as it flops wildly in her hand.

"Do I have you two to thank for returning her to us?" the water nymph asks.

"You have Princess Sorcha to thank. In all honesty, I wanted to leave her behind while she slept," Thorne says a little briskly, standing up and walking downstream.

The water nymph hums and slides off the rocks, heading in my direction. I'm too tired to stand, so I shift to face her fully, pulling my cold feet from the river and rubbing the tender soles with my hands. She walks slowly, feet gliding through the water.

"I've heard of you, Sorcha, dagger-giver. A naïve little human princess who gave promised quite a lot to one of my sisters, along with an exquisite dagger. 'Such an uncommon offering' said the whispers on the water. But you are no longer a naïve little human, are you? This land has changed you. The Goddess has changed you." She leans down, looking into my face, black eyes scanning my eyes, slightly pointed ears, sharper bone structure.

I look from her to Opal, uncomfortable with her scrutiny.

She slides down to sit next to me on the banks and dangles her feet in the water next to mine. She smells like clean water and fresh grass, and her body is covered in tiny iridescent scales, glittering in the dying light of the afternoon. Her long hair brushes my arm in the breeze, and a shockwave of power travels down my spine. I catch her eyes, and she smirks knowingly. "Sorcha, I think you're more than what you present in this world."

"More?"

She hums the same lullaby tune as she returns to the water, submerging to her neck and turns around. "You are returning home, then. Fulfilling the prophecy." She looks from me to Thorne.

"*Prophecy?*" I mouth to Thorne. They shift their attention to the water nymph, ignoring me completely.

"Opal will join you on your journey, see you through the boulders, and then return to the waters with us before the river runs through the boundary. She is a powerful half-breed and will ensure you will make it to the boundary safely. The water nymphs owe you, Sorcha, for your service in returning what is rightfully ours." She looks pointedly at Opal, who smiles and continues eating her fish, then slips away underneath the water.

"Yet another encounter with the water nymphs." I groan, standing up on cold-numbed feet. "How much farther, Thorne, until we get to the boundary and you tell me about this *prophecy*?"

They shirk a little. "Is it too late to ask forgiveness?"

"What prophecy, Thorne?" I ask again.

"Well, there's this prophecy that the rightful heir to the Earth

Fae kingdom will bring about an era of peace, or restore the magic to the stones or some other silly Fae nonsense." They wave their hand in the air, turning away from the conversation and following the river downstream to the west.

"No, no, this isn't happening again." I run to catch up, Opal trotting behind me. I reach out and grab Thorne's sleeve, stopping them. "Stop avoiding this. I don't want to be in the dark anymore. That didn't do me any favors back at the castle, and I *really* hate the idea that you're lying to me. That's so… so far below you."

They don't speak, just look at me intently. So I continue, "What am I doing here, Thorne? What is going on with this so-called magic I have? And what prophecy?"

They rub a hand over their face, walking slowly next to me as they explain. "I was really hoping we had more time to dive in to all this back at the castle. But everything kind of went to shit, didn't it?"

I nod.

"Right, well. Where do I start?" They sigh, stretching their neck. "You know that lullaby you sing? Supposedly, a prophecy was crafted into its lyrics, but we have lost it to time. Only the ancients who worked with the stone circles knew the entire song. Some say it tells of stones being raised around the true ruler. Others think it is finding the magic that comes inside the stones, being a conduit for their energy. Theories have changed over the centuries, but I believe your grandmother was working on solving this riddle before her disappearance over the Border. Evidently, she and her sister did something to their ancestral lands to ensure that the secrets stayed protected there until the time was right."

"Aerona…" I muse, thinking back to the family tree. "She died right around the signing of the treaty. She didn't have children, either. What does she have to do with anything?" I shake my head, not comprehending where all of this is headed.

"Aerona was King Achill's fated mate, Sorcha," Thorne says.

I stop dead in my tracks. A whooshing fills my ears, and my jaw drops open. "Fated mate…"

"Yes, his *true* fated mate. It would never be you, though I'm sure he made you think you were." They tsk and shake their head. "Aerona… well, she killed herself to save everyone from King Achill's twisted war."

As we continue walking west, Thorne tells me more about Aerona and Cariad's plans to end the Border War and figure out how to fulfill the prophecy. Aerona, a powerful water Fae, and Cariad, my grandmother, came from the ancient Deoir Fae. Aerona, none too keen on living on land, refused to acknowledge the mating bond, citing Achill's ever-growing untenable view on humans. Her parents, however, still made them wed. Cariad, the younger sister, had yet to be fated to any Fae and was free to continue researching the prophecy under the guise of trying to decipher the magic of the stone circles. However, when the Border War escalated, both Deoir girls devised a plan to help end the war, solve the prophecy, and unseat King Achill.

As the story goes, Aerona went to the battlefield to bargain with King Achill, who was still madly in love with her and hoping that she'd accept the mating bond. As she rode out that morning, she held in her hand a treatise—one that stated that upon her death, he would have to marry the first female human heir, hoping a war-prize marriage would end the fighting. Unbeknownst to him, however, she planned on dying that day after he made a blood oath and signed the treaty. She walked out into the thick of the battlefield, unarmed and surrounded by humans. King Achill watched as they showered her with arrows, each one piercing her like pins in a cushion. She never fought back.

☾☽❦☾☽❦☾☽

We continue westward, downstream, stopping now and then for Opal to snatch a fish out of the water. After her soak in the water, she shifts closer to her nymph heritage, and her teeth have grown fully back in—tiny and sharp compared to the thick bone-crunching teeth of the ogre. Her arms are full by the time we stop to set up camp for the evening. Everyone is quiet, not wanting to disturb my pensive mood while I finish putting the pieces together.

"We should reach the boundary by midday tomorrow morning," Thorne says to no one in particular. Opal is cleaning and gutting fish, tossing each one into a pan that's already sizzling near the fire. I sit back, the world fades to a hum, and I look at my hands, the fingertips glowing faintly. My eyes grow unfocused, and I can see faint tendrils of light trailing from them as I wave them in the air, playing with the sparks as I flick my fingers back and forth.

"They look like sunbursts," I say out loud. The more I focus on the tendrils, the longer they grow, reaching and stretching out into the fading light as if they're seeking a connection with the natural world.

"Like this?" Thorne asks, flicking their own hand up into the sky. Tendrils of light trail from their fingers, silver and sparking, reaching up into the air like their magic is grabbing the wind itself. They come sit next to me, holding out their hands, as I bring mine over. We sit there, our hands ebbing and flowing together, weaving our magic together in the air.

"This is... far beyond what I imagined I'd be doing right now." I laugh, disbelievingly. "Mere weeks ago, I was still a human. Powerless against my fate, magic-less, friendless. I just... It's so much to take in. I feel like my chest is going to collapse."

Thorne nods, looking out at the river beyond, watching Opal sit and soak in its waters as the fish sears in the pan. "It's an adjustment. No one would blame you for feeling overwhelmed, Sorcha. We've all grown up with magic. It's entirely different when you've just found it."

"I doubt anyone has felt magic quite like this, I say, looking at my hands. "What am I doing here? Being here, I feel like I'm helping the war continue. Innocent people are dying right now, their crops are burning, their houses destroyed. And I'm off gallivanting through the forest, trying to get to my supposed ancestral lands to fulfill some prophecy, to figure out what the stone circles mean, to close a loop that might not actually close?"

"Sometimes, Sorcha, it's in these uncertain times that we have to dig deeper than we've ever had to do before, find our own True North, to discover who we are and what we're supposed to do on this earth," Thorne says, looking up at the dusk-colored sky. The harvest moon rises slowly, casting an ethereal honey-colored glow across the horizon.

It's then that I hear a lone wolf call, howling off into the darkness. My head snaps around, looking behind us into the depths of the meadows, and a wolf streaks across.

Conall! My heart leaps, but this wolf is grey and much smaller, running at top speed.

And then I hear the shouting, a clamoring of armor. Horses in the distance neigh. I look at Thorne, wild-eyed. Opal has doused the fire with a surge of water from the river, washing away all evidence of our previously set-up camp, the river claiming everything into its depths.

Thorne stands, air whisking around us, as we run. Opal rides the water, diving under, and then I've lost her. Stumbling, Thorne reaches down and yanks me back up as we continue running down the river.

"You need to get to the boundary markers. Whatever you do, just make it to your family land. You'll be safe there. I'll buy you some time," they say, their eyes finding mine in the growing dark. Their purple eyes glow with an imposing, ancient power. They reach into their robes, pulling out a tiny tincture. It glints the moonlight.

"What is that?" I pant.

"You take this when all else feels lost. When you fear that the worst is yet to come. You drink this and then, only then, will you finally understand everything that passes." Their voice is low but soft, so soft I almost miss what they say next. "Trust in the stones."

I wrap my fingers around the tiny bottle, shoving it down between my breasts, next to the hagstone, and nod. A deep quiet fills the surrounding air, weighing me down, and that's when I know.

This is goodbye.

A gust of air blows past, and they shift into their falcon, taking off into the night air. The grey wolf yips, leaping ahead of me and I chant as I run with it, "Trust in the stones."

34

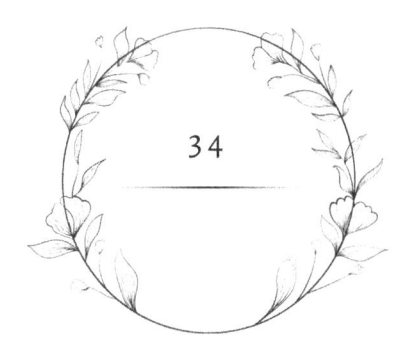

The moon reaches higher in the sky and the terrain changes from grassy meadow to hills with shrubs almost instantly, a great forest looming in the distance. The grey wolf has long since left my side, my pacing having slowed a while back despite my best efforts to keep going. My feet are numb from hitting the rough ground, my lungs heave, and I slow to a stop, bracing my hands on my knees. I'm slick with sweat and my hair hangs heavy around my head, curtaining my fiery face in its depths and sticking to my sweaty skin.

Stars dance in my vision as I take in deep lungfuls of air to catch my breath and bring my heartbeat down. The river has grown in size, its wild roaring usurping any other sounds in the distance as it rushes over large boulders. Opal pops her head up, her gaze trailing the path that I came from and then I hear the faint whinnying of horses in the distance. I fold in on myself, in no form to keep running at the pace that I have been, and exhaustion fills my body. Picking my feet up now feels like trying to move mountains.

I turn to the forest, eyes following the river as it cuts right through its dark depths leading to the stones that mark the boundary to my ancestral home.

The horses whinny closer, and I panic, refusing to look behind and instead look at Opal. She smiles and waves, swimming back upriver. Large waves of water roll upstream behind her, and I know what she's going to do. The powerful half-ogre, half-nymph swims with such force, the water churning and swirling behind her.

"Opal, no. Stay with me!" I shout as she disappears, pulling the river upstream with her into a tidal wave of power. My heart shatters as fear sings in my veins. My only hope is that she can hold off the horses a little longer. Despite my leaden limbs, I keep moving, trudging through the shrubs, and slip into the darkness of the forest.

Large, heavy boughs hang low to the ground, covered in lichen and mistletoe. A bird chirps every now and then, their whistle echoing among the trees. Goose flesh travels up my arms. I hesitate, a part of me scared to traverse this ancient forest alone.

Not everything is as it seems. Conall's voice echoes in my head, pulling at my heart strings. Where is he? Why isn't he here?

My head whips to the right seconds before I hear a tree move, creaking and groaning with the effort of pulling its roots up out of the soil.

"Welcome home, Daughter of Deoir." A resonant voice sings into my head and a face appears in the moving tree.

My jaw drops open. Vines grow from nowhere, snaking across the land to push me up and meet the tree spirit face-to-face.

"Hello." My voice sounds meek and quiet compared to the ancient baritone.

"I see you have offered a blood rite for safe passage." The voice sounds again in my head.

"I...?" And then I think of my bleeding feet and, Goddess Above, for the first time since they started bleeding, I am thankful for the blisters. "Yes, I offer a blood rite to pass through this forest. Please. I need to get to the stones. I need to get home."

The spirit shakes its leaves, releasing a shimmering green dust that travels on an invisible wind, settling on every tree that I can see. Where the dust settles, the trees shake their leaves in response, the canopy of the forest waking from a long slumber.

"I will forever grant you passage through, Deoir-blood." And just like that, the face disappears, roots sinking back down into the soil, and the vines gingerly place me on the ground.

I wince as the dirt grinds back into the soles of my bare feet. Before me, a mossy path grows, guiding me through the ancient woods. The ancient power thrums here, and my hands glow a bright green, lighting my way as the earth magic travels up my shoulders. The river is far below, carving out a chasm so high that I don't trust myself to walk too close to it for fear of fainting from exhaustion and falling down the cliffs.

I climb carefully over large downed trees and enormous ferns that stretch across the forest floor. Any kind of quick movement through this place is treacherous. The winds pick up, slicing through the trees and the cool air from the river rushes over my sweat-drenched skin.

A wolf howls from my left.

Though the harvest moon shines high above, the light doesn't penetrate beyond the uppermost canopy. Another wolf howls from behind me, and strands of damp hair plaster my face, whipping at my neck in the winds as I turn my head, trying to track the wolves.

Their howls punctuate the overgrowth, a warning call for my ears alone.

Picking up the pace, I try leaning into the gift of my earth magic, listening intently as a low humming leads me instinctively toward the stones. The moss grows thicker below my feet, and the ferns bow out of the way, revealing an ancient verdant trail leading that leads to the west. My heart lifts and I step quickly, weaving my way through. I thank the plants with my hands as I move past, vines and flowers growing where my fingers touched the trees.

More wolves cry, I count four separate, distinct howls coming from every direction, almost like they're herding me.

The farther into the woods I go, the clearer the path gets, finding the determination to run. I can still hear the river, the path meandering back towards its cliffs. I lean against a tree for a moment, looking down into the gushing water when a horse neighs in the distance and the rider's shouts carry on the gusts of wind.

I push off the trunk, fingers leaving little budding flowers in their wake, and trudge down the pathway again. Up ahead, a few bushy tails weave amongst the undergrowth and a wolf's head pops up occasionally, looking back at me as if to make sure I'm still following.

Fog crawls around my ankles, slow like ghostly fingers, despite the increasing gusts of wind that tear through the woods. The forest floor disappears underneath the thick blanket of fog, forcing me to slow down and find my way over fallen logs and debris that I can't see.

The wind gushes through again. I can almost see a few large boulders, and a clearing appears through the bending trees.

My breath catches in my throat.

There!

It was only a moment, but a few standing stones shone in the moonlight. I am so close. Just get to the clearing...

The hair on the back of my neck stands on end as the creeping fog mutes all sounds, blanketing the forest in quiet.

No wolf howls, no wind in the trees. Just eerie silence, as if the forest has gone to sleep.

I slow to a crawl, holding my breath, sliding my feet carefully along the forest floor, mindful to not make much of a sound. Not like it would matter, anyway. The fog weighs on each inch of the forest and all I can hear is my heart beating loudly in my ears. I slide my blistered feet along the mossy undergrowth and I'm racing across the virgin ground, clambering over downed trees and branches, rocks, and dead fauna.

A wolf snuffles and grunts, sounding like it's a few scant yards away to my right. The fog creeps farther into the forest, dragging all sounds with it.

I can't trip… not now. Keep going. Keep going. Get past this fog, get into the clearing. Get past this fog, get into the clearing. Get past the—"Aargh!"

I slip on a slick rock and my grunt echoes throughout the eerily quiet forest. My left foot slides down a muddy hillside and the rest of my body follows, and then I'm falling, falling. My hands strike out, and I scramble and grapple at fallen branches, trying to find purchase without success. Branches whip at my face and pull my hair as I tumble down into an old creek bed, landing on my stomach with a breath-stealing *THUMP*. I lie still while I try to calm my breathing at the bottom of the gully, taking stock of any injuries. My cheeks sting where the branches snagged, and I definitely have a sprained ankle. I take a deep breath, getting my hands underneath my shoulders, and push myself up.

The fog hasn't reached this part of the forest… *yet*, and the wind continues to roar through the trees.

Limping and exhausted, I crawl over moss-covered rocks and fallen trees, still hopeful that I'm heading in the right direction of the stones. A wolf howls again at the top of the gully and I can barely make out a shadowy figure running against the trees. A few more shouts echo behind me, still quite a way off, but too close for comfort.

My breathing is labored, my ankle throbbing with the increased movement, but I force myself up to run again. A wolf snuffles closer. They've stopped howling now but keep pace with me, stopping when I struggle to find my way through the bracken.

The fog crawls down the sides of the gully and up the creek bed towards me. Scramble. Limp. Scramble. Limp. Up and to my left, there is a small game trail heading up the other side of the forest. Reaching, I grab on to slippery tree roots and haul myself up the muddy embankment. The trail meanders through the rest of the woods towards the standing stones and — Oh my goddess! I'm almost there.

The magic pulls me closer and the boundary stones look like

they're glowing in the moon's light, beckoning me to come touch them.

The wind tickles my ear, and I swear I hear it say, "*Come home.*"

My fingers tingle, and the tips of my nails turn a light shimmering green with the budding magic recognizing familiar kin. The limp in my ankle slowly fades to a dull ache with every step I take that's closer to the clearing. My feet, no longer cracked and bleeding, throb less, and I feel... revitalized.

This is just like my dream...

Shaking my head in disbelief, I look down at my feet and notice the fog creeping through the forest again, wrapping its icy fingers around my ankles, thicker this time. Quieting the forest once more, the fog advances and climbs up my legs. My steps slow, feet dragging behind, feeling like I'm walking through knee-deep mud.

I'm... so... tired. I just... need to... catch my breath... I have time for that... don't I?

I lean against a tree and slump against the rough bark. The tree itself groans, and I think I see a sleeping face form in the trunk next to my hand. Should this bother me? I'm too tired to be scared anymore.

A wolf howls ahead of me on the trail. I drag my eyes slowly away from the face in the tree and see the wolf dash between the trees, its black coat shimmering in the moonlight. This isn't the same wolf, though. This one is black, it's thick luscious coat I know well from the stone circle.

Conall. Is this what I'm supposed to be ready for? Has he finally come to help me?

He reaches the stones and turns, piercing green eyes boring into me that glow so brightly I can see them from yards away. Stretching his neck skyward, he presses his ears against his head, a howl escaping from his maw. It cuts through my exhaustion, igniting a fire deep in my soul.

My heart feels like it's about to burst as I watch him vanish behind the trees, the howl echoing for a few beats. It's only after it fades that I realize the rest of the forest is deadly quiet. No wind rustling. No wolves howling. It's as if the entire forest is waiting with bated breath for something.

And then...

—CRACK—

A portal rips open. The king steps out, his white hair billowing around him. The smoke from the forest mingles with the plumes of smoke that swirl around his body. Behind him, in the wavering lines of the portal, I see the giant towers of his castle and the elaborate ironwork conservatory looming behind his shoulder. Vines creep over the parapets, through windows and broken doors, and prickly shrubs cover an old walkway.

Those vines weren't there before.

What happened to the windows?

I shake my head slowly; the fog creeping up to my stomach. It lingers, a thick coat of mist keeping me against the tree. Why am I so tired?

The black wolf howls once again. My head snaps up and I meet its gaze between the trees by the stone circle.

It opens its maw and I hear, "SORCHA."

Looking back into the portal as the king steps closer, a deep feeling of dread presses in around me. The outlines of a stone sarcophagus sits over his shoulder, its earthy coffin overgrown with vines and flowers blossoming throughout the conservatory.

I know that place.

No, no, no, I can't go back to that place.

I shake my head, reaching down into my bosom, uncapping the tincture bottle that rested snuggly in my stay. The fog creeps up into my stomach. It lingers, a thick coat of mist keeping me against the tree. Finally, the vetiver and lemon scent fills my lungs and I know now why I am so tired.

Fear claws at my throat, coursing through my veins, as the king steps forward. His smoke plumes around him, sweat beads on his brow.

I look down at my hands that glow a bright green and the small purple bottle in my hands. I pop the cap off and raise it to my lips. He stops walking forward, the smoke retreats slightly.

I can't go back there. I know what will happen to me if I go back there. Do I take what's in the bottle?

"I won't go," I say out loud, shooting my hands out, but the king keeps advancing, my vines going through his body like he's a specter.

"*Not everything is as it seems, Sorcha.*" Conall's voice reverberates in my head, down into my spine, flaring around my chest.

Then Conall's voice screams, "Now, Sorcha!"

I let out a primal scream, clenching my fist around the purple bottle. Bright green light swirls around me, my hair whips about my face, and for a few seconds, I can't see anything as I am encased in a bubble of green luminescence.

"I am not going back there!" I yell at Achill, then clap my hands together, green sparks shooting outward, tendrils of magic flying from my fingertips.

The portal to the castle closes, snapping shut, and another opens in its place, the tendrils of my magic rip it open with green fingers shredding into the air. White light shoots out from the space within and a smell of dirt and rocks emanates from beyond. A sleeping figure appears in the haze and my breath catches.

Awareness shakes through my body and I look one last time at Achill. He stands in front of me, frozen in place next to where his portal had been, shimmering like a specter as the rest of the world fades behind me. I step through the portal I just made, my vines caressing my skin as I walk through, and a great booming sound echoes all around me.

"Is she awake?" a tiny, familiar voice whispers.

Hazel? I ache. Everywhere. My head throbs with the echoes of the cracking rocks. The smell of dirt permeates my nose and dust clogs my throat. I cough, trying to bring my hands up to my face but my arms are stiff, unused to movement.

My fingers twirl lazily in tufts of fur, marveling at the softness and the warmth they provide. I am trapped underneath heavy blankets, making it nigh impossible to move comfortably without shifting all the furs off of me. But it's so warm that I snuggle in deeper and slowly move my hands up toward my face…

Wait a minute.

These furs have ears…?

My hands fly to my face, brushing the dust and rubble from my eyes as I'm met with a cold, black nose that is nearly touching mine. Green eyes like emeralds glinting in the sun stare back at me. Flecks of auburn and grey hair line the muzzle and the soft hair near the ears.

"Oh, hello, Conall. It's been quite a while, hasn't it?" I smile so wide my lips crack and bleed. I gently nudge the wolf's nose with my own, savoring finally being in the same room as Conall. Light filters through a dense, heavy canopy of trees, glass, and silver framing.

Conall's black wolf nudges me back and a familiar voice reverberates in my head. "See something you like, Sorcha?"

CONTENT & TRIGGER WARNINGS

In an effort to be transparent, this is an adult dark fantasy romance, intended for audiences eighteen years and older. Please read the trigger warnings carefully.

This book contains scenes that may depict, mention, or discuss: animal death, assault, attempted murder, blood, bones, death, decapitation, fire/smoke, implied non-consent/sexual coercion, violence, and discussions of slavery and war. There are several adult scenes with sexually explicit material as well as explicit language.

This book also contains: enthusiastic consent, positive body image language, nonbinary representation (a character with they/them pronouns), found family, healthy family systems, and older protagonists.

ACKNOWLEDGMENTS

This book could not have been written without the unwavering support from my husband, Steven, my two sweet children, my mom and step-dad, brother (my first beta reader, ever, and I promise I will never make you read anything I write ever again), and my best friend beta reader, Brittney (without your notes, the story would not be what it is today!).

Jo, my editor, is one-of-a-kind with her ability to help me really flesh out this story in the best way possible. She took an absolute trash draft and, with her guidance, helped me make this into a legitimate story.

A special thanks to Becks, the best alpha/beta/friend a newbie author could ever ask for. The enthusiastic support, hilarious conversations, and late-night TikTok videos helped keep me going and I hope this is the beginning of a lifelong friendship.

I also want to give a special shout out to the awesome team of readers and supporters near and far! Hopefully you have enjoyed reading this story as much as I have enjoyed writing it. I have so many more stories to tell and, because of all of you and your gracious support, I can actually write them.

Thank you all, so much, again and again and again!

xo

O.

ABOUT OPHELIA WELLS LANGLEY

Ophelia Wells Langley is the pen name of a mother to two boys. She loves reading, writing, knitting, and you can almost always find her chasing after her high-energy children pretending to be a dragon or a dinosaur.

Her goal is simple: create character-driven stories within lush fantasy worlds that satiate our need for escapism. Ophelia strives to create female characters that are older, and wiser, but still have quite a bit of growing to do. She writes about male characters that are complex and diverse (also with a lot of growing to do). And she incorporates inclusive bodies as well as gender identities and romantic experiences in order to fully reflect life as we know it. Plus, she loves spice ;)

Join OWL's Newsletter for updates and free stories on her website: www.opheliawlangley.com

- tiktok.com/@opheliawellsauthor
- instagram.com/opheliawlangleyauthor
- twitter.com/opheliawlangley
- pinterest.com/opheliawlangley
- amazon.com/Ophelia-Wells-Langley
- facebook.com/opheliawlangleyauthor

ALSO BY OPHELIA WELLS LANGLEY

The Stone Circle Queen: Book Two in The Stone Circle Series
Coming Spring 2023!

Of Smoke and Shadows - A Stone Circle Series Prequel Novella
Read about King Achill and how he became the villain we all love.
Find it on Amazon and Kindle Unlimited

Love Tastes Like Blood & Honey, Sapphic Short Story
SACRED: A Romance Anthology for Bodily Autonomy
Available October 31, 2022

CPSIA information can be obtained
at www.ICGtesting.com
Printed in the USA
BVHW041342311022
650735BV00007B/141